Dear Readers,

Many years ago, when I was a kid, my father said to me, "Bill, it doesn't really matter what you do in life. What's important is to be the *best* William Johnstone you can be."

I've never forgotten those words. And now, many years and almost 200 books later, I like to think that I am still trying to be the best William Johnstone I can be. Whether it's Ben Raines in the Ashes series, or Frank Morgan, the last gunfighter, or Smoke Jensen, our intrepid mountain man, or John Barrone and his hard-working crew keeping America safe from terrorist lowlifes in the Code Name series, I want to make each new book better than the last and deliver powerful storytelling.

Equally important, I try to create the kinds of believable characters that we can all identify with, real people who face tough challenges. When one of my creations blasts an enemy into the middle of next week, you can be damn sure he had a good reason.

As a storyteller, my job is to entertain you, my readers, and to make sure that you get plenty of enjoyment from my books for your hard-earned money. This is not a job I take lightly. And I greatly appreciate your feedback—you are my gold, and your opinions *do* count. So please keep the letters and e-mails coming.

Respectfully yours,

WILLIAM W. JOHNSTONE

AMBUSH OF THE MOUNTAIN MAN

WRATH OF THE MOUNTAIN MAN

PINNACLE BOOKS
Kensington Publishing Corp.

http://www.kensingtonbooks.com

PINNACLE BOOKS are published by

Kensington Publishing Corp.
850 Third Avenue
New York, NY 10022

All Kensington Titles, Imprints, and Distributed Lines are available at special quantity discounts for bulk purchases for sales promotions, premiums, fund-raising, and educational or institutional use. Special book excerpts or customized printings can also be created to fit specific needs. For details, write or phone the office of the Kensington special sales manager: Kensington Publishing Corp., 850 Third Avenue, New York, NY 10022, attn: Special Sales Department, Phone: 1-800-221-2647.

Pinnacle and the P logo Reg. U.S. Pat. & TM Off.

First Pinnacle Books Printing: September 2006

10 9 8 7 6 5 4 3 2 1

Printed in the United States of America

AMBUSH OF THE
MOUNTAIN MAN

1

Smoke Jensen and his friends, Cal, Pearlie, and Louis Longmont, turned their horses' heads south and rode out of the town of Noyes, Minnesota. They rode slumped in their saddles, dog-tired after the months they'd spent in Canada working for William Cornelius Van Horne.

Cal, still excited about the adventures they'd had and the unforgettable scenery of the northern Rocky Mountains, jabbered on and on about how he wished he'd been born in the days of the mountain men.

Louis and Smoke just looked at each other and smiled, for they knew those days hadn't been nearly as romantic as they'd sounded in the stories Cal had heard around the campfire from Bear Tooth and Red Bingham and Bobcat Bill.

Of course, they weren't about to tell the young'un that and ruin his ideas about the "good old days."

They rode on for about two miles, until they came to the railroad station that was their goal.

As they reined in their mounts in front of the station-master's office, Louis stretched and observed, "That was very nice of Bill Van Horne to arrange for us to ride all the way back to Big Rock on the train instead of on horseback."

"Yeah, it'll sure save some wear an' tear on my back-side," Pearlie agreed as he stepped down out of his stirrups. "The way I feel now, if'n I never see another saddle as long as I live it'll be all right with me," he added, rubbing his butt with both hands.

Smoke laughed. "Not only that, but Bill said we could ride in James Hill's own private car on our trip south."

"Hill?" Cal asked. "Ain't he the man Bill said bought up all the railroads in this part of the country?"

Smoke nodded. "That's right, Cal. Hill owns just about every inch of railroad track between here and home."

"Jiminy, then his own private car ought'a be somethin' to see."

"I would imagine it will be rather lavish," Louis said as he got down off his horse.

"I don't know what lavish means," Pearlie said, "but I hope it means it's stocked right well with food, 'cause I'm hungry enough to eat a bear."

"Well, now, that's a surprise," Cal said sarcastically to his friend. "From the way you was talkin', I figured you'd be too tired to eat an' you'd just go right to sleep once we got to the train."

Pearlie looked at the young man as if he'd uttered a blasphemy. "What? Go to sleep without eating? What kind of man would do that?"

After Smoke spoke to the stationmaster, and their horses and gear were stowed in the cattle car, the man showed them into James Hill's private car. As they entered, he told them to just pull the bell rope next to the door if they needed anything and a steward would take care of it.

Just before he left, he stopped in the door and looked around the car, shaking his head. "You boys must be powerful friends of Mr. Hill's," he said, " 'cause this is the first time I've ever seen him loan his car out to anyone." He paused and grinned. "Hell, when the President came out here last year on a tour, Mr. Hill gave him another car. Said this one was too good for politicians to use."

"Thanks for all your help," Smoke said, smiling and shutting the door behind the man.

As the stationmaster stepped down out of the car, a man

moved out of the shadows next to the station building and stood there staring at the train.

When the stationmaster approached him, the man ducked his head and put a lucifer to the cigarette dangling from the corner of his mouth. He looked up, tipping smoke from his nostrils, and gave the stationmaster a lopsided grin. "Howdy," he said in a friendly tone of voice.

"Hello," the stationmaster answered. "If you're here to buy a ticket on this train, you need to see the man in the ticket booth inside the building."

"Thanks," the stranger answered. "I might just do that." He turned toward the building, hesitated, and then he looked back over his shoulder at the stationmaster.

"Uh, by the way, was that man I just saw getting on the train named Smoke Jensen?"

The stationmaster nodded absentmindedly, already thinking about the dozens of things he had to see to before the train could leave the station.

The stranger cut his eyes back at the train before he went into the station to buy a ticket. His eyes were filled with hate.

When he got to the ticket booth, he pulled a wad of cash from his vest pocket and placed it on the counter.

"Can I help you, sir?" the ticket man asked.

"Yeah. Can you tell me how far Smoke Jensen and his friends are going?"

The ticket salesman looked down at an open book in front of him and pursed his lips for a moment. "I believe they're ticketed all the way through to Big Rock, Colorado," he said, glancing back up at the man standing in front of his window.

"Then give me a ticket to the same place," the man said, pushing his money under the gated window.

"Yes, sir."

"And I need to know if I have time to send a wire before the train leaves."

The ticket man pulled a watch from his vest pocket and

shook his head as he looked at it. "No, sir, I don't believe you do."

"Damn," he muttered.

"But I'd be happy to send one for you after the train leaves if you wish."

When the man nodded, looking relieved, the ticket man pushed a piece of paper and a pencil under the window gate. "Just write out who you want me to send it to and what you want to say and I'll get it on over to the telegraph office just as soon as the train leaves the station."

"Uh," the man stammered, his face burning scarlet. "I can't write too good."

The ticket man pulled the paper back and smiled. "Then just tell me what you want to say in your message and I'll write it for you."

"It's to Angus MacDougal in Pueblo, Colorado." The man thought for a moment and then he said, "Just say our friend is headed for home . . . should be there in ten days."

"Will there be anything else, sir?" the ticket man asked as he folded up the paper.

The man grinned through thin lips. "No, I think that ought'a 'bout do it."

After Smoke closed the door and turned around, he saw Louis pouring himself a glass of brandy into a bell-shaped crystal goblet from Hill's private bar in the corner. Louis swirled the amber liquid for a moment, and then he sniffed delicately of the aroma. His face relaxed and he smiled, as if he had died and gone to heaven.

Cal had taken his boots off and was lying back on the overstuffed sofa, poking the cushions with his hands, feeling how soft they were.

Pearlie was over in the opposite corner and he had his hands on the bell rope, about to pull it.

Smoke cleared his throat loudly. "Pearlie, what are you doing?"

Pearlie glanced over at him, his face blushing slightly and looking embarrassed. "Uh . . . I'm just ringing this here bell to see if the man who answers it can get us some food 'fore I faint from hunger."

Smoke shook his head, pointing to the corner of the car where a coffeepot was steaming on a fat-bellied stove. "Why don't you have a cup of coffee to fill your gut until the train leaves the station? Then we can see about getting some grub."

"Coffee?" Pearlie asked, as if he'd been offered something horrible to eat.

Louis looked up from where he stood at the bar. "And Pearlie, there's a bowl of sugar and a pitcher of cream here on the bar to sweeten it up with."

Pearlie grinned halfheartedly and moved toward the potbellied stove. "Well, now," he said amiably. "I guess now that you mention it, that coffee will do for a start."

"Coffee does sound good," Cal said, getting up from his perch on the couch. "But Louis, you'd better dole that sugar out to Pearlie a little at a time if'n you want any left for the rest of us to use," he added as he followed Pearlie toward the stove.

"You sayin' I'm a sugar hog, boy?" Pearlie asked, poking Cal in the shoulder with his fist.

"No, not exactly," Cal answered, rubbing his shoulder and frowning. "It's just that sometimes you like to put a little coffee in your sugar."

Two hours later, the men had finished their meal and were sitting around a table in Hill's private car getting a poker lesson from Louis. Luckily for Cal and Pearlie, they were playing for pennies instead of dollars, because Louis and Smoke were each winning just about every hand.

Just as Louis was leaning over to rake in another pot, the train suddenly slowed, its steel wheels screeching as the engineer applied the brakes with full force.

"What the . . ." Louis began to say when the chips and cards all started to slide across the table from the sudden slowing of the train. Cal moved his head to the side toward the nearby window and called out, "Looky there!" and pointed off to the side of the train.

A group of men could be seen suddenly appearing from a copse of trees near the track, all riding bent down low over their saddle horns, guns in their hands and bandanna masks over their faces.

"Well, I'll be hanged," Smoke said, his lips curling into a slight grin of anticipation. "It looks like the train is going to be robbed."

Louis unconsciously reached up and patted the wallet in his coat breast pocket, thick with the money William Cornelius Van Horne had paid them for helping with the surveying for his Canadian Pacific Railroad the past six months. "I'll be damned if any two-bit train robbers are going to take any of my money!" he exclaimed.

Smoke pulled a Colt pistol from his holster and flicked open the cylinder, checking to see that it was fully loaded. "No one's gonna take any money from any of us, Louis," he promised, the grin slowly fading from his face.

"I'll get our rifles from our gear in the next car," Pearlie said, referring to the sleeping car next door where they'd stored their valises and saddlebags.

"Bring some extra ammunition too," Smoke said, glancing out of the window. "It looks like there're fifteen or twenty riders out there we're gonna have to contend with."

He ducked down out of sight, motioning the others to do the same, as the train slowed and the group of riders drew abreast of the car they were in.

A gunshot rang out and the window next to Smoke's head shattered, sending slivers of glass cascading down onto his back and causing a tiny, solitary drop of blood to appear on his neck. He reached up and wiped it with his finger. "First blood to them," he said in a low, dangerous voice.

The train continued its rapid deceleration—probably because the robbers had dynamited or obstructed the tracks in some manner, Smoke thought as Pearlie came scuttling back into the car with his arms full of long guns. Smoke took the Henry repeating rifle from Pearlie, and watched as Louis took the ten-gauge sawed-off express gun and an extra box of shells from him.

"You're gonna have to get awfully close for that to do much damage," Smoke said.

Louis grinned. "I thought I'd wait until they came knocking on our door and then give them a rather loud greeting," he said in a light tone of voice that was belied by the dark fury in his eyes.

Smoke nodded. "Good idea. I think I'll take Cal and Pearlie and slip out the far side of the car when the train stops. When the bandits get off their horses to make their way through the cars, it'll give us a chance to scatter their mounts."

Pearlie nodded, grinning. "And then they'll be trapped out here in the middle of nowhere with nothing to ride off on. Good idea, Smoke."

When the train finally ground to a complete stop, Louis turned a big easy chair around until it was facing the door, and then took a seat, the express gun across his knees and his pistols on a small table next to the chair. He pulled a long black cigar out of his coat pocket and lit it, sending clouds of fragrant blue smoke into the air. He pulled his hat down tight on his head and leaned back, crossing his legs and smoking as if he were waiting for a friend to visit.

"Good hunting, gentlemen," he called as he eared back the twin hammers on the shotgun.

"You be careful, you hear?" Smoke said, tipping his head at his friend.

"It is not I that should be careful, pal," Louis replied, his voice turning hard. "It is those miscreants that are interrupting our trip who should be saying their prayers at this time."

As Smoke and the boys slipped out of the car and moved slowly down the line of cars toward the front of the train, Cal asked in a low voice, "Smoke, what's a miscreant?"

Smoke chuckled. "It's someone without a shred of decency in their character, Cal."

"Oh," Cal said, glancing at Pearlie walking next to him.

"You mean like someone who'd take the last spoonful of sugar in the bowl and not leave any for his friends?"

"Now Cal, boy," Pearlie said in a soothing voice, "that there bowl wasn't near half-full to begin with."

As they neared the car just behind the engine that contained wood to be burned in the boiler, Smoke heard a harsh voice say, "Watch the hosses, Johnny. We'll get the passengers' money and be right back."

Smoke gave the robbers time to climb aboard the train before he put the Henry in his left hand, sauntered out from between two cars, and walked slowly toward the outlaws' horses, which were being tended by a large, fat man with a full beard and a ragged, sweat-stained hat set low on his head.

The outlaw's eyes widened and his hand moved toward his belt as he said, "Who the hell . . . ?"

Smoke drew his Colt in one lightning fast motion and shot the man in the face, blowing him backward off his horse to land facedown in the dirt next to the track, his gun still in its leather.

The other horses jumped and crow-hopped at the sound of the pistol shot until Cal and Pearlie untied them from where they had been hitched to the rail on the railroad car and they shooed them away by waving their arms and shouting.

Soon, only the dead outlaw was left next to the tracks, blood still oozing into a puddle under his head.

Smoke moved up to the engine and found the engineer lying on his side, holding his left arm, a bullet hole in his left shoulder.

Smoke knelt next to him. "Are you gonna be all right?"

The engineer nodded. "Yeah, but somebody needs to put some wood in the boiler or we're gonna lose all our steam."

Smoke glanced over his shoulder. "Cal, would you help this man and do what he says while Pearlie and I go after the robbers?"

"Aw shucks, Smoke," Cal groused as he climbed up into the cab of the engine. "Pearlie gets to have all the fun."

"We just don't want you getting yourself shot again an' bleedin' all over Mr. Hill's fine car," Pearlie teased, "you bein' such a magnet for lead an' all."

"Now Pearlie," Cal argued, his face turning red. "I ain't been shot in over three weeks now."

Smoke laughed. "That might be because we haven't been in any gunfights for three weeks, Cal."

Cal bent and helped the engineer to his feet as Pearlie and Smoke jumped down out of the engine and headed back along the tracks toward the passenger cars.

They eased up into the first one, and Smoke was surprised when a female passenger threw up her hands and screamed, "Oh, no, they've come back to rape and kill us!"

Smoke smiled and motioned for her to put her hands down. "No, ma'am. We're here after the robbers," he explained as he and Pearlie moved down the aisle between the seats.

She took one look at Smoke's handsome face and broad shoulders and her voice seemed a mite disappointed when she said, "Then you aren't going to rob the men and rape the women?"

"Not this time," Smoke called back over his shoulder with a grin.

Smoke and Pearlie moved through three more cars before catching up to the robbers in the car just before Hill's private one that Louis was in.

Smoke motioned for Pearlie to kneel down in front of the door, and then stood over him as he jerked the door open.

The crowd of robbers in the aisle collecting passengers' money and jewels glanced back over their shoulders in time to see Smoke and Pearlie open fire, Smoke working the lever of the Henry so fast his shots seemed to be one long explosion.

Six outlaws went down before the others could return fire, and then it was wild and poorly aimed as they shouted and screamed and backed through the far door of the car, which was so filled with gunsmoke they could barely be seen.

The bandits in the lead jerked open the door to Hill's car and rushed inside, to be met by the thundering explosion of twin ten-gauge barrels hurling buckshot at them.

Four more men went down, shredded and almost cut in half by the horrendous power of the express gun.

The seven men remaining alive dove off the train out of the connecting door to the cars, and began running as fast as they could back up the tracks to where they thought their horses were tied.

They slowed and looked around with puzzled expressions when they came to Johnny's dead body.

"Where the hell are the hosses?" one of the men hollered, whirling around and looking in all directions.

From thirty feet behind him, Smoke said, "They're gone, you bastards!"

The robbers turned and saw Smoke and Pearlie and Louis standing there, side by side, their hands full of iron.

"There's only three of them, boys, let's take 'em!" one of the men shouted.

"Uh-uh," came a voice from behind the outlaws. Cal stood there just outside the engine, his Colt in his hand. "There's four of us," he said, a wide grin of fierce anticipation on his young face.

Nevertheless, the outlaws swung their pistols up and opened fire.

In less than fifteen seconds it was all over and every gunman lay either dead or dying next to the train. Blood pooled and saturated the dry earth of the tracks.

Smoke and Pearlie and Louis approached the group of bodies on the ground cautiously, kicking pistols and rifles out of reach of the wounded men who were groaning and writhing on the ground.

Cal said softly, "Dagnabit!" as he glanced down at his thigh, noting a thin line of red where a bullet had creased his upper leg, burning rather than tearing a hole in his trousers.

He quickly turned to the side so his friends couldn't see the wound, calling, "I'm just gonna go on up and make sure the engineer is all right."

When the engineer looked at the blood staining Cal's pants leg, Cal shook his head. "Don't say nothin' 'bout this to my friends, all right?"

The wounded engineer just grinned, having heard what Pearlie and Smoke had said about Cal being a magnet for lead. "I promise not to say nothin', if you'll be so kind as to build me a cigarette while we wait for the steam to build."

2

Carl Jacoby sat staring out of the train window next to his seat, sweat beading on his forehead and running down his cheeks as he thought about just how fast with a gun Smoke Jensen and his friends had proved to be.

Jacoby was one of Johnny MacDougal's best friends . . . or at least he had been until Jensen and his men had shot his friend down in the streets of Pueblo, Colorado, last year. Jacoby hadn't been there, being sick with the grippe at the time, but he'd been told Jensen had shot Johnny down in cold blood without even giving him a chance to clear leather.

Being also hopelessly in love with Johnny's older sister, Sarah, Jacoby had at once told the family he would do anything they wanted to help them get even for Johnny's untimely death. He'd hoped this would endear him to Sarah, but she hadn't seemed to notice him when he made the offer just after her brother's funeral. She'd been quiet and kind of off in her own world, as if she was thinking of something else.

Old Angus MacDougal, eaten up with grief and the need for vengeance, had questioned Sheriff Wally Tupper about where Jensen and his friends had been heading after they'd killed his son. Sheriff Tupper had said that one of the men, a William Cornelius Van Horne, was a famous Canadian railroad builder.

Angus had done some checking, and afterward he'd sent Carl up to Canada to follow Jensen and his men and to let the old man know when they headed back to the States so he could avenge his son's death.

He'd told Jacoby to stay out of Jensen's way, not to brace him or to let him know he was being watched, but just to keep an eye on him and make sure they didn't leave Canada without Jacoby knowing about it.

Jacoby had done so gladly, sure that no one could have bested Johnny in a fair fight, him being the quickest man with a short gun Carl had ever seen—that is, until the gunfight he'd just now witnessed.

He was watching out the window as Jensen and the three men with him went up against outlaws who outnumbered them two to one. He'd gasped in disbelief when he'd seen the cowboys blow the outriders off their feet without even breaking a sweat.

Hell, he thought, sleeving sweat off his forehead, I was watching Jensen when he drew and I still didn't see his hand move, it was so fast, and the gents with him were just a hair slower, if that.

He didn't think the outlaws would've gotten a single shot off if they hadn't already had their guns in their hands, and still they hadn't managed to draw blood from Jensen or any of his friends.

Jacoby shook his head, remembering how many times he'd been tempted over the past six months to just step up to Jensen and draw his gun and shoot the bastard. His stomach grew queasy at the thought of what would have happened had he been so foolish—he'd be lying dead and buried in the godforsaken wilderness above the border, that's what. He snorted. Hell, as fast as Jensen is and as slow as I am, he'd have had time to build and light himself a cigarette and still could've shot me deader'n yesterday's news.

He turned his head from the sight of the men from the train picking up the dead outlaws' bodies and stacking them in an empty boxcar, and thought about what he was going to do next. He knew that if he continued on his mission for Angus MacDougal, sooner or later he would have to go up against Jensen and his friends, and that thought scared him half to death.

On the other hand, if he quit now and headed back to Pueblo with his tail between his legs, he was sure Sarah MacDougal would never give him another look—at least not the kind of look he'd want her to give him. She'd more than likely think him a coward and a fool, and would never again give him the time of day.

Damn Johnny to hell, he thought angrily. *If he'd just kept his mouth shut and hadn't tried to play the big man like usual, I wouldn't be in this mess.*

Jacoby looked up as the conductor came down the aisle, telling all the passengers that they would be on their way shortly and that all of their money and valuables would be returned to them at the next stop, thanks to Smoke Jensen and his friends.

"Uh, sir," Jacoby asked, raising his hand like a schoolkid to get the conductor's attention.

"Yes, sir?" he asked, stopping next to Carl's seat.

"Will there be a telegraph at the next stop?" Carl asked, almost hoping the man would say no.

"Why, yes, I believe there is, sir."

"Thanks," Carl replied, turning his mind to just what he was going to say to Angus. He knew he'd better warn him about Jensen's ability with a gun, but he didn't want to come off sounding like he was afraid of the man, even though the plain truth of the matter was that he was more frightened of Jensen than of anything else he could imagine. Carl scrunched down in his seat and pulled his hat down over his eyes. This was going to take some heavy thinking before they got to the next stop if he was going to get it right.

After all, he remembered, Angus MacDougal didn't exactly take kindly to being told he was wrong about anything, and especially not about this.

Angus MacDougal sat on his porch smoking a corncob pipe, still wearing his black mourning suit, even though it'd been more than six months since his only son had been shot down in the streets of Pueblo, Colorado.

He glanced up from his reverie at the sound of hoofbeats rapidly approaching his ranch house. He nodded slowly to himself when he recognized the portly figure of Sheriff Wally Tupper riding toward him. Must be some news from Carl, he thought, getting slowly to his feet and stretching to get the kinks out. He felt like he'd aged ten years since Johnny died, but then the death of a loved one will tend to do that to a person, he reasoned as he walked down the porch and waved a greeting at the sheriff.

Tupper climbed down out of the saddle and held up an envelope in his hand as he climbed the steps to the porch. "Got this here wire for you from Carl Jacoby, Angus," he said, his voice deferential as if he worked for Angus instead of the town of Pueblo. "It came in on the telegraph just this mornin' and I rode right out here to bring it to you first thing," Tupper said.

Angus took the paper, his eyebrows knitting together over a scowling face. "What's it say?" he asked.

"I dunno," the sheriff replied, his face screwing up in fright. "I wouldn't presume to read a wire addressed to you, Angus. You know that."

Angus smiled a half smile, reveling in the look of fear and trepidation on the sheriff's face. He couldn't help it, he just loved to intimidate other men, especially men who were supposed to be in authority.

"I know you'd better not, Wally," he said in a low, hard voice. "Now go on into the kitchen and have the cook fix you some coffee while I read this, and then we'll talk."

Angus slit the envelope with a thumbnail and pulled out the folded sheet of paper. It was indeed a telegram from Carl Jacoby. Angus squinted his eyes—it looked to be from some pissant town in Minnesota that he'd never heard of before. Sighing at the indignities old age put on him, Angus reached into the breast pocket of his coat and pulled out a pair of reading spectacles he'd taken to using in the last year when he found he was unable to read the local newspaper without holding it way out at arm's length.

The telegram read:

HAVE SEEN JENSEN AND HIS MEN IN ACTION STOP VERY IMPRESSIVE STOP DO NOT THINK THEY WOULD HAVE TO BACKSHOOT ANYONE STOP PLEASE CHECK SITUATION AGAIN BEFORE PROCEEDING STOP SHOULD ARRIVE BIG ROCK SEVEN TO TEN DAYS DEPENDING ON WEATHER END
CARL

Angus crumpled up the paper and gritted his teeth so hard his jaw creaked. He whirled around and stomped across the porch and into his house. He found Sheriff Tupper drinking coffee out of a mug and flirting with his Mexican housekeeper, Lupe.

Angus took a deep breath and tried to calm down as Lupe poured him a cup of coffee and put it on the table in front of him.

"Would you excuse us, Lupe?" he asked, struggling to keep his voice soft. "Man talk."

"Certainly, Señor," she said, and quickly vanished from the dining room.

Tupper raised his eyebrows when he saw the crumpled sheet of paper in Angus's hand. "Bad news?" he asked over the rim of his cup.

Angus didn't answer until he'd gotten to his feet and walked over to the cabinet against the wall. He opened the door, took out a bottle of whiskey, and poured a dollop into his coffee, pointedly not offering any to Tupper.

"Tell me again about the day my boy Johnny was shot down, Wally," Angus ordered shortly as he took a sip of his whiskey and coffee.

"You sure you want to hear all that again?" Tupper asked, his face showing his discomfort. The day he'd brought Johnny's body home to Angus, he'd thought for a moment the old man was going to kill *him*, as if *he'd* done something wrong.

"I asked, didn't I?" Angus responded angrily, slamming his cup down so hard the coffee sloshed over the rim.

"Well," Tupper began quickly, trying to picture that day in his mind, "from what I heard from those who were there, Johnny and the boys had been drinking a mite, an' they proceeded to tease Jensen and the men with him about how they smelled. Shortly, one of those old mountain men riding with Jensen jumped up and . . . uh . . . " Tupper hesitated, trying to decide how graphic to get with his description of the events. Finally, he decided to be a bit vague. "Jumped up and knocked Johnny to the floor."

"And Johnny hadn't drawn on the man up till then?" Angus asked, his eyes full of sorrow and anger.

"Nope," Tupper replied. "Matter of fact, Johnny was flat on his back after the man attacked him without no warning," he said, shading the truth a mite because he knew that was what the old man wanted to hear.

"What happened then?"

"Well, sir, Johnny's friends took him outside an' they waited for Jensen and his men to come out of the Feedbag an' into the street."

"And when they did?"

"This is where the stories all get a mite different," Tupper said. "Johnny and his friends all had their guns in their hands when I got there, but only Johnny's had been fired, an' he'd only gotten off the one shot. But the man with Jensen, a William Cornelius Van Horne, said Johnny and his men had fired at them first an' started the fracas."

Angus drained his cup, his face pale at hearing once again how his boy had died. "And you believed him, even though none of the boys managed to get a shot off?"

"I didn't have no choice, Angus. This Van Horne man carries a lot of weight in the state, an' he knows the governor personally."

"And tell me again, just how many times was my boy shot?" Angus asked.

"Uh, the undertaker said he had over six slugs in him, Angus."

"And you honestly think, knowing how fast Johnny was with a six-gun, that he could be standing there with his guns out and only get off one shot whilst someone else has to take the time to draw and ends up shooting him six times?" Angus asked, his voice incredulous. He shook his head. "No, sir! There ain't nobody alive that fast," he finished without waiting for an answer.

"Well, what do you think happened then?" Sheriff Tupper asked.

"I think those bastards shot my boy and his friends down in cold blood, and then they took out their guns and put them in their hands so it'd look like a fair fight," Angus said, his voice tight with anger.

Before Sheriff Tupper could answer saying there'd been plenty of other witnesses to dispute Angus's version of the gunplay, the door opened and a pretty young woman in her mid-twenties walked into the room, her face a mask of anguish. It was obvious she'd been listening to Tupper and Angus from the other room.

"That's not all they did to him, Daddy," Sarah MacDougal said through jaws tight with anger.

Angus cut his eyes to her. "What do you mean by that, Sarah?" he asked.

"Sarah, do you really think this is necessary?" Sheriff Tupper began, a worried look on his face.

"Yes, Wally, I do!" she answered. "My father deserves to know the truth about what was done to his son and my little brother."

Angus slammed his fist down on the table, causing the coffee cups to leap into the air and spill dark liquid all over the wood.

"Damn it!" he shouted. "Don't talk about me like I wasn't even in the room!" He turned his gaze to the sheriff. "Wally, if you know more than you've been telling me for the past six months, you'd better spit it out now or I'll make you wish to hell you had."

Tupper reached out and turned his coffee cup back

right-side-up, clearing his voice. "Well, Angus, when I got to Johnny's body, I saw a deep cut on his cheek and saw that his two front teeth had been knocked out."

"What?" Angus shouted, half-rising to his feet.

Tupper held out his hand, palm out. "Now hold on, Angus. I asked around and it seems Johnny was raggin' the men with Jensen 'bout them being smelly and dirty, an' one of the old mountain men took offense at it and pulled out his Colt and pistol-whipped Johnny with it." Tupper took a deep breath. "I didn't say nothing about it 'cause it was plain to see that Johnny had picked the fight in the first place."

Angus sat back down, slowly nodding his head. "Now I see why Johnny was waiting outside for those men to leave the saloon. His pride was hurt because of the beating he took in front of his friends."

Sarah stepped over and laid her hand gently on Angus's shoulder. "That doesn't alter the fact that Johnny was shot down in cold blood, Daddy, and that was after they slashed his face and knocked his teeth out."

Angus turned sad eyes to his daughter and covered her hand with his. "You're right, Sarah. Even though Johnny was spoiled and a hothead who never knew when to shut his mouth, he didn't deserve to be shot down in the street like a stray dog for it, him and his friends both."

Tupper leaned forward, his arms on the table. "Now Angus, don't go off half-cocked. Johnny's dead, and there ain't nothing you can do gonna change that." He took out his handkerchief and wiped his sweaty forehead with it as he continued. "Killing Jensen and his men won't change anything, Angus."

Angus looked over at the sheriff and his lips curled in a deadly smile. "No, I can't change it, Wally, but I can sure as hell make sure someone pays for what they did to my boy."

Sarah blinked back tears, and turned and walked slowly from the room and out the door to stand on the front porch, staring at the mountain peaks in the distance. She'd always hated Johnny, ever since they were little kids.

Up until she was five years old, she'd been the apple of her daddy's eye and he'd taken her everywhere with him, teaching her to ride and shoot like a man.

Then, Johnny had been born and her life had changed forever. All of a sudden, it was as if she ceased to exist and her daddy's world revolved around his new son.

It hadn't been fair; from the beginning, she could ride and shoot better than Johnny, and was smarter in the bargain. But that didn't matter to Angus MacDougal. All he cared about was having a son to carry on his name. Well, that was over now, Sarah thought bitterly. His precious son's big mouth had finally gotten him into some trouble their daddy couldn't buy his way out of.

Sarah shook her head and entered the house again, and walked into her room and began to pack her bags. She planned to be in Big Rock when Smoke Jensen and his friends arrived. She had it all worked out in her mind: She'd move into town using a fake name, get a job, and no one would know she'd come there to put Smoke Jensen in his grave.

As she flung her clothes into the valise, she thought that maybe then Angus would again give her the respect and attention she deserved.

3

Sheriff Monte Carson was waiting at the station in Big Rock when Smoke Jensen and his friends, Cal, Pearlie, and Louis Longmont, got off the train.

The four men looked tired and their faces were drawn from the long train ride from up near the Canadian border, and it looked as if they'd all lost weight on their journey to Canada and back.

As they stepped down out of the passenger car, Monte turned to his deputy. "Jim, why don't you see to their horses and luggage and I'll take them over to Longmont's Saloon." He chuckled. "They look like they could do with some good food for a change."

Monte walked over and slapped Smoke on the shoulder, smiling at the men standing next to him. "Well, boys, I'll bet it's good to get home, ain't it?" he asked.

"It is certainly good to get my posterior off of those torture devices the railroad calls seats," Louis said, stretching and rubbing his butt at the same time. "I do believe they stuff those seats with rocks," he added, wincing at the pain in his buttocks.

"Just think how bad it would'a been if we would'a had to sit in regular seats 'stead of those padded ones in Mr. Hill's car," Pearlie said.

"I rather not think about that eventuality, if you don't mind," a grouchy Louis rejoined.

Monte's deputy tipped his hat and said hi to the men before he walked off down the platform toward the baggage and livestock cars.

"Jim's gonna get your hosses and luggage and all," Monte said. "Why don't we head on over to Louis's place and get some good grub into you boys," he said, hesitating before adding, "You all look like you been starved half to death up there in the North Country."

Pearlie's tired face broke into a wide smile. "Did I hear somebody say grub?"

Smoke nodded. "That sounds awfully good, Monte. I could use some coffee that I don't have to chew before swallowing." He smiled. "After riding with mountain men for a spell, any coffee that won't float a horseshoe is considered too weak to bother with."

"Yeah," Cal added. "Like they said, their coffee don't take near as much water as you think it do," he said, doing a fair imitation of Bear Tooth's growl.

Daniel Macklin sat on a bench at the far end of the platform, whittling on a stick and watching the men as they moved off toward the downtown area. He'd been on this same bench watching the arrival of each and every train that'd pulled into Big Rock for the past three months. His lips curled into a slow grin as he realized his job was just about over.

The fingers of Macklin's right hand twitched as they hung just above the butt of his pistol, tied down low on his right thigh. He forced the hand to relax, deciding to wait until he'd contacted Angus MacDougal before he braced Jensen. He hoped that when Angus found out Jensen was back in town he would wire him back giving him permission to kill the son of a bitch. That would be fitting, he thought, since the men Jensen had killed had been some of his best friends.

He got slowly to his feet, dropped the sharpened stick to the ground as he leaned his shoulder against the corner of the building, and waited for Carl Jacoby to get off the train. Angus had wired him Jacoby was trailing Jensen, so Macklin figured he'd be somewhere on the same train.

Sure enough, a few minutes after Jensen and his friends had left, Macklin saw Jacoby exit a car further down the track. As Jacoby put his bag down and looked around, Macklin gave a low whistle and grinned. Jacoby was also a good friend of his, though Macklin thought he was a dumb ass for mooning over Sarah MacDougal like a hound dog in heat. Sarah would never give ordinary cowhands like them the time of day—she had been groomed since she was just a pup for finer things, men more important than country boys. Of course, that was before her brother had been killed. Who knows what was going on in her mind at this stage?

Jacoby nodded, picked up his bag, and walked toward Macklin. "Hey, Mac, how're you doin'?" Jacoby asked.

Macklin looked down at the large pile of wood shavings from his whittling and grinned. "I'm doin' a mite better now that you and Jensen are here," he replied, glancing over his shoulder at Jensen's group as they walked down the street away from the station. "I'm sick of coolin' my heels here for the past few months waitin' on y'all to get back from the North Country."

"I hear that," Jacoby said, nodding his agreement. "Come on," he added, "show me to the nearest saloon. My mouth's so dry I'm spittin' cotton."

Macklin pursed his lips and narrowed his eyes. "Don't you think we'd better wire ol' Angus first and tell him everbody's here?"

"Naw," Jacoby said, waving his hand in dismissal of the thought. "I wired him from along the way tellin' him when we were gonna get here. Besides, there's some things I gotta tell you 'fore we decide on just how to proceed with this matter, important things."

Upon hearing that his boss and friend was back, Andre rushed from the kitchen in Longmont's Saloon and wrapped his arms around Louis's shoulders, giving him a quick kiss on both cheeks in the French manner.

"Thank you, Andre," Louis said, smiling at the man who'd been both his chef and his good friend for many years. "I'm glad to see you also."

"But Monsieur Louis," Andre said, clucking his tongue and shaking his head as he stepped back and took a good look at Louis. "You have lost much weight on your journey. Did not those railroad men up there in Canada feed you?"

"Not nearly enough, Andre," Pearlie piped up from the rear of the group of men.

Andre glanced up and smiled. "Ah, Monsieur Pearlie, my most ardent customer."

"If ardent means 'hungry,'" Pearlie said, "you sure got that right, Andre." He took his seat at the table and stared at the chef with anticipation. "How long before we can get some lunch?"

Andre laughed. "I will get to work immediately," he said. "I will see that fresh coffee is prepared while I fix you a lunch that will put some weight back on your bones and some strength back in your muscles."

The men all took seats at Louis's regular table just as the young black man who was the head waiter appeared carrying a tray with a silver coffee service and five mugs on it.

As they drank their coffee, Monte leaned back and said, "All right now, boys, tell me all about your adventures up there north of the border."

"First, Monte," Smoke said, "I want to know if you've heard from Sally."

"Oh, dagnabit, I almost forgot," Monte said. "I got a wire yesterday that said she'd gotten your telegram saying you were on your way home. She said her father is doing much better and she will probably be here in the next week or so."

Smoke didn't answer, but the smile on his face showed he was pleased at the news. Before he'd left for Canada a few months back, his wife Sally had gone back east to be with her ailing father. Smoke was glad to hear the man was better and that she'd be home soon, for he missed her terribly.

Pearlie stuck a cigarette he'd built into his mouth, leaned back as he got it going, and proceeded to give a slightly exaggerated account of the men's adventures in the Canadian wilds over the past six months. He ended his narrative with the tale of the train robbers. "And Cal here actually got into the gunfight with us without getting wounded, if you can believe that!" Pearlie said, taking a breath and finally getting around to sampling his coffee, which was cooling by now.

Cal unconsciously reached under the table and rubbed the sore spot on his thigh where he had in fact been slightly wounded, something he'd managed to keep from his friends. It wasn't his fault that bullets just naturally seemed to seek him out, no matter how careful he was in the gunfights. Luckily, though he was a frequent target, none of the wounds had been overly serious.

Monte laughed and slapped Cal on the back. "Well, now, that is something. Maybe your luck's changing, Cal," he said just as Andre appeared followed by two waiters with platters of heaping food in their hands.

Pearlie hurriedly stubbed out his cigarette and rubbed his hands together. "All right!"

Andre caught Louis's and Smoke's eyes and winked. "I am glad to see that you are so hungry, Monsieur Pearlie," he said, nodding his head.

"I'm so hungry I could eat a horse, Andre," Pearlie said, straining in his chair trying to look and see what the platters held.

"That is good, my friend, for I have just acquired a new supply of frog legs and escargot from my supplier in Denver this very morning."

Pearlie made a face and sat back in his chair. "Uh, Andre, no offense, but I think I'll just skip the frog legs and try some of that es-car-go, or whatever it is. It shore smells good, I'll tell you that."

"And I assure you, Monsieur, it will be a taste you will

never forget, especially when you dip the little creatures in the melted butter I've made."

"Uh . . . did you say somethin' 'bout little creatures, Andre, or did I misunderstand?" Pearlie asked, his face suddenly showing signs of suspicion.

"Mais oui, Pearlie, I did say creatures."

"But, Andre. Just what are es-car-go?"

"Snails, my friend, large, plump, juicy snails," Andre replied.

Pearlie put his hand over his mouth and started to get up from the table until he saw what was on the platter the waiter was setting down.

He grinned and pointed. "That looks like beefsteak to me, Andre."

Everyone at the table laughed, even Pearlie, and they all grabbed knives and forks and dug in.

4

Macklin took Jacoby by his hotel, arranged for him to get a room there and dropped off his luggage, and then showed him to a restaurant that served both liquor and food.

While they drank a glass of whiskey and waited for their food orders to arrive, Jacoby told Macklin about the gunfight on the train between Jensen and his friends and the outlaws who'd outnumbered them.

Jacoby shook his head and drained his glass, sleeving whiskey off his lips with his arm. "It was the damnedest thing I ever seen, Mac," he said, his eyes wide with wonder. "One minute Jensen an' his friends are standing there in front of maybe ten outlaws, an' 'fore you could spit, they hands was full of iron and they was blasting the shit outta those hombres."

"Just because a man's an outlaw don't necessarily mean he's fast on the draw, Carl."

"That's just it, Mac. All of them bandits already had their guns in their hands when Jensen and his men drew down on 'em."

"And you're sayin' none of those outlaws managed to draw any blood?"

Jacoby held his glass up and pointed at it so the waiter would bring him another. "That's just what I'm saying, Mac. Jensen and his men walked away from that fracas clean as a whistle. And what was even more funny is they didn't wait for the bandits to make a play at them or try to take their money. They went looking for the outlaws as if they kind'a enjoyed the thought of a good fight."

Macklin's eyes narrowed as he stared at Jacoby. "Just what are you sayin', Carl? You sayin' Jensen is faster on the draw that Johnny MacDougal was?" he asked, his face showing his doubt that such could be the case.

"Hey, Mac, I'm telling you the truth," Jacoby insisted. "I know Johnny was fast with a six-killer 'cause I've drawed against him in contests before, but Jensen is faster, by a long shot!"

Macklin stroked his jaw as he let his eyes drop to stare into his whiskey. "So, you think it may've been a fair fight when Jensen shot Johnny down in Pueblo?" he asked, keeping his voice low so the nearby diners wouldn't hear him mention Jensen's name.

Jacoby shrugged. "Hell, I weren't there, Mac, so's I can't say for certain. All I know is Jensen could snatch a quarter off'n a rattler's head and leave two dimes an' a nickel in change 'fore the snake could strike." He raised his hand to the waiter and indicated he wanted another drink and he wanted it fast. All this talk about how fast Jensen was with a gun was making him nervous. Sweat formed on his forehead when he remembered how he'd once planned on bracing Jensen himself.

After the waiter placed two more glasses on the table in front of them, Jacoby glanced down at the way Macklin was wearing his gun low on his right hip. "And by the way, Mac," he said, pausing to take a deep draught of his drink, "I've seen you draw before too. So if you're planning on going up against Jensen, you'd better plan on shooting him in the back from a long way off, or I'll be taking your dead body back to Pueblo with me when I leave this burg."

Macklin's face flushed and he gritted his teeth for a sharp retort, but was interrupted by the waiter reappearing with a platter containing their food orders on it in his hands. When the waiter left, Jacoby, who'd noticed the angry expression on Macklin's face when he warned him not to try and outdraw Jensen, wisely decided to change the subject before Macklin got really pissed off.

He cut his steak and stuck a piece in his mouth, asking around it, "You been here long enough to ask around, so what is Jensen's reputation in this town?"

Macklin busied himself with cutting his own steak and didn't look up at the question, though he snorted derisively through his nose. "Hell, around here they think he's better than homemade apple pie," he answered. "I couldn't find a single person in this entire town had a bad word to say about Jensen or the men riding with him." He stuck the meat in his mouth and added, "Hell, seems Jensen himself founded this town some years ago, so naturally nobody's gonna say nothing against him."

Jacoby sighed. "That's what I figured you'd say," he said as he used his fork to rake some corn onto his knife and then stuffed it into his mouth. "From what I seen on the train, Jensen is pretty much a square shooter," he added as he chewed thoughtfully.

Macklin shrugged and asked, "So what? Angus Mac-Dougal didn't send us here to check out his character. He sent us here to let him know when he got home an' possibly to put a bullet in him and his friends."

"But Mac," Jacoby said, shoving his plate to the side and leaning forward, "what if his fight with Johnny was fair an' it was like they said, that Johnny fired off shots at them first? Hell, we all know what an asshole Johnny could be when he was all liquored up."

"Don't make no never mind to me what happened back in Pueblo," Macklin answered, his eyes burning. "All I know is, Johnny and the others that died with him were friends of mine, an' I aim to see Jensen in his grave for what he done to them!" He paused for a moment, staring at Jacoby as if he were an enemy instead of one of his oldest friends. "An' I aim to do it with you or without you, Carl, so don't be getting in my way or you're liable to catch some lead too."

Jacoby snarled back, "Don't go playin' the big man with me, Mac. Remember, I seen you draw before an' I ain't all that certain you could take me, even if you was crazy enough to try."

"Well, then, how 'bout I put it like this. Old Man Mac-Dougal been pretty good to both of us, it seems, so if'n he wants Jensen dead, for whatever reason, it's plenty good enough for me."

Jacoby started to reply, but Macklin added, "And what do you think Sarah is gonna say when she hears you've gone all soft and sweet on Jensen, the man what killed her baby brother?"

Jacoby let his eyes drop to what remained of his meal, his appetite squashed by the question. "Maybe if I explain to her that—"

"Explain what?" Macklin burst out. "That the man who put six slugs in her little brother after bashing out his front teeth is really a nice feller and we should just forget about the whole thing?"

Jacoby leaned his head back and rubbed the back of his neck with his hand, trying to ease the sudden pain there that Macklin was causing. "You're right, Mac, she'll never understand," he said wearily. "She's like her father. She don't never forget a slight, and she sure as hell won't care what I think about Jensen's character, that's for sure."

"If you're finished with that steak, maybe we'd better get on over to the telegraph office and wire Angus and see what he wants us to do," Macklin said, stuffing the last piece of his meat into his mouth, thinking Jacoby was a fool for caring so much about a lady that would never ever give him the time of day.

Sally Jensen eased out of her seat on the train when it pulled into the station at Pueblo, Colorado. The next stop would be Big Rock, and she wanted to freshen up a little before arriving home. She hadn't seen Smoke for more than half a year, and she wanted to look her best when he met her at the station. She could already imagine him throwing his arms around her and squeezing her tight against his hard body.

When she looked into the mirror in the women's parlor compartment as she applied a light dusting of powder and just a hint of lip rouge, she noticed that the thought of seeing her man again after so long was making her cheeks flush and burn as if they were on fire.

She grinned, speaking at her image in the looking glass. "Why, Sally Jensen, you're acting like a hussy instead of an old married woman!"

"Pardon me?" a young woman who was just entering the compartment asked, raising her eyebrows at the sight of Sally talking to herself in the mirror.

Sally laughed, her cheeks flushing even more at being seen acting so strangely. "Oh, don't mind me, miss," she said, waving a hand at the young girl. "I'm just returning home after a long absence, and the excitement of seeing my husband and home again after so long has me behaving a bit silly."

The young woman stepped in front of another mirror across the room and spent a few moments adjusting her hat and dress. Sally thought the girl probably wasn't used to wearing such nice clothes, the way she picked at the buttons and continually fussed with the ruffled collar on the neckline. And she certainly didn't know how to wear a frilly hat. She had it at completely the wrong angle.

"Here, let me help you with that," Sally said, moving over to smooth out the ruffles in the back of the dress and make it a bit more comfortable for the young woman and to adjust the tilt of the hat to a more rakish angle.

"Thank you," the girl said, smiling. She stuck out her hand. "I'm Sarah . . . uh . . . Sarah Johnson," Sarah Mac-Dougal said, stammering a bit over the false name she'd decided to use on her trip to Big Rock to see what she could do about making Smoke Jensen pay for what he'd done to her little brother.

"Hello, Sarah," Sally said, taking her hand and shaking it. "I'm Sally Jensen."

Sarah flushed when she heard Sally's last name, and ducked her head as she tried to think of something to say. She'd had no idea the man might be married, and to such a refined-looking woman as Sally obviously was. If she'd thought about it at all, she would've thought a gunman like Smoke Jensen would probably be keeping company with a dance-hall gal or one of the fallen doves in a house of ill repute somewhere.

Sally, seeing the girl's discomfort but not knowing what was behind it, asked, "Are you traveling far, Sarah?"

"Uh . . . just to Big Rock, Mrs. Jensen," Sarah answered in a hoarse voice with just a trace of a tremor in it.

"Oh, just call me Sally, Sarah," Sally said, smiling and returning to her own mirror for a last-minute adjustment. "We're not very formal in Big Rock, as you'll find out when we get there."

"All right, Sally," Sarah said, bending to pick up her valise.

Sally put her arm through Sarah's as they left the compartment. "Why don't you sit with me, dear, and you can tell me all about your trip to Big Rock," she said, leading Sarah to her row of seats.

After Sarah had stashed her valise on the overhead rack, she sat down next to Sally and they began to talk.

"Are you visiting friends or family in Big Rock?" Sally asked, wondering to herself what would make a young woman set out all alone on such a trip.

"Uh, not really, Sally," Sarah answered. "I just had to get out of Pueblo, and Big Rock seemed like a nice place to move to."

Sally's eyebrows rose at the tone in Sarah's voice, as if she were in some kind of trouble, and Sally wondered how Sarah would have heard of Big Rock in the much larger city of Pueblo.

"I hope I'm not being too nosy, Sarah, but just why do you have to get out of Pueblo?"

When Sarah hesitated and stared past Sally out the window as the train began to move out of the station, Sally patted her on the arm. "Never mind, dear," Sally said, turning and looking forward. "Your reasons are none of my business and I fear I'm intruding on your privacy."

Sarah, not wanting to make Sally suspicious, decided to

tell her the story she'd made up to account for her moving from Pueblo to Big Rock.

"Oh, don't worry, Sally, it's nothing all that mysterious," Sarah said, making her voice light and carefree. "It's just that I was engaged, until recently, to a prominent member of Pueblo society. When we decided to cancel our engagement, people began to talk, and my family thought it best if I moved away, for at least a little while, to let matters settle down," she finished.

"Ah," Sally said, nodding, "an affair of the heart often makes tongues waggle, especially tongues of the gossip mongers who like nothing better than to besmirch someone else's reputation." She clucked and shook her head. "Now, even though the people of Big Rock are very nice, Sarah, I wouldn't be too quick to tell anyone your story. It is after all a small town, and it does have its gossips just like all towns do."

"That's it exactly, Sally. Oh, I knew you'd understand," Sarah said, blushing in shame at deceiving this woman who was being so kind to her.

"Of course I understand, dear," Sally said. "I'm not so old that I cannot remember what it was like when my husband first began courting me, and how the gossip flew hot and heavy around my town at the time."

Sarah realized she needed to find out if Sally Jensen's husband was Smoke Jensen. She figured he was, but Jensen wasn't all that uncommon a name and she wanted to be sure. After all, she still couldn't believe someone as nice as Sally seemed to be would be married to a gunfighter like Smoke Jensen, a man who killed defenseless boys.

"Tell me about your husband, Sally," Sarah said, leaning back in her chair a bit so she wouldn't seem too anxious. "What's his name?"

Sally laughed. "Well, his name is Kirby, Sarah, but he goes by Smoke, or at least that's what everyone including me calls him."

"Smoke?" Sarah asked, "My, what an unusual name." It was him. She was married to a monster.

Sally's eyes became distant as she thought back to what Smoke had told her of his early days in the wild West . . .

Sarah stared at Sally, who seemed lost in a pleasant memory for the moment. This wasn't what she'd expected. Most gunmen, at least all that she'd been acquainted with or told about, didn't have wives. They were for the most part a sorry lot of drunkards and malcontents who drifted from one place to another, selling their guns and their willingness to kill without reason to the highest bidder. And the women they did take up with, when they weren't busy killing, were nothing like Sally Jensen. *Why, she and I could be friends if things were different,* Sarah thought wryly. *I just can't believe she's married to a man as evil as Smoke Jensen and doesn't realize how bad he really is.*

After a moment, Sarah reached over and gently touched Sally's arm. "Mrs. Jensen," she said tentatively.

Sally started and seemed to come out of her reverie. "Oh, excuse me, Sarah," she said, smiling almost sadly. "I fear my long journey has tired me considerably and I was daydreaming for a moment."

"No, that's all right," Sarah said, returning the smile. "You seemed to be someplace else for a minute . . . someplace nice."

"I was just remembering some tales my husband told me of his first days out here in the wilderness, back when he was no more than a child."

"Oh?"

"Yes. Things were very different then, and Smoke had to learn to use both his wits and his guns at a very young age." Sally laughed softly. "Thank goodness we're much more civilized nowadays and things are different."

Not so different as you think, Sally, not so different at all, Sarah thought, struggling to keep the hatred she felt for Smoke from showing in her eyes or in her voice.

5

Sarah decided it would be best if she could find out all she could about this man she planned to kill, this man who went by the unlikely name Smoke. She didn't like taking advantage of a nice woman like Sally, but it wasn't her fault the lady had married a monster and didn't seem to realize it. Perhaps if she could get her to talk about him, she would find out how best to get close to him and then take him out.

"Please, Sally," she said, "if you're not too tired, tell me some of those tales about your husband's early days out here and how he got such an unusual name as Smoke."

"Well," Sally said, hesitating, "I wouldn't want to bore you."

"Oh, you won't," Sarah promised. "My father used to tell my brother and me about how he got started years ago, back when things were very different in Colorado Territory, and his stories always fascinated us."

Sally smiled. "We're a lot alike, Sarah," she said. "I too have always been interested in the history of the Old West."

The only difference is my father is a respectable rancher and your husband is cold-blooded killer and gunman, Sarah thought.

Sally settled back in her seat and closed her eyes, letting the memories of the stories Smoke had told her come to the front of her mind. . . .

* * *

Smoke was sixteen years old when his father returned to their hardscrabble farm in Missouri from fighting for the Gray in the Civil War. When young Kirby told his father that his mother, Emmett's wife, had died the previous spring, Emmett put the farm up for sale and he and Kirby moved off headed west.

They rode westward, edging north for several weeks, moving toward country controlled by the Kiowa and Pawnee Indians. When they arrived at the Santa Fe Trail, they met up with a mountain man who called himself Preacher. He was dressed entirely in buckskins, from his moccasins to his wide-brimmed hat. Young Kirby thought him the dirtiest man he'd ever seen; even his white beard was so stained with tobacco as to be almost black.

Soon after their meeting, the three men were ambushed by a group of Indians that Preacher said were Pawnees, and took refuge in a buffalo wallow just behind a low ridge.

Suddenly the meadow around them was filled with screaming, charging Indians. Emmett brought one buck down with a .44 slug through the chest, flinging the Indian backward.

The air had changed from the peacefulness of summer quiet to a screaming, gun-smoke-filled hell. Preacher looked at Kirby, who was looking at him, his mouth hanging open in shock, fear, and confusion.

"Don't look at me, boy!" he yelled. "Keep them eyes in front of you!"

Kirby jerked his gaze to the small creek and the stand of timber that lay behind it. His eyes were beginning to smart from the acrid powder smoke, and his head was aching from the pounding sound of the Henry .44 and the screaming and yelling. The Spencer rifle Kirby held at the ready was a heavy weapon, and his arms were beginning to ache with the strain.

His head suddenly came up, eyes alert. He had seen

movement on the far side of the creek. Right there! Yes, someone was over there.

Kirby was thinking to himself that he really didn't want to shoot anyone when a young brave suddenly sprang from the willows by the creek and lunged into the water, a rifle in his hand.

As the young brave thrashed through the water toward him, Kirby jacked back the hammer of the Spencer, sighted in on the brave, and pulled the trigger. The .52-caliber pounded his shoulder, bruising it, for there wasn't much spare meat on Kirby. When the smoke blew away, the young Indian was facedown in the water, his blood staining the stream.

Kirby stared at what he'd done, then fought back waves of sickness that threatened to spill from his stomach.

The boy heard a wild screaming and spun around. His father was locked in hand-to-hand combat with two knife-wielding braves. Too close for the rifle, Kirby clawed out the .36-caliber Navy Colt from leather. He shot one brave through the head just as his father buried his Arkansas Toothpick to the hilt in the chest of the other.

And as abruptly as they came, the Indians were gone, dragging as many of their dead and wounded with them as they could. Two braves lay dead in front of Preacher, two braves lay dead in the shallow ravine with the three men; the boy Kirby had shot lay facedown in the creek, arms outstretched, the waters a deep crimson. The body slowly floated downstream.

Preacher looked at the dead buck in the creek, then at the brave in the wallow with them . . . the one Kirby had shot. He lifted his eyes to the boy.

"Got your baptism this day, boy. Did right well, you did."

"Saved my life, son," Emmett said, dumping the bodies of the Indians out of the wallow. "Can't call you a boy no more, I reckon. You're a man now."

A thin finger of smoke lifted from the barrel of the Navy .36 Colt Kirby held in his hand. Preacher smiled and spit tobacco juice.

He looked at Kirby's ash-blond hair. "Yep," he said. "Smoke'll suit you just fine. So Smoke hit'll be."

"Sir?" Kirby finally found his voice.

"Smoke. That's what I'll call you now on. Smoke."*

Sarah's face was flushed and she was fanning herself with a small handkerchief as Sally finished her tale of how her husband came to be called Smoke and of his introduction to the Wild West.

The story had been very exciting, and somehow it reminded Sarah of the stories Cletus and her father had told her as she was growing up, about how they'd had to hold off Indian attacks and bandit attacks while still trying to raise crops and cattle and babies.

"My, my, Sally," Sarah said, taking a deep breath. "That was quite a story."

Sally smiled as she patted Sarah's thigh next to her on the seat. "Things were quite different in those days, Sarah. The Indians were still around and hated the intrusion of the white man, and there was no law to call upon when you got in trouble. People had to learn to take matters into their own hands, and they became very tough in the doing."

Kind of like me, Sarah thought as she turned her face to stare out of the window. Since the law is unable to do what is right, I'm taking matters into my own hands, and I'm going to kill Smoke Jensen for what he did to my brother.

After a moment spent composing herself and forcing her face into an expression of friendship, Sarah turned back around and faced Sally. "And did this country make your husband tough, Sally?" she asked, trying to keep the venom out of her voice and her expression pleasant.

Sally pursed her lips as she thought about the question. She didn't quite know how to answer it. True, Smoke was as tough a man when provoked as she'd ever met, but with

The Last Mountain Man

her he was invariably gentle and kind, and she knew that there was no man more loyal to his friends than her husband, or more fearsome to his enemies. So, she guessed Smoke was tough when he needed to be and gentle and kind when he was allowed to be.

Unable to put all this into words without sounding like a fool, she just shrugged. "I suppose Smoke became as tough as he needed to be to survive in those days, but thankfully, those days are gone now and he has little need for that ability nowadays." She smiled at Sarah. "Nowadays, he spends his time with me on our ranch just outside of Big Rock, raising cattle and horses and being a boring old homebody."

She glanced over Sarah's shoulder and pointed. "And speaking of Big Rock, I do believe we're pulling into town right now."

Sarah followed Sally's gaze, hoping her friends already stationed there wouldn't be foolish enough to try to meet her at the station. She'd told Sally she didn't know anyone in town, and she didn't want them to make a liar out of her. She realized if she was to have any chance to get close enough to Smoke Jensen to do him in, she was going to have to have the trust of his wife.

She sighed. "Well, here I go about to start a new life for myself," Sarah said. She looked at Sally. "I hope I'll be able to find a nice place to stay and a good job soon."

Sally didn't hesitate. "I'm sure that won't be a problem," she said. "I know that Ed and Peg Jackson, who own the town's largest general store, are always looking for someone to help out so that Peg can spend more time at home with the children, and there's a very nice boardinghouse right on Main Street that caters to young, single women."

Sarah forced herself to smile brightly. "Oh, thank you, Sally. I don't know what I'd have done if we hadn't met."

Sally added, "Of course, if money is tight, you could always stay out at our ranch for a while until you've worked long enough to afford your own place."

Sarah paused, considering Sally's offer for a moment. True, it would give her plenty of access to Smoke Jensen, and would make it much easier when she finally decided to kill him, but she would be severely limited in being able to contact her friends in town or to keep in touch with her father about the details of what was going on. She finally decided against accepting Sally's offer, but she wanted to leave the door open for visits out to the ranch just in case.

"Oh, that is so kind of you, Sally, but my father made sure I had plenty of money when he sent me here. I have enough to tide me over until I get a few paydays behind me, but I would appreciate the chance to see your spread and visit with you if I get too lonely."

Sally patted her arm and stood up, getting her valise from the overhead rack. "Well, you know that you're always welcome, Sarah, and I'll be sure to have you out to dinner once you're settled in."

As they moved down the aisle when the train had ground to a halt, among much screeching of brakes and hissing of steam, Sally said, "I'll stop by the Jacksons' place on my way out of town and tell them that you'll be calling for a job."

Sarah nodded, her mind elsewhere as she searched the small crowd on the platform looking for either Carl Jacoby or Dan Macklin. If she saw them, she was going to have to give them some sign to stay away until they could meet later, when no one was around to see them.

Fortunately, there were no familiar faces in the group waiting on the platform, and Sarah let herself relax as she handed a porter her claim ticket for her luggage.

Still, it wouldn't hurt to be extra careful. Sarah decided to take her time exiting from the train so she wouldn't be next to Sally in case her friends were out there waiting for her.

She went back into the ladies' parlor room, and pretended to be fussing with her hat and dress in front of the mirror, giving Sally plenty of time to leave the car ahead of her.

6

Sally too was anxiously scanning the crowd, looking for her husband as she stood on the platform, her heart beating a little faster than usual in her anticipation of seeing and holding him again.

Just as she was about to give up, thinking that perhaps he hadn't gotten her wire stating her arrival day, she saw him on the edge of the crowd, leaning up against the wall of the station house.

Gosh, but he looks good, she thought, flushing at the sight of his wide shoulders, heavily muscled arms, and tanned, handsome face. Even though his ash-blond hair was beginning to be streaked with touches of gray at the temples, he was still the best-looking man she'd ever seen, and the most desirable to boot.

She was glad to note the way his eyes lit up and his lips curled in a wide grin when he spied her. She dropped her valise and ran into his arms, inhaling the musky man-scent of him and sighing deeply with contentment. She was where she belonged, finally, and it had been a long time since she'd felt so safe and happy. She wondered briefly if he could feel the way her heart beat wildly in her chest at the touch of his arms around her.

She leaned back and looked up at his hair. Usually unruly, with a lock or two falling down over his forehead in a most appealing manner, it was shiny and slicked back and smelled faintly of pomade.

She grinned at him. "I see you've changed your hair," she said, running her hands through it and mussing it up just as she liked it.

He blushed. "Oh, I thought I'd get a trim in honor of your arrival, so I let the barber whack a little bit off the sides." He winced. "He put that smelly stuff in it before I could stop him, and I didn't have time to wash it out 'fore your train was due to arrive."

She locked an arm in his and walked with him toward the baggage car to collect her luggage. "Well, don't worry. I'll heat us up some water when we get to the Sugarloaf and we'll have a bath."

He turned to her, a slight flush on his face. "We?" he asked.

She too blushed. "Of course. I have to wash the grime of my journey off, and you have to get that pomade out of your hair." She hesitated. "If we share the bath, you won't have to work so hard to bring extra water into the cabin," she said, her face bright red at the brazenness of her proposal. Not that they hadn't shared an intimate bath before. It was just that they didn't usually discuss it out in public beforehand.

He smiled slowly. "So, I see that you've missed me as much as I've missed you."

She cocked one eye up at him. "More!" was all she said, but her tone caused him to rush the porter to get her luggage and put it on the buckboard so they could get back to the Sugarloaf as soon as possible. He had some serious welcoming-home to attend to, and he wasn't sure he could wait the few hours the trip home would take!

Sally looked around at the crowd of people near the baggage car, hoping to see Sarah. She wanted to introduce Smoke to her new friend, but Sarah was nowhere to be seen. Oh well, Sally thought, there'd be plenty of time for that later.

She made a mental note to tell Smoke to be sure and stop by the general store on their way out of town so she could tell Peg Jackson about the girl who wanted to work there. Peg would be ecstatic, since that would allow her more time at home with their children.

At that very moment, standing only a couple of dozen feet behind Smoke and Sally, Sarah put her hand in her handbag and closed her fingers around the butt of a snub-nosed Smith and Wesson .36-caliber revolver. Her eyes narrowed as she saw for the first time the man who'd killed her brother. Her heart beat fast, and she began to tremble at the sight of the monster who'd ruined her family. Perhaps it would be best to get it over with and kill him now. After all, she might never get a better chance.

She started to pull the weapon out and put a bullet in the back of his head, but a hand closed over her arm.

She whirled around, her hate-filled eyes glaring as Carl Jacoby whispered in her ear, "Not here and not now, Sarah. Don't be a fool."

She struggled against his grip for a moment, and then she relaxed as the killing fever left her. She slumped against him and let him pull her out of sight around the corner of the station building.

"You're right, Carl," she said as he leaned her back against the wooden wall. "A shot in the back with no warning would be too easy for that man. I want to look into his eyes when he knows he's about to die and tell him just why I'm going to kill him. I want him to suffer, to think about never seeing his wife again, to know what his dastardly act in Pueblo cost him."

Carl glanced around to make sure no one was watching. Sarah was really worked up, with her red face and animated talk. He knew he'd better get her out of sight before someone came up and asked what was going on.

"Come on, Sarah. I've got a room reserved for you at the hotel."

She stopped him with a hand on his chest. Nice girls

didn't stay at hotels, especially by themselves without any other family around.

"Uh-uh, Carl. I think I'll get a room at a boardinghouse Mrs. Jensen recommended to me."

"What?" he asked, his eyes wide and his face paling at her words. "What do you mean Mrs. Jensen . . . ?"

Sarah smiled, calmer now that her thoughts of an immediate kill were over, and she began to walk up the street. "I'll explain it all to you later, over dinner." She looked at him. "This place does have an acceptable eating establishment, I take it?"

He nodded, his expression worried. He still couldn't believe she'd been talking to Smoke Jensen's wife on the train. He hoped she hadn't given anything away. He knew that if the people of this town thought that anyone was going to try and harm their favorite son, Smoke Jensen, they'd most likely string them up from the nearest maple tree.

Cal and Pearlie were lying around the bunkhouse, mending socks and sewing buttons on shirts and doing all the things that needed doing after a few months away from home, when they heard the buckboard pull up in front of the ranch house.

Cal jumped to his feet and looked out the window. "Hey, Pearlie," he called, turning with a big grin on his face as he headed for the door. "It's Smoke and Sally."

"Hold on, pard, just where do you think you're goin'?" Pearlie drawled from his place at the table next to the pot-bellied stove.

Cal stopped and looked back over his shoulder. "Didn't you hear me, Pearlie? Miss Sally's back from her trip," he said. "I'm gonna go out there an' tell her hello."

Pearlie grinned and shook his head. "No, you're not, young'un," he said firmly.

Cal put his hands on his hips. "And just why not?" he asked angrily. "It's been almost a year since I seen her and I want'a tell her how much I missed her."

"Son, I know you ain't had a whole passel of experience

with womenfolk like I have, so I guess I'll just have to excuse your ignorance on the subject and maybe try an' explain a few things to you."

Cal raised his eyebrows and moved toward Pearlie. "And just what does my experiences with females have to do with anything, 'ceptin' your dirty mind?"

Pearlie sighed and took a drink from his coffee mug that was sitting on a small pine table next to his bunk, along with some spare change, a pocketknife, and his tobacco pouch and papers.

"Think about it, Cal. Smoke and Sally have been away from each other for the better part of a year now, and they're fixin' to be alone together for the first time in a lot of months." He raised his eyebrows as if that explained everything to the young man.

"So?" Cal asked, clearly not getting Pearlie's drift. "That's what I been sayin'. Miss Sally's been gone a long time an'—"

"Do I have to spell it out for you, Cal?" Pearlie said with a heavy sigh, speaking as if he were talking to someone not quite right in the head. "Who do you think Sally wants to spend time with right now, you or Smoke?"

Suddenly, it dawned on Cal what Pearlie was trying to hint at.

"But you don't think they're gonna . . . ?" he said, his eyes wide and his face flushing bright red.

Pearlie laughed. "Well, if'n I was Smoke an' I hadn't been with my wife in over six, seven months, I sure as hell would first chance I got."

"But . . . but it's daylight outside!" Cal argued, aghast at the very idea.

Pearlie sighed again and looked down into his coffee cup, his eyes crinkling at the corners as he smiled. "Boy, do you have a lot to learn, Cal, more than you can ever imagine."

A couple of hours later, after Sally had heated enough water to fill the oversized tub they kept in their spare bedroom, and after they'd both managed to get freshened up from their trip and their rather exuberant welcome home, Smoke knocked on the bunkhouse door.

Pearlie answered it, since Cal was in the middle of trying to mend a hole in one of his socks that was almost big enough to put a fist through.

Smoke leaned inside. There was no one there except Cal and Pearlie, the other hands not in from the fields yet.

"You boys interested in some real home cooking for a change?" he asked.

Pearlie shook his head, a sorrowful expression on his face. "You don't mean you're gonna make Miss Sally cook her first night back home, do you, Boss?"

Smoke shrugged. "I offered to eat leftovers from Cookie's dinner meal, but she insisted on cooking. Said it'd been a long time since she cooked for her family and she wanted to do it."

"You sure she intended for you to ask Pearlie an' me over too, Smoke?" Cal asked from his bunk.

Smoke grinned. "When Sally said she wanted to cook for her family, who the heck do you think she meant?"

Pearlie beamed at him and Cal being included in the term family by Sally, and quickly nodded. "You bet, Smoke. Give us a few minutes to clean up an' we'll be right over."

Smoke looked back over his shoulder and sniffed loudly through his nose. "Well, don't take too long. If my nose isn't wrong, I think her fresh apple pie is just about ready."

Pearlie's eyes opened wide and he whirled around and headed for the pitcher and washbasin in the corner, already rolling his sleeves up. He hadn't had any of Sally's wonderful home cooking for a long time and he could hardly wait.

"Course you're gonna have to wait until you finish the fried chicken and mashed potatoes and green beans and fresh-baked rolls before she's gonna let you have any of the pie," Smoke added from the doorway.

"Fried chicken?" Cal asked, licking his lips over the thought.

"And mashed potatoes and fresh green beans and oven-baked bread," Pearlie finished, his eyes dreamy as if he were talking about a lovely woman who'd just asked him out.

"Outta the way, Cal," Pearlie called as he hurried toward the door, "'less you want'a get runned over."

7

Carl Jacoby carried Sarah's luggage as she walked down Main Street until they came to a white clapboard building with a sign next to the front door that read ROGERS' BOARDING HOUSE.

Sarah knocked on the door, and a rotund woman wearing a white apron sprinkled with flour answered it. She was wiping her hands on a cup towel, and looked angry at being interrupted.

"Yes?" she asked, irritation in her voice.

"Hello," Sarah said. "My name is Sarah Johnson. Mrs. Sally Jensen referred me to you. She said you rent rooms to young single ladies."

The woman in the doorway broke into a big smile, all traces of irritation vanishing immediately. "Well, howdy, Sarah," she said, sticking out her hand. "My name is Melissa Rogers, but everyone calls me Mamma. Come on in."

Sarah took the hand, which seemed as big as a ham, and shook it as she entered the door.

"You can just put the luggage down here in the parlor, boy," Mamma Rogers said to Carl Jacoby, who grimaced at the term "boy" but kept his mouth shut as he unloaded the suitcase and valise.

Sarah stepped over to him and handed him a bit of change from her purse, as if she were tipping a stranger for carrying her bags for her. With her back to Mamma Rogers, she mouthed the words "I'll see you later."

After Sarah had told Mrs. Rogers the same lie about her reasons for coming to Big Rock as she'd told Sally, Mamma showed her to a room on the second floor overlooking Main Street.

"I'm sorry 'bout this room, Sarah," Mrs. Rogers said, moving over to open the drapes and let some light into the room. "It's a mite noisy on weekends when the local cowboys are in town celebrating, but it's the last one I have available, and you do catch a nice breeze through the window."

Sarah stepped to the window and peered out. In her mind she could see herself taking careful aim with a rifle down at Smoke Jensen as he passed on the street below—it wouldn't be as gratifying as looking into his eyes as she killed him, but it would do for a backup plan in case she wasn't able to get him alone long enough to do it face-to-face.

She turned back around to Mamma, smiling, all traces of her murderous thoughts gone from her innocent visage. "Oh, this room will do nicely, Mamma, and I do like the view of Main Street."

An hour later, after she'd unpacked her luggage and paid Mamma Rogers for the first two weeks, she asked about a good place to eat.

"Well, you're welcome to eat here most nights," Mamma said, "but if you need a place to have a good home-cooked meal at lunch or breakfast, you can't beat the Sunset Café over on Second Street."

"Thank you," Sarah said. "I think I'll take a walk around town and get acquainted with my new home."

After she left Mamma Rogers's place, she stepped into the hotel where Carl had told her he was staying, and left a note with the desk clerk telling him where to meet her.

Thirty minutes later, after walking around doing some sightseeing, she joined Carl Jacoby and Daniel Macklin at the Sunset Café on Second Street. It was past lunchtime and before dinnertime, and so the place was practically deserted, which was just fine with Sarah because she didn't want too many people to see her conversing with the two new men in town.

"Hello, Daniel," she said as she approached their table, glad to see another familiar face from her hometown.

Daniel dipped his head. "Howdy, Sarah. I see you made the trip all right."

Carl, who was bursting with curiosity about her earlier comments about Mrs. Jensen, butted in. "Now, what's this about you an' Smoke Jensen's wife becomin' such good friends on the train?"

"What?" Macklin said. Jacoby hadn't told him of her comments about Mrs. Jensen.

Sarah smiled secretively as she waved the waitress over and told her she would have the lunch special and a cup of hot tea to drink.

Jacoby and Macklin had already ordered beefsteaks and fried potatoes.

After the waitress put her tea and food on the table and gave her a small jar of honey to use in her tea, Sarah told the two men what had happened on the train while she ate.

"You were taking an awfully big chance, talking to Mrs. Jensen like that," Jacoby said as he picked at his steak, a worried expression on his face.

Macklin fixed him with a scornful glance as he said, "Our friend Carl here seems to have come up with a sudden lack of courage where it comes to Smoke Jensen," he said, a sneer in his voice.

Sarah raised her eyebrows and gave Carl a questioning look as she sipped her tea. "Well, Carl, for your information, I didn't know whose wife she was when we struck up a conversation, and after she told me she was married to Smoke Jensen, I couldn't very well just get up and leave, now could I?" she said.

"I guess not," he admitted, still not able to look at her.

"Now, what's this Mac is saying about you being afraid of Smoke Jensen?" she asked, her voice getting hard.

Carl, flushing, argued back, "That's not true!" He fussed with his steak for another moment. "It's just that everything I see and hear about this man don't fit the picture of a backshooter or a man who'd kill someone without giving them a fair chance."

Sarah pursed her lips and slowly put her teacup down on the table. "So," she said in a low voice, her eyes boring into Carl's. "Now you're an expert on Smoke Jensen and you think what he did when he shot my brother and your friend was all right?"

Carl shook his head. "That's not what I'm tryin' to say, Sarah," he said, a pained expression on his face as he tried to make himself understood. "It's just that I don't think it went down like everybody in Pueblo seems to say it did."

Macklin gave a short, harsh laugh. "Yeah, Sarah," he said, his voice dripping with scorn. "Carl here thinks this Jensen is so quick with a handgun he could draw and put five or six slugs in Johnny an' his friends 'fore they could even get a shot off, even though they already had their guns out."

Sarah shook her head and turned her gaze back to Carl. "Is that really what you think, Carl?"

He nodded, leaning forward and putting his elbows on the table as if by getting closer to her he could make her believe what he was saying. "You got to see him draw to believe it, Sarah. The man is fast as greased lightning."

"So was Johnny, Carl. You know that," she said, her eyes beginning to tear up at all this talk about how her brother got shot and killed.

Carl shook his head, sorry he was making her sad but determined to make his point. "No, Johnny wasn't in Jensen's class, Sarah. Johnny was quick, all right, but Jensen is as fast as I've ever seen, bar none."

Now it was Sarah's face that flushed as she leaned across the table toward Carl until their faces were inches apart. "Well, it really doesn't matter, does it?" she said in a bitter tone. "Whatever happened that day in Pueblo, Smoke Jensen put lead in my brother and then he walked away like it never happened, and for that we're going to kill him!" She hesitated, and leaned back to take a sip of her tea before adding, "Unless you really have lost your nerve like Mac says you have."

Macklin threw his napkin down on the table. "Now you're talkin', Sarah. I say we go look for him and get this over with right now."

Jacoby didn't answer her accusation; he just looked at her with lovesick eyes, knowing he'd probably lost any chance for her to ever think of him in a favorable way again.

Sarah sighed and shook her head, a thoughtful expression on her face. "No, Mac. I want this done right. When I put the fatal bullet in Smoke Jensen's heart, I want to be looking in his eyes while I do it, and that is going to take some planning."

Macklin's eyes widened. "Sarah, you can't be serious. Carl's right about one thing. From what everybody around here says, Jensen is snake-quick on the draw. You wouldn't have a chance goin' up against a man like Jensen face-to-face."

She smiled and took a delicate sip of her tea. Her eyes had a mischievous twinkle in them. "Not if he didn't know I was coming after him," she said softly.

After Sarah finished her meal and left the café, warning the boys not to approach her in public but to leave a message in the mail slot at her boardinghouse when they needed to speak, Macklin shook his head.

"That little filly's gonna get in a world of trouble the way she's goin' after Jensen," he said, a sour expression on his face.

Jacoby, who had to struggle whenever he was around Sarah not to let his feelings for her show, nodded in agreement. "Yeah, an' if anything happens to her while we're supposed to be watchin' out for her, her old man will have our hides nailed to his barn door 'fore the week's out."

Macklin leaned back in his chair and slipped the Colt from his holster. He held the gun down out of sight from the waitress and opened the loading gate, checking the cylinders to make sure the pistol was fully loaded.

Jacoby frowned. "What the hell are you doin', Mac?"

"I'm getting ready to save Sarah and do what old man MacDougal sent us here to do in the first place—kill Jensen 'fore Sarah has a chance to get herself hurt trying that damn fool plan of hers."

Jacoby laughed harshly. "You're crazy, Mac. I done told you that you won't stand a chance against Jensen. He's too damned fast for you or me to handle." He hesitated. "Heck, I don't think we'd have a snowball's chance in hell if we drew down on him at the same time."

Macklin snorted. "Hell, Carl, I didn't say I was gonna challenge him to a duel face-to-face." He smiled grimly. "There's more'n one way to skin a cat, as they say."

"You're not going to backshoot him, are you?" Jacoby asked, his lips puckered like he'd tasted something sour at the very thought. It was only the lowest type of men in the West who would deign to shoot another man in the back, and Carl Jacoby couldn't believe Macklin would stoop that low, no matter the reason.

Macklin shook his head. "No, but I'm not gonna give him much warnin' either. I'll just walk up to him when he's not expecting any trouble and hook and draw."

"But you'll be arrested and hung."

"Naw, 'cause as soon as I fire I'm gonna hightail it outta there and be on my horse ridin' outta town 'fore he hits the floor."

Jacoby thought about it as he finished his coffee. After a moment, he said, "You might just have a chance." And even if he gets caught, at least he'll save Sarah from trying to do it herself, Jacoby thought to himself, but didn't say out loud.

Macklin slid his six-gun in its holster and then he got to his feet. "Now, let's go see if we can find Jensen," he said, wanting to get it done before he had a chance to think about it and change his mind.

8

Smoke was finishing his second cup of coffee at the breakfast table while Sally stood behind him, kneading his shoulders.

"Well, sir," she said, a teasing note in her voice, "how does it feel to be back from the wilds of Canada working as a boring old married rancher again instead of an intrepid explorer risking life and limb to carve a railroad out of a remote wilderness?"

Smoke laughed out loud. "Intrepid?" he asked. "Now that's a new one on me." He looked over his shoulder at her and grinned. "I suppose that means incredibly handsome and desirable?"

"No, sir, it certainly does not mean that. It means fearless, very brave," Sally, the ex-schoolteacher, informed him, putting on a highfalutin air.

He half-turned in his chair and pulled her down on his lap. "To tell you the truth, lady," he said, a twinkle in his eyes, "if I hadn't had you to come home to, I just might have stayed up there in the Canadian mountains." He paused, and his eyes got a faraway look in them. "They reminded me of the way it was out here twenty years ago, before all the pilgrims came from back East and spoiled it all."

"So," she said, leaning her head on his shoulder, "you gave all that up for little old me?"

He bounced her up and down a couple of times, grinning and patting her hip with his hand. "Oh, I don't know about 'little' anymore."

She straightened up with a frown. "Are you insinuating I gained weight while I was visiting my parents? That my hips are suddenly too big?" she asked, frost in her voice and her eyes flat and dangerous.

Realizing his mistake, he tried to get out of it, and of course that just made it worse. "Uh, no, dear, of course not. I was just teasing . . ."

"That does it, Smoke Jensen," she said, scrambling to her feet and smoothing her dress down over her hips. "I'm going to go on a diet right away."

"Now sweetheart . . ." Smoke began, knowing from past experience that when Sally dieted, everyone dieted. It was not a pleasant experience by any means.

She turned her back to him and began fussing with the leftover biscuits and sausage patties on the counter. "You'd better get a move on, Smoke," she said, her voice still cool and flat. "Pearlie said there were lots of supplies you needed to go get from town."

Smoke sighed. He'd really put his foot in it this time. Why were women so sensitive about their weight? he thought. Men weren't.

He got up from the table and put his guns on. As he got ready to leave, he walked over and put his arms around her from behind, holding her breasts as he leaned down to kiss the back of her neck.

"You don't need to diet, darling," he whispered, hoping she'd relent and give him a reason to put off his trip to town. "You've got the best figure in the territory."

"Or at least the biggest," she finished, her body stiff in his arms and her neck red and flushed.

He sighed and left the kitchen. Maybe she'd be in a better mood when he got back from Big Rock with the supplies. Maybe he'd get lucky and she'd forget all this nonsense about her needing to diet.

As he walked over to the bunkhouse, he chuckled. Pearlie was going to be mighty disappointed if Sally refused to make any more pies or bear sign for a while, that was for sure.

Smoke rode his big Palouse stud while Cal and Pearlie rode in the buckboard. Pearlie, after talking to the men he'd left in charge while they went on their jaunt up to Canada, found they were in dire need of several rolls of wire, some nails, and various other assorted supplies to make the repairs that always seemed to be necessary to keep a ranch in good order.

As they rode into town, Smoke said, "I got some bad news, boys."

"What's that?" Cal asked.

"Sally thinks she's getting fat, so she's going to go on a diet."

"What?" Pearlie exclaimed. He remembered the last time Miss Sally went on a diet. He'd about turned into a rabbit; they'd eaten so many salads and greens and carrots. "Please don't tell me that, Smoke," he said, a pained look on his face. "I was just getting used to having home cooking again." He rubbed his stomach. "I don't know if I can stand to go back to eating all them greens again."

"You and me both, pal," Smoke said as they pulled up in front of the general store.

When they entered, Cal saw what he thought was the most beautiful girl he'd ever seen in his life behind the counter. Her hair was long and fell down over her shoulders, and framed a face that belonged to an angel.

"Hello, sir," she said with a smile when she saw him gawking at her. "What can I get for you?"

"Uh . . . er . . ." he stuttered, not knowing what to say since he'd plumb forgotten why they were there. All he could think of was how pretty she was, and why had he never seen her before?

"Hello, miss," Smoke said, moving toward the counter. "You must be Sarah Johnson."

Sarah's eyes narrowed and a slight flush appeared on

her cheeks. "Do I know you, sir?" she asked, her voice hardening and her neck stiffening.

Smoke held up his hands, a flush appearing on his face at her reaction. "I didn't mean to give offense, Miss Johnson," he said quickly, looking around to see if Peg or Ed Jackson was around to rescue him. "It's just that my wife, Sally Jensen, said she met you on the train the other day, and she told me to tell you hello when we got here."

Sarah's eyes stayed hard for a moment, and then she made a conscious effort to soften her expression. "Oh, of course, you must be Mr. Jensen," she said, sticking out her hand and forcing her lips into a cordial smile.

Smoke shook it. "Yes, I am, but my friends just call me Smoke."

Sarah forced her eyes off Smoke, lest she give away the hatred she felt for him. "And who are these gentlemen with you, Mr. . . . uh . . . Smoke?"

"This is Calvin Woods, and the skinny one over there is my ranch foreman, Pearlie," Smoke said, inclining his head at the two men.

Sarah nodded her head at Pearlie and smiled demurely at Cal, causing the boy to blush furiously.

"Are you here alone?" Smoke asked, looking around the shop as he loaded his arms with supplies and piled them on the counter.

"Yes," Sarah answered. "Mr. and Mrs. Jackson took the morning off to take their children on a picnic." She glanced over at Cal, who was still standing there staring at her with his mouth half open. "Mr. Jackson said he might even do a little fishing on the creek up north of town. Mrs. Jackson will be in later."

"They must trust you very much to leave the store in your hands all alone."

She dipped her head, embarrassed by the compliment, especially as it came from a man she was all set up to hate. "Yes, sir, I guess they do."

Cal moved up next to Smoke and also dumped a load of supplies on the counter, almost stumbling over his feet since he seemingly couldn't take his eyes off Sarah.

When the boy just stood there staring, Pearlie, standing behind him with his arms also loaded down, cleared his throat loudly. "If you don't mind, podnah," he said with a hint of a laugh in his voice, "I'd like to put these down when you're finished gawkin'."

Cal whirled around, his face bright red. He leaned forward and thrust his face out. "I ain't gawking, Pearlie, an' don't you dare say I am."

"Calvin," Sarah called, "do you want me to add those things you're holding?"

Cal turned back around and put his supplies on the counter. "Uh, yes, ma'am, but everybody just calls me Cal."

Sarah smiled, forgetting for the moment her hatred of Smoke Jensen and everyone who worked for him. Cal was very cute, she thought, and he seemed so shy, she just wanted to grab him and cuddle him like a little puppy.

Her soft mood was ruined when Smoke stepped up to the counter and said, "Just put it on the Sugarloaf bill, if you would, Sarah."

When she nodded, not looking at him for fear her hatred would show in her eyes, Smoke and Cal and Pearlie began to pick up the supplies and carry them out to the buckboard in front of the store.

Once the wagon was fully loaded, Smoke climbed up on his horse and inclined his head toward Louis Longmont's saloon. "Why don't we grab lunch over at Louis's?" he asked.

"You don't have to ask me twice," Pearlie said, "though we'd better save some room for Miss Sally's bear sign. She told me yesterday she was gonna cook up a batch today."

"Uh, I wouldn't count on that, Pearlie," Smoke said as he spurred his horse toward Louis's saloon.

Pearlie slapped the reins on the butts of the horses pulling the buckboard and caught up with Smoke. "Oh, that's right. You said Miss Sally was fixin' to go on one of her diets." He looked over at Smoke. "Now what in blazes could make Miss Sally think she was getting too fat?"

"Well, to tell the truth, it's my fault."

"What do you mean?"

"This morning I was fooling around and I teased her that she wasn't as light as she used to be."

Pearlie groaned. "Oh, no! Don't tell me you was fool enough to say somethin' like that to a woman?"

Smoke nodded. "Yep."

"Damn!" Pearlie groaned. "You 'member last time Miss Sally got to feelin' fat?" Pearlie asked.

Smoke glanced at him, wondering how any of them could forget that terrible time.

"She didn't cook no biscuits nor bear sign nor pancakes for near about two months." Pearlie shook his head in sorrow. "Greens an' carrots an' vegetables was all we had to eat, an' I swear I 'bout had to threaten the hands with my six-gun to keep 'em on the job till she got over that foolishness."

"I remember," Smoke said. He forced a hopeful look on his face. "Maybe this time she won't stay on it too long."

"Yeah, an' maybe pigs'll learn to fly too," Pearlie added morosely.

Cal gave a short laugh. "I guess ol' Pearlie'll be findin' lots of reasons to come to town. 'Member last time, Smoke? He came to town at least ever' two or three days so's he could eat at Louis's."

"It was the only way I could keep my weight up enough to keep my pants from falling down around my ankles," Pearlie said, laughing at the memory.

"Yeah, an' you spent just about all your wages on food, so when you needed a new pair of boots you had to borrow the money from me," Cal said, laughing.

As the three men entered Louis Longmont's saloon, Daniel Macklin and Carl Jacoby watched them from an alley up the street.

"Now's my chance," Macklin said, pulling out his Colt and checking the loads once again, even though he'd just done it back at the hotel that morning. He was nervous as a cat in a roomful of rocking chairs, but he was too proud to back down now that he'd told Jacoby what he had in mind.

"You're not gonna try for him in Longmont's, are you?" Jacoby asked. "He's in there with all his friends. You won't stand a chance."

"No, I'm not gonna take him in there. I'm gonna wait until he comes out of the batwings. His eyes won't be used to the brightness an' he'll be half blind for a minute or two. That's when I'm gonna pull iron on him. Once he's down, I'll jump on my horse and hightail it toward Pueblo."

"How will you know when he's coming out?" Jacoby asked, watching the front of the saloon. "You can't just hang around the doorway an' wait. Someone'll see you and get suspicious. Hell, you might even get arrested for loitering."

"You're right," Macklin said, his brow furrowed as he thought about how to do it. Jacoby was right. He couldn't just stand at the window peeking in, or Jensen would surely see him and get suspicious.

"I know. I'll go in an' have me a beer or two at the bar. When I see Jensen getting up to leave, I'll walk out right ahead of him and when he comes through the batwings, I'll be waitin' for him out front."

He turned to Jacoby and stuck out his hand. "I know you don't much agree with me on this, but it's the only way I can think of to keep Sarah from getting herself hurt by trying to do it herself." He paused. "Besides, I owe it to Johnny and our other friends he cut down to do something about it," he added, his voice trembling just a bit.

"I know," Jacoby said, taking his hand. "And once you're gone, I'll explain it to Sarah and send old man MacDougal a wire tellin' him you're on your way."

As Macklin nodded and turned to leave, Jacoby added, "Good luck, Mac." He thought but didn't say out loud, *you're gonna need it!*

He didn't really think he'd have to wire Angus that Macklin was on his way, for he knew as sure as shooting that Macklin was going to die this day.

Jensen hadn't survived this long by letting men surprise him outside saloons.

9

Louis and his chef Andre were laughing at Smoke's description of how life was going to be on the Sugarloaf with Sally on a diet. "You know, fellahs, dieting seems to make women cranky, and when Mamma's not happy, nobody's happy," Smoke said, a morose expression on his face. "I just can't believe it," he added. "I come back from six months out in the wilderness eating with mountain men and trappers"—he paused and looked at them—"and you have no idea of just how bad that can be, and then I come home and say something stupid and kill any chance I have of getting something good to eat for a change."

"Well, my friend, from what you've told me," Louis observed dryly, "it's your own fault she feels like she has to lose weight."

"I know, I know," Smoke said. "Why couldn't I keep my big mouth shut?" He looked around, seeking support. "I was just teasing. Hell, Sally isn't fat. In fact, she's trim compared to most other women her age."

Louis laughed and shook his head while holding up his hand. "Now hold on, Smoke boy. Don't tread on that snake."

"What do you mean?"

"A woman is even more concerned with age than with weight, so don't ever say 'a woman of your age' to Sally."

The men at the table all laughed at this, realizing Louis

was correct. "In fact," Louis added, "were you to make such a grievous mistake, I predict you'd not only not be eating, you'd not be doing anything else with Sally for quite some time, if you get my drift."

Smoke nodded. "Yeah, I know. Sleeping in the bunkhouse. Wouldn't be the first time either."

Andre interrupted the banter. "Monsieur Smoke, I will gladly make up a series of box lunches for you and the boys. You can send Cal or Pearlie into town every few days, and they can take them out to the Sugarloaf where you can sneak into the bunkhouse for a snack whenever you get to feeling weak from lack of sustenance."

Smoke was about to reply when he noticed a tall, heavy-set man at the bar watching him while trying not to show it. Years of living as a fugitive from some untrue wanted posters had taught Smoke to listen to his instincts, and they were screaming at him to be careful of this man.

While the others at the table gave Andre their orders, Smoke leaned back in his chair, extended his right leg under the table, and unhooked the rawhide hammer thong on his right-hand Colt.

Whenever he glanced in the cowboy's direction, he noticed the man was sweating up a storm, though the temperature in the saloon was mild and cool.

Uh-huh, Smoke thought to himself, he's definitely up to something. Probably trying to get up the nerve to come over here and call me out. He'd seen this kind of behavior before, mainly when some young buck had bragged to his friends that he could take the famous gunfighter Smoke Jensen and then they'd had the effrontery to call him on it.

They usually sweated like a pig until they finally either got up the nerve to actually try their hand, or ran out in the alley and puked their guts out. He hoped this man was a puker instead of a caller. He had no desire to kill anyone today, especially someone he didn't even know.

While Cal and Pearlie and Louis reminisced over some of their adventures of the previous six months in Canada,

Smoke kept his attention riveted on the man at the bar, but he did it so the man didn't know he'd been seen.

The other thing Smoke noticed that made him even more certain the cowhand was up to something was the fact that the man nursed one beer for almost thirty minutes, not ordering another but not leaving the bar either. In Smoke's experience, men at a bar either drank continually or they left. They didn't stand around sneaking looks while they sipped a beer until it was warm and flat.

Once the meal was served, Louis, who was almost as experienced in the ways of the gun as Smoke was, leaned over and said in a low voice, "What is going on, my friend?"

Smoke raised his eyebrows as he cut into the incredibly juicy and tender steak Andre had prepared. "What do you mean?" he asked, his voice innocent.

Louis smiled, though there wasn't a lot of mirth in it. "I've been watching the man at the bar, and he seems inordinately interested in you and what you're doing. Do you recognize him—perhaps someone you've come across before or someone who perhaps has a grudge against you for some reason or other?"

Smoke shook his head. "No, not that that means much. He could be a relative of someone I've had trouble with, or he could be a young gun looking to get a reputation the quick way. I just don't know."

Louis shook his head. "No, I don't think he's a gunny. He has the look of a working cowboy to me, not someone who's riding the owlhoot trail." Louis reached across the table to get the silver coffeepot, and used the act of refilling his coffee cup to observe the man better.

"In fact," Louis said as he took a drink of his coffee, "his gun is old and worn and his boots are dirty. This man is no gunslick out to make a name for himself. He doesn't dress well enough."

"Yeah, I know. I agree," Smoke said, "but he's sure as hell on the prod for me, for whatever reason."

Louis leaned back and pulled a long, black cigar from his coat pocket. As he put a match to it, he looked over the glowing tip at Smoke. "Well, what are you going to do about this impasse we find ourselves in, partner? You're not going to let him pick the time and place, are you?"

Smoke smiled at Louis. "No, you're right, Louis. That wouldn't be very smart."

Since he didn't know if the man had friends waiting outside, Smoke looked around the table until he had Cal and Pearlie's attention. "Boys," he said in a low voice while keeping his expression bland and innocent, "keep your gun hands empty and keep a watch on the door for me. There's a gent over at the bar that's been eyeing me and I'm going over to have a talk with him. Watch my back in case he's got friends outside."

Cal and Pearlie nodded. "You got it, Boss," Pearlie said, letting his hand drift down to release his hammer thong while he continued to stuff his face using his left hand.

Smoke took a final sip of coffee and got up from the table. Before the man at the bar could move, Smoke turned and walked directly toward him.

As he approached, Smoke noticed sweat dripping from under the man's hat and running down the sides of his face. When he dropped his gaze to the man's right hand, he saw it had a fine tremor in it. The man was definitely on edge, and Smoke knew such men, though rarely effective, were still extremely dangerous because one never knew what they were going to do.

Smoke walked up and stood at the bar next to the man, facing forward with his elbows on the bar and his chin in his hand while he watched him in the mirror behind the bar.

"What do you want?" the man asked, his voice hoarse and gruff, his legs fidgety as he shifted his weight from one foot to the other and wiped sweat off his brow.

"Well, now, that's exactly the question I was fixing to ask you, friend," Smoke said, keeping his voice friendly while turning slightly so he was facing the man.

"Why . . . uh . . . what do you mean by that?"

Smoke smiled gently, his eyes interested but showing no animosity or anger. "You've been watching me for the past half hour, and you're sweating like a racehorse, so I thought I'd just end the suspense and come over here and introduce myself. I'm Smoke Jensen."

The man scowled. "I know who you are, Jensen," he growled as he picked up his warm beer and drained the mug.

"Do you have some business with me?" Smoke asked in a level voice, with no trace of challenge or fear.

"I don't do business with killers and murderers," the man said.

Smoke shrugged. "Well, I have to admit, I've killed some men in my day, though I've never murdered anyone, and those I've killed have all tried to kill me first."

"That's a lie!"

Smoke's face flushed. He didn't ordinarily let someone talk to him like this, but he wanted to find out what the man's beef was.

"Now ordinarily, friend, a man who spoke to me in that tone and with those words would either be flat on his back with a busted jaw, or he'd be bleeding all over the floor," Smoke said evenly, trying to control his temper. "However, you've obviously got something weighing heavily on your mind that concerns me, so I'll hold off on taking any offense for now. You want to tell me what you got stuck in your craw, Mister . . . uh . . . I didn't get your name?"

The man reached into his vest pocket and pulled out a couple of coins and threw them on the bar. "Not yet, Jensen, but when I'm ready, you'll know. And the name's Macklin, Daniel Macklin."

Smoke sighed and stepped away from the bar. "Well, we can settle this right now, if that's what you really want," he said, his eyes flat and hard. His hands hung loose by his thighs, his expression expectant.

Macklin's eyes strayed to the table across the room, where Cal and Pearlie and Louis all sat watching the show.

"Yeah, with your friends over there all set to gun me down if I make a play. No, thanks."

"My friends won't interfere if it's a fair fight," Smoke said, his eyes never leaving Macklin's.

Macklin sneered. "That's not the way I hear it, Jensen.

In fact, I hear they usually take a hand and join right in when you kill someone."

Smoke frowned. He had no idea what this Macklin was talking about. "Mister, I don't know what you're getting at or where you get your information, but I'm telling you flat out that's a lie, and I'm willing to back my words up any way you choose." Smoke waited just a beat. "Are you?"

Macklin let his hand drop to his side, and before he could blink, Smoke's Colt was in his hand, cocked, and pointing at his chest from a distance of two inches.

Macklin's face turned pale and he took a step back. He'd never seen anything like it. He hadn't even seen Jensen's hand move before it was holding a gun.

Macklin slowly raised his hands. "You gonna shoot me down in cold blood too, Jensen?" he managed to croak through a throat that was suddenly very dry.

Smoke shook his head and holstered his gun. "I still don't know what you're talking about."

Macklin turned and walked away, saying over his shoulder, "Well, I'll be sure and remind you next time we meet."

Smoke watched him leave the saloon, and then he went back to the table and took his seat.

"You find out what he wanted?" Louis asked.

Smoke shook his head. "No, but he's got a powerful hate for me going on. Seems to think me and my friends shot someone close to him down in cold blood."

"Where'd he get that crazy idea?" Cal asked.

Smoke shrugged. "He wouldn't say."

"You don't think it's about that fracas we had up in Canada, do you?" Louis asked.

Smoke shook his head. "No, I don't see how anyone could think we were the aggressors in that fight."

"Well, like you say, he's got a powerful hate on," Pearlie said, glancing at the batwings. "I could see it in his eyes."

"Yeah," Cal added, a worried look on his face as he stared at the batwings the man had just pushed through. "I'd sure watch my back if I was you, Smoke. A man as pissed off as that man is ain't gonna think twice 'bout shooting you in the back."

10

Carl Jacoby, who was watching the doorway to Longmont's Saloon from an alley down the street, was
astonished when Dan Macklin walked hurriedly out of the
batwings, jumped on his horse, and hightailed it around
the far corner onto a back street leading to their hotel.
His back was stiff and he didn't even glance behind him
as he rode away like his pants were on fire.

Carl had been expecting some fireworks from Macklin,
but he hadn't heard any gunshots and there didn't seem
to be a crowd forming or anyone coming out of the door
looking for Macklin. Couldn't have been much of a gunfight with this little a reaction.

"Well, I'll be damned," he muttered to himself as he
turned and walked quickly up the alley toward the hotel's
back entrance, hoping to find Macklin and find out what
had gone on in the saloon. He could tell something had
happened from the way Macklin looked as he rode down
the street, but he couldn't imagine what it could be.

When he got to the rear of the hotel, he saw Macklin's
horse tied to a hitching rail there and the back door par-
tially open.

He went inside, and stopped as he passed the doorway to
the hotel bar when he saw Macklin standing at the bar with
a bottle of whiskey in front of him and a glass to his lips.

Jacoby moved next to him at the bar, noticing his face

was flushed and he was covered with sweat. His hand holding the glass was shaking so much that Jacoby was afraid Macklin would spill it all over himself if he tried to drink from it.

Without speaking, Jacoby took the whiskey bottle, poured himself a small drink, and stood there as he sipped, waiting for Macklin to speak and wondering just what the hell had happened to shake his friend up so.

After a moment, and after he'd slugged down another drink, without spilling too much, Macklin turned toward Jacoby and leaned his elbow on the bar. "Carl, you were right 'bout Jensen." He shook his head. "I ain't seen nothin' like it in all my born days."

"What happened in there, Mac?" Jacoby asked, wondering how Macklin had been able to see Jensen's draw since he hadn't heard any gunfire.

Macklin poured himself another drink, but this time he sipped it instead of swallowing it down in one gulp. "I think the man must have eyes in the back of his head. I followed him and his friends into the saloon, and I took up a station at the bar and commenced to drink me a beer while I kept a look on him out of the corner of my eye. He must've noticed me watchin' him or something, 'cause he come over to the bar where I was standin' and he braced me."

"What do you mean?"

"He asked me what was it I wanted. When I didn't exactly answer his question and I accidentally let my right hand move toward my gun, he drew his pistol."

Jacoby let his lips curl in a small smile, knowing what was coming next. "Pretty fast, huh?"

"Fast ain't exactly the word I'd use, Carl. More like lightning, I think. One second I was looking in his eyes, as cold and black as a snake's, an' the next second his hand was full of iron and I was staring down the barrel of a Colt—and the thing is, I didn't even see his hand move." He took another sip of whiskey, his hand more stable now.

"You know how when you're facing somebody an' they're fixin' to draw, you can usually see a twitch of their arm muscle or a shift in their eyes 'fore they hook and draw?" he asked, his face pale.

Jacoby nodded. He knew what Mac meant. There was almost always some telltale sign before a man committed himself in a gunfight. Knowing this and recognizing it was what gave professional gunfighters the edge in such contests.

"Well," Macklin continued, "there was nothing about Jensen that even hinted he was going for his gun. One minute he's looking me in the eye, just talking as natural as you please, and the next he's somehow got a gun in his hand stuck against my chest and his eyes are hard and black as flint."

Jacoby's eyes narrowed. "And he didn't threaten you or hit you or anything like that after he drew his pistol and had the drop on you?"

Macklin shrugged, dropping his gaze to stare into his whiskey. "Who needs to threaten when you can draw a six-killer like that?"

"But Mac," Jacoby said earnestly, "can't you see what I've been trying to tell you? Jensen ain't no cold-blooded killer. He had the drop on you in front of his friends. If he was a showboat or looking to impress 'em, he could've pistol-whipped you or even shot you down. Hell, this is his town. No one would've blamed him. But he didn't."

Macklin's expression became thoughtful. "No, he didn't, an' you're right. There wasn't nothin' I could do to stop him from doing whatever he wanted to."

Jacoby turned back to the bar and downed the rest of the whiskey in his glass. "Maybe we'd better try and talk some sense into Sarah, or at least get her to hold off until we can figure out what we got to do."

Macklin smirked and drained his glass in one long swallow. "Hell, there ain't no need in worryin' ourselves over that, Carl, my friend. Old Man MacDougal wants Jensen dead, an' so does his daughter Sarah. As far as them two are concerned, once they've made up their minds on something, it's as good as gold."

"But maybe we can convince them they're wrong about him," Jacoby argued.

Macklin laughed. "You ever try to tell Sarah anything she didn't want to hear, boy?"

Jacoby nodded. "Yeah, I see what you mean. She is a mite stubborn at times."

"No, Carl. A mule is a 'mite' stubborn. Sarah is full-on-all-the-time stubborn."

"So, what are we gonna do?"

Macklin sighed. "I guess we got to do like you say and at least try to make her see reason." He chuckled. "Hell, worst she can do is chew our ears off."

"Maybe if we get her to hold off for a while and to watch how Jensen operates around town. Maybe she'll start to see that he ain't exactly the monster she thinks he is."

"I still think we're whistlin' in our hats, but like you say, it won't hurt to try and talk some reason into her, though the words 'reason' and 'woman' don't ordinarily belong together."

Macklin headed on over to the café while Carl walked to the general store down the street. Once inside, he caught Sarah's eye, mouthed the words "Sunset Café," and then left, hoping she'd understand that he needed to talk to her.

Sarah waited until Carl had been gone for a few minutes and then she went over to Peg Jackson, who was stocking a shelf in the rear of the store.

"Peg," she said, "I'm going to go over to the Sunset Café and get some coffee. I'm a little sleepy today and I need something to pick me up. Would you like for me to bring you back a cup?"

"That would be delightful, Sarah, and could you also get me a piece of one of those sweet cakes they make so well over there?"

"Certainly," Sarah said, and she took off her apron and walked down the block and around the corner to the café.

Carl and Dan were sitting in a corner booth toward the back away from any windows. Macklin didn't want to be seen with Sarah now that he'd managed to arouse Jensen's suspicions.

Sarah joined them at the table after making sure that no one she knew was in the place. After the waitress had taken their orders and placed coffee for all of them on the table, Sarah spoke. "Now, what's so all-fired important that you wanted to meet here in the middle of the day where everyone in town can see us together?"

Jacoby sat back, waiting for Macklin to speak. "Well, I had a talk with Jensen today," Macklin said.

"You what?" she exclaimed, almost yelling. When several patrons turned to glance at her, she sat back and tried to calm herself down. "What did you do, Mac?" she asked in a calmer tone of voice, but it was clear she was still furious.

"Don't get upset, Sarah," Macklin said, shushing her as he looked around to make sure no one was watching them any longer. "I didn't tell him anything. I just wanted to get a feeling for the feller, that's all."

Sarah's face was flushed with anger. "And did you, Mac?" she asked in a lower voice this time. "Did you get a feeling for the man who killed my brother?"

Macklin glanced at Jacoby, who nodded, and then he leaned forward, speaking earnestly. "Yes, I think I did, Sarah, an' I don't think he did what everybody in Pueblo thinks he did."

She sat back, a look of astonishment on her face. "You don't think he shot Johnny down?"

Macklin also sat back, trying to think how he could convince her of what he felt was the truth. "Oh, I think he probably shot Johnny," he said. "But I don't think it was in cold blood or that he ambushed him. Jensen is too fast to have to do that. In fact, he's plenty fast enough to have killed Johnny and all the others in a fair fight."

Her mouth fell open in astonishment. "And just how did you determine this, Mac?" she asked sarcastically. "Did you walk up to him and say, "By the way, Mr. Jensen, I'd sure like to see how fast you are on the draw. Could you oblige me and show me your moves?"

Macklin flushed in embarrassment. He wasn't used to anyone talking to him like this, especially not young women who were still wet behind the ears. "No, Sarah, I didn't do that. I just prodded him a little until he drew on me. That's when I saw how fast he was, and believe me, it was plenty fast."

Sarah looked around, shaking her head. "I don't believe this," she muttered, as if to herself. Then she looked up and stared into Macklin's eyes. "Let me remind you of something you've evidently forgotten, Mac. You work for my dad, and he sent you here for one reason, and that is to kill Smoke Jensen or to guard my back while I do it. Isn't that right?"

Macklin nodded reluctantly. "Yes, but I think Angus and you are both wrong about what happened that day. And if Jensen killed Johnny in a fair fight, which Johnny probably started, then I don't think Jensen should be killed for it."

Sarah slowly sipped her coffee, her eyes burning into Macklin's. After a moment, she turned her gaze to Jacoby. "Is this how you feel also, Carl?"

Jacoby nodded. "Yes, it is, Sarah. We've both looked into this before you got here, and everyone in this town thinks Jensen is straight as an arrow. They don't have one bad thing to say about him, and no one in this town would ever believe he's a backshooter or ambusher."

"Well, I'll tell you what I think," she said, her voice low and hard. "I think you're both full of . . . well, hot air."

Jacoby reached his hand across the table and tried to put it on hers. "We just don't want you going off half-cocked, Sarah, and either killing an innocent man or getting yourself shot up."

Sarah moved her hand away from Jacoby's, her lips tight. "This is going to take some thinking about," she said. "I'll send a wire to my dad and see what he thinks about all this. I may have to ask him to send me some more help, men who know their place and are loyal to him."

"Be careful what you say in a telegram," Macklin warned. "Remember, everyone in this town knows Smoke Jensen."

"Don't you worry about that, Mac. You got other things

to be worried about, like what my daddy's going to say when I tell him you've gone over to the other side."

"Aw, Sarah," he said, but she held up her hand.

"Now, get out of here, the both of you. I've got some thinking to do."

After they left, she called the waitress over and ordered two pieces of the sweet cakes. One for Peg and one for her.

While she waited for her order, she sat there thinking on how she could word a telegram so her daddy would know what was going on without letting the telegrapher know what she was doing.

As she sat there, she wondered just what it was about Smoke Jensen that enabled him to fool so many people into thinking he was a good man. It never crossed her mind that perhaps they were right about him and that she and her father were wrong.

11

Cletus Jones pulled his mount to a stop in a cloud of dust in front of the MacDougal ranch house and jumped to the ground. He had a feeling the telegram he'd picked up in Pueblo from Sarah MacDougal was important enough to need Angus's immediate attention.

Cletus had been MacDougal's foreman for as long as he could remember. They'd both come out here to Colorado Territory back when there were more Indians than white men, and had fought hard to carve a ranch out of the wilderness.

Cletus had been best man for Angus MacDougal's wedding, and he was godfather to both of the old man's children—now there was only Sarah since Johnny was dead.

As he ran through the front door, Mrs. MacDougal called out, "Cletus, don't you go running on my hardwood floors that've just been waxed!"

He tipped his hat and smiled, but didn't slow down appreciably as he headed toward the study/office where Angus could always be found this time of day.

Angus swiveled around in his leather high-backed chair and regarded Cletus with raised eyebrows. "Who lit a fire under your saddle, boy?" he asked in his rough, gravelly voice. Cletus was just about the only man on the ranch that Angus would allow to burst in on him unannounced.

"I got this here message from Miss Sarah, Boss," Cletus

said, pulling a wrinkled yellow envelope from his breast pocket. It was wet with sweat from his rapid ride from town. "The telegraph man said it came in yesterday but it was too late to get it out here by then."

Angus frowned, but didn't say anything as he slit the envelope with a thumbnail and pulled out the telegram. At first, he'd been very angry at her for taking off after Smoke Jensen on her own without consulting him. But after thinking about it, he'd realized he would have expected a son to do it, and Sarah had always been as good as, and often better than, his son had been at managing the ranch.

He smiled and opened up the folded yellow sheet of paper. After a moment spent reading it, he swiveled around and stared out the window, thinking.

Cletus was bursting with curiosity to find out what Sarah had done about Smoke Jensen, but he knew better than to interrupt the old man while he was thinking. Even though Cletus had been with Angus MacDougal since the early days when they'd fought off Indians and rustlers and road agents together while founding the MacDougal spread, and even though he was the kids' godfather, since they were pups he'd never thought much of Johnny. He knew he was and always had been a spoiled brat. However, Cletus thought Sarah was one of the prettiest and nicest womenfolk he'd ever known. Hell, if he'd been twenty years younger and hadn't been like family to her, he'd've made a run at her himself.

After a moment, Angus turned his chair back around, crumpling the paper in his fist. "Get your gear together and gather up the best ten men you can find, Cletus. You're gonna take a little trip down to Big Rock."

When Cletus nodded, Angus turned back to his desk and picked up a pencil and paper. "And send little Jimmy in here. He's gonna need to ride to Pueblo and send my daughter an answer to her wire."

"Uh, Boss, what do I tell the men we're gonna go to Big Rock for?" Cletus asked.

Angus MacDougal smiled grimly. "Tell 'em you're

gonna go down there and pick up a skunk and bring him back here to me to deal with."

"Yes, sir," Cletus said, though he really didn't understand just what the old man meant about picking up a skunk. Hell, they had plenty of those around here if'n he wanted one.

Cletus was loyal to the bone, but sometimes he was dumb as a post.

Three days later, days Macklin spent holed up in his hotel room lest he run into Smoke Jensen or one of his friends again, a bellboy knocked on the door to Jacoby's room and handed him a handwritten note.

Jacoby opened it and read, "Meet me at our usual dining place after the noon rush at three o'clock." It was signed with only an *S*.

Jacoby tipped the boy a nickel and went next door and knocked on Macklin's door. When he answered, Jacoby showed him the note. "We've got about an hour till three o'clock. That ought to give you time to get freshened up a mite," Jacoby said, wrinkling his nose as he looked at Macklin's disheveled attire and unshaven face.

His friend had been in a funk ever since the day Jensen scared him half to death by drawing on him and Sarah had chewed his butt about going against her father's wishes.

"Yeah, all right," Macklin said in a dull voice.

"You got to snap out of it, man," Jacoby said. "We got work to do." He knew that Macklin was still ashamed that he hadn't had the courage to draw down on Jensen when he had the chance. Jacoby had tried to explain to him that it wouldn't have done any good, and that the only result would have been that Mac would now be deader than yesterday's news. Still, his friend was not accustomed to backing down from anyone, least of all the man who'd killed his best friend and his boss's son.

"That is, if I ain't been fired," Macklin said, and shut the door in Jacoby's face.

* * *

It was five after three and the Sunset Café was almost deserted when Macklin and Jacoby joined Sarah at their usual table in the rear. Jacoby was thankful that Macklin had shaved and washed up before the meeting. He didn't want Sarah to see how his friend had declined in mental attitude since his run-in with Smoke Jensen.

Sarah had already ordered, so the men sat down across the table from her and told the waitress to just bring them whatever she was having, though they both wanted coffee instead of the hot tea she favored.

After the waitress left, Sarah placed a telegram on the table so they could both read it. It said:

I AGREE FULLY WITH YOUR IDEA STOP WILL SEND SOME MEN TO HELP YOU ROUND UP STOCK AND BRING THEM BACK HERE TO RANCH FOR FURTHER EXAMINATION AND FINAL DETERMINATION OF THEIR DISPOSITION END

Macklin raised his eyebrows. "Just what does this mean, Sarah?"

She took a bite of her food and washed it down with her hot tea. "I telegrammed my father and told him I was having trouble rounding up the stock he was interested in and that I needed some more help, and that the beeves should be transported to the ranch rather than being slaughtered here." She inclined her head at the paper on the table. "You can see his reply for yourselves."

Jacoby leaned forward. "So what are you saying? Your dad's gonna send some men here to take Jensen prisoner and bring him back to the ranch in Pueblo?"

She smiled and wiped her mouth with a napkin. "Yes, that's exactly what it means. I didn't figure the three of us would be able to get the drop on Jensen and get him all the way back to Pueblo by ourselves." She hesitated, glaring at them through narrowed eyes. "Especially considering the rather friendly feelings toward him you two have been showing."

"Sarah," Macklin said, shaking his head. "This is crazy. Kidnapping is a hanging offense."

"So is murder, in case you've forgotten what he did to my brother," she snapped in reply. After a moment, she took a deep breath and tried to calm herself. She needed their help, and there was no need getting them so angry that they might refuse it.

"Besides, since both of you seem to have some notion that Jensen is not guilty where it comes to my brother's death, I would think that you'd be glad Daddy has consented to us bringing Jensen out to the ranch and letting him tell his side of it."

Jacoby and Macklin glanced at each other. They both knew that wasn't the reason old Angus MacDougal wanted Jensen brought to him—it was more likely so the old man himself could have the pleasure of putting a bullet in Jensen, or worse, torturing the poor son of a bitch. Knowing the old man as they did, they didn't figure he'd just shoot Jensen and be done with it without first causing the man a good deal of pain and humiliation. Angus had been around long enough to have fought Indians in the old days, and to hear him tell it, he'd learned some interesting ways to torture a man from them.

"All right, let's say for the sake of argument that you are right," Jacoby said. "Just how do you think a gang of men are going to show up here in Big Rock and not bring a lot of attention to themselves so that when Jensen disappears they are not suspected?" He shook his head. "Hell, they'd have a posse on our tails 'fore we got fifty miles."

"That's easy," Sarah said, a note of triumph in her voice as she bent her head and began to eat her meal. "They're not coming into town."

"What?"

"That's right, because you and Mac are gonna ride out on the trail from Pueblo and camp out until the men get here. You'll tell them to wait out there until I can bring Jensen to them."

"And just how in blazes do you expect to do that little trick?" Jacoby asked, while Macklin just stared at her through bloodshot eyes.

Sarah leaned back and smiled seductively while fluffing the lace ruffles on the front of her blouse. "Well, a woman's got her ways to get a man to do what she wants."

Jacoby laughed. "Bullshit, Sarah!" he exclaimed, flushing at his use of profanity in front of a woman. "Jensen may be a lot of things, killer included, but I can tell you this: the man is no womanizer. He doesn't even look at other women, ever!"

Sarah blushed and went back to her meal. "Well, don't you worry, Mr. Smart-aleck. You just go out there and wait for the hands my daddy is sending. I'll get Jensen there one way or another, and I'll do it so it'll be a while before anyone knows he's missing."

Jacoby and Macklin looked at each other, both thinking that Sarah had gone round the bend. There was simply no way she could get the drop on a man like Smoke Jensen, no way at all, they thought.

As they walked back to their hotel, Macklin shook his head. "Now I know I should have killed Jensen." He turned tortured eyes on Jacoby. "Sarah is gonna mess around and get herself hurt or put in jail."

Jacoby smiled grimly. "I think you underestimate Sarah, Mac. Remember, she's Angus MacDougal's daughter, an' she's always been twice as smart and four times as tough as her brother ever was."

"Yeah, but Jensen's an experienced gunslick, Carl, an' he didn't get to be as old as he is by letting anyone, girls included, get the drop on him." He sighed. "Hell, I couldn't even watch him in a crowded saloon without him knowing exactly what I was doing. The man has eyes in the back of his head and the instincts of a mountain cougar."

Jacoby shrugged. "You may be right, but I don't know what the hell we can do about it." He smiled again. "Of course, you're more than welcome to go over there an' tell Sarah she's full of beans and that you think she ought to stick to cookin' an' such an' leave the rough stuff to us real men if you want to."

This last made even Macklin throw back his head and laugh. "No, thank you, Carl, 'cause I do relish my *cojones*, and Sarah would sure as hell rip them off if I ever suggested there was something Angus MacDougal's daughter couldn't do as well as any man working for 'em."

As they walked up the stairs to their hotel room to get packed and do as Sarah had told them to, Jacoby glanced sideways at Macklin. "Tell you what, pardner. I'll bet ten dollars Sarah does get Jensen out there, an' I'll give you two-to-one odds."

Macklin shook his head. "Nope. I learned a long time ago not to waste my money bettin' against a MacDougal, male or female." He sighed as he came to his door, and looked back over his shoulder at Jacoby. "You got any idea how she's gonna do it since, like you say, Jensen don't chase no skirts?"

Jacoby gave a short laugh. "No, but knowing Sarah, I wouldn't put it past her to just walk up to him and pull a gun out of her purse and stick it in his face."

"You really think so?"

Jacoby wagged his head. "Hell, Mac, I don't know. Predictin' what a woman's gonna do is like predictin' which way a frog's gonna jump—you're gonna be wrong at least half the time."

12

After Angus straightened him out on the real reason he was sending him to Big Rock, Cletus picked ten of the toughest, meanest men they had working for them on the ranch. More than a few of them had once ridden the owl-hoot trail and knew their ways around firearms. A couple had even spent time in the territorial prison for murder and mayhem.

As the gang of men sat on their horses in front of his house, Angus addressed them from the front porch. "Each of you men will receive a healthy bonus for this work. In fact, I'll pay you two months' wages for what should only be a couple of weeks of easy work."

Jason Biggs, one of the men who'd done time in prison and had no compunctions about killing, called out, "What if this man Jensen should give us some trouble or try to escape?" He grinned, revealing brown cigarette-stained teeth. "You want us to shoot him if'n that happens?"

Angus stared at Biggs through flat, hard eyes, noting that unlike most cowhands, Biggs wore his six-shooter down low on his hip. Angus shook his head. Back in the old days, punks like this would've been run out of town on a rail by the citizens. "Should any of you take it upon himself to kill this man and deprive me of the pleasure of getting my hands on him, I will personally see that you experience what one of our bulls does when it is gelded. Do I make myself clear, Mr. Biggs?"

"But what if—"

"No buts, Biggs," Angus interrupted. "There are eleven of you and you're meeting up with three more, including my daughter, Sarah. That should be more than enough to keep Mr. Jensen under control." He shook his head. "And if it's not, then God help you when I get through with you."

Biggs clamped his jaws shut and busied himself with building a cigarette.

Later, on the trail, Biggs rode up next to Cletus, who was leading the group of men.

"Clete," Biggs said.

"Yeah?"

"Did the boss tell you anything about this Jensen feller 'fore he told you to go down to Big Rock and pick him up?"

Cletus shook his head, not looking at Biggs directly. He didn't like the man and never had. If it weren't so hard to find hands to stay at work through the brutal winters of Pueblo, then he'd never have been hired. "No, Jason, he didn't." Now he turned and glanced at the man riding next to him. "Why? Do you know something?"

Biggs nodded. "Yeah, I heard of this Smoke Jensen when I was in the territorial prison a while back."

Cletus continued to stare at Biggs, wondering just what the man had on his mind. Cletus didn't trust Biggs and never had, but surprisingly, he'd been a steady worker, even if he did tend to get into fights with the other hands. Luckily for him, he'd never gone so far as to pull his weapon, or he would've found out just how hard a boss Cletus could be.

"What'd you hear, Jason?" Cletus asked. He was curious about the man who'd shot Johnny. He'd heard the usual: that Jensen was pretty famous with a gun and that he'd once had some posters out on him, but that was about all he knew. He didn't get to town to listen to local gossip too often, being much too busy trying to keep the ranch going.

Biggs let his reins drop while he used both hands to build himself a cigarette. Once he'd gotten it going, he screwed it in the corner of his mouth and let it dangle there while he talked. "Well, first off, I heard he's rattlesnake-quick with a short gun."

Cletus shrugged. "That don't surprise me none, since he somehow managed to shoot down Johnny and some of his friends, an' Johnny was no slouch with a handgun either." Smelling the smoke coming from Biggs made him want a cigarette too, so he commenced to make himself one. "Besides, there's plenty of men who're quick with a gun out here, Jason. This territory just seems to be a magnet for men who think they can make a living off their six-shooters."

Jason smirked, realizing this was directed against him, since he'd been one of those men until he'd gotten caught and sent to prison. He continued. "I also heard he's mean as a two-peckered Billy goat if you cross him or any of his friends." He inhaled and let smoke drift from his nostrils. "I shared a cell with a man who'd tried to brace Jensen once in a saloon."

Cletus laughed sourly. "If this Jensen is so fast and so mean as you say, how come the man braced him and lived to tell about it?"

Biggs smiled back. "'Cause Jensen didn't need to kill him. When my mate went for his gun, Jensen used his fists instead. He beat this guy so bad, he's gonna be eating through a straw for the rest of his life. He not only knocked all of his teeth out, he broke his jaw so bad his gums don't even come together right." Biggs laughed. "Poor sumbitch is skinny as a rail, and he used to weigh over two hundred pounds, an' he has this kind'a funny whistle when he tries to talk."

Cletus eyed Biggs. He'd never before seen Biggs give anyone the least amount of respect. "You sound like you're halfway a'feared of this man, Jason."

Biggs's face flushed scarlet and he sat up straighter in his saddle, trying to look tough. "I ain't a'scared of no man, Clete!"

Cletus wasn't fooled. He could see it in the man's eyes, lurking deep in them, like a sore that won't heal. "Well, then, why're you tellin' me all this? We're being well paid to take this little trip."

Biggs cleared his throat. "A couple of months' pay ain't so much when you're dealin' with a man like Jensen," he said, rubbing his chin with his hand.

"Well, like the boss says, fourteen of us ought'a be able to handle one man, Jason," Cletus said, trying to keep the scorn out of his voice. "But if you're so worried, then maybe you ought'a turn your mount around and head on back to the ranch where it's safe."

Biggs snorted through his nose. "Thirteen men, Clete, and the boss's little bitch, who looks plenty good to play in the hayloft with, but who ain't near as tough as the old man seems to think."

Before Biggs could blink, Cletus backhanded him with a fist the size of a ham, knocking him backward off his horse to land sprawling in the dirt.

When Biggs jumped to his feet and grabbed for his gun, he found himself looking down the barrel of Cletus's big Walker Colt. Cletus wasn't known as a fast draw, but he'd been handling men like Biggs for more years than he cared to think about, and he knew most of them were cowards when they didn't have an edge.

"You shouldn't ought'a talk about Miss Sarah like that, Biggs," Cletus said, his voice soft but all traces of friendliness gone from his manner. "I don't much like it, an' I hate to think of what the boss would do if'n he happened to hear about it."

Biggs relaxed and let his hand move away from his pistol. He tried a grin, but there was little humor in it and his eyes blazed with hate and humiliation. He wiped the blood off his lip with the back of his hand. "Aw, I was just funnin' with you, Clete. I know you got a soft spot for the girl. I didn't mean nothin' by what I said."

"It ain't that way, Biggs. I knowed her since she was born, so watch your mouth when you're around me, you hear?"

"Yes, sir," Biggs said, throwing an insolent half-salute.

"I mean it, Jason," Cletus added, "or your friend from jail won't be the only one eating his meals through a straw."

"Is it all right if I get back on my hoss?" Biggs asked, his face flaming scarlet.

Cletus holstered his gun and leaned over in the saddle until his face was close to Biggs's. "Sure. Just don't go getting any ideas about putting a lead pill in my back, Biggs, 'cause I'm gonna tell the other men if that happens, to string you up to the nearest tree. You get my drift?"

"Come on, Clete," Biggs said with a sickly smile as he climbed into the saddle. "You know we've always been friends, even if I do let my mouth override my ass ever' once in a while."

Cletus smiled back, his face equally devoid of humor. "No harm then, long as you keep your thoughts about Miss Sarah to yourself."

He jerked his horse's head around and proceeded on up the trail, whistling softly to himself while the other members of the group looked from him to Biggs, unsure of how to take this altercation.

Behind him, Biggs rode along, keeping his face bland, but his teeth were so tightly clenched together it made his jaws creak. If Cletus could have read his mind, he would not have been so cavalier about turning his back on the ex-prisoner and murderer.

Just outside the city limits of Big Rock, on the trail to Pueblo and points north, Carl Jacoby and Daniel Macklin were having some trouble. The late fall temperatures had begun to drop, and there was even the smell of snow in the air, though it was early in the year for that.

They'd stopped at the general store and bought provisions for their camp, while Sarah pretended not to know them as she waited on them with Peg Jackson working nearby. Along with foodstuffs, they'd bought a couple of small one-man tents that would keep the worst of the weather off them, though the thin oilcloth of the tents' walls would do little to keep them warm in the dropping temperatures.

Working as ranch hands and cowboys for many years, they were both experienced in camping out under the stars, but neither particularly enjoyed it, having become accustomed to the niceties of bunkhouse living over the past few years working for Angus MacDougal.

They'd also become quite accustomed to having a camp cook make their meals for them, so neither was particularly looking forward to doing his own cooking.

Jacoby gathered some hat-sized stones and made a small circle in the middle of their camp, which they'd placed on a hill overlooking the trail a quarter of a mile below them. There were some maple and oak trees in a small copse nearby that would help keep the worst of the wind off them, but it was clear that it was going to be a cold night nevertheless.

Macklin dumped an armful of deadwood he'd picked up under the trees into the campfire area, and squatted next to the stones as Jacoby put a match to some moss and dry leaves to get it going. He reached into his pocket and took out his makin's, and proceeded to build himself a cigarette as he waited for the coffeepot on the edge of the fire to begin to boil.

"How long you reckon 'fore the men from the ranch get here?" he asked.

Jacoby shrugged. "Who knows? If'n they left the same day Angus sent the wire, they could be here as early as tomorrow mornin', but that's unlikely. They'd have to get provisioned up and all, so I don't really 'spect them for another couple of days."

Macklin shivered as a cold wind blew up inside his jacket, and he reached for the coffeepot, which was beginning to put out some steam. "Damn," he said as he poured them both mugs of dark, strong coffee. "That means we're gonna sit out here freezin' our balls off for two or three more days."

Jacoby blew on his coffee to cool it. He glanced up at

lowering, dark clouds overhead that were scurrying across the sky under heavy winds. "That's about the size of it."

Macklin shook his head, letting cigarette smoke trail from his nostrils. "I should'a taken my chances with Jensen and drawn down on him when I had the chance."

Jacoby smiled over the rim of his mug. "Then you wouldn't be out here freezing your balls off, Mac. You'd be planted forked-end-up in boot hill being food for the worms."

"Hell, maybe not. Maybe I could've taken him," Macklin argued, though it was clear from the way his face paled at the thought of bracing Jensen that he didn't believe a word of it.

"Yeah," Jacoby snorted, "an' maybe pigs can fly too."

Macklin took the cigarette out of his mouth and stared into the red-hot end for a moment. "Carl, why do you think a man like Jensen would trouble himself with a nobody like Johnny MacDougal?" He cut his eyes at Jacoby as he stuck the butt back into his mouth. "Hell, it ain't like he was gonna get more famous for killin' him."

Jacoby sipped his coffee, turning it over in his mind. "You ever think maybe Jensen didn't have no choice in the matter, Mac, that just maybe Johnny pushed the man too far and had to pay the price for it?"

"Whatta you mean?"

"Just that the men with Jensen claimed they acted in self-defense, that Johnny got pissed when one of Jensen's party beat the shit out of him, and that he drew down and fired on them first without givin' them no warning."

Macklin pursed his lips as he thought about this. "I can see it happenin', if Johnny had a snootful of liquor an' was actin' the big man like he usually did when he was drunk an' showing off in front of the boys."

He hesitated, and then he looked at Carl. "You try tellin' that little story to his sister, Sarah?"

Jacoby shook his head. "No, she wouldn't listen to anything bad about Johnny. Her and the old man both always turned a blind eye to his shortcomin's, though he certainly had plenty of 'em."

"Maybe that's why he's dead," Macklin said, flipping his butt into the coals of the fire. "If Angus would've kicked his ass a few times when he was growin' up, 'stead've lettin' him get away with being a horse's ass, maybe he'd of learned to keep his mouth shut."

Jacoby stared at Macklin. "I thought you was his best friend."

Macklin shrugged. "I was, but that don't mean I didn't see how dumb he could be sometimes. Hell, my old pappy used to take a razor strop to me if'n I got outta line, an' I soon learned to keep my mouth shut if'n I didn't have something worthwhile to say."

He yawned and got to his feet. "I'm gonna get those tents ready. Why don't you fry us up some fatback and beans so's we can eat 'fore it gets too late?"

Jacoby grinned. "I want to know who elected me the cook of this little expedition."

Macklin looked back over his shoulder as he began to unload their tents off their packhorse. "Hey, it don't make no never mind to me. You can set up the tents an' I'll cook if'n you want."

Jacoby thought about this for a moment. At least he'd be near the warm campfire if he was cooking.

"No, that's all right. You do the tents, I'll do the cooking."

13

Sarah finished with the last customer of the day and proceeded to lock up the general store. Ed and Peg Jackson had been so impressed with her work that they were now giving her almost complete authority in the running of the store when they weren't there.

Peg had grown to like her so much she'd even been hinting that if Sarah would like to attend Sunday services at their church, there were some interesting single men she would like to introduce her to.

When Sarah had finished putting the money and charge slips in the drawer behind the counter and extinguished all the lanterns, she stepped out the back door and pulled it shut behind her, turning a key in the lock. Moving quickly, she walked down the alleyway to the buckboard she'd put there in the early hours of the morning. She'd stolen the wagon from the livery stable the night before instead of just renting it. She didn't want anything pointing to her to give a posse or any of Jensen's friends any leads on where to look for him when he turned up missing.

She climbed up onto the hurricane deck and kicked the brake with her foot, releasing it. Clicking her tongue, she whipped the twin reins against the horses' butts and urged them to get moving. It was just before five o'clock and the daylight was fading fast, and Sarah had a long way to ride—all the way out to the Sugarloaf Ranch.

She wasn't sure just how she was going to handle getting Smoke Jensen under her control, but she knew she'd figure out something. She always had in the past. Her daddy had taught her well, never telling her how to do something, just telling her what he wanted accomplished and letting her figure out the best method to get it done.

About the only thing that bothered her about what she was about to do was the thought of Sally Jensen and how it was going to affect her. She'd liked the lady from the first moment she'd met her, and Sally had been kind and considerate to her. It was a shame that Sarah was going to have to break her heart, but it couldn't be helped. Smoke Jensen was an evil man; he had to be to have done what he'd done to her brother.

As she bounced along in the buckboard, slowing as the light faded and the potholes in the road became less visible, she wondered how it was that an intelligent woman like Sally Jensen couldn't see how bad her husband was. She shook her head. She'd seen it before, women so besotted with love that they took up with men no decent lady would even talk to, much less marry or fall in love with.

She often saw these pathetic creatures when she went to town, where they walked around with heavy makeup on trying to hide the bruises the brutes they'd married seemed to give them on a regular basis.

She tried to salve her conscience by thinking how much better off Sally would be without a man like Smoke Jensen. Heck, she thought, he probably beat her when he got drunk, like a lot of those men in Pueblo did to their wives. In time, Sally would probably thank her lucky stars that he was gone.

Feeling better, Sarah turned her mind to ways that she might be able to get the drop on Jensen without any of his hands or his wife knowing she was involved. Sally knew too much about her, including the city she was from, to let her know she was involved. She needed to get the drop on

Jensen and get him out to the trail without anyone from Big Rock realizing she had anything to do with it.

She slipped her hand inside the purse lying on the wooden seat next to her, and let her fingers curl over the walnut handle of the snub-nosed .38-caliber Smith and Wesson pistol that lay nestled there. Though she'd never shot anyone before, she knew she was capable of it, especially when she thought of how pale and shrunken her brother had looked in his coffin when they'd buried him out on the ranch where they'd both grown up.

Her eyes filled with tears when she pictured Johnny lying there, looking somehow smaller than he had when he was alive and being his usual obnoxious self. Angrily wiping the tears away, she leaned forward and urged the horses on, anxious to do what needed to be done.

She pulled the buckboard to a halt when she saw the lights from the Jensens' cabin through the trees. She knew from talking to Ed and Peg Jackson that the Jensens didn't have any dogs or chickens near the house to raise an alarm, so she shouldn't have any problem getting close to the house without being heard, as long as she was careful. She wasn't sure what she'd do then, but figured she'd think of something—she always did.

She climbed down off the buckboard and bent over, pulled the rear hem of her dress up between her legs, and stuck it under her belt to make the dress look like trousers. She didn't want it getting caught on any underbrush to leave traces of her having been there.

She took her pistol out of the purse, stuck it under her belt in the small of her back, and began to walk quietly toward the house in the distance, being as careful as she could so as not to step on any sticks or piles of leaves.

When she got to the house, she moved over under one of the windows and slowly raised her head up to peek inside. She saw Smoke and Sally talking quietly together as they ate supper at the kitchen table.

Occasionally, one or the other would smile and laugh

softly at something the other said. Sarah pulled her head down and squatted under the window, wondering what she was going to do now. If worse came to worst and she didn't get another chance, she'd have to go inside the house and take them both, though she really didn't want to do that if there were any other way. Sally wasn't involved in this, and Sarah didn't want to have to scare her half to death. It'd be much better for the both of them if Jensen just disappeared and was never heard from again and Sally never found out what happened to him. That way, maybe she'd think he'd just got tired of married life and run off to live alone somewhere.

Just as she'd about resigned herself to going into the house, she heard Sally say, "I'm going to bed, dear. Are you coming?"

Sarah's heart began to beat faster when she heard Smoke reply, "Not just yet, sweetheart. I think I'll have a cigar out on the porch and another cup of coffee first."

Sarah peeked in the window and saw Sally give Smoke a quick kiss. "Good night then. I'll see you in the morning."

Smoke laughed. "Unless I wake you up when I come to bed," he joked.

"Don't you dare," Sally said with a mock frown. And then she smiled coyly and added, "Unless you plan to make it worth my while."

"Don't I always?" Smoke called as he laughed and moved out onto the front porch with a coffee cup in his hand.

Sarah waited until Smoke had finished half his cigar and most of his coffee, giving Sally time to get to sleep, before she moved around and walked up to the porch.

When Smoke noticed her, he got to his feet, a slight frown on his face. "Why, hello, Sarah," he said, concern in his voice. "Is anything wrong?"

"Please, Mr. Jensen," Sarah said in her most helpless voice, keeping it low so as not to awaken Sally. "Come with me quickly. I need your help."

"Let me just wake Sally up," Smoke began.

"No! There's no time for that," Sarah pleaded. "Come

AMBUSH OF THE MOUNTAIN MAN   101

quickly. My buckboard is just up the road a ways and I have something in it you need to see."

She turned around and moved at a fast pace down the road away from his house, not giving him time to think about it as he followed her down the dark path.

"Is someone hurt?" Smoke asked as he caught up with her and walked by her side.

"You'll see," Sarah said, avoiding the question. "It's just around the corner here."

When they came to the buckboard, Smoke leaned over the side, looking into the bed of the wagon. All he saw was a pile of blankets and some rope coiled up in the corner of the wagon. "I don't see . . ." he began, turning around to find Sarah standing a few yards away with a pistol in her hand aimed at his gut.

"What the . . . ?"

"Kindly put your hands up, Mr. Jensen," she said, her voice suddenly hard and flat.

He took a tentative step toward her and she eared back the hammer on the pistol with an audible click. "Please, Mr. Jensen, don't make me shoot you here. Just do as I say and you may live to see morning."

Smoke frowned as he raised his hands over his head.

"Now, turn around and climb into the back of the buckboard," Sarah ordered.

"Why don't you tell me what this is all about?" Smoke said as he climbed up into the bed of the wagon.

"Don't you turn around, just keep looking in that direction," Sarah ordered.

Smoke shrugged and did as she said. "Is it all right if I ask you what this is all about?" he said without turning to look at her.

Instead of answering him, Sarah reached under the seat of the buckboard and pulled out an iron crowbar she'd put there earlier. Swinging as hard as she could with one hand, she hit Smoke in the back of the head, knocking him unconscious onto his face.

She put down her gun and climbed up into the wagon with him. Taking some short lengths of rope she'd prepared earlier, she tied his hands together behind his back and then tied his feet together. Once that was done, she took some fence wire and wound it tightly around the rope, so that he couldn't possibly undo the knots she'd tied.

When she was finished, she noticed blood was pouring from a wound in the back of his head, so she took a handkerchief from her purse and tied a makeshift bandage around his head to slow the bleeding. Once it stopped, she checked to make sure he was still breathing. After all, she didn't want him to die on her—that would be too easy. She wanted him to suffer for a while, and then she wanted him to know why he was being killed before he died.

She wanted him to know that killing her brother Johnny had caused his death.

She climbed up into the seat and turned the buckboard around. She had to hurry. She wanted to be a dozen miles away before Sally Jensen woke up tomorrow morning and found her husband missing. By the time the alarm was raised and they figured out what had happened, she should be almost home.

Moving as fast as she could over the road in the near-total blackness, Sarah took almost three hours to make her way to the outskirts of Big Rock, where she hoped to find the men from her father's ranch waiting for her along with Carl and Mac.

It'd been three full days since she'd sent Mac and Carl out to wait for them, so the men certainly should have been able to make the trip from Pueblo to here in that time.

Even looking for them and expecting to see them, Sarah almost jumped out of the heavy coat she was wearing when a dark figure materialized out of the darkness and grabbed the reins to the horses pulling the buckboard.

"Is that you, Miss Sarah?" a gruff voice called.

She took a moment to catch her breath and try to calm her racing heart. "Yes. Who are you?"

"I'm Jimmy Corbett, ma'am," the voice called back as the figure moved closer so she could make out the face.

She recognized the man then. He'd been with her father for several years, though she didn't know him all that well personally. He was a little older than she and her brother, so Johnny had never run around with him much like he had some of the younger hands on the ranch.

"Well, Jimmy, you scared me out of two years' growth coming up on me out of the darkness like that," she complained, but her voice was level and there was no malice in it.

"Sorry, ma'am," he said, taking his hat off and standing there like a schoolboy. "Clete told us to make sure it was you 'fore we called out or anything, an' in the darkness it was kind'a hard to tell."

"That's all right, Jimmy. Where is Clete?"

Jimmy pointed up a slight rise off to her right. "He's up the top of that there hill, ma'am." He hesitated. "It's gonna be kind'a bumpy ridin' that buckboard up there. You want I should take the reins and let you ride my hoss?"

Truth to tell, Sarah's butt was aching from the long ride on the hurricane deck of the wagon, so she readily agreed. Even a saddle was better than the hard boards of the wagon seat and the continual bouncing of the wagon.

"Sure, Jimmy. Show me the way."

It didn't take long to get Cletus and the other men awake and some fresh coffee brewed. Though Sarah much preferred hot tea, she gratefully accepted a tin mug of the strong brew to help ward off the chill of the frigid night air. She hadn't realized how cold it was when she'd left town heading out to the Jensen spread, and now she was about frozen clear through.

She was about half through with her cup when Cletus finished checking out Smoke Jensen in the back of the buckboard and approached her next to the fire. Carl Jacoby was sitting next to her and Dan Macklin was on the other side. Neither had asked her how she'd managed to get Jensen in the back of the wagon, both figuring she'd tell them soon enough.

"Sarah, Jensen's more dead than alive in the back of that wagon. What'd you hit him with, an anvil?" he asked as he squatted next to her and poured himself a cup of coffee.

She cast worried eyes in the direction of the wagon. "No, just that iron crowbar under the seat."

Cletus blew on the coffee to cool it, and then took a deep swig. He glanced at her over the rim. "I'd say it's 'bout fifty-fifty whether he makes it through the night, what with the blood he lost and the fact that he's not really dressed for this cold. The man's 'bout near froze to death."

"Sarah, didn't you think to cover him with a blanket or something?" Jacoby asked from beside her.

Angry with herself for not realizing how dangerous it would be to transport him the way she did, Sarah snapped back, "No, I didn't, Carl! It's not every day I kidnap a killer and have to drive him halfway across the country in the dead of night." She shook her head. She'd put blankets in the back of the buckboard, but those were to cover him with if anyone approached, and she simply had been too miserable with her own discomfort to think much about his.

She glanced over at the buckboard, hoping she hadn't inadvertently killed the man before she could tell him why she'd kidnapped him.

"Calm down, Sarah," Cletus said in his usual unruffled tone of voice. Sarah reflected she couldn't ever remember Cletus being riled up about anything in all the years she'd known him.

"I'm havin' a couple of the boys carry him over here next to the fire, an' I'm gonna see if we can wake him up enough to get some hot coffee down him."

She felt her face flush with shame when she saw them carry Smoke Jensen's pale, limp body over and lay it next to the fire. Cletus was right, she thought. He does look more dead than alive.

"But Clete," she said, glancing back and forth from

Smoke to him, "we've got to get moving. Come morning, his wife is going to wake up and realize he's missing. We need to be as far away when that happens as we can be."

Cletus took a deep breath and sipped more of his coffee. "Won't matter none if we kill him in the takin', Miss Sarah. If we don't get him warmed up a little an' some fluids down to replace the blood he lost, he won't make it five miles in the back of that wagon."

Just then, Smoke moaned and moved his head slightly, wincing at the pain the movement caused.

He looked around him at the campfire and the men gathered around it until his eyes landed on Sarah.

"Why?" he croaked, trying to make some sense of her attack on him.

Blushing, she got to her feet and moved to stand over him. "Does the name Johnny MacDougal mean anything to you?" she asked, venom dripping from her voice.

14

Smoke struggled up on one elbow and looked up at the angry young woman standing over him. His head felt like a blacksmith had been pounding on it, and his eyes kept blurring and trying to cross. He concentrated, pushing the pain and nausea aside, and thought about her question. The name Johnny MacDougal did stir some memories, but he couldn't quite put his finger on them just yet.

He started to shake his head in a negative reply, but he stopped when the movement caused a red-hot pain to shoot through his skull. He reached up and gingerly felt the back of his head. There was a large, squashy lump there with what felt like dried blood scabbing it over. Evidently someone, probably the very same young woman standing before him now, had hit him from behind. He'd have to get to feeling better to die, he thought.

In a hoarse voice, he croaked, "Sarah, the name is familiar to me, but I don't quite remember just why."

At her astonished glare, her eyes filled with even more hatred, he asked gently, "You want to tell me about it?"

She opened her mouth to speak, and he held up his hand, swaying slightly back and forth on his elbow as he lay there. "Just a minute, Sarah," he said, coughing. "Could I first have some water or coffee? My throat feels as dry as the desert right now."

Sarah glanced at Cletus without saying anything, and he

got to his feet, poured some coffee into a tin mug, and handed it to Smoke. "Here ya go," he said, "but drink it slow so it don't come back up on ya."

While Smoke drank, Sarah put her hands on her hips and stared down at him. "For your information, Mr. Smoke Jensen, Johnny MacDougal was my brother, and last year about this time you beat him up and knocked out his teeth and then you shot him and some friends of his down in cold blood in Pueblo."

Smoke's eyes widened over the rim of the cup. He slowly lowered it and struggled up to a sitting position, trying to move his head as little as possible, his face wincing at the pain the movement caused. "That was your brother, the one dressed all in black?"

Sarah nodded, her eyes as hard as flint. Smoke let his head fall into his hands and fought back nausea the coffee had caused as he thought back about that day the previous year when William Cornelius Van Horne had offered to take Smoke and his friends to lunch. . . .

Van Horne pulled the head of his Morgan toward a dining place with a sign over the door that said simply THE FEEDBAG, and the others followed, tying their mounts and packhorses to a hitching rail in front of the building.

The Feedbag was set up similarly to Longmont's Saloon back in Big Rock. It consisted of a large room with eating tables on one side, and a bar and smaller tables for the men who just wanted to drink their meals on the other side. It was about three quarters full. Most of the men wore the canvas trousers of miners, but there was a smattering of men dressed in chaps and flannel shirts and leather vests who were obviously cowboys from nearby ranches.

Van Horne pushed through the batwings and walked directly toward a large table in the front corner of the room, while Smoke, Pearlie, Cal, and Louis spread out just inside the door with their backs to the wall waiting for their eyes to adjust to the gloomy lighting. The two mountain men stopped and eyed Smoke with raised eyebrows.

"You expectin' trouble, Smoke?" Rattlesnake Bob asked, his hand dropping to the old Walker Colt stuck in the waistband of his buckskins.

Smoke smiled as his eyes searched the room for anyone who might be giving him special attention. "No, Rattlesnake, but I've found the best way to avoid trouble is to be ready for it when it appears."

When he saw no one was looking their way, Smoke walked on over to the table where Van Horne was already sitting down talking to a waiter, and took his usual seat with his back to the wall and his face to the rest of the room.

As they all took their seats, Bill said, "I ordered us a couple of pitchers of beer to start with while we decide what to order for lunch."

Bear Tooth smacked his lips. "That sounds mighty good, Bill. I ain't had me no beer since last spring."

Before Bill could answer, a loud voice came from a group of men standing at the bar across the room. "God Almighty! What the hell is that smell?" a man called loudly, looking over at their table. "Did somebody drag a passel of skunks in here?"

The young man, who appeared to be about twenty years old, was wearing a black shirt and vest with a silver lining, and had a brace of nickel-plated Colt Peacemakers tied down low on his hips. He had four other men standing next to him, all wearing their guns in a similar manner, and all were laughing as if he'd just said something extremely funny.

Rattlesnake Bob glanced at Bear Tooth and grimaced. "I hate it when that happens," he said in a low, dangerous voice. "Now we're gonna have to kill somebody 'fore we've even had our beer."

"Take it easy, Rattlesnake," Smoke said. "He's just some young tough who's letting his whiskey do his thinking for him."

Rattlesnake eased back down in his chair. "You're right,

Smoke," he said, smiling. "If'n ever' man who was drunk-dumb got kilt, there wouldn't hardly be none of us left."

Smoke continued to keep an eye on the man across the room as the bartender tried to get him to be quiet, without much success.

When their waiter appeared with the beer and glasses, Smoke asked him, "Who's the man with the big mouth over there at the bar?"

The waiter glanced nervously over his shoulder, and then he whispered, "That's Johnny MacDougal. His father owns the biggest ranch in these parts."

"Well, I don't care if'n his daddy owns Colorado Territory," Bear Tooth growled. "You go on over there an' tell the little snot if'n he wants to see his next birthday he'd better keep his pie-hole shut."

The waiter's face paled and he shook his head rapidly back and forth. "I couldn't do that, sir," he said.

"Why not?" Rattlesnake asked.

"Just last week Johnny shot a man for stepping on his boots." The waiter hesitated, and then he added, "And the man wasn't even armed at the time."

"How come he's not in jail then?" Louis asked.

"Uh, his father carries a lot of water in Pueblo," the waiter said. "The sheriff came in and said it was in self-defense, though it was plain to everyone in the place that the man wasn't wearing a gun."

"So that's the lay of the land," Van Horne said, pursing his lips.

"Yes, sir," the waiter said, and hurried off back to the kitchen before these tough-looking men could get him in trouble, or worse yet, get him shot.

A few minutes later, after he'd downed another glass of whiskey, the young tough and his friends began to swagger across the room toward Smoke's table.

Smoke and Louis both eased their chairs back, took the hammer thongs off their Colts, and waited expectantly for the trouble they knew was coming. Smoke eased his right leg out straight under the table so he'd have quicker access if he had to draw.

MacDougal stopped a few feet behind Rattlesnake's chair and made a production of holding his nose. "Whew, something's awfully ripe in here," he said loudly, looking around the room to make sure he had an appreciative audience. "I think something done crawled in here and died."

Rattlesnake eased his hand down to the butt of the big Walker Colt in his belt, and as quick as a snake striking he whipped it out, stood up, and whirled around, slashing the young man viciously across the face with the barrel.

MacDougal screamed and grabbed his face as blood spurted onto his vest. Before the other men could react, Rattlesnake grabbed MacDougal by the hair, jerked his head back, and jammed the barrel of the gun in his mouth, knocking out his two front teeth.

As MacDougal's eyes opened wide and he moaned in pain, Rattlesnake eared back the hammer and grinned, his face inches from the young tough's. "Now, what was it you was sayin', mister?" he growled. "Somethin' 'bout somebody smelling overly ripe, I believe?"

As one of MacDougal's friends dropped his hand to his pistol, Bear Tooth stood up, and had his skinning knife against the man's throat before he could draw. "Do you really want some of this?" he asked, smiling wickedly at the man. "'Cause if'n you do, you'll have a smile that stretches from ear to ear 'fore I'm done with you."

"Uh, no, sir!" the man said, moving his hand quickly away from his pistol butt.

MacDougal's eyes rolled back and he almost fainted from pain and embarrassment, and he sank to his knees on the floor of the restaurant.

Rattlesnake shook his head in disgust, pulled the Walker out of his bleeding mouth, and pushed him over with his boot until MacDougal was lying flat on his back, crying and moaning with his hands over his face.

Rattlesnake waved the Walker at MacDougal's friends, who cringed back, and he said, "You boys better take this little baby off somewheres an' get him a sugar tit to suck on 'fore he pees his pants."

The men all bent down, picked MacDougal up, and helped him stagger out the batwings, their eyes fixed on the barrel of the Walker as they left.

Rattlesnake stuck the gun back in his belt and turned back to the table. "Now then, where's my beer?"

After they'd all eaten their fill of beefsteak, potatoes, corn, and apple pie for dessert, Van Horne threw some twenty-dollar gold pieces on the table and they walked toward the door.

Smoke hung back for a moment and whispered to Cal and Pearlie, who broke off from the group and exited through a side door.

He glanced at Louis and nodded. Louis nodded back and kept his hand close to the butt of his pistol. Both of them knew the trouble wasn't over yet. Men like MacDougal didn't take treatment like he'd received without trying for revenge, especially when they'd been shamed in front of their friends and neighbors.

Just before Van Horne got to the batwings, Louis and Smoke stepped in front of him. "You'd better let us go out first, Bill," Smoke said, his eyes flat and dangerous.

Smoke and Louis went through the batwings fast, Smoke breaking to the right and Louis to the left, their eyes on the street out in front of The Feedbag.

Sure enough, MacDougal and his friends were lined up in the street, pistols in their hands, cocked and ready to fire.

As they raised their hands to aim and shoot, Smoke and Louis drew, firing without seeming to aim. An instant later, Cal and Pearlie joined in from the alley where they'd come out to the side of the men in the street.

Only MacDougal, out of all the men with him, got off a shot, and it went high, taking a small piece off Smoke's hat.

The entire group of men dropped in the hail of gunfire from Smoke and Louis and the boys, sprawling in the muddy street, making it run red with their blood.

"Damn!" Rattlesnake said in awe. He had started to

draw his Walker at the first sign of trouble, but it was still in his waistband by the time it was all over. "I ain't never seen nobody draw an' fire that fast," he added, glancing at Smoke and Louis with new respect.

Smoke and Louis walked out into the street and bent down to check on the men. They were all dead, or so close to dying that they were no longer any risk.

A few minutes later a fat man with a tin star on his chest came running up the street. "Oh, shit!" he said when he saw who had been killed.

He looked over at Smoke and the group and moved his hand toward his pistol, until Smoke grinned and waggled his Colt's barrel at him. "I wouldn't do that, Sheriff," Smoke said, jerking his head at the group of people standing at the windows and door of The Feedbag. "There are plenty of people in there who will say we acted in self-defense, so there's no need for you to go for that hog-leg on your hip."

"But . . . but that's Angus MacDougal's son," the sheriff stammered.

Van Horne moved forward. "I don't care if it's the President's son, Sheriff. These men drew on us first."

"And just who are you?" the sheriff asked.

"My name is William Cornelius Van Horne," Bill said, pulling a card from his vest pocket and handing it to the sheriff. "And if you'd like to send a wire to the United States marshal over in Denver, I'm sure he will vouch for me."

The sheriff eyed the men standing in front of him, and wisely decided not to make an issue of it. "All right, if it went down like you say, you're free to go." He took his hat off and wiped his forehead. "But I don't think Mr. Mac-Dougal is gonna like this."

Rattlesnake bent over and spit a stream of tobacco juice onto Johnny MacDougal's dead face. "If'n the man has any sense, he'll be relieved that we took that sorry son of a bitch off his hands," he said. "If he'd had any sense at all, he would'a drowned him in a barrel a long time ago."

* * *

Smoke hadn't remembered Johnny MacDougal's name, but he still remembered the young man's lifeless, cold eyes that barely held a hint of humanity in them as he shot off his mouth in the saloon that day. The boy was evidently spoiled rotten, and had never had to face up to the fact that people feared him because of his father's wealth, not out of any respect for him or because of any doing of his own.

He raised his eyes to Sarah's. "But his name was Mac-Dougal and yours is . . . "

"Mine is MacDougal too," Sarah said. "I lied when I told your wife it was Johnson."

Smoke sighed and drained the last of his coffee from the cup, hoping it would stay down. "Well, if Johnny was your brother, then you know how unreasonable and stupid he was when he was drinking," Smoke said, though his gentle voice took some of the sting out of what he said.

"What?" Sarah almost screamed, stepping closer to Smoke and raising her hand as if she was about to hit him.

Smoke smiled grimly at her. "Think about it, Sarah," he said. "How many times before had he gotten drunk and caused trouble, assaulted or hurt someone? Why, the day he forced us to draw on him, I heard he'd killed an unarmed man the week before."

When Sarah's face flushed, Smoke continued. "Did anyone from your family go and tell that poor man's wife and kids you were sorry for what your brother had done, or did you just use your father's influence to sweep it all under the rug?"

"You son of a—" Sarah began.

"And did anyone from that man's family come out to the ranch and try and take Johnny prisoner or shoot him for what he'd done to their father?" he asked, his eyes boring into hers as he spoke.

"You know that was different," she almost screamed. "The man drew on Johnny first . . . " she was saying.

Smoke started to interrupt her, but his vision suddenly narrowed and everything became dark and fuzzy, and then he tipped over and fell headfirst into a deep, black pool.

Cletus rushed to his side and felt the pulse in Smoke's neck. "He's just fainted," he said, looking up at Sarah. "Probably from loss of blood, though God only knows if you've managed to scramble his brains with that crowbar."

"It'd serve the bastard right," Sarah said, moving toward the fire and the coffeepot to get herself another cup. "Especially after what he said about Johnny."

Cletus's eyes softened with sorrow, for he knew that Sarah knew that what Jensen had said was the truth, as painful as it was for her to hear it spoken out loud.

They'd all tried to maintain the fiction that the man Johnny killed had been armed, but they'd never spoken of it, and the sheriff had covered up the truth from the townspeople. But out at the ranch they'd all known how it really went down.

15

Sarah sat there, staring into the campfire over the rim of her cup, with an occasional sideways glance at Smoke. He lay still, his chest barely rising and falling, his skin as pale as the moon on a summer night. He could hardly have looked any more lifeless if he were dead.

How dare that man denigrate the memory of her brother, a man he'd callously shot down in the streets of his own town! Why, just because Johnny was a little spoiled and liked to drink and throw his weight around a little too much, that didn't mean he was a bad man. And as for that man he'd shot and killed the week before he died, her father had told her the man had a gun and that Johnny hadn't had any choice but to shoot him in self-defense.

Jensen was lying about him being unarmed—he must be, she thought as she swallowed the last of her coffee. Otherwise, the sheriff would surely have arrested Johnny. "Cletus, come here a minute, will you?" she asked as she got to her feet and moved away from the fire and the other men from the ranch.

Cletus followed her over into the darkness at the edge of camp. "Yes?"

"What Jensen said about that man Johnny shot being unarmed, that was a lie, wasn't it?" she asked, hating the whining, hopeful tone in her voice, as if she didn't really believe it herself.

Cletus pursed his lips and avoided her gaze, staring up at the stars while debating within himself how to answer her question. On the one hand, he wanted to tell her the truth, but on the other, Angus had sworn him to secrecy.

Sarah was no fool. She heard him hesitate and saw the pain in his eyes when he turned them back to her. "Oh, Clete," she said before he could answer. "Why didn't Daddy tell me the truth?"

He shrugged, glad he hadn't had to lie to her after all. "I don't know, Missy," he said, using the pet name he'd given her when she was just a toddler. "I suppose he felt it was best that you didn't know."

She looked over her shoulder at Jensen, who still hadn't moved. "Then he was right about Johnny, wasn't he?" she asked, her voice low and sad.

Cletus put his hand on her shoulder. "Now, Missy, just because Johnny was a little rough around the edges sometimes didn't give anyone the right to shoot him down in cold blood, no matter how drunk he was or what he may have said to them."

Sarah nodded distractedly, but she was thinking, What if Johnny did more than just shoot his mouth off? What if he'd drawn on Jensen and his men as Jensen maintained he did? What would she do then? Could she stand to take this man to her father where he would be killed if he were in fact innocent of any wrongdoing?

She moved over closer to the fire, chilled by more than the freezing air around her. She had some tough decisions to make, and for once, she wouldn't have her father to guide her in the making of them. Somehow, before they arrived back at the ranch, she would have to decide just who was telling the truth about what had happened last year in the streets of Pueblo.

She turned to Cletus. "We'd better get a move on, Clete," she said. "Jensen's wife is going to wake up before too long, and then we're going to have a posse to deal with if we're not a lot of miles away from here."

Cletus looked over at Jensen, whose chest was rising and falling rapidly with shallow breaths. "I don't know, Missy. If we move him now, he's liable to start bleedin' inside his head or something." He turned back to her. "Angus ain't gonna like it if'n we bring him back a corpse."

She turned to face him, putting her hands on her hips and looking him right in the eye. "He also won't like it much if his only daughter is arrested and hung for kidnapping, Clete. Now, either we get a move on and Jensen takes his chances, or we shoot him here and leave him for the buzzards to find."

Cletus shook his head and spit out, "Damn, but you're just like your old man—headstrong and stubborn as a mule!"

Sarah smiled and reached up to pat Cletus's cheek, something a man would have gotten shot trying. "I take that as a compliment, Clete. Now, get a move on . . . Please."

Three hours later, just as the sun was edging over mountain peaks to the east, Smoke rolled over in the back of the buckboard and got up on his hands and knees. His head hung down, and he vomited until he thought he was going to bring up his toes.

Cletus, who was riding on the hurricane deck, looked back over his shoulder and grimaced at the nasty sight. "Shit," he said, "now you're gonna have to ride in that the rest of the way home."

Smoke glared up at him, his face pasty and pale, his eyes sunken and surrounded by black. Suddenly, his lips curled in a smile that made the hair on the back of Cletus's neck stand up. He'd never seen anything as dangerous in his life.

"What're you grinnin' at, Jensen?" Cletus asked. "It 'pears to me like you got precious little to smile at."

"Mister," Smoke croaked through dry and cracked lips, "I was just thinking about how good it is gonna feel when I make all of you pay for this." He coughed and leaned his head to the side as he spit out a clot of old blood.

"Ordinarily, I get no pleasure from killing men, but for this group, I'm gonna have to make an exception."

"Only one's gonna get kilt around here is you, Jensen," Cletus said before he turned back around to face the horses before Jensen could see the fear in his eyes—eyes that had never been made to show fear before.

"Better men than you and these mangy coyotes riding with you have tried to plant me forked-end-up, mister," Smoke said as he struggled to get turned around so he could put his back to the sideboard of the wagon. After a moment, he succeeded, and he leaned there with his elbows on his knees. "And I'm still kicking," Smoke added after a moment spent getting his breath from the exertion his moving had caused.

Sarah gently spurred Cletus's horse she was riding, and pulled the animal up next to the bed of the wagon where Smoke sat with his back to her.

Neither Cletus nor Smoke could see her as Cletus called back over his shoulder, "Yeah, but you ain't never killed no MacDougal before neither, Jensen."

Smoke snorted. "If you're talking about that man named Johnny I shot in Pueblo last year, the only thing special about him was his capacity to drink enough liquor to make him both stupid and dangerous."

Cletus nodded, his attention on the horses in front of him. "Yeah, Johnny could put the tonsil paint away, all right. But that didn't give you no right to beat him near half to death an' then shoot him full'a lead."

Smoke sighed. "What's wrong with you people?" he asked, his voice low as if he were talking to himself, exasperated at their unwillingness to learn the truth. "Didn't anybody ask the sheriff what had happened? There were plenty of witnesses to the whole thing."

"All we heard was that Johnny got pistol-whipped and all his teeth were knocked out, and then he and his friends got shot down without being able to get off any shots themselves." Cletus looked back over his shoulder again. "That don't exactly sound like no fair fight to me, Jensen."

Smoke held his head. All this talking was making his

head feel as if it was going to explode. What was it about self-defense that these people didn't understand? Surely they must have known what kind of a man Johnny was.

"I'll try one more time, then I'm done talking," Smoke said. "Johnny had a snootful of liquor and came over to our table and braced the men I was with, saying they stunk like skunks and garbage. Well, it's no surprise that one of the mountain men I was with took offense at his remarks and proceeded to beat the shit out of him, which he no doubt deserved. After Johnny got knocked flat on his back, his friends came over and carried him outside. Later, after we'd finished our supper, we walked out the door. Johnny and all his friends were standing there in the street with their hands filled with iron—we had no choice but to shoot."

Cletus turned his head. "You that good, Jensen, you can draw and kill a man who's already got his pistol out?"

Smoke chuckled. "Why don't you try me, mister, and find out for yourself, or do you let a mob do your fighting for you? You got the balls for it, give me a gun and we'll see if I'm fast enough to take the lot of you."

Cletus gritted his teeth and looked ahead. A lot of what the man said made sense. He'd loved Johnny like his own son, but that didn't mean the little bastard wasn't mad-dog mean when he'd been drinking. He shook his head. It could well have gone down just like Jensen said, but if it did, why didn't Sheriff Tupper tell it that way to Angus?

Sarah, who was wondering the same thing, flicked her riding crop at Smoke and got his attention. When he turned his head to look at her riding alongside the wagon, she said, "That isn't exactly the way the sheriff tells it, Mr. Jensen, and why would he lie about it?"

Smoke smirked and turned back around, speaking over his shoulder. "Your father has a reputation of not listening to people who tell him what he doesn't want to hear, Sarah. My guess is, the sheriff was too scared to tell him his little boy got killed because he got drunk and let his mouth override his butt. Truth be told, Johnny wasn't near as tough or as fast with a gun as the liquor made him think he was, and he seemed too busy showing off for all of his friends to think straight about it."

Sarah swiped at the back of Smoke's head with her crop. "You bastard!" she yelled, and spurred her horse into a full gallop, riding off in a cloud of dust.

Cletus shook his head as he watched Sarah gallop off up ahead of the column of men. "Boy, you sure know how to end a conversation."

"I guess her father's not the only one doesn't like to be told the truth, especially when her mind's already made up on the subject."

16

Sally woke up just as the sun was coming up and brightening the bedroom. She yawned and, as she did every morning, stuck out her right hand and felt around the bed for her husband. When she didn't feel Smoke next to her, she opened her eyes and rolled on her side. His side of the bed was smooth, and his pillow was unwrinkled.

She sat up straight, rubbing sleep out of her eyes. Evidently, he hadn't come to bed last night, because she'd never known him to get up early and make his side of the bed while she was still sleeping.

Something was wrong.

She jumped out of bed and got dressed. As she was heading for the door, she noticed that Smoke's hat and guns were hanging on the peg next to the front door. He would never have gone anywhere without them.

She crossed the porch and ran to the bunkhouse. She pounded on the door until Cal opened it, yawning widely. It was just about time for the cowboys to rise, but it was evident he hadn't had his morning coffee just yet.

"Oh, hi, Miss Sally," he said, his voice still husky from sleep.

"Cal, have any of you seen Smoke this morning?"

"Uh, why, no, Miss Sally. We just got up an' ain't seen nobody yet."

"Damn!" she said, thinking furiously. "Did you see or hear anything out of the ordinary last night?"

Cal shook his head, his expression changing to one of alarm at her questions.

Without saying anything else, she turned back toward the barn and took off at a dead run. She wanted to go and see if Smoke's horse was still there, though she knew he'd never have gotten on his horse and left without saying something to her, or at least grabbing his hat and guns from the cabin.

Cal glanced over his shoulder and called out, "Pearlie, somethin's wrong. Get on out here." Then he took off at a run after Sally, tucking in his shirt on the go.

Twenty minutes later, the three of them sat at the kitchen table in the ranch house. Sally had put some coffee on to boil while she told them about Smoke's mysterious absence.

"And he didn't say nothin' 'bout goin' nowheres when you went to bed last night?" Pearlie asked as she handed him a steaming cup.

She shrugged and shook her head. "No. He went out on the porch to have a cigar and a cup of coffee before he came to bed, and he said he'd see me in a while."

"It ain't like Smoke to just take off without tellin' nobody," Cal said, getting up from his chair. "Especially if there was trouble brewin'."

He moved out onto the front porch and began to look around, even getting down on his knees to get a better look at the ground around the porch.

"Look here," he said to Sally and Pearlie, who were standing behind him. He pointed to a half-smoked cigar lying on the ground next to the porch, and a cup that still held a third of a cup of cold coffee in it on the arm of a wooden chair.

"Looks like somethin' spooked him, or at least made him throw down his cigar and leave his coffee 'fore he was through with either one," Cal said.

"You see any tracks, Cal?" Pearlie asked, moving over to lean over his shoulder. Cal was smart and quick, but Pearlie was the more experienced tracker by far.

"Yeah. Most of 'em head over toward the bunkhouse," Cal replied, "but it looks like two sets go off down the road that'a way. And see, one set looks smaller, like it might'a been a woman, or maybe a boy."

Pearlie bent down and gently fingered the tracks. "You're right, Cal, and these are from last night too."

"How can you tell that?" Cal asked.

"Here, see how the other tracks are crusted over where they've been wet by dew that's dried a few times?"

When Cal nodded, Pearlie added, "Well, these here fresh tracks are still soft and damp, so they've only had the dew fall on them once and they haven't dried yet, so they must've been made last night."

"Pearlie," Sally said, reaching inside the door and pulling a gun from Smoke's holster, "follow the tracks and show us where they lead."

Pearlie followed the tracks, walking bent over like an old man as the tracks led him down the road away from the Jensens' cabin. Finally, he stopped and pointed. "Look there, Miss Sally. Tracks of a buckboard right here where these two sets stop."

"Shoot!" Sally said. "That's not much help. Everyone in the valley has a buckboard."

"Yeah," Cal added. "An' followin' those buckboard tracks once they get on the main road will be impossible."

Pearlie, who was still staring at the tracks, shook his head. "Maybe, but these tracks show the iron on the wheels to be brand-new. Lookit how sharp the edges of the tracks are. They ain't worn at all." He looked up at Sally and Cal, who weren't following him. "Don't you see?" he asked. "All we have to do is ask Jed the blacksmith who's had their wheels re-ironed lately and we'll know who was here."

Sally grabbed Pearlie and hugged him, causing him to blush furiously. "Pearlie, you're a genius," she said, and she turned and ran back toward the cabin.

* * *

By the time they got to Big Rock, it was almost nine o'clock in the morning, and they rode directly to Jed Blankenship's blacksmith shop.

"Oh, no," Sally said when she dismounted and walked up to the door. There was a sign on it that was too small for the boys to read from their horses.

"What's it say, Miss Sally?" Cal asked.

"Jed's not here. He's gone to Silver City to help his brother who broke his leg. He won't be back for at least a week."

"You want me to hightail it over to Silver City and see what he has to say?" Pearlie asked.

Sally thought about it for a moment. "No, it'll probably be quicker just to divide up the ranches around town and all of us ride around asking whose buckboard it might be."

"Maybe it's something simple, like one of your neighbors came by last night askin' Smoke for help," Cal observed.

Sally shook her head. "No. If that were the case, Smoke would still have had time to either wake me up or to get his hat and guns from the rack next to the door. You know he never leaves the house without them."

Both Cal and Pearlie nodded. "That's right, Miss Sally. An' if'n one of the neighbors needed Smoke's help, he would've asked either you or Cal or me to come along," Pearlie said.

"Yes, so I suspect Smoke is in some kind of trouble, and it's up to us to figure out who took him and then to make sure we get him back."

"You know, it might be kind'a dangerous for you to go ridin' up to the ranches askin' 'bout where Smoke is," Pearlie advised. "If'n they took him an' you show up, you're liable to get shot."

Sally smiled grimly and patted the snub-nosed .36-caliber Smith and Wesson revolver on her hip. "It won't be dangerous for me, boys. It'll be dangerous for whoever took Smoke."

"Speakin' of that," Cal said, "why don't we ask Monte and Louis to help us look for him? That'd sure cut down the time it's gonna take to find that buckboard."

"Hell, they might even know whose it is," Pearlie added.

"Good idea, Cal. Let's ride on over to Longmont's and see who's in there."

Sally sent Pearlie to the sheriff's office while she and Cal walked directly to Longmont's Saloon. As much a café as a drinking and gambling establishment, the place was half-full of patrons eating one of Chef Andre's magnificent breakfasts.

Louis was, as usual, sitting at his private table drinking strong coffee and smoking a thin, black cheroot. When he saw Sally and Cal, he immediately put the cigar out and got to his feet, motioning them over to his table.

He gave a very slight bow. "Good morning, Sally, Cal."

He pulled a chair out and as Sally took a seat, he asked, "Will Smoke be joining us this morning?"

She shook her head, and he noticed her eyes were wet with unshed tears. "No, Louis, but Pearlie will be here shortly with Sheriff Carson."

Louis sat down, glancing at Cal for some clue as to what was going on.

"Smoke seems to have disappeared sometime last night, Louis," Cal said.

Louis held up four fingers to the young black waiter without taking his eyes off Sally. "Do you have any idea what happened?" he asked while the waiter put four coffee mugs on the table and began to pour them all coffee.

She shook her head. "No. Everything was normal when I went to bed last night. Smoke said he was going to have a cigar and a cup of coffee on the porch and he would be right in." She took a moment to wipe daintily at her eyes with a handkerchief, and then she continued. "I fell asleep, and woke up this morning and he was nowhere to be found."

Just then Monte Carson, sheriff of Big Rock, joined them along with Pearlie.

"Pearlie's told me the gist of things, Sally," he said. "Are you sure Smoke didn't leave of his own accord, maybe 'cause this woman or boy came by needin' help?"

She shook her head. "No, Monte. His guns and his hat were still on the peg next to the door."

Monte glanced at Louis. They both knew Smoke would no more leave his house without his hat and guns than he would walk down Main Street naked. There were just too many men roaming around the country who'd like nothing better than to catch Smoke Jensen unarmed and defenseless.

Monte nodded. "You're right, Sally. I'm sure foul play's involved here."

"Sheriff, we found some tracks of a buckboard with new iron rims on the wheels. The tracks make it look like Smoke went off in the buckboard," Pearlie said.

"New rims, huh?" Monte said, stroking his jaw before picking up his mug and drinking some coffee. "Guess I'd better go on over to Jed's and see who's had new rims put on lately."

"Won't do, Monte," Cal said. "We've been there. Jed's out of town for a few days on over to Silver City."

"He at his brother's place?" Monte asked.

When Sally and the boys nodded, Monte got to his feet. "I'll go by the telegraph office and send a wire to the sheriff there askin' him to take a ride out to Jed's brother's place and see if he can find out what we need to know."

Louis nodded. "Meanwhile, we can split up and ride out to some of the nearby ranches and take a look at their wagons."

Monte scratched his jaw again. "I don't know if that's such a good idea, Louis," he said in his slow drawl. "If'n Smoke was took against his will, whoever took him ain't gonna welcome any questions with open arms."

Louis frowned. "You're right, Monte. We'd need to go in posse strength at least since we don't know how many men we're dealing with here."

Monte took his ever-present pipe out of his shirt pocket and began filling it with sweet-smelling tobacco from a leather pouch. "Why don't you all just sit here and have some breakfast? It shouldn't take more'n a couple of hours to get an answer from the sheriff over at Silver City. Then we can all go together to find out just what's goin' on."

Sally looked up at him. "I don't know if I can just sit here without doing something, Monte, not while Smoke is in danger."

Monte patted her shoulder as clouds of blue smoke whirled from his pipe. "I know it's tough, Sally, but you won't be doing him any good if you go out and get caught by the same people."

"You're correct, Monte. I'm being foolish."

"No, you're not," Louis said, waving his hand at the waiter to come and take their orders. "You're just being a wife who's worried about her man. Nothing wrong with that."

"You know, Sheriff," Pearlie said, scratching his head. "I just don't hardly think it's anybody from around here took Smoke. Hell, ever'body that lives within fifty miles of Big Rock is good friends with Smoke and Sally."

Monte nodded. "You're probably right, Pearlie. But there ain't been no suspicious strangers hanging around town for the past couple of weeks, and we got to start looking somewhere."

Sally nodded. "You're right, Monte. Why don't you go on over to the telegraph office while we have some breakfast?"

17

As they rode down the trail toward Pueblo and home, Sarah MacDougal struggled with her conscience. The more she was around Smoke Jensen, the less he seemed like a crazed gunfighter out to kill anyone who got in his way and the more he seemed like an honest, decent human being.

She thought back to when Sheriff Tupper had come to give her and her father the news of Johnny's death. As she went over what he'd said on that visit, she realized that she and her father hadn't really heard what he was trying to say.

He'd tried to tell them, in his own mealymouthed way, that it was Johnny's fault he'd been shot. Of course, neither she nor her father had been willing to listen to that explanation, not when their kin was lying dead in the back of Tupper's wagon, his teeth knocked out and his body full of a stranger's lead.

"Missy," Cletus called from the seat of the buckboard alongside her.

"Yes?"

"I think it's time we took a noonin' an' rested our mounts. We keep goin' at this pace, we're gonna lose a couple of 'em 'fore too long." He grinned. "An' I don't hanker to carry none of these boys on my back."

"All right," she agreed, pointing to a copse of trees off

to the right about a hundred yards ahead. "Pull over there and we'll fix up some grub for the men and give the horses some grain and water."

She glanced down sideways at Smoke, who was riding in the back of the wagon. "Jensen, don't you go getting any ideas about trying to make a break for it. My father wants you brought back alive, but he won't quibble if you're killed trying to escape."

Smoke shrugged. "This is your party, Sarah. I'm just along for the ride." He gingerly felt the large knot on the back of his head. "Besides, if I tried to run right now, I think my head would fall off."

"You keep thinking like that and you may just survive this trip," she said, blushing a little at his mention of the damage she'd done to his head.

He glanced up at her and smiled, no fear at all evident in his eyes. "What about the homecoming?" he asked. "Will I survive that too?"

Sarah's face flushed even more, and she spurred her horse on up ahead to tell the men to ready the camp without trying to give him an answer.

While Cletus oversaw the cooking of fatback and beans and the heating of coffee, Sarah walked over to stand next to Smoke, who was sitting with his back to a tree while two men held pistols on him from a short distance away.

"You understand why I'm doing this, don't you, Mr. Jensen?" she asked.

He glanced up at her. "Of course I do, Sarah. You've lost a brother, and your father has lost a son. Neither one of you wants to admit to yourselves that it might have been your fault for not making him grow up better, so you're planning on taking it out on me." He smiled, though there was no mockery in his expression. "It's simple when you think about it. I'm to be a scapegoat for your dad's failure as a parent and your failure as a sister."

She flushed, angered by the way he was continually turning things around and trying to shift the blame to anyone but himself. "That's not true. I'm taking you back because you must be punished for what you did."

"Punished for defending myself?" he asked, the grin still on his face. "For doing what the law should have done a long time ago when your brother killed his first man?"

"Oh, you're just impossible," Sarah said, stamping her foot and walking quickly over to stand next to Cletus at the campfire.

"It's not easy being judge, jury, and executioner, Sarah," Smoke called to her back. "I don't think you're going to like the job much."

Cletus glanced up at her as he poured her a cup of coffee and handed it to her, noticing the redness of her eyes and her hunched-over shoulders and stiff neck. "He getting your goat, Missy?" he asked gently.

"Yes," she said, taking the cup and blowing on it to cool it down enough to drink. "He twists everything around so you'd think he should get a medal for shooting Johnny, instead of . . ." She paused, not wanting to put into words what was waiting for Smoke at her father's ranch.

"Instead of being killed in cold blood by your daddy or you?" Cletus asked, getting to his feet.

"I didn't say that!"

He shook his head. "No, but you know that's what's gonna happen, don't you?" he asked. "You're not fooling yourself into thinking anything different, are you?"

She hung her head. "I . . . I guess I know what's going to happen," she finally answered, her voice low.

"Good," he said. "'Cause if you're gonna do this, you better be able to live with it, or it'll eat you alive. You'd better figure you're right and it needs doin'. Otherwise, well, otherwise maybe you ought to ride on ahead and let me take him the rest of the way."

"Don't treat me like a baby, Clete."

"I'm not, Missy. But I can see by lookin' in your eyes you got some doubts 'bout all this." He sighed as he drank his coffee. "I've known men out on the trail did something that got one of their friends killed. Most of 'em knew it comes with the job of cowboying, but a few never got over it. Their lives were plumb ruined by one little mistake that could've happened to anybody." He stared hard at her. "I don't want that to happen to you, Missy."

"Yes, I do have some doubts, Clete," she admitted. "What if what he says happened is the true story? What if he had no choice but to shoot Johnny in self-defense?"

Cletus shrugged. "What really happened don't make no never mind to me," he said. "I take my orders from your daddy, an' he said to bring this man to him. Far as what happens then, it ain't no concern of mine."

"So, you won't feel responsible when Daddy shoots this man you're taking to him?"

Cletus looked surprised. "Responsible? Hell, no, not unless I pull the trigger myself."

"And would you do that, if my father told you to?" she asked, peering at him over the rim of her mug as she drank.

He looked down at his feet. "I don't know, Missy, I just don't know."

"I'm ashamed of us both, Clete. You for not being man enough to take responsibility for what you're doing, and me for not finding out the truth about what happened before taking Jensen prisoner."

After they'd eaten and fed the horses, Cletus called three men over to him. "Bob, you and Billy and Juan head on back down our back trail. Take your rifles and plenty of ammunition along with you. Anybody comes up the trail looks like they following us, you slow 'em down."

"What if'n it's a big posse, Clete?" Bob Bartlett asked.

Cletus looked around at the rising ground on either side of the trail. "There's plenty of places along here where you boys can get the high ground, Bob. You do that and you ought'a be able to hold the trail against a dozen men or more if'n you have to."

"You want we should kill them, Jefe?" Juan Gomez asked, grinning like that was something he wouldn't mind doing at all.

Cletus shook his head. "Not unless you absolutely have to, boys. Just shoot close enough to make them think twice about following us. I don't want to start a war here by killin' some lawmen and deputies, not unless there's no other way."

"But Boss," Billy Free said, "if there is no other way, then what should we do?"

Cletus shrugged. "Try for the horses first, the men last, but keep them off our backs until we get to the ranch. Understand?"

Several hours later, longer than the "couple of hours" Monte had promised, Jimmy from the telegraph office came running into Longmont's, where the group was gathered impatiently waiting for word from the blacksmith.

They'd all drunk so much coffee they felt as if they were floating, and even Andre's sumptuous breakfasts hadn't done much to cheer them up.

Jimmy handed the wire to the sheriff, who thanked him and slowly unfolded the yellow foolscap paper. He snorted when he read it, and got to his feet.

"Damn, I should'a knowed as much," he said, a wry look on his face.

"What does it say, Monte?" Sally asked, also getting to her feet.

"Jed says the only new rim he's put on in the last month was for the livery rental wagon."

Louis snapped his fingers. "Of course. We should have known that Pearlie was right and that no one who lived around here would be a party to any action against Smoke. It had to be an outsider."

"But Monte," Sally said, a puzzled look on her face. "Why would someone be so dumb as to come into town and rent a wagon to kidnap someone as well known as Smoke is?" She shook her head. "That would leave a trail pointing straight back to them as soon as we talked to the livery agent."

"Sally," Monte said, "when you've been a sheriff as long

as I have, you'll soon learn that most men who ride the owlhoot trail are as dumb as a post." He chuckled as he settled his hat on his head. "Hell, if'n they was smart, they'd get a job as sheriff like me an' get rich."

They all laughed nervously as they hurried down the street toward the livery stable.

Fred Morgan shook his head when they asked him who had recently rented his wagon with the new iron rim on the wheels. "Can't rightly say, Sheriff," he drawled in his backwoods accent, a long piece of straw hanging from the corner of his mouth that bobbed up and down as he chewed the wad of tobacco stuck in his cheek.

Monte sighed. Sometimes, talking to Fred was like pulling teeth. It took a lot of effort, and the results were usually less than satisfying. "Why not, Fred?" he asked, trying to be patient.

Fred shrugged. "Why, 'cause nobody *rented* the buckboard, Sheriff. They stole it night 'fore last."

Monte cocked his head and put his hands on his hips. "You mean someone took the wagon without paying you for it?"

"That's right."

"Well, why in hell didn't you report it to me?" Monte asked, getting red in the face.

Morgan held up his hands to calm the sheriff. "'Cause it happens all the time, Sheriff. Lots of times folks will find they need a wagon in the middle of the night 'cause theirs broke down, so instead of waking me up, they just take one of mine. Heck-fire, they always bring 'em back in a day or two."

Monte smirked. "I think this time your wagon is gone for good, Fred."

"But who round here'd do something mean like that?" Fred asked in a whining voice.

"They probably weren't from around here, Mr. Morgan," Sally said, her voice sad.

As they walked slowly back to Longmont's, she asked,

"Monte, what do you think we ought to do now? That wagon with the new rim was our only clue as to who may have taken Smoke."

Monte pursed his lips. "Well, there's only four ways they could have gone, so I guess the best thing to do is send riders out along each of the trails leading from town. Sooner or later, they've got to come across those wagon tracks."

"And until they do?" Sally asked.

"I'd suggest you go on back to the Sugarloaf and get packed up for a trip," Monte said. "Soon as the men find out which way they've gone, we'll get a posse together and go after them."

Sally thought about this for a moment, and then she shook her head. "No, Monte, I don't think that's a very good idea."

"And why not, Sally?"

"A large posse would be too easy to spot, and it would move too slow. I think just five or six men should be enough." She glanced around at Louis, who smiled and nodded his head. "I think Cal and Pearlie, Louis and you, and of course me will be more than enough."

"But Sally," Monte argued. "We don't even know how many men we'll be going up against nor which way they went."

She smiled. "Monte, outside of Smoke himself, you four men are the best men I know to have on my side in a fight. No matter what the odds are, I think the five of us will be able to handle it, and from what I hear, Pearlie can track a mouse in a blizzard. We should be all right."

Monte nodded, his lips tight. "I hope you're right, Sally."

18

The next morning, with their saddlebags packed for a long trip, Sally and Cal and Pearlie rode back into Big Rock. As they were passing the general store, Peg Jackson stepped out on the boardwalk in front and waved to Sally.

"Sally, can I talk to you for a minute?" she called.

"Why don't you boys go on over to Longmont's while I have a few words with Mrs. Jackson?" she said.

Cal and Pearlie tipped their hats to Peg and rode off down the street. Sally climbed down off her horse, tied it to the hitching rail, and then turned to Peg.

"Yes, Peg?"

"I was just wondering if you'd seen Sarah Johnson in the last couple of days," Peg said.

Sally thought back. "Why, no. In fact the last time I saw her was the last time I was in your store."

"That's strange," Peg said, looking worried. "I really don't believe she has any other friends in town she might be staying with."

"What do you mean?" Sally asked. "Is she missing?"

"Oh, I don't know as I'd go that far," Peg answered. "It's just that she hasn't been to work for the past couple of days, and she didn't tell me she wasn't going to come in."

Sally shrugged. "Maybe she quit, or got a better job."

"I don't think so," Peg said. "I still owe her for three

days' work. If she was quitting, don't you think she'd come by for her money?"

"Yes, I do," Sally said. "Have you checked with her landlady?"

"No, not yet," Peg said. "I just assumed she was sick or under the weather or something."

"Well, she's been staying at Mamma Rogers's place. I can go by there on my way to Longmont's," Sally said. "I'll just stick my head in and see if she's all right."

"Oh, thank you, Sally. That would put my mind at ease," Peg said. "After all, she's such a nice young woman."

Mamma Rogers opened the door and smiled at Sally. "Oh, howdy, Sally," she said. "Come on in."

As Sally entered the parlor, she asked, "Melissa, is Sarah Johnson in her room? I'd like to talk to her."

Rogers frowned. "Funny you should mention that," she said. "I think she moved out."

"Why is that?" Sally asked.

"Well, I didn't see or hear her for a couple of days, so I peeked into her room. The bed hadn't been slept in and all of her clothes were gone."

"Did she leave owing you rent?"

"Oh, no. Matter of fact, she's paid up through next week. It is kind'a funny, though, that she didn't ask for a refund if she was leaving for good."

Sally began to get an itch at the back of her neck that told her something was wrong. She remembered the smaller set of tracks they'd found along with Smoke's "Did Sarah have any callers while she was here?" she asked.

Rogers frowned. "Well, you know I don't allow gentlemen visitors to my women boarders, but a couple of times two men did stop by and leave messages for her."

"Citizens of Big Rock?"

Rogers shook her head. "No, they were strangers. Far as I know, they were staying over at the hotel on Main Street."

"Strangers, huh?" Sally asked.

"Yeah, and come to think of it, I haven't seen the two of them the past few days either."

"Maybe I'll just stop by the hotel and see what's going on," Sally said.

The desk clerk smiled at Sally as he flipped through the pages of his register book. "Oh, here it is, Missus Jensen. Their names were Carl Jacoby and Daniel Macklin. Macklin's been here a few months. Jacoby arrived not too long ago."

"Could I see that book, Mort?" she asked.

"Certainly," he said, turning it around so she could read the names.

It was just as she'd suspected. Both men had signed a home address of Pueblo, Colorado.

"Thank you, Mort," she said as she turned and rushed out the door toward Longmont's.

As she approached the table where Louis and Monte Carson and the boys were sitting, the sheriff stood up. "I'm sorry, Sally, but the boys haven't been able to find those wagon tracks yet."

"I think we need to look along the trail that goes toward Pueblo, Monte."

"What? Why do you say that?" he asked.

Sally shook her head and sat down. "I don't know exactly, but there are some very strange things happening that concern a young lady that is from there."

She went on to tell them all she'd found out before coming to the saloon.

She noticed Cal and Pearlie looking at each other, and sighed when Pearlie nudged Louis with his elbow.

"All right, men," she said. "Just what is going on?"

"Uh, Sally," Louis began, "Pearlie just reminded me of something that happened when we went through Pueblo on the way up to Canada last year."

"Uh-huh?"

"There was a gunfight and some men from Pueblo were killed by our group."

"Any of them named Johnson, or Jacoby, or Macklin?" she asked, her stomach doing flip-flops.

"No, not as I recall," Louis said.

Sally glanced at Monte, who was sitting next to her. "Monte, I think Smoke's disappearance ties in somehow with that of the girl who called herself Sarah Johnson. Now that I think about it, she was awfully curious about Smoke when we met on the train. I didn't catch it at the time, but she asked a lot of questions about him."

"And you think that ties in with the killing in Pueblo last year?" he asked.

She shrugged. "Probably, but it doesn't matter. We have four people who've disappeared from Big Rock in the last few days, so there's got to be some connection."

"She's right, Monte," Louis said. "What are the odds of that happening and it not being related?"

Monte got up from the table. "I agree. Let's get moving up the trail to Pueblo."

"I'll bet you a dollar against one of Miss Sally's bear signs that we find those buckboard tracks 'fore we go ten miles," Pearlie said to Cal as he got to his feet and set his hat low on his head.

"I won't bet, but I hope you're right," Cal replied, following him toward the door.

Meanwhile, Cletus and Sarah and their men were getting closer to Pueblo, where Angus MacDougal had some plans for Smoke Jensen.

Sarah was beginning to feel less and less sure that she was doing the right thing. The more she talked to Smoke, the harder it was for her to see him as a cold-blooded killer. In spite of how she'd tricked and betrayed him in order to take him to her father, he seemed to bear her no malice. When she asked him about this, he just shrugged. "I guess I'd probably feel much the same way if I were in your shoes," he told her. "Matter of fact," he added, thinking of the time he'd gone after the men who'd raped his wife and killed her and his son, "I have done pretty much the same thing—the only difference was, I knew I was right and you don't."

That night they stopped and fixed camp for the last time. By the end of the next day, Cletus said they'd be at the MacDougal ranch.

Exhausted from the ride and her mental battle with herself about the rightness of what she'd done, Sarah flopped down on the ground near the fire and stared into the flames, as if she could find some answers there.

Smoke, who was standing a few yards away with his hands tied, glanced her way. His eyes widened and he took two quick steps and launched himself at her headfirst.

His body slammed into hers, knocking her to the side and almost into the flames.

Cletus, seeing this and hearing Sarah's cry of surprise and pain, whipped out his Walker Colt and aimed it at the back of Smoke's head.

Before he could pull the trigger, he saw Smoke twist his body around and lift his boots into the air. A dark brown, mottled shape flashed into the light and a five-foot-long timber rattler struck at Smoke's boots, its fangs slashing a double groove in the soles of the shoes.

"Damn!" Jimmy Corbett yelled as he jumped to the side to get out of the way of the angry critter.

Smoke brought the heels of his boots down hard, smashing the snake in the head and dazing it.

Cletus, finally seeing what was going on, stepped over and put a bullet between the snake's eyes, blowing its head off.

"What . . . why . . . ?" a startled Sarah cried from where she lay, a few feet away.

Cletus holstered his pistol and moved to her side, helping her to her feet. She leaned over Smoke, looked at the dead snake, and shuddered.

"You saved my life," she murmured.

"Naw, probably not," Smoke said, struggling to sit up, the task difficult with his hands still tied behind his back. "The poor critter was just trying to get to the fire to warm himself up a bit. When it's this cold outside, they can't move very fast."

Cletus snorted. "Hell, boy," he said. "He didn't look all that slow when he struck at your boots."

Smoke just shrugged. "Now that the excitement is over, how about a cup of that coffee that's boiling over by the fire?" he asked.

Cletus nodded, and moved over to squat next to the pot and pour a mug. He looked at Sarah, who was standing next to him. "You're right, Missy," he said in a low voice so only she could hear him. "That boy did save your life, and at some risk to his own."

"I know," she said, squatting next to Cletus and holding out her mug for some of the steaming brew.

Cletus glanced over his shoulder at Smoke. "You know, Missy," he said, "this is the first time in more'n twenty years I been workin' for your daddy that I feel like he's dead wrong 'bout somethin'."

"What are we going to do, Clete?" she asked, holding the mug in both hands to warm them up.

"I don't know, Missy," he said, his voice heavy and sad. "I'm afraid we've both got some thinkin' to do on it 'fore we get home tomorrow."

He got slowly to his feet, and carried the mug of coffee over and handed it to Smoke, who nodded his thanks.

"Uh . . . I want to thank you for what you done, Jensen," Cletus said, the words coming hard.

Smoke eyed him. "Sarah means something special to you, doesn't she, Cletus?" Smoke asked.

"I'm her godfather, and I've knowed her all her life," Cletus answered.

Smoke nodded slowly, sipping the coffee. "Then, you're welcome, Cletus."

Later that night, after everyone had eaten and while even the sentries were dozing in their appointed spots, Sarah slipped out of her blankets and crawled over to where Smoke lay curled up next to the coals of the fire.

Sometime in the last couple of hours, the lowering clouds had released their burden and it had begun to snow fairly heavily.

Sarah glanced around in the darkness and could see no one stirring. The only sounds were the hissing of the fire as snow fell into it, and the occasional snorting and snoring of the sleeping cowboys all around them.

She reached over and nudged Smoke with her hand, holding her finger to her lips when he came instantly awake and stared at her face in the meager light of the coals.

Without saying a word, she slipped a clasp knife into his hand. When he raised his eyebrows in question, she pointed toward the nearby mountains, even though they were not visible through the storm.

Smoke nodded and eased the knife open. It took him less than five seconds to saw through the ropes on his wrists and scramble to his feet.

He looked toward the line of horses tied to a rope stretched between two trees, but Sarah saw his glance and shook her head.

He shrugged, smiled, and grabbed up his blanket from the ground. Throwing it over his shoulders, he waved to her, and seconds later he had disappeared into the billowing white clouds of the snowstorm.

Sarah took another look around to make sure no one had seen what she'd done, and then she crawled back to her blankets, mussing the snow behind her to hide her tracks.

On the other side of the fire, Cletus shook his head and smiled at her actions. He had never been more proud of her in all the years he'd known her.

Sighing, he lay his head back down on his saddle and pulled the blanket up to his chin. Maybe, with a little luck, Jensen could get to the mountains before daylight and their moral dilemma would be solved.

"Can't kill a man who ain't there," he mumbled to himself, and fell fast asleep.

19

Monte Carson, acknowledging Pearlie's superior tracking skills, let him lead the way up the trail northward toward Pueblo.

Pearlie leaned over the side of his mount, and sometimes he even dismounted to squat next to some tracks, as he looked for the telltale signs of the passage of a wagon with new iron rims on the wheels. This caused the group to move slowly, something Cal in his youthfulness chaffed at.

"Jiminy, Pearlie, can't you go no faster'n that?" he complained.

Louis glanced over at him. "It won't do much good to race along, making good time, if we're going in the wrong direction, Cal." Louis looked up at the sky. "And this snow covering up the tracks isn't helping matters any either."

"I know, I know," Cal agreed. "It's just that I'm really worried about Smoke."

Sally smiled grimly. "We all are, Cal, but we mustn't let that keep us from doing the right thing in searching for him. It is very difficult to keep a clear mind when one is worried or frightened, but that is precisely when it is most important to do so."

Suddenly, up ahead, Pearlie got down off his horse and knelt next to some tracks just to the side of the road. "Looky, here," he called, pointing down. "Here's where the wagon got off the road a little bit an' outta all the other tracks. It's our buckboard, all right," he said, swinging back up into the saddle.

Monte grinned, taking out his six-gun and opening the loading gate to check his loads. "Now, we can ride full out and see if we can catch up to those . . . owlhoots," he said, glancing at Sally and editing his last few words so as not to offend her.

"But not too fast, Monte," Louis advised. "We don't want to ride so fast we run up on the scoundrels without being ready for them, something easy to do in a storm like this. That could get Smoke killed in a hurry."

Monte nodded and set his hat down tight on his head. He leaned over the saddle horn, spurred his horse, and kicked it into a gallop, with the others following right behind with bandannas tied over their noses and faces to help against the frigid north wind they were riding right into.

Meanwhile, up ahead a few miles, Bob Bartlett, Juan Gomez, and Billy Free had taken up positions on either side of the trail where it narrowed between two large outcroppings of boulders. The forest on either side of the trail was very thick with brush and the land there had a steep slope to it, which would make it almost impossible for anyone to move around and flank them without becoming targets from the high ground.

"How're we gonna know who to stop, Bob?" Billy asked. "How're we gonna be able to tell if they're trackin' Jensen or not, especially in this storm? Hell, I can't see shit through all this snow."

"Don't much matter, Billy," Bob answered. "For the next twelve hours or so, till it gets full on dark, we're gonna stop anybody an' everbody who tries to come up that there trail. That way we can be sure nobody can catch up to us 'fore we get to the ranch in Pueblo."

"But I don't hanker on killin' no innocent people, Bob," Billy said, his forehead creased in a frown. "I know

Jensen deserves what he's gonna get, but shooting down some regular men who just happen to be in a posse just don't seem right to me," he complained.

"I didn't say nothin' 'bout killin' nobody, Billy," Bob said. He looked around at the spot they had chosen to defend the trail. "From up here, we can keep anybody from passin' without having to kill 'em. We just shoot a couple of hosses out from under the riders, hit some rocks close by 'em, an' I have a feelin' they gonna be hightailin' it back to Big Rock." He paused and added, "An' the way this snow is fallin', they'll play hell getting a clear shot back at us."

Billy nodded, relieved. He glanced across the trail to where Juan Gomez was sitting looking over a large rock. "You think Gomez got that message too?" he asked. "Ol' Juan likes to use his gun a little too much for my taste."

Bob followed his glance. "He'd better of gotten the message, since I told him flat out if he killed anybody Angus would have his scalp. The old man don't want this to turn into a range war. He just wants his revenge on the man that killed his son."

Suddenly, from across the trail came a low whistle. When they looked, they saw Juan pointing down at the trail as it rose to meet them.

A couple of hundred yards away, five riders could barely be seen riding at speed up the road into the teeth of the storm. Bob held up his hand to keep Juan from firing too soon, and he and Billy lay down across the top of the rock they were behind and took careful aim with their Winchesters.

Once the riders got in range, Bob gently squeezed the trigger on his long gun.

Down below, the rider in the lead was thrown head over heels as his horse swallowed its head and collapsed underneath him.

As the other riders jerked their mounts to a halt, both Billy and Juan fired at the same time. Billy missed, but the horse Juan was aiming at screamed and crow-hopped for a few seconds before it too fell to the ground.

Louis struggled to get his leg out from under his big Morgan. When the horse fell, it trapped Louis's leg underneath it.

Sally jumped off the big Palouse she was riding and ran to Monte's side. She gently rolled him over and found he was conscious, but barely. The unexpected fall had clearly stunned him badly.

She looked around quickly. There was no good cover nearby. They'd have to retreat at least a hundred yards back up the trail to find someplace to hide.

Pearlie jumped down off his horse and ran to help her, while Cal did the same with Louis. In minutes, supporting him between them, Sally and Pearlie were moving Monte back up the trail and away from the ambushers.

Louis, once Cal had helped him get up, took a moment to put a bullet into the head of his wounded horse so he wouldn't suffer. One look at Monte's mount told him the gelding was already dead, so Louis swung up into the saddle behind Cal and they galloped back up the trail heading for cover.

When they came abreast of Sally and Pearlie, who were still struggling with a dazed and incoherent Monte, Louis swung out of the saddle and took Sally's place helping Pearlie, while Sally rushed to get control of hers and Pearlie's horses and keep them with them.

As they hustled Monte up the trail, Louis looked back over his shoulder toward the place where the shots had come from. The snow was blowing so hard he could barely see the spot, and he was surprised there hadn't been any more gunplay. He knew the men hiding up there could have killed them had they so desired, even with the reduced visibility of the snowstorm. Why they hadn't was a mystery he didn't have time to puzzle out now. He had to get Monte under cover and then determine if he needed immediate medical help.

Up on the ridge, Bob nodded in satisfaction. They'd done a good job stopping those pilgrims from getting up the trail. He had no idea who they were, whether they were a posse after Jensen or not, but it didn't make any difference. No one was going to pass their way on this day, no matter who they were.

"You see that, Bob?" Billy asked.

"What?"

"I think one of those people was a woman," he answered. "I could see her long, black hair hanging out from under her hat when she ran to that man that was on the ground."

"So?" Bob asked.

"I just can't believe if'n that was a posse that they'd let a woman ride along. Leastways, I ain't never seen no woman on a posse before."

"Like I said before," Bob said, "it don't matter none who's down there. The fact is, it's our job to keep everybody from passing."

He looked back over his shoulder. "Now, I'll keep an eye on those galoots down there, an' you can get back there an' stir up that fire. I'm thinkin' some hot coffee'd sure go down good right now to take the chill out of my bones."

Down below, Sally had laid Monte down on his back and was sponging his forehead with cool water from her canteen. As snowflakes began to accumulate on his shirt, she had Pearlie cover him with a blanket.

"How are you feeling, Monte?" she asked when he began to shiver.

"I . . . I don't rightly know, Sally," he said with a confused look in his eyes. "Where are we and what happened to me?" he asked with a groan.

"We're on the trail after Smoke's kidnappers, Monte, and someone shot your horse out from under you, causing you to take a bad fall."

"Smoke's kidnappers?" he asked, clearly still confused and unsure of what was going on.

Louis frowned and touched Sally on the shoulder, indicating he wanted to talk with her out of Monte's hearing.

She got up and they walked a short distance away, turning their backs to the north wind to lessen the chill. "I think he's got a concussion, Sally," he said. "I've seen it before when someone got hit on the head. It makes them forget what they've done the past few days, and it can be very serious."

"I know," she said, glancing back over her shoulder at Monte's pale face. "We've got to get him back to Big Rock where Dr. Spalding can take a look at him."

"You think he's fit to ride a horse?" Louis asked, doubt in his voice.

"Not by himself," she answered. "But if you ride behind him and help hold him in the saddle, I think he can do it." She glanced up at the snowflakes drifting down. "He's going to have to, Louis. This storm looks like it's going to be pretty bad, and I don't know if he will survive a night of freezing temperatures, not in his condition."

"I agree," Louis said. He looked around at the terrain surrounding them. "Anyway, they've got us pretty well boxed in here, and I don't see any way past them without a larger force of men." He grinned sourly. "And especially not with the five of us having only three horses left."

Sally went back over to Monte. "Monte, we're going to try and get you up on a horse," she said. "Louis is going to ride with you on the way back to Big Rock."

As Pearlie and Cal helped Monte to his feet, he leaned over and vomited in the weeds. Louis glanced at Sally and shook his head. He knew from past experience this was not a good sign in men with head injuries.

It took both Cal and Pearlie to get Monte up on the horse and to hold him there while Louis climbed up behind him. "You just hold on to the saddle horn, Monte, and I'll do the riding for both of us," Louis said, putting his arms around Monte to grab the reins.

Since she was the lightest, Sally rode double with Cal while Pearlie had his own horse to himself.

"Pearlie, since you're riding alone, why don't you hightail it on back to Big Rock and see if you can get the doc to come out to meet us with a buckboard? That way he can get to see Monte sooner," Louis suggested.

Pearlie touched his hat and put the spurs to his mount, heading back down the trail as fast as he could ride.

It was slow going as they rode toward home. Louis was afraid to push the horse too fast lest he stumble in the snow or jar Monte and cause more problems inside his head.

"Who do you think that was back there that shot us up?" Cal asked as they rode.

"It must have been some of the people that took Smoke," Sally said.

"I wonder why they didn't try and kill us," Louis said. "They certainly had a good chance to do so."

Sally shook her head. "I don't know, Louis. Perhaps their only quarrel is with Smoke and they don't want to kill anyone else unless they have to."

"But if they're that angry with Smoke, why take him?" Louis asked. "Once they had the drop on him, why didn't they just kill him and be done with it? That would have been a lot less dangerous and would have made a lot more sense than taking him prisoner."

"I don't know, Louis," Sally said, "but I do intend to find out, and God help whoever is behind this."

Louis glanced at Sally and felt the hairs on the back of his neck stir. He'd seen that look before in Smoke's eyes, and it always meant someone was about to die.

Suddenly, he felt very sorry for whoever had taken Smoke, for he knew their days were numbered.

20

Smoke moved through the night as fast as he could, considering the snowstorm made the darkness almost absolute and he was running through snow that was getting deeper by the minute. It was only his excellent night vision that kept him from breaking an ankle or impaling himself on a tree limb or other natural obstruction in the heavy forest he was traversing.

Knowing the storm, like most early fall storms, was coming almost directly out of the north, he realized all he had to do to keep on track was to keep the wind directly in his face. That way he avoided traveling in circles as most inexperienced men did when moving in unfamiliar territory.

Smoke knew the mountain ranges all around them were closest directly to the north, and getting up into the High Lonesome was his only chance to avoid the men who would surely be on his trail no later than daybreak.

He knew from earlier in the day that the closest mountain was about seven miles away and that he had absolutely no chance to make it before daylight, not on foot traveling through darkness in snow that was rapidly getting up to his mid-calves. The only good thing about his rapid advance was that the exertion was keeping his body temperature high enough to avoid frostbite due to exposure to the extreme cold.

The bad news was that his only weapon was a five-inch

clasp knife and he was completely without any other supplies or food. He laughed out loud into the freezing north wind. Only a mountain man, and a crazy one at that, would think that he had any chance at all against more than a dozen well-armed men on horseback on his trail under these conditions.

Well, this crazy old mountain man still had a few tricks up his sleeve, and if he could keep from freezing to death long enough, he'd show them a thing or two.

The wind was howling and the snow was blowing almost horizontally when the camp began to wake up the next morning. Dawn was evident only through a general lightening up of the snow since there was no morning sun to be seen.

Cletus, as usual, was the first to arise, and he piled fresh wood onto the smoldering coals of last night's campfire. He filled pots with water and heaping handfuls of coffee in preparation for an early breakfast. He knew from his observation the night before that Smoke Jensen had escaped his bounds, but he pretended not to notice the empty space where Smoke had lain the previous night as he busied himself around the fire.

As men slowly gathered around the fire, holding out hands to get them warm and gratefully accepting mugs of steaming coffee, he told Jimmy Corbett to get started cooking some fatback and beans in the large skillets they'd brought along.

"Don't worry with trying to make biscuits in this storm," he said. "We've still got some left from last night's dinner that ought'a do."

"Gonna have to dip them sinkers in coffee to get 'em soft enough to chew," Jason Biggs said, grinning. "Otherwise you're liable to break a tooth on 'em."

Cletus was about to reply when Wally Stevens hollered from over near the tree Smoke had been under, "Hey, ever'body, Jensen's gone!"

Cletus forced a surprised look on his face and ran over to

where Smoke was supposed to be lying. "Well, I'll be damned," he exclaimed, straightening up and looking around with his hands on his hips. "The bastard's not here."

"I don't see no ropes," Stevens said, looking around on the ground and pushing mounds of snow aside, "so maybe he couldn't get them loose and his hands are still tied."

"What's going on here?" Sarah asked as she appeared out of the blowing snow.

"Looks like Jensen has somehow managed to escape from the camp," Cletus said, trying to appear disgusted with the turn of events.

"Escaped?" Sarah asked, her voice astounded. "How in the world was he able to do that?"

"I don't know, Miss MacDougal," Biggs said, "but he can't have gotten far in this storm, not on foot."

"How do you know he didn't take one of the horses?" she asked, causing everyone to make a mad dash off to the side where the horses were all tied to a tether rope.

After a quick count, Cletus assured everyone that Smoke hadn't in fact taken any of the mounts.

The men went back to the camp and began to make a circle around the periphery, trying to locate any tracks Smoke might have left.

After an hour of searching, they all decided the storm had covered any traces he might have made.

They gathered around the fire to get warm again and to discuss what they ought to do. "You got any bright ideas, Clete?" Biggs asked. "'Cause I surely don't relish going back to the ranch and having Mr. MacDougal chew my ears off for letting Jensen get away from us."

Cletus thought for a moment as he finished off his mug of coffee. Finally, he looked around. "All right, here is what I think. Jensen could have gone in only two directions, north or south."

"Why do you say that?" Stevens asked.

"'Cause if he headed either east or west, all he's gonna find is a big prairie with almost no cover to speak of. Jensen's too smart to put himself in that position, 'cause in this weather, no cover means he'd freeze to death. Now, if he heads south back towards his home, we got three men behind us guarding the trail. If, on the other hand, he heads north towards the nearest mountain range, then he's got a good chance of hiding out from us if he makes it."

"So," Sarah said, "you think he's probably gone north toward the mountains?"

Cletus shrugged. "It's what I'd do in his place." He made a grimace of disgust. "'Course, we're gonna have to cover all the directions, just in case he tried to fool us by going someplace we wouldn't think he'd try."

"That's gonna split us up pretty good," Stevens said.

"Not really," Sarah said. "Remember, Jensen's on foot and doesn't have any weapons. We can send one man east and one man west. If he's out there in the open, they should be able to run him down before nightfall and take him prisoner again."

"What about south?" Cletus asked.

"I think one man should be able to get back down the trail and warn Bartlett and Gomez and Free to be on the lookout for him," she said. "That should leave us plenty of men to undertake a campaign to catch him before he can get too far into the mountains if he headed north."

Cletus shook his head in admiration. "Missy, I wish I'd had you running my outfit during the war. You plumb got a mind for tactics."

"Well, I'd suggest we get a move on," she said. "Clete, you pick the men to go east and west and south, and I'll see to getting their canteens filled with hot coffee to keep them from freezing to death on the way."

"We got time to eat first, Miss MacDougal?" Stevens asked, his face hopeful.

"Certainly. We can't go out into this storm on a man-hunt with our bellies empty, now can we, men?"

Cletus laughed. "Jimmy, get those beans to cookin', boy, we got a man to catch."

"Yes, sir," Corbett answered, using a long stick to stir the coals under the trestle that contained the pot of beans and fatback.

As Sarah began to fill canteens with hot coffee, Cletus

looked at her and shook his head. He'd never seen a better performance. No one would ever suspect that she'd let Jensen go herself, and he damn sure wasn't going to enlighten anyone.

He stepped over to the edge of the fire and stood looking into the north wind, in the direction Jensen must have gone if he was to have any chance to avoid capture.

What would it take for a man to have the courage to take off on foot into a blizzard like this with no weapons and no warm clothes to speak of? he wondered.

He chuckled to himself, knowing full well the answer to that question. A man would otherwise have to be completely without hope of survival to take a chance like that, and Jensen certainly knew that for him to stay in camp would mean certain death.

As Sarah called to him that the beans and fatback were ready, he turned and shook his head. The man didn't stand a chance in this weather, he thought, but at least freezing to death was probably less painful that a bullet.

21

Pearlie jerked his horse to a stop in front of Dr. Colton Spalding's office, bounded out of the saddle, and raced through the front door without bothering to knock.

Spalding, who was called Cotton by all of his friends due to his ash-blond, almost white hair, looked up from his rolltop desk in the corner of his parlor. When he saw the agitation in Pearlie's face, he got to his feet and began putting on his coat before the young man had a chance to speak.

"Doc, you gotta come!" Pearlie gasped, still out of breath from his breakneck ride into town.

Cotton picked up his black bag and a pair of gloves from the side table in the hallway. "Of course, Pearlie," he said. "Is there trouble out at the Sugarloaf?"

"No, Doc, it's Monte Carson," Pearlie answered. "His hoss was shot out from under him and he took a terrible fall. He hit his head an' he ain't been exactly actin' right since then."

"Where is he?" Cotton asked as they exited his door, followed by his wife Mona, who'd heard the commotion and joined them in the parlor. He gave Mona a quick kiss good-bye and told her he'd be back as soon as possible. When she went back in the door, he didn't bother to lock it in case someone needing his care wanted to come in and wait for his return, in which case his wife Mona, who was also his nurse, would take care of that person.

"Out on the road north of town, 'bout five or six miles by now," he answered.

"By now?" Cotton asked, raising his eyebrows. "Don't tell me he is being moved."

"Uh . . . yes, sir," Pearlie said. "Louis is riding double with him to keep him on horseback."

"Oh, sweet Jesus," Cotton said under his breath as he climbed up into his wagon that was hitched in front of his office.

"You'd better take me there as fast as you can, Pearlie, and let us hope we're not too late and that moving him has not caused irreparable damage to his brain."

When they met up with Louis and Sally and Cal on the road into town, Cotton pulled his wagon to the side of the road. "Pearlie, scrape that snow out of the back of the wagon and get those blankets out from under the tarp there under the seat. Make a bed for Monte as best you can."

Monte was sitting unconscious in front of Louis, being held in place by Louis's hands around him. The sheriff's head lolled limply to and fro as the horse moved.

"Cal, get over here and help me take Monte down and get him in the back of my wagon, but be as gentle as you can," the doctor ordered.

Moments later, Monte was lying on his back in the rear compartment of Cotton's wagon and the doctor was leaning over him, checking his pupils and feeling his pulse.

"Has he had any violent purging . . . uh, vomiting?" he asked Sally.

"Yes, once, right after he tried to get up after the fall," she answered.

Cotton shook his head. "That's not a good sign. It means he's definitely had a concussion."

Sally, standing at his side, said, "I know a head injury shouldn't be moved, Cotton, but I thought the time saved getting him under your care and out of the cold was worth the danger of moving him." She gave Monte a worried look. "There was no shelter on the trail and we had no way of keeping him warm in this storm."

"You're probably right, Sally," Cotton said, not looking away from his patient. "At any rate, it's hard to say which is worse, exposure to the elements or movement."

He straightened up after tucking the blankets around Monte to keep him as warm as possible. "Now, I need to get him back to my office where he can be properly cared for."

As he climbed up onto the seat of the wagon, he looked back down at Sally. "Perhaps you'd better swing back by Monte's house and tell Mary what is going on," he said. "She can come to my office and sit with him if she wishes."

"How serious is it, Cotton?" Sally asked.

The doctor shrugged. "Well, it's a good sign that he survived the trip on horseback. He's obviously had some minor bleeding in his head and a severe concussion. The only question now is will he have any more and just how much damage that he's already had has done to his mind." As he took up the reins, he added, "He's going to need some luck."

After Cotton slapped the reins on his horses' rears and moved off down the trail, Louis asked Sally, "What do we do about Smoke?"

She shook her head. "First, I need to go talk to Mary and tell her what happened." She hesitated. "We can't do Smoke any good right now, not with those men blocking the trail."

"Miss Sally," Cal said, "we could get a big posse together in less time than it takes to say it. Heck, just about ever'-body in Big Rock would go along if'n they thought Smoke was in trouble."

"He's correct, Sally," Louis agreed. "With a large number of men we could get by that ambush and go after the men who took Smoke."

Sally turned tortured eyes to Louis. "Yes, Louis, I believe we could do that. But how many men would get hurt or possibly killed trying to get past that ambush site?"

When he paused, unable to answer, Sally smiled sadly. "See what I mean? Do you think Smoke would want a lot of townspeople getting hurt trying to rescue him?"

Louis reluctantly shook his head. "No, I guess not, Sally."

She put a hand on his shoulder. "Look at it this way. If whoever took him wanted to kill him, he's already dead. If he's still alive by now, then there is some other reason for taking him and keeping him alive. Either way, waiting until morning to continue our trip after them won't make much difference."

"You think the men guarding the trail will be gone by then?" Pearlie asked.

She nodded. "Probably. They cannot hope to hold the trail forever. My guess is they were just trying to give whoever has Smoke time to get to where they're going. We should be able to get by in the morning."

"I just hope we're not too late for Smoke," Cal said, his voice heavy.

Sally swung up into the saddle and smiled. "Cal, you should have more faith in Smoke. He has managed to survive much worse than this for a lot of years."

Louis laughed as he kicked his horse to follow Sally. "That's a fact!" he said.

Just as Cletus and Sarah and their men were saddling up their mounts, Daniel Macklin approached Cletus. "Say, Clete, I think somebody ought'a ride on over to the ranch and tell Angus what's goin' on," he said, his eyes flicking from Sarah to Cletus, not sure who was in charge of the men since she'd arrived.

Cletus tightened the cinch-belt on his saddle and said over his shoulder, "And just why would you think that, Mac, since Angus put me in charge of this little fracas?"

Macklin rubbed his jaw. "Well, for starters, you got four men coverin' our back trail, an' two more headin' off east and west, so that only leaves six or seven of us to head out after Jensen in the mountains."

"So, I say again Mac, what is your point?"

"I done some talkin' 'bout Jensen when I was in his town waiting for Sarah to make up her mind what to do," Macklin said, glancing at her out of the corner of his eye to make sure she wasn't taking his talk wrong.

"Yeah, so?"

"What I found out was this Jensen is not only a famous gunfighter, he was a mountain man from the time he was a little boy until just a few years ago."

Now Macklin had Cletus's full attention. "Is that a fact?" Cletus said, his lips tight.

"Yep, an' you know that a handful of us cowboys ain't gonna be no match for a mountain man up in those mountains," Macklin said, glancing off in the direction of the snow-covered peaks to the north, barely visible in the light snowfall.

Cletus followed his gaze. "You may be right, Mac. Of course, I'm hoping to catch up to Jensen 'fore he gets a chance to get up into those mountains."

Macklin shrugged. "If you do, then you'll be able to handle him with no problem, assuming you catch him out in the open." He hesitated. "Of course, if you don't, you're gonna need all the help you can get."

Cletus glanced at Sarah, who was busily cinching up her saddle and pretending not to be paying any attention to their talk. Cletus was caught in a dilemma. He wanted Jensen to do exactly what Macklin said he was worried about, that is, get up into the mountains and disappear so they couldn't find him and take him back to Angus. But he didn't want Angus to suspect as much, so he had to play the game of doing his best to capture the gunman.

"I guess you're right, Mac. Why don't you hightail it on ahead to the ranch and see if Angus wants to hire more men to come out here and help us hunt Jensen down if he makes it to the mountains? That way, we can leave it up to Angus how much he really wants Jensen."

Macklin nodded. "My thoughts exactly, Clete."

Cletus thought for a moment, and then he added, "If you do bring more men, plan to meet up with us at that old line cabin at the base of the mountain near where that stream comes out onto flat ground."

Mac nodded and he swung up into his saddle, tipped his hat, and put the spurs to his mount, heading up the road toward the MacDougal ranch in Pueblo.

Cletus looked over at Sarah to see how she was taking this, but all he could see was that her jaw was set and her lips were tightly squeezed together as she finished setting her saddle and throwing her saddlebags across the animal's rump.

"That all right with you, Sarah?" he asked.

She turned to look at him, still not realizing he knew she'd been the one to turn Smoke loose. "Sure, Clete. What Mac said made sense, and we may well need some help if Jensen makes it up into those slopes."

Cletus put his foot in his stirrup and eased up onto the back of his horse. "I just hope Angus don't send a bunch of flatlanders that don't know which end of a gun the bullet comes out of to help us. Otherwise, we're gonna need more'n one wagon to carry all the bodies back in."

22

Instead of trying to run the entire several miles to the lower slopes of the nearest mountain and exhausting himself, Smoke alternated walking at a fast pace with jogging for fifty yards. He kept his head lowered and his eyes squinted against the blowing snow and wind in his face, but even so, it wasn't long before his eyes began to burn and itch from the drying effects of the constant wind.

He'd known men up in the mountains who'd had their eyes frozen shut by blizzards like this, and he didn't want to take any chances, so he kept the brim of his hat down low and his head bent down, glancing up occasionally to make sure he wasn't about to walk into a crevice or boulder.

Soon, the snow had accumulated to a depth almost up to his knees, and it was beginning to make walking extremely difficult and running impossible. He knew he was going to have trouble getting to deep cover on the mountainside before dawn. The only good thing about the amount of snow falling was that it would completely obliterate his tracks so if the gang of men tried to follow them, they wouldn't be able to find him, and it would slow them down as much as it was him.

Normally, faced with a storm such as this and no horse, Smoke would cut some branches off pine trees and build himself a lean-to to weather out the storm out of the wind. With ten or so angry men on his trail, this wasn't an

option, but if he didn't do something to get out of the
weather, he was going to freeze to death while he walked.
His only hope was to make it until dawn lightened the eastern sky so he could find something else that would do to
both hide him and keep him out of the cold.

By the time the eastern sky began to lighten enough for
him to see his surroundings, Smoke was shivering with
cold and was weak from dehydration. His sweat had
frozen on his skin and his mouth was so dry he couldn't
work up a good spit.

He resisted the urge to eat snow, as that would only
lower his body temperature. He knew of several mountain
men who'd made that mistake and hadn't lived to tell
about it.

As the day got brighter, Smoke noticed a fallen ponderosa pine off to his right. It appeared to have been
struck by lightning, as there was a jagged, blackened scar
along its trunk.

He slogged over to it, and saw to his relief that the giant
had taken out several other smaller trees around it when
it crashed to the ground. Smoke moved along the trunk
until he came to the jumble of broken and crushed limbs
at the top of the tree. Sure enough, it was as he'd hoped.
The tangle of tree limbs and trunks and roots made a perfectly acceptable place to get out of sight and weather out
the rest of the storm.

With any luck, the men chasing him would just ride on
by if they came this way.

Smoke pushed aside a thick branch and bent over to
worm his way into the thick tangle. He froze when he
heard a low growl from in front of him. He realized immediately what it was. It was the sound of a mountain cougar
who'd had the same idea of using the tree for shelter as
Smoke had.

Moving slowly, Smoke took out the small clasp knife
and worked the blade open, trying not to provoke the big
cat into a charge. He couldn't see the animal in the gloom
of the enclosure, but he could smell its fetid breath and
musky odor as if it was very close.

Suddenly the cat snarled and rushed at him out of the darkness of the jumble of tree limbs. Smoke jumped back and let go of the branch he'd been bending back to enter. The branch snapped forward, catching the cougar in the face as it leapt at Smoke.

Smoke dove onto the cat before it could regain its balance and slashed to and fro with the small knife, praying he'd hit the throat before the cat got his arm in its powerful jaws.

They rolled over a couple of times, Smoke almost screaming at the burning pain as the cat raked his back with its claws. Luckily, the intervening branch kept the cougar from gutting Smoke with its hind feet as cougars usually did.

Moments later, it was over. The cougar gasped its last breath as Smoke's knife tore its throat open almost to the spine.

Unable to see the damage to his back, Smoke did the next best thing. He pulled his shirt up and lay on his back in the snow, rocking back and forth and letting the coldness stop the bleeding and wash out his wounds.

The pain was almost unbearable, but he counted himself lucky to be alive and a little pain was a small price to pay for shelter, and now food. He sat up and pulled his shirt back down over his back, wincing as the deerskin scraped the raw wounds. He had no way of knowing if the bleeding had stopped, but figured he'd find out soon enough if the blood soaked the shirt.

He didn't dare start a fire, so he quickly skinned the cougar and gutted it. Since liver has the most nutrients, Smoke ate as much of the raw liver as his stomach could take. Once he'd filled his belly, he scraped the skin as best he could and cut it into wide pieces he could wrap around his lower legs as leggings, to keep from getting frostbite when he walked through deep snow. It wouldn't smell very good, he thought with a smile, but that was the least of his worries.

With the still-warm liver in his stomach, he risked eating enough snow to slake his thirst, and then he curled up in the crown of the fallen tree under a blanket of pine boughs and the rest of the cougar skin. He was asleep instantly.

Cletus took the lead, with Sarah right behind him, as the group headed through the forest toward the mountain whose peak couldn't be seen through the driving snow.

Even though they were on horseback, they couldn't move much faster than Smoke had been able to because of the depth of the snow and the uneven, wooded terrain.

"Hey, Boss," George Jones called from the middle of the pack.

"Yeah, George?" Cletus answered, twisting in his saddle to see what the man wanted.

"Maybe it'd be a good idea if we spread out 'stead of riding in a line like this. In this storm, it's better'n even odds Jensen froze to death last night. It'd be a shame to ride past his carcass and not know it."

Cletus had to admit the man had a good point. Though he didn't for a minute think a mountain man would ever freeze to death in a minor storm like this, Cletus knew that Jensen might well have gone to ground somewhere between here and the mountain hoping they'd ride right on past him.

"That's a good idea, George," Cletus said, stopping his horse. He waved his hands to both sides. "I want you men to spread out, and keep a sharp eye for any sign of Jensen along the way," he called. "And be sure to stay in sight of the men on either side of you. I don't want Jensen to be able to slip between us."

In a lower voice, he said, "Sarah, I want you to stay next to me. Your daddy'd have my hide if I let anything happen to you."

Sarah gave him a gentle smile. They both knew she could shoot every bit as straight as him and she was probably a lot faster on the draw. Still and all, he'd been a good and loyal friend to both her and her father, so she didn't point this out to him. "All right, Clete. I'll stay close so you can protect me from the big, bad Smoke Jensen."

He frowned at her, knowing she was putting him on. "Don't underestimate this man, Sarah. I know you don't think he is a really bad man, but men who are desperate to live will sometimes do things they wouldn't ordinarily do—and that includes Smoke Jensen."

Sarah had a hard time imagining Smoke Jensen would ever be desperate, but she kept her mouth shut and rode alongside Cletus as he moved northward toward the nearest mountain. She pulled her heavy, fur-lined deerskin coat tight around her shoulders as they rode into the freezing wind, wondering how Jensen, who was dressed only in buckskins, would be able to survive the brutal conditions.

Even though they were downwind, Smoke heard the approaching riders when they were still over a hundred yards away, and he came instantly awake. Years living in the High Lonesome had trained him to be able to hear and see things most normal men couldn't, and he could respond to them instinctively without having to think about it beforehand.

It was a trait that'd saved his life on more than one occasion when he and Preacher were living up in the High Lonesome.

He eased to the edge of his tree-limb hideout and glanced around to make sure the snow had covered all signs of the struggle with the big cat. He nodded in satisfaction to see a pristine blanket of fresh snow around the jumble of fallen trees he was in. He was also relieved to see that the storm was still fairly heavy. He was counting on it to mask his next moves.

He readied himself by moving to the very edge of his hideout so that he could exit it quickly and silently when the time came, and then he got out the clasp knife and opened it. He was going to need it very soon now.

* * *

Trying to keep a straight line of riders going into a storm and weaving back and forth in a fairly thick forest is impossible. Thus, the line of riders coursing through the woods toward Smoke was ragged and uneven, with some men being fifty or sixty yards ahead of or behind the others on either side of them. The fury of the storm kept conversation between the riders at a minimum, and most were riding with their heads down and their hats pulled low over their brows to try to keep the worst of the wind and snow out of their faces.

Smoke knew he could just lie still, and odds were that the men would pass him by and he'd be safe for a while. But he'd still be without a horse, and this put him at a terrible disadvantage in the deadly game of hide and seek they were playing. No, he couldn't afford to let them go by. He needed both weapons and a horse if he was going to survive this death hunt.

He hated the idea of killing a man he didn't even know, but the man must've known what he was doing when he signed on to take another man to his certain death. Smoke knew it was much too dangerous with the other men so close to try to take a man's guns and horse and leave him alive, so he steeled himself to the inevitable; he was going to have to hit fast and hard and not worry about the consequences.

Smoke waited until a figure on horseback was directly opposite his hiding place. As the man moved just past him, Smoke eased out of the tree limbs and took a running jump up on the back of the man's horse. As he landed, he wrapped his left arm around the man's face and, with the knife in his right hand, he made a rapid slashing motion across the man's throat.

The horse reared up and whinnied, but the sound was lost in the howling of the wind.

Smoke held on tight as the man's body struggled for a few seconds and then became limp as his hot blood spurted across Smoke's forearm.

When he was completely limp, Smoke eased the man's hat off and put it firmly on his own head, throwing his own hat to the ground. Next, he took the man's gun belt and holster and put it around his waist. The hardest part was removing the man's thick rawhide and fur coat without letting his body fall off the horse, which Smoke kept moving by gentle nudges of his heels, guiding the animal with his knees.

When he had the man's hat, guns, and coat on, Smoke started to let the body fall, and then thought better of it. Leaning to the side, he felt in the man's right boot. Sure enough, there was a long-bladed skinning knife there. It would be of much more use to Smoke than the small clasp knife he'd used to kill the man.

Looking to both sides to make sure he'd been unobserved so far, Smoke waited until a particularly strong flurry of snow came, and then let the man's body fall to the side, where it landed in a snowbank with a soft thud inaudible from more than a few feet away.

Slowly, so as not to draw too much attention to himself, Smoke let the horse he was riding ease on out ahead of the line of men. Before long, the men on either side of him were barely visible in the blowing snow. Smoke knew the storm couldn't last too much longer, and he planned to be well away before the snow stopped and he became fully visible to the others. He hoped with the limited visibility of the storm, the man's hat and coat would fool his friends into thinking Smoke was him.

Suddenly, a voice called from about forty yards behind him. "Hey, Charlie, what's your hurry?"

Smoke hunched over, tightening his grip on the reins. He knew he didn't have much longer before his ruse was discovered.

"Yeah, Blake," another voice on the other side hollered. "Get your ass back here with the rest of us 'fore we accidentally put a bullet in your butt thinkin' you're Jensen."

As he passed a tight grove of trees, Smoke leaned forward and dug his heels into his mount, causing it to break into a full gallop ahead.

"Hey, what the . . . ?" a voice yelled.

And then, another screamed, "Yo, Clete! Somethin's wrong with Charlie Blake. He's ridin' like a bat outta hell!"

The man on Smoke's right kicked his horse into a gallop also, wanting to see why his friend was racing ahead. As he pulled closer, he realized it wasn't Charlie Blake on the horse ahead of him.

"Damn! That ain't Charlie, fellers, that's Jensen," he screamed, pulling his pistol out and opening fire.

He might have caught Smoke, but a branch suddenly appeared in front of him and whipped across his face, drawing blood and making him slow his horse to keep from falling off.

The ghostly figure on horseback in front of him disappeared into the gloomy snowstorm ahead.

Cletus and Sarah rode over to Sam Jackson. "You all right, Sam?" Cletus asked.

Jackson sleeved blood off his face where the tree limb had slashed his cheek. "Yeah, I'll be all right," he growled, leaning over to spit blood from his mouth.

"You say that wasn't Charlie up there?" Sarah asked, looking ahead into the snow flurries.

"Naw, I don't think so," Jackson said. "He had Charlie's coat on, but he didn't sit a horse like Charlie an' he looked to be about thirty pounds heavier and five or six inches taller."

"But how did he get Charlie's coat and horse?" Cletus asked.

Jackson looked back over his shoulder. "I don't know, Boss, but I'll bet we ain't gonna find out what happened from Charlie either."

Cletus nodded. "All right, men, let's double back a ways and see if we can find Charlie's body."

Sarah took a deep breath and felt a deep sorrow. She didn't know Charlie Blake well, but if he was dead, then it was her fault for letting Smoke Jensen escape.

She shook her head as she pulled her horse's head around. How was she going to live with herself if more men were killed because of her? she wondered.

23

As he rode hell-bent-for-leather through the deepening snow and into the teeth of the freezing north wind after capturing the man's horse, Smoke leaned as close to his mount's head as he could to avoid being scraped out of the saddle by a tree limb. He had to trust the horse's instinct not to run headlong into a tree or off a cliff, and so all he could do for the first couple of hundred yards of their flight was to hang on for dear life and hope for the best.

At least it beat a bullet in the back.

After about ten minutes at a full gallop, Smoke raised his head and looked back over his shoulder. The snow was still blowing, and all he could see was a solid sheet of white behind him.

He slowed the horse and cocked his head to the side, listening to see if he could hear any pursuit over the howling of the wind.

Nothing. He turned back around, pulled his hat down tight, and rode on into the wind toward the mountain up ahead, moving slower now to give his horse a rest. He knew that if he could make the slopes up ahead before his captors caught up to him, he would have the advantage for the first time since this adventure began.

He smiled grimly. And then it would be time to pay them back.

* * *

Angus MacDougal was just sitting down to a solitary supper, served by his housekeeper/cook, when the door banged open and a breathless Daniel Macklin barged in.

Angus threw down his napkin and smiled, evidently thinking the group of men had arrived with Smoke Jensen as their prisoner.

"Where is that son of a bitch?" Angus growled, moving toward the hat rack in the corner with his belt and holstered pistol hanging on it.

Macklin didn't understand at first what Angus was referring to. "Uh . . . where is who?" he asked, taking his hat off and holding it in front of him like a shield.

Angus sighed as he buckled on his gun belt. "Jensen, of course," he answered. "You remember him, don't you? The bastard who gunned my Johnny down? The man you went to Big Rock to get for me?"

"Uh . . . that's what I come to tell you, Mr. MacDougal." Few men in the world called Angus MacDougal by his first name, and certainly not an employee as low as Daniel Macklin.

Angus knew something was wrong. "Well, spit it out, man. What the hell's going on?"

"We were 'bout half a day's ride from here when Jensen somehow managed to get loose and run away," Macklin finally managed to say.

"What?" Angus yelled, advancing on Macklin as if he were about to kill him.

Macklin held up his hands. "Now wait a minute, Mr. MacDougal. He ain't gotten away—leastways not all the way away."

Angus slapped his thigh with his hand. "Now just what the hell does that mean?" he growled.

"He didn't get no horse, an' he's on foot in a bad storm some miles from the nearest mountain. He's runnin' on foot through the woods with Cletus and the rest of the men on horseback after him."

The redness began to fade a little bit from Angus's face

at this news. "Oh, well, then, it shouldn't take Clete long to run him down then, should it?"

Macklin shook his head. "No, sir, I don't think so."

Suddenly Angus cocked an eyebrow at Macklin. "If that's so, then why did Clete send you here?"

"Well, the fact of the matter is that Jensen used to be a mountain man, sir, and we . . . that is, Cletus thought that if he did manage to make the mountains, we might ought'a have a few more men out looking for him."

Angus took a couple of long, slow breaths to try to calm himself. He found he did his best thinking when he was calm, not when he was in a fit of rage.

After a moment, he nodded. "I guess I can't argue with that logic," he said. "Let me see, you got about ten, eleven men up there now. Another ten or so ought'a be plenty. With twenty men I can run a search of the mountain that a squirrel couldn't get through."

He pulled out his pocket watch and opened the gold clasp. "Well, it's too late now to round up any good men. We'll get to bed early and be in Pueblo at dawn. We should be able to find ten men who want to make a little extra money without any problem."

Or who want to make the richest rancher for a hundred miles happy, Macklin thought.

"You have anything to eat 'fore you got on the way here?" he asked, suddenly in a better frame of mind now that he knew he'd have the personal pleasure of hunting Jensen down like the dog he was. Hell, it might even be fun running the bastard down like a deer or a bear.

"No, sir," Macklin answered, his mouth watering at the smell of the pot roast and fresh vegetables he could smell on the table in the next room.

Angus nodded. "Well, then, head on over to the bunkhouse and I'll have my cook send you over a plate."

"Thank you, sir," Macklin said, trying to hide his anger. Here he was busting his butt to help the old man out and he wasn't good enough to break bread with him in his house. The ungrateful asshole!

* * *

The next morning, just as the sun was peeking over the eastern slope mountains, Angus and Macklin were knocking on Sheriff Wally Tupper's door in Pueblo.

A sleepy Wally opened the door, his hair disarranged and his face creased with wrinkles from his pillow. "Yeah?" he asked gruffly before he saw who was on his doorstep.

Then it was, "Oh, I'm sorry, Mr. MacDougal. Come on in and I'll have the wife fix you up some coffee and breakfast."

"Don't have time for that, Wally," Angus said, brushing past the sheriff into his house as if he owned it. "I need you to get dressed and help me round up ten or fifteen hard men to go on the trail with me."

"You mean, like a posse?" Wally asked, covering a wide yawn with the back of his hand.

"Kind'a," Angus replied enigmatically.

"Why . . . what for, Mr. MacDougal?" Wally asked as he pulled his trousers up under his nightshirt and sat on a couch to put on his socks.

"We're going polecat hunting," Angus said with an evil grin.

"What?" Wally asked again, pausing with one sock on and the other in his hand.

"My men were on the way back here with Smoke Jensen in tow, when he managed to get away. He's on foot and running for the mountains as we speak. I need some men to help me roust him out of those woods if Cletus doesn't find him first."

"But Mr. MacDougal, Jensen ain't broke no laws that I know of."

"So what?" Angus asked.

"Well, I can't hardly send no posse after a man who ain't done nothing wrong."

Angus reached over, grabbed the front of Wally's nightshirt, and jerked his face close. "Wallace Tupper, if you don't want to spend the rest of your miserable life shooting stray dogs for fifty cents a piece in this town instead of being sheriff, you'd better make up your mind who you're

gonna listen to . . . me or those goddamned law books
you're always reading!"

"But Mr. MacDougal," Wally protested.

"But nothing, Wally," Angus growled. "Now I'm gonna
go on over to the café on Main Street and have myself
some coffee and maybe some eggs and bacon. If you
aren't there with at least ten good men, by the time I
finish, I'll assume you're out hunting for dogs to shoot."

Less than an hour later, while Angus was still sopping
up egg yolks with a folded piece of pancake, Wally Tupper
appeared at the café with twelve men. All of the men had
a hard look about them and all were armed to the teeth.

Wally walked into the café, his hat in his hands. "Uh, I
managed to get you twelve men, Mr. MacDougal," he said,
not willing to meet Angus's eyes directly.

"That's a good man, Wally. I knew you'd come through
for me as usual."

"I told 'em since this wasn't an official posse, that you'd
be paying them for the trip," Wally said, his voice low and
uncertain, as if he were asking Angus instead of telling
him how it was going to be.

Angus waved a hand. "No problem, Wally. Since this is
personal, I really can't expect the town to pay for it, now
can I?"

"Uh . . . no, sir. I guess not."

"Now, while I'm finishing up here, I want you to get a
couple of packhorses and go on over to the general store
and get a couple of crates of dynamite, some cans of black
powder, lots of extra ammunition of various calibers, and
enough grub for the men to be gone a week or so."

"Is there anything else?" Wally asked, struggling to keep
his anger at being ordered around like he was one of
Angus's employees out of his voice.

Angus shook his head. "No, I think that ought to do it
for right now."

Wally put his hat on and walked from the café. As he
walked toward the general store, he thought to himself,

Crazy old coot! Serve his ass right if Jensen somehow manages to blow his fool head off. And just where does he get off ordering me around like I'm some ranch hand anyway?

By the time he got to the store, he was so mad he could hardly unclench his teeth to say hello to the proprietor when greeted.

He pointed behind the counter at the hundreds of boxes of ammunition. "Seymour, I'm gonna need a bunch of cartridges and other things, and I'm gonna need 'em fast."

24

Sally sat on a wide settee in Dr. Spalding's parlor holding Mary Carson's hand. Mary was quietly sobbing into a lace handkerchief. Across the room, Pearlie and Cal sat in high-armed easy chairs, both of them acutely uncomfortable in the presence of a crying woman.

Finally, after what seemed like years but was only a couple of hours, Cotton Spalding emerged from his inner treatment room drying his hands on a towel. He looked dog-tired, with red, bloodshot eyes and dark circles under the eyes. He'd been continually by Monte's side during the long night, and it showed.

Mary looked up quickly, an unspoken question in her eyes. Cotton smiled at her and moved to take her hand. "He's going to be just fine, Mary. He's awake now and I can find no evidence of any brain damage or other infirmity, other than a complete amnesia about the events of the last couple of days, which isn't unusual in these cases."

"Oh, thank God!" Mary breathed, looking skyward.

Sally Jensen looked over at the boys, her eyes brimming with tears of thankfulness, while both Cal and Pearlie grinned from ear to ear.

"Now, he's going to have to remain quiet for a week or two, and I'm going to want you to feed him plenty of beef stew and soup with cream in it to get his strength back," Cotton said, his manner becoming more professional.

"Don't you worry, Doc Spalding," Mary said, nodding her head as she spoke. "I'll make sure that ornery galoot does exactly what you tell him to."

"It isn't going to be easy, Mary," Cotton said. "He's already chomping at the bit to get back to work. He asked me who was going to take care of his town if he lay around on his butt all day."

They all laughed at that. It was just like Monte Carson to put the welfare of the townspeople ahead of his own well-being. It was one reason why he'd never had any serious opposition for reelection as sheriff since Smoke had recommended him for the job when the town was first formed.

After the doctor went into another room to see to another patient, Mary turned to Sally. "Thank you for staying here by my side until he woke up, Sally, but now it's time for you to go see about your man."

"Will you be all right?" Sally asked as she got to her feet, anxious to get back on the trail and go after the men who'd taken her Smoke.

"Of course I will, now that I know Monte is doing all right," Mary said. "Now you and the boys go on and bring Smoke back here safe and sound."

Sally leaned down and gave Mary a hug. "You tell Monte we'll be thinking of him and to get well soon," she said, and then she led the boys out the front door.

"You want us to go get Louis to ride with us, Miss Sally?" Pearlie asked.

She looked up at him. "Of course, Pearlie. Louis would never forgive us if we left him out of this fracas," she answered.

An hour later, they'd picked up their horses at the livery and the four of them were on the trail toward Pueblo, hoping against hope that they were going to be in time to find Smoke alive.

"Hey, men, over here!" Wally Stevens yelled through his cupped hands.

As Cletus and Sarah and the other men rode slowly up to him, they found him standing over the snow-covered dead body of Charlie Blake. Blake was lying on his back with a gaping hole in his throat and frozen blood all around him. Luckily, they'd gotten to him before the scavengers did.

The storm was winding down, and there was even the hint of sunlight peeking through the clouds as the snow disappeared and the wind began to die down. They'd spent an uncomfortable night before the dawn came and they could resume the search for Charlie's body.

Cletus felt a raw knot of anger in his gut. Damn Angus MacDougal and damn Smoke Jensen for this. A good man lay dead whose only fault was trying to help out a friend.

Sarah brushed away tears from her eyes. She didn't want the men to see her crying or to guess the reason. If she hadn't helped Smoke Jensen escape last night, Charlie Blake would still be alive.

Of course, she was intelligent enough to know that Jensen would by now be dead at the hands of her father, but that was only one life. She had a feeling that Jensen was going to cause a lot more deaths before this little trip was over. She wondered what her father would think about that and whether he would consider Johnny's death the equal of the deaths of so many other good men.

She grimaced. Of course he would. In Angus's mind, there was no one who was nearly as important as a member of the MacDougal clan. No, she thought with disgust, he wouldn't worry one bit if it cost ten men their lives as long as he got a chance to avenge Johnny's death.

"Pick him up and put him across one of the pack-horses," Cletus said.

"And be quick about it!" Billy Free growled, pulling out his six-gun and checking the loads. "That bastard Jensen has to be made to pay for this!"

Sarah looked over at the young man, whose face was flushed and red in the morning light.

"He was only defending himself, Billy," she said in an even tone, glancing from Billy's face to the mountain slopes a couple of miles off in the distance where Jensen had disappeared.

"How can you take his side?" the boy almost screamed. "Charlie Blake was a friend of mine!"

"Charlie was my friend too, Billy," Sarah answered. "And Johnny was my brother and I've got to tell all of you, I'm beginning to wonder if he was worth all this."

The men began to look around at each other, wondering what the hell Sarah was talking about.

"I'm sure Sarah means that she hates to see anyone else get killed because of her taking Jensen prisoner, isn't that right, Sarah?" Cletus said, trying to change her meaning to one the men could understand.

Sarah lowered her head and quickly blinked away the tears in her eyes. "Yes, of course that's what I mean," she said in a firm voice. "I have no sympathy for murderers and gunmen, but I also don't want to put the rest of your lives at risk to avenge the death of one of my family members."

"Don't you worry none, Miss Sarah," Bob Bartlett called. He and Juan Gomez and Billy Free had joined up with the group right after Smoke had ridden off into the storm. "We ain't gonna let no gunslick get away with killin' our friends and neighbors. We ain't gonna stop until we've dragged him outta those mountains feet-first—right, boys?" he yelled, raising his rifle into the air.

The crowd all hollered their assent, and a couple even shot off their weapons into the air.

Lord help us, Cletus thought, looking around at the men as they yelled and hollered. We've gone from a posse to a lynch mob and all it took was one death. I wonder what we'll become after several more of us are killed. Will we still be human, and will we ever be able to forget what's about to happen here in the mountains in the next few days?

"Come on, Clete!" Jason Biggs yelled. "Let's go get that bastard!"

Cletus held up his hands for silence, trying to quiet the mob the men had become. "Listen up, men," he said, keeping his voice level and emotionless. "Take a look at

Charlie's body lyin' across that packhorse," he said, inclining his head toward the mount. "You'll notice he ain't wearin' no guns, and if I'm not mistaken, he probably had a long gun or two in his saddle boots on his horse."

"Yeah, so what?" Biggs asked sarcastically. "That just means that son of a bitch Jensen stole 'em."

"What it means," Cletus tried to explain, "is if we go charging up into those mountains, Jensen is gonna pick us off like flies. He's an experienced mountain man who knows what he's doing, and now that we know he's armed with a long gun and a couple of six-killers, we have to be smarter and more careful than we've ever been before or most of us ain't gonna be coming home."

"You sound like you're plumb scared to death of that son of a bitch, Clete," Sam Jackson said, disgust in his voice.

"Respecting the abilities of your enemies ain't being scared, Sam," Cletus answered, not rising to the bait in Jackson's tone, "it's being smart. You want to go hightailing it up into those woods, yelling and screaming and not paying caution no mind, you go right ahead. I'll do my best to find your dead carcass and get it back to your wife so she and your kids can plant you proper."

Cletus's words sobered the men and quieted them down a bit so they weren't so boisterous. "Now, I'm still the leader of this group, an' anybody don't think so is welcome to mosey on along by themselves, but whoever stays is gonna do what I say or I'll put a bullet in their head myself. You all got my drift?" he asked.

There were mumbles of assent, but no one left and no one disputed his right of leadership. "Now, here's what we're gonna do," he said, motioning the men to draw closer so they could hear his plans.

"First off, we're gonna pair up. No one rides alone or gets out of sight of his partner. Secondly, we're gonna ride with our weapons in our hands, loaded up six and six and the hammer cocked at all times. We're not going to give Jensen a chance to take any more of us out without a fight."

As the men nodded their agreement, he went on with

his attack strategy. "Now that the storm has quit, he won't be able to move around the mountain without leaving tracks, so we've got to be careful not to get crosswise with one another and spoil his trail. We're gonna spread out, each pair staying in eye contact with another pair, and we're gonna criss-cross those woods until we pick up his trail, and then we're gonna dog him until we catch him."

"And then we're gonna blow his damn head off!" Billy Free shouted.

Cletus silenced him with a glare. "No, and then we're going to try and capture him, if we can do it without losing any more men," Cletus said. "Angus MacDougal is still paying for this trip and he wants Jensen alive, if at all possible. So, if we can, we're going to try and take him back to the ranch in one piece."

"What if he don't agree to that proposition, Boss?" George Jones asked.

Cletus smiled grimly. "Then we'll blow his ass to hell and back!"

When the men all laughed at this, Cletus said, "Now, let's make a quick camp and get some hot coffee and some good grub into our bellies. It's gonna get awful cold tonight, and I don't want to give our position away by making any campfires. We'll eat a hot meal now, and tonight we'll try and have a cold camp."

"And I want to add another hundred dollars to the man who gets the drop on Jensen so we can capture him," Sarah said.

"What does a man get who puts lead in the son of a bitch?" Billy Free asked sarcastically.

Sarah stared at him. "I'll let my daddy deal with that man," she said, "but I don't think he'll appreciate what my daddy does."

25

Smoke had a problem. The storm had stopped and the day was clearing off, clouds disappearing as fast as they'd appeared days before. He knew that with no storm to cover his tracks, the deep snow would lead the gang that had taken him prisoner right to him. Also, his dark clothes were going to stand out against the white snow like a road sign. He was going to have to be very careful moving around to make sure he stayed under cover.

The good news was that he was a good mile and a half up the lower slope of the mountain he'd been heading for. Now the gang was going to have to come after him in his territory, where he was right at home and where they were interlopers.

As he rode, he checked his weapons. He had two pistols, each with six cartridges, and a rather old and beaten-up Winchester that looked as if its owner hadn't cleaned it in years. He shook his head, knowing he wouldn't be able to trust it for accuracy at much over a hundred yards.

He leaned forward, took the canteen off the saddle horn, and pulled its cork, taking a sniff of the contents. He wrinkled his nose. The man he'd killed had had his canteen filled with whiskey instead of water or coffee. That's no good, he thought. His experience had taught him that men who drank whiskey when the weather was below freezing didn't last too long. Instead of warming a body up, as many flatlanders thought, whiskey actually lowered the body's resistance to freezing temperatures.

He guided the horse into the middle of a small copse of trees, so he'd be out of sight from the slopes below, and dismounted. He opened the saddlebags to see what else he'd inherited with the dead man's horse.

Good news at last. The man had a large chunk of bacon wrapped in waxed paper in a sack along with several biscuits and a couple of pieces of jerky. There was also a small can of Arbuckle's coffee, but no pot or skillet to use to cook either the bacon or the coffee in.

No matter, he thought. A good mountain man can always improvise.

In the other saddlebag was an old monocular scope, the kind you pulled out and looked through with one eye. It wasn't as good as a decent pair of binoculars, but it would do. Nestled in the bag was a box of .44 cartridges for the rifle and for the pistols as well. That was an additional fifty rounds he had to add to what was already in the weapons.

In addition to the shells, there was a folded-up yellow rain cape and a small woven blanket and a box of lucifers. Along with the waterproof ground blanket folded behind the saddle, he would at least have some protection against the cold when night fell.

He nodded, grinning. All in all, not too bad, he thought. He had managed to escape and to acquire not only transportation, but also weapons and food and some shelter against the elements. He was ready now to go to war.

He took the telescope and moved to the edge of the copse of trees. He panned the scope all around the downslope area that he could see. There was no sign of any pursuit just yet, which meant he probably had enough time to fix a fire and to eat and make some coffee.

He took the reins of the horse and led it around and through the trees until he found some boulders sitting so there was a small protected space out of the chilly wind on the mountainside.

Using his boot, he scraped the snow down to where the

horse could forage enough grass to fill its belly. Unfortunately, the man hadn't carried any grain for his mount, but a few days on grass wouldn't hurt the horse.

He took the saddle and blanket off, and used the reins to fashion a makeshift hobble for the animal, since he didn't know if he could trust it to remain nearby if only ground-reined.

Once his horse was taken care of, he gathered up an armful of dead tree limbs and deadfall from around the boulders. He made a small pile between the boulders, with the smaller sticks on the bottom and the larger ones on top.

He opened the saddlebags and took out the woven blanket. Since the grass around was all covered with snow, it couldn't be used to start the fire. It was too wet. So, he unraveled an inch or so of the blanket, wadded up the yarn, and stuck it under the kindling. When he lit it with a lucifer, it was only moments before he had a small fire going.

He'd picked up only long-dead wood, so there was very little smoke, though there was enough to spot if the men below were looking, and he knew he'd have to make this nooning fast.

He took out the bacon, sliced it with the skinning knife he'd taken from the man's boot, and laid the strips out on a wide, flat rock. This he laid gently in the edge of the fire.

While the bacon was cooking, he poured the contents of the can of Arbuckle's coffee into the sack the bacon and jerky and biscuits had been in, and then he filled the empty can with snow. He placed it near the fire so the snow would melt.

As the bacon cooked and the water began to boil, Smoke dumped a handful of coffee grounds into the water in the can. Using the skinning knife, he cut one of the biscuits open, and then speared the bacon and put it between the halves of the biscuit and began to eat.

The biscuit was very hard, but it softened a bit as the grease from the bacon soaked into it, and soon he could chew it without worrying about breaking a tooth off.

When the coffee was boiling, he wrapped the blanket

around his hands and pulled the can away from the fire. He set it down and waited for it to cool down enough so he could drink it.

"All the comforts of home," he mumbled to himself, happy to be free at last.

Thirty minutes later, he kicked snow into the fire to put it out and got back in the saddle. He'd dumped the whiskey out of the canteen after taking a sip or two, and replaced it with hot coffee. He'd also saved some of the biscuit and bacon sandwiches for an evening meal, since he doubted he'd be able to make a fire after darkness came.

He spurred the horse into motion and as it walked up the slope, he glanced behind him. Sure enough, the pine tree limbs he'd tied to the horse's tail were dragging along, smoothing over the prints the horse was making in the snow. It wasn't perfect, and if the men chasing him had a good tracker along, they could still follow him. But to see and follow the tracks, the tracker would have to walk—they couldn't be seen from horseback. This would slow their chase considerably, and for every minute they delayed, the high winds of the High Lonesome were making his tracks that much harder to follow.

He moved farther and farther up the slope, wrapping his blanket around his shoulders as the temperature got colder and colder the higher he went. He glanced upward and smiled to see dense, dark clouds again forming around the distant peaks, whipped around and around by the high winds up on top of the mountain. He knew this meant more early winter storms were on the way, along with temperatures many degrees below zero.

"We'll see how those boys like mountain weather," he said to the back of the horse's head as they slowly ascended toward the snow-covered peaks above them.

Several miles away, Cletus got to his feet as his men finished their noon meal. He moved over next to where the horses were tied and found Jason Biggs standing there, a pair of binoculars to his eyes.

"You see anything, Jason?" he asked as he began to build himself a cigarette.

"Couple'a elk an' a bear, but nothin' that looked like a rider on horseback." He hesitated, and then he added, "I did see what looked like a thin plume of smoke, but with the winds up there it was hard to tell."

Cletus put a match to his cigarette and nodded his head through the smoke. "Yeah, there's just too many trees up there. A hundred men could be ridin' around up there and if they was careful, we wouldn't see nothin' from down here in the flats."

Biggs turned to him. "So, you ready to go upland an' get us a son of a bitch?" he asked, still angry over the death of his friend Charley Blake.

Cletus nodded. "Yeah, I guess so. I was kind'a hoping Mac would'a been back from talking to Angus, but we can't wait any longer if we want'a get up the side of that mountain 'fore dark."

"Good, 'cause I'm itchin' to get that sumbitch in my sights."

Cletus put his hand on Biggs's shoulder. "Jason, you know we're going up there to capture Jensen, not assassinate him, don't you?"

Biggs showed his teeth, but it was more a grimace than a real smile. "You do what you got to do, Clete, an' I'll do the same."

Cletus decided to let it drop. He too was pretty pissed off about Blake, though he could understand why Jensen had done what he'd done. As he'd told Sarah, a man running for his life will do just about anything he has to in order to survive.

Cletus got his men saddled up and headed toward the steep slopes of the mountain in the distance. Like Smoke, he too noticed the clouds whipping around the peaks, and knew they were going to be in for some rough weather before too long.

When the group came to the trail leading up into the

forest on the side of the slope, Cletus stopped them across the stream from a rotting one-room log cabin that looked like it hadn't been used for years.

"Jimmy," he said, pointing to Jimmy Corbett, "I want you to wait over there by that cabin for Mac to get here. He'll probably have some more men from Mr. MacDougal, an' I want you to bring 'em on up after us when they get here."

"Yes, sir," Jimmy said, jerking his horse's head to the side and riding toward the shallow, ice-encrusted stream.

"And Jimmy . . ."

"Yeah, Boss?" the boy said, looking back over his shoulder to see what Cletus wanted.

"You'd better fire a couple of shots when you get close to let us know it's you coming." Cletus smiled. "I figure we got more'n a few itchy trigger fingers in this group, and you wouldn't want to sneak up on none of 'em."

Jimmy grinned and touched the brim of his hat as he rode into the stream and over toward the log cabin.

"We gonna sit here all day jawin' or we gonna go up there and git Jensen?" Jason Biggs called from the front of the group of men, where he sat impatiently in his saddle.

Cletus clenched his teeth and walked his horse over next to Biggs's without answering.

He leaned over to put his face close to Biggs's and said in a low voice, "You open your pie-hole like that at me one more time, Jason, an' we're gonna see who the best man with a gun is! You hear me boy?" he asked, his face red and his voice harsh. His flat, dangerous eyes let Biggs know he wasn't kidding in what he said.

"Uh, I didn't mean nothin' by what I said, Clete, you know that," Biggs answered, his eyes looking down and not meeting Cletus's.

"Remember, Jason, one more time is all it's gonna take. I won't remind you again."

"Yes, sir."

As Cletus rode off, his back turned, Biggs let his hand fall to the butt of his pistol. No one could talk to him like that and get away with it.

Then he looked around at the men gathered nearby. He knew they'd blow him out of the saddle if he shot Cletus, so he relaxed and kicked his horse into following Cletus's. There'd be plenty of time later for Clete to have an accident.

26

Sheriff Wally Tupper handed the dally rope he had attached to the two pack animals behind him to Jack Dogget, one of the men riding with Angus MacDougal.

"Here's your dynamite and gunpowder and extra shells, Angus," he said, trying as hard as he could to keep his anger out of his voice.

Angus MacDougal tipped his head. "Come on with us, Wally," he said, though this time it was more in the way of an offer instead of an order. "I promise you it's gonna be fun. After all, hunting a man is much more exciting than hunting elk or bear, and I'm offering a bonus of five hundred dollars to the man who catches that son of a bitch."

Wally shook his head. "No, thanks, Angus. I think I'll stay here."

Angus stared at him, his eyes narrowing. "I get the feeling you don't think much of what I'm doing, Wally. Am I right?"

Wally nodded. "Yep, you're right as rain, Angus. I told you, Jensen ain't done nothing wrong—leastways nothing against the law. Everybody there that day says he fired in self-defense—that Johnny prodded him and drew on him without any provocation."

"Bullshit!" Angus screamed, making his horse stomp and crow hop a time or two. "He killed my boy, and he's going to pay for it!" Angus's face was beet red and his eyes were wide and full of madness. He looked like he was about to have a stroke.

Wally shook his head sadly. "Maybe he did kill him, Angus, but Johnny wasn't no boy. He was a growed man who shot his mouth off and got himself killed for drawing on the wrong man at the wrong time. It was bound to happen sooner or later, and if it hadn't have been Jensen, it would've been somebody else."

"You saying my boy deserved to get killed, Wally?" Angus asked, his voice suddenly low and dangerous but the madness still in his eyes.

Wally sat up straighter in the saddle, tired of being a whipping boy for this crazy old man. "Yeah, I guess that's what I am saying, Angus, and it's long past time someone told you like it is."

Angus smiled grimly. "This is a dangerous time to try and grow a backbone, Wally."

"Maybe, Angus, but I'll tell you this straight. If you go up in those mountains and kill Jensen, that's your business 'cause it's out of my jurisdiction. But if you bring him back here and do it, then I'll see that you hang for it."

"Those are awfully big words, Sheriff," Angus said, looking around at the twelve men sitting on their horses with him. "I hope you can back them up."

Wally looked around at the men, his face paling just a bit. "These men all agreed to go out with you to catch a gunman, Angus. I don't think they agreed to kill an officer of the law."

Angus snorted through his nose. "Well, we'll just have to see about that when I get back."

Wally nodded. "Things are going to be different when you get back, Angus. That's what you'd better be thinking on while you're up in those mountains."

Angus growled and spurred his horse right at Wally, waiting for him to jump out of the way. But Wally stood his ground, and it was Angus who had to pull his horse to the side and ride off toward the mountains in the distance.

Wally sat watching him as he rode off with his hired gunmen. He felt sorry for the old man, but his day was dead and gone, like his son. From now on, Wally intended to be a sheriff for all of the people of Pueblo, not just the MacDougals. And if they didn't like it, then they could just lump it.

As they rode up the mountain slope past the log cabin at its base, Cletus followed the tracks of a lone horse in the knee-deep snow.

"Spread out, men," he hollered. "Ride in pairs, but keep within sight of the pairs on either side of you and keep your hands on your guns. If Jensen fires on us, everyone take off after him."

As his men spread out, Sarah stayed next to Cletus, riding as his partner. He rode slowly, flicking his eyes from the tracks in the snow in front of him to the mountainside up ahead of him, trying to see if there was any movement up there where a man might be lying in wait.

He felt the sweat start to ooze out of his pores and freeze on his forehead, and the hand that was holding his pistol developed a slight tremor. Damn, he'd never been afraid of a man before, and he'd gone up against some of the meanest men in the West in his day. Maybe he was just getting old—too old to go traipsing through the woods after a man who'd saved Sarah's life only a couple of days before.

Sarah saw the sweat glistening on Cletus's face, and felt ashamed of the situation she'd put him in by bringing Jensen up here and then setting him loose. Cletus had been like a father to her for more years than she cared to remember. In fact, he'd been more of a father to her than her real dad. Angus had always had eyes only for Johnny, and he'd made it clear that he was going to leave the ranch to him, not her.

Sarah tried to think of some way to get them all out of this mess, get the men to give up and go on home. But for the life of her she couldn't think of anything to say that would make them give up the hunt. They were all too afraid of Angus MacDougal. They knew if they returned to the ranch without Jensen, Angus would make their lives miserable, or he'd kill them. The old man wouldn't like his orders being disobeyed, especially when they concerned the man who'd killed his favorite child.

She could only hope that Jensen would keep right on riding and they'd never find him. If he stayed and fought and more men were killed, more men like Charlie Blake who were friends of hers, she didn't know if she could live with herself for what she'd done.

As they rode, she offered a silent prayer that Jensen would never be seen or heard from again.

Up ahead, Smoke had used his time to good advantage. He'd explored the area of the mountainside, and now he knew his way around as well as if he'd lived there for years. As he rode around exploring and learning the various trails, he spent his time preparing traps and deadfalls to bedevil his enemies.

Sharpened stakes were set in shallow holes along the trail, and then snow was thrown over them to hide them. Heavy branches were pulled back and tied to rope along the ground so they'd release and knock men off their horses when they were on narrow trails next to cliffs and ledges. He'd found and remembered where there were large boulders that could be pushed down the mountain to start landslides in case the men following him got too close.

He was ready for war. He wondered if the men riding up the hill after him knew what they were getting into. He doubted they did, or they would've turned tail and ridden away as fast as they could.

Cletus slowed and held up his hand when he saw a man's footprints next to the horse's in the snow. Evidently Jensen had dismounted here for some reason.

Signaling the men on either side of him to circle around in front, he got off his horse and walked it slowly along toward a thick copse of trees up ahead, his pistol out and the hammer cocked.

When he entered the grove of trees, he found the boulders and the remains of Jensen's campfire. He knelt and felt the coals. They were still warm, but not hot. Jensen had been gone from this place a while now.

Cletus holstered his gun, but signaled Sarah to keep hers out. He walked around the camp and searched the ground on all sides of the copse of trees. That was strange, he thought. There were tracks coming into the grove of trees, but none leaving it.

He stood there, looking around, scratching his head. Damn! The man couldn't just fly out of here without leaving any traces, could he?

He glanced up at the sky as the sun suddenly darkened. Heavy, black clouds were whirling around the sky, and the temperature was dropping while the chilly north wind was picking up. A storm, and a big one from the feel of it, was definitely coming soon.

He stood there thinking. Jensen only had two ways to go. He could go up, or he could've circled around and be heading back down the mountain on their flanks.

For his money, he felt Jensen would go higher. Jensen was an old mountain man, this was his playground, and he wasn't about to give up his advantage by heading for the flatlands. No, Cletus knew Jensen was up above them somewhere, and he was probably looking down at them at this very moment.

Well, the hell with him, Cletus thought, getting angry. Sarah had given the man a chance to get away clean. If he chose to stay and fight, then Cletus planned to give him a fight he wouldn't soon forget. And he surely didn't intend for any more friends of his to get killed in the doing of it.

He swung back up into his saddle and waved his men forward and upward.

27

Smoke was indeed watching the group as Cletus's men weaved in and out of the forest on their way higher up onto the mountainside.

"Time to sow a little hate and dissent," he mumbled to himself as he took the telescope from his eye and picked up the old Winchester he'd stolen.

Instinctively he aimed a little lower than it looked like he should, since he was shooting downhill. He was a good three hundred yards up the hill and was well hidden, lying on his stomach behind a ponderosa pine that'd been felled by lightning. He'd stacked snow on the brim of his hat so the only thing visible from below would be his dark eyes. Not much of a risk since his targets were so far away.

He put the bead on the end of the rifle barrel about three inches above the head of one of the men far off to the right, and slowly squeezed the trigger. He didn't expect to hit the man, but he hoped the rifle was accurate enough to at least come close enough to scare the man.

The rifle exploded and kicked back against his shoulder. Smoke immediately pulled the gun back to him and lowered his head a couple of inches. He knew it'd take the sound of the gunshot a second or two to reach the men below, after the bullet had already landed.

The man Smoke had aimed at screamed at the top of his lungs and pitched sideways off his horse. Suddenly, most of the men below were firing their pistols and rifles in all directions as the sound of Smoke's gunshot echoed and re-echoed around the mountainside, distorting the direction from which it had actually come.

The man Smoke knew as Cletus rode rapidly over to the wounded man, lying low along his mount's neck to make himself less of a target.

As soon as Cletus got to the man, he jumped off his horse and held his hands up in the air, hollering, "Stop shooting, cease firing!" as loud as he could.

The gang's shooting slowed and finally stopped, but it was clear to Smoke from the way the men turned their heads back and forth that they were frightened. It was also clear that most of these men weren't gunslicks or hired guns, but merely cowboys who were out of their depth in this kind of fracas.

When the men had stopped their firing, Cletus told the ones nearby to keep a sharp lookout and he bent down over Billy Free, who was lying in the snow, holding his right arm with his left hand and moaning and groaning as he writhed on the ground.

Cletus said, "Hold on, Billy. Let me take a look at where you got hit."

Free moaned again, but moved his left hand. Cletus saw a hole in Free's right arm just below the shoulder that was leaking blood slowly. A good sign that no major artery had been hit.

Cletus raised the arm, causing Free to clamp his jaws together and to almost shout out in pain. The bullet had gone through the arm, and was sticking in the heavy leather of Free's fur-lined winter coat.

Cletus took Billy's bandanna from around the boy's neck and wrapped the arm tight enough to stop the bleeding, making Billy groan again. "Good news, Billy," Cletus said. "The bullet went right on through and the bone ain't broken. You should do all right if'n it don't get infected."

"Did anybody see where the bastard fired from?" Billy asked as he struggled to sit up in the snow.

Cletus shook his head. "No. Evidently, he was far enough away that nobody saw the muzzle flash nor heard the report until he'd ducked back in hiding."

Suddenly, there was a loud thumping sound followed immediately by the sharp report of a rifle shot, and Wally Stevens's horse screamed and reared up before collapsing onto a shouting Wally.

Wally hollered as loud as he could for somebody to get his damn horse off his leg.

"I . . . think it's broken," he sobbed, grimacing and holding his right thigh with both hands.

George Jones and Sam Jackson jumped off their horses, and struggled to lift Wally's horse enough for him to slide his leg out.

Sure enough, the leg just below the knee was bent at an unnatural angle. Luckily, there was no bone sticking out, but the leg was going to have to be set, and it was a sure thing that Wally was not going to like that, nor the long ride back to the ranch on horseback.

Cletus waved his arms. "You men get off your horses and take cover behind trees," he shouted. "And for God's sake, see if you can spot where the gunshots are coming from."

The men complied with Cletus's order, and soon all of them were hugging trees in a wide semicircle, their eyes pointed up the hill as they looked for any sign of Jensen.

Up above, Smoke smiled and eased back away from the tree trunk he was behind. Now, he had all the men that were after him sitting around watching for him. As the temperature dropped they'd get colder and colder since they weren't able to move around. Just what he wanted, and they wouldn't dare gather around a fire because it would make them perfect targets.

He grinned as he eased up into his saddle and walked his horse over a ridge and away from the men below. Now, he had to find a good spot to make a fire so that when darkness fell, he'd be able to heat some coffee and finish off the last of his bacon and jerky and get some of the chill out of his bones.

* * *

An hour later, after Wally's leg had been set and a couple of tree limbs used as a splint, Cletus looked around at his men. They were all shivering and slapping their arms against their chests as they hid behind trees looking for any sign of movement up above them.

It suddenly dawned on Cletus what Jensen was up to. The sly son of a bitch wanted his men half-frozen to death and scared to move.

Damn, he thought. He got to his feet, feeling an itchy sensation in the back of his neck as he imagined the mountain man drawing a bead on him. "Come on, men," he shouted, waving them to their feet. "It's gonna be dark 'fore long an' we gotta find a place to make camp."

Bob Bartlett, whose face was red and chapped from the cold, stammered out, "It's gonna get colder'n a well-digger's belt buckle tonight, Clete."

"Yeah," Carl Jacoby agreed, looking up at the darkening sky, which was full of dark roiling clouds. "And it looks like more snow's on the way too."

"Exactly," Cletus agreed. "That's why we've got to find a place we can defend that's protected from above so we can make a fire and get warm."

"I ain't sittin' next to no fire an' makin' myself an easy target," Sam Jackson said grimly.

Cletus shrugged. "Good, Sam. Then when morning comes we'll throw your frozen carcass on the coals to thaw you out so you can sit a saddle."

By the time darkness had fallen, Cletus had managed to find a series of large boulders that were lying in a line across the slope of the hillside. He had his men make a camp on the downhill side where they'd be safe from gunshots from above, and he built a large fire.

"Clete," Sarah said when she saw the pile of brush and limbs he'd stacked up. "Jensen will be able to see that fire for miles."

He shrugged and grinned. "You think he don't already know exactly where we are, Missy?"

"Uh . . . I guess he does at that," she agreed.

"Now, I'm gonna build this here fire and get some hot vittles into the men, 'cause if'n I don't, they're gonna freeze to death. But while we're eating, I'm going to have some sentries out so that Jensen won't be able to sneak up on us or take any potshots at us."

"You think sentries will stop him?" Sarah asked.

"Probably not, but I think Jensen's gonna be doing just what we're doing tonight. Trying to stay outta the storm and get some heat into his body. I don't care how long he was a mountain man. That don't keep his blood from freezing just like anybody else's."

When she nodded, he slapped her on the back. "Now, get on over there and help the men get some coffee made and some beans and fatback cooked up so's we can eat."

"Yes, sir, Mr. Cletus, sir," she said, snapping off an insolent half salute and grinning as she turned and moved over to the packhorse that carried their supplies.

They'd just finished eating when a gunshot came from down the hill, followed quickly by a shout, "Yo, the camp!"

The men sitting around the fire all jumped to their feet, their pistols in their hands and worried looks on their faces as Cletus shouted, "Put those guns away, men. That's Macklin's voice."

Moments later, Angus MacDougal and the men with him rode slowly into the light of the campfire. Daniel Macklin was riding at MacDougal's side.

"Damn, Clete," Angus said as he dismounted and walked over to stand near the fire with both his hands outstretched in front of him. "That fire feels good. I'm froze clear down to the bone."

Clete looked over at Juan Gomez. "Juanito, would you boys cook up some more beans and fatback and put some more coffee on to boil. Looks like we got company for supper.

"How'd you find us in the dark?" Cletus asked Angus.

"Hell, boy, you can see this fire for five miles," Angus answered. He looked around at how Cletus had arranged the fire behind the boulders so his men were protected from above.

He nodded in approval. "Right smart move, Clete, making your camp here."

Cletus smiled and turned to pour himself some coffee from the pot. Guess the old man's forgotten all the times we camped out surrounded by hostile Indians in the old days, he thought.

28

As they sat by the fire next to each other, Angus told Cletus that he was taking over the hunt for Jensen.

"You're welcome to it, Angus," Cletus said, relieved that he wouldn't be in charge any longer. "I got no more stomach for this anyway."

"What do you mean by that?" Angus asked around a mouthful of bacon and beans.

Cletus drank his coffee, staring over the rim at the fire without looking at Angus. "I just don't think Jensen is the killer you make him out to be, Angus."

Angus swallowed his food. He couldn't believe what he was hearing. "You mean you don't believe he killed my Johnny?" he asked.

Cletus turned to look at him. "No, I know he killed Johnny, Boss. It's just that I think Johnny probably didn't give him no choice in the matter, that's all."

"Bullshit!" Angus growled. "He shot my boy down in cold blood."

Cletus shook his head. "First off, Angus, Johnny weren't no boy, he was a full-growed man, though I got to admit he often didn't act like it."

Angus glared at Cletus, hate in his eyes at this desecration of his son's memory.

Cletus went on. "Not only that, but on the ride back

here, after Sarah betrayed him and took him prisoner, Jensen risked his own life to save hers."

Angus opened his eyes wide in disbelief. "What?"

Cletus told him the story of Smoke and the rattlesnake and how he'd thrown himself in front of Sarah.

Angus clamped his jaws shut. "That don't make no never mind. Fact is, he killed Johnny and for that he's gonna die, no matter what he did for Sarah."

From the other side of Angus, Sarah interjected, "Daddy, I think you ought to listen to Clete. He's right about Jensen. He isn't a cold-blooded killer like you say."

Angus's face twisted up in hatred and he swung a backhand, slapping Sarah across the face.

"Don't you dare say nothing against your brother, girl," he snarled. "He was worth two of you."

As Sarah's hand went to her face, Cletus reached across Angus and grabbed his wrist, twisting hard until Angus groaned in pain. "That tears it, Angus. I'm through with you and your little gang of killers. And if I ever hear of you laying another hand on Sarah"—Cletus paused and looked over at her—"I'll personally come out there and beat the living shit out of you!"

Cletus got to his feet and helped Sarah to hers. He put a palm against the side of her face, his eyes sad. "I'm sorry, Missy."

She glanced from Cletus back down to her father. "Me too, Clete. Come on. Let's get out of here."

The two walked over to the string of horses and began to saddle their mounts.

"You leave me now, Clete, and you'll never work in Colorado again!" Angus shouted at their backs.

As Cletus and Sarah swung up into their saddles, Cletus shook his head at the old man. "I wouldn't make threats you ain't gonna be able to carry out, Angus. For my money, I don't think you got one chance in ten of riding off this mountain alive."

"And just where do you think you're going, young lady?" Angus growled at Sarah.

She sat up straight in her saddle. "I'm going home to

pack my things. It's about time I left home and made my own way in the world."

"Well," Angus snorted, "good riddance to the both of you. You'll both come crawling back to me when you realize I'm right about all this."

Cletus shook his head. "No, Angus, we won't be back. And I don't think you've been right about anything for a very long time."

They jerked their reins and rode off alongside one another without looking back, leaving Angus staring after them as the darkness swallowed them up.

Smoke heard this exchange from where he stood in the darkness less than a dozen yards away. It had been no trouble for him to sneak near the camp, moving between the sentries as silent as a ghost in the pitch-black night. He could have snuck up to any of them and killed them before they knew what was happening, but he wanted to end this with as little loss of life as he could. There'd already been too much killing.

The knee-deep snow helped to cover any sounds he might make, but would show his tracks later in the morning light. He smiled to himself, unworried about that. He planned to give the men in the gang plenty of other things to be thinking about before the sun rose in the morning.

Moving slowly and staying out of the light of the campfire, Smoke snuck over to the string of horses where they were tethered along a rope stretched between two trees. He walked along the broncs, his hands lightly touching their rumps so they wouldn't get nervous and whinny, until he came to the pack animals. Their packs had been removed and sat on the ground next to them, and he was lucky the men hadn't bothered to take the boxes of supplies and ammunition and explosives up near the fire where they would have been safe.

It took Smoke five trips to carry all of the boxes of dynamite and gunpowder and extra cartridges a couple of hundred yards away from the camp. He needed them to be that far away for what he had planned. On his last trip, he used his clasp knife to cut the rope holding the horses, but made no effort to scatter them. That would come later.

When he was far enough away, he opened the boxes and took out fifteen or twenty of the sticks of dynamite, along with their fuses and detonators, and stuck them in a saddlebag. He then took a fuse, cut it two feet long, and stuck it and a detonator into a stick of dynamite. He took a can of gunpowder and, using his skinning knife, he opened the top, wincing at the scraping sound the knife made.

He set the can between the boxes of dynamite and gunpowder and cartridges and put the stick of dynamite in it, nestling it down into the powder. He struck a match and lit the fuse, and then ran as fast as he could around the edge of the camp until he was on the opposite side from where he'd set the supplies.

While he waited for the fuse, he took out one of the sticks of dynamite from his saddlebag and stuck a detonator and a very short two-inch fuse into the end of it.

Three minutes later, the dynamite and gunpowder and cartridges all went up with a tremendous bang. The fireball from the explosion rose fifty feet in the air, and set the top of one of the ponderosa pines on fire.

The force of the explosion blew men off their feet and tossed them about like rag dolls, causing several to suffer broken arms and lacerations from flying debris.

The extra cartridges in the pack were set off by the blast, and bullets flew through the air like a swarm of angry hornets, wounding two men. The rest of the gang threw themselves on the ground with their hands over their heads while they screamed in fright and terror as slugs whined past their ears.

Smoke kept his head down until things had quieted down. Men slowly got to their feet, shaking their heads and pulling their pistols from their holsters as they moved off in the direction of the explosion.

Suddenly, Daniel Macklin shouted, "Hey, Mr. MacDougal, the horses are all gone!"

Angus got to his feet and brushed himself off, his ears ringing and his nose running from all the dust and dirt in the air.

"Well, just don't stand there, men. Round 'em up!" he shouted, pointing with both hands as horses ran around in the forest, as frightened as the men were.

Once all of the men had stumbled out of the camp and out into the woods looking for horses, Smoke leaned over the boulder he was hiding behind and pitched his stick of dynamite into the campfire.

He'd managed to run only a dozen yards when the dynamite went off, exploding in the campfire and blowing what was left of the camp into smithereens.

At least half of the men's saddles were destroyed, along with most of their sleeping blankets and ground covers. All of the rest of the food supplies were ruined, with the exception of several cans of Arbuckle's coffee, which were smashed and dented but remained somehow intact.

As the bedraggled group of cowboys and gunslicks limped their way back into what was left of their camp, a light snow started to fall.

Angus gritted his teeth and glared at the skies above. "This is perfect," he growled, "just perfect!"

By the time morning came, Angus's men had managed to find about three quarters of the horses, and the injured and wounded had been patched up as best they could with what supplies they had remaining.

Another campfire had been built, and the men breakfasted on coffee made with melted snow. There wasn't any food left that was worth eating.

The snow continued to fall, but at least the wind was not too strong, and the temperature actually seemed a bit warmer than it had been the night before.

All in all, the men counted themselves lucky there'd been no loss of life in the explosions of the night before.

29

As the bedraggled group of men sat around the camp-fire drinking their coffee, Angus got to his feet. "I'm not gonna let that bastard Smoke Jensen get away with making Angus MacDougal look like a fool," he said in a loud voice.

Off to one side, George Jones whispered to Sam Jackson, "Don't seem to me like the old man got much choice. The deed's done been done."

Angus glared at the men for interrupting his speech, though he couldn't hear what they'd said. "As I started to say, Jensen ain't gonna get away with this. I'm offering five hundred dollars to the man what puts a bullet in Jensen."

Carl Jacoby glanced at Daniel Macklin, sitting next to him. He shook his head and stood up. "But Mr. MacDougal, that makes us no better'n bounty hunters."

"So what, Jacoby?" Angus asked belligerently. "You got a problem with that?"

"Yeah, I do," Jacoby answered. "Me and most of the boys here signed on to help you get Jensen 'cause we knew he'd killed your boy and thought he deserved to be punished." He paused. "Now a lot of us ain't all that certain of the facts of what happened in Pueblo last year, and we damn sure didn't sign on as hired killers."

Angus's face turned beet red and he shouted, "You keep your mouth shut, Jacoby, or you'll be fired."

Jacoby shrugged. "That's all right, Mr. MacDougal. I don't think I want to work for you any more anyway." He turned to the group of men sitting around the fire. "I don't know about the rest of you, but Mac and me, along with Sarah MacDougal and Cletus Jones, all think Jensen wasn't at fault for killing Johnny MacDougal. Now maybe that don't matter to some of you, but I ain't gonna hunt down and kill a man what don't deserve it, no matter how much money Angus offers." He turned back to Angus. "I quit."

"Go on, you coward!" Angus shouted. "None of the rest of the men are going with you."

"I don't know about that, Mr. MacDougal," Macklin said as he got to his feet. "I ain't no bounty hunter, and I sure as hell ain't no killer neither. Wait up, Carl, I'm coming along too."

Slowly, almost all of the men around the campfire got to their feet and made their way over to the few remaining horses, some looking at MacDougal with disgust, others with pity, but none looking afraid of him as they used to be.

Jacoby looked back over his shoulder. "We'll take the buckboard for the injured men and try and double up on the mounts so we can leave you enough to get back to the ranch on," he said as they began to hitch up a couple of horses to the wagon and put blankets on the backs of a few others.

By the time the men had all gone, Angus realized he only had four men staying with him. Jason Biggs and Juan Gomez from his ranch, and Jack Dogget and Joshua Stone from the group that Wally Tupper had gotten from town.

He nodded and rubbed his hands in front of the fire to get them warm. "You men won't regret staying," he said, his eyes gleaming with madness. "I'm gonna make you rich."

After the men and Angus had gathered up as much ammunition as they could find that hadn't been destroyed, they climbed up on their horses and began to follow the tracks Smoke had left when he bombed the camp.

Angus was in the lead, riding up a narrow trail that skirted the edge of a precipice along the side of the mountain. He could look to the side and see a drop of four hundred feet over the side.

Suddenly, his horse stumbled, its legs falling into the hole Smoke had filled with sharpened stakes. The horse screamed in pain as the wooden stakes pierced its legs, and it bucked and jumped to the side, falling off the cliff.

Luckily, Angus had been thrown from the saddle, and fell on the edge of the cliff, his arms wrapped around a cluster of small pine trees and holding on for dear life. Dogget and Stone jumped off their mounts and pulled Angus up and over the edge until he was standing on firm ground.

Angus looked down into the hole and saw the stakes, slapping his thigh and cursing. "That tricky son of a bitch!"

Dogget and Stone got back on their horses and walked them around the hole and up the trail, ignoring Angus standing there.

As Biggs and Gomez rode by, Biggs leaned over and offered his hand. Angus took it and swung up on the horse's back behind him. "Don't you worry none, Mr. MacDougal," Biggs drawled. "We'll get that bastard for you."

Angus nodded, but he was beginning to have his doubts. So far, Jensen seemed much smarter than the men he'd hired to go after him.

Maybe it hadn't been such a good idea for him to come up here and lead the group himself.

Thirty minutes later, as they continued to follow Jensen's tracks in the snow of the trail along the edge of the cliff, going slow so as not to fall into any more holes, Jack Dogget's horse tripped a rope stretched across the trail and hidden just under the snow. As the rope was tripped, it let go of a large branch that had been pulled back and tied in place. The branch whipped forward, catching Dogget full in the chest. The force of the blow slammed him backward off his horse and over the cliff in an instant.

The men riding behind him barely had time to blink before he was out of sight, and all they could hear was his screams as he fell four hundred feet to his death.

"Sweet Mary Mother of God!" Juan Gomez whispered, crossing himself as his face broke out in a heavy sweat. "Jensen is *el Diablo!*"

"What'd you say, Juan?" Angus asked.

"He said Jensen is the devil," Biggs answered, his eyes wide, "and I don't know as what but I agree with him."

Suddenly, from up ahead, Gomez whispered, "Madre de Dios!"

"Now what are you saying?" Angus asked, until he saw where Juan was staring.

Up ahead, standing in the middle of the trail, was a man dressed in buckskins. He had a pistol in a holster tied down low on his right leg, and another pistol stuck in his belt facing his left hand. He was standing in the trail as cool and composed as if he were out for a walk.

"Jensen!" Angus hissed as he looked over Biggs's shoulder at the man.

"That's right, Mr. MacDougal. Now that the odds are fair, I'm ready to face you and your men head-on."

"Odds fair?" Josh Stone asked incredulously. "But it's four to one."

Smoke shrugged. "That's about right, I 'spect. I want to give you men at least a fighting chance."

"Holy shit!" Biggs whispered.

"Now, you can hook and draw, or you can turn tail and ride on off and live to enjoy another beautiful day in the High Lonesome," Smoke said, seemingly unconcerned about their decision. "It's your choice."

"Son of a bitch!" Stone yelled and went for his gun, as did Biggs and Gomez.

Angus had never seen anything like it. One minute Jensen was standing there, as cool as a cucumber; the next his eyes were on fire and his hands were full of iron and he was blazing away at them.

Stone was hit in the throat, the slug blowing out the back of his neck and almost decapitating him. His body fell to the side, the head flopping back and forth on a slender thread of tissue.

Gomez didn't even clear leather before he was hit twice, once in the left chest and the other bullet hitting him right between the eyes, blowing the back of his head off and leaving a cloud of red mist hanging in the air as Angus and Biggs were showered with bits of skull and brains.

Biggs actually managed to get his gun out and cocked before Jensen's fourth slug took him in the gut, bending him over with a loud grunt. The fifth shot entered the top of his head and stopped his groaning as if a switch had been turned off.

As Biggs's body fell off the horse to land facedown in the snow, Angus stuck his hands straight up in the air, his face a frightened mask of terror.

"I've got one bullet left, Mr. MacDougal," Smoke said calmly, seemingly unaffected by his killing of three men in less time than it takes to tell it. "You want to try your luck?"

Angus shook his head violently from side to side. "Uh, no, please don't shoot me," he cried, tears running down his cheeks.

"You're a pathetic excuse for a man, MacDougal," Smoke said, holstering his pistol as he walked toward the broken man. "Your son was an asshole, but at least he fought his own battles. He didn't hire other men to do his dirty work for him."

Angus held his hands out in front of him like he was warding off an evil spirit as Smoke walked up to him.

Smoke reached up, took Angus's gun from its holster, and threw it over the cliff. He leaned to the side and spit into the snow, as if he were getting rid of a bad taste in his mouth.

"You'd better go on home, MacDougal. To what home you have left, that is," Smoke said, his voice filled with disgust as he turned and walked away.

30

Sally and the men riding with her, Louis, Cal, and Pearlie, finally reached Pueblo after a hard few days' ride. They'd encountered no resistance along the way, which surprised Louis but not Sally.

"There's no reason for them to be watching their back trail, Louis," she'd said when he remarked on the absence of any sentries or guards. "They've already got Smoke where they want him, or he is already dead."

Louis had looked at her, his mouth open, his eyes sad.

She'd smiled grimly at him. "Oh, don't think I don't know that is a possibility, Louis, old friend," she'd said, her eyes blazing. "I hope to find him well and alive, but if I don't, I will survive it." She'd hesitated, her face set. "I will survive it, but the men who carried this out will not."

As they rode into town, Louis said, "I think we ought to start with the sheriff. He's bound to know this Sarah Johnson and where her parents live."

They rode up to the sheriff's office, and all got down off their horses and walked through the door.

A rotund man of average stature was sitting behind his desk, his feet up on one corner, drinking coffee when they entered. Upon seeing Sally, the man jumped to his feet, grinning his most engaging smile.

"Howdy, ma'am, my name's Wally Tupper. I'm sheriff of Pueblo. How can I be of assistance to you?"

"Hello, Sheriff Tupper," Sally said, equally engaging. "My name is Sally Jensen. I'm from the town of Big Rock and I'm looking for a young woman named Sarah Johnson."

They all saw the blood drain from Tupper's face as his smile faded like a snowflake on a hot stove. "Uh, I don't know any Sarah Johnson, Mrs. Jensen," he said, his voice croaking on the words.

Louis stepped forward. "Maybe her name's not Sarah Johnson, Sheriff," he said. "She's about this high, attractive, with long brown hair, and is in her mid-twenties. You know anyone fits that description around here?"

"Uh . . . no. Why are you looking for this woman?" the sheriff asked, sweat appearing on his forehead.

Louis cocked his head. "Why would you need to know that if you don't know anyone by that description, Sheriff?" Louis asked, his eyes boring into Tupper's.

"I guess . . . I guess I don't," the sheriff answered weakly.

Sally said, "Come on, men, let's go ask around town."

Louis set his hat on his head and glared at the sheriff. "Tell you what, Tupper," he said in a low dangerous voice. "We're going to make our way around town asking everyone we meet about this girl. If I find out she lives here and you lied to us, I'm going to come back here and have another talk with you—and I promise you won't like the results."

As Sally put her hand on the door, the sheriff wiped his face with a handkerchief and flopped into his desk chair. "There's no need for that," he said in a defeated voice.

Sally turned back around. "Sheriff, I believe this woman has something to do with the kidnapping of my husband. I think she and her friends mean him harm, so you had better tell us what you know or I will have the U.S. marshals down here to see just what part you played in all this."

Tupper nodded slowly. "You are right, Mrs. Jensen," he said. "The woman you describe is named Sarah MacDougal, daughter of Angus MacDougal. About six months ago, your husband was here with these gentlemen and shot and killed a young man named Johnny MacDougal." He sighed and wiped his face again. "I do believe the

MacDougals are interested in revenging that death by killing your husband."

Louis stepped forward. "Sheriff, you know from your investigation that Johnny MacDougal started that fight and was killed in self-defense. Didn't you tell the Mac-Dougals that?"

Tupper nodded. "Yes, I did, but they wouldn't believe me. Old Angus, and now his daughter Sarah, has been on the warpath for Smoke Jensen ever since the shooting. None of them will listen to reason."

"But Mr. Tupper," Sally interrupted. "You are the sheriff of this county. Why didn't you do something to stop them from attacking my husband?"

Tupper held out his hands. "You don't understand, Mrs. Jensen. Angus MacDougal owns the biggest spread in these parts and is a very powerful man. You just don't go up against him if you want to keep your job."

Louis snarled and reached over and jerked the tin star off Tupper's chest, ripping a large hole in his shirt. He contemptuously tossed the star in the wastebasket next to Tupper's desk. "You don't deserve to wear that badge, Tupper. You were elected to represent all of the people and uphold all of the laws, not just those agreed to by the rich and powerful."

Tupper hung his head, his face flaming scarlet. "I know, don't you think I know that? I thought I had the guts to stand up to Augus. But I guess I'm not the man I thought I was."

"Where is this MacDougal ranch, Mr. Tupper?" Sally asked. "And what is the fastest way to get there?"

At that moment, Smoke was riding up to the MacDougal spread, his shoulders slumped with fatigue.

He had pushed his horse as hard as he could, taking a shortcut over the mountains to get to the MacDougal ranch before any of the hands could arrive. He knew the approximate location from the talk he'd heard around the campfire when he'd been prisoner.

He rode directly up to the barn and got down off his horse. Working as fast as he could, he got two horses out of the corral next to the barn and hitched them up to a wagon.

He drove the wagon over to the ranch house and pulled it to a halt. Stepping down, he walked up on the porch and knocked on the door.

An elderly lady answered the door, and looked at him with startled eyes. "Yes, may I help you?" she asked.

Smoke took off his hat and held it in front of him. "Are you Mrs. MacDougal?" he asked politely.

The woman straightened up and looked over at him regally, as if she were royalty. "Yes, I am. My husband and I own this ranch. As I said before, what can I do for you?"

"Is anyone else in the house?" Smoke asked, glancing over her shoulders."

"Sir, that is certainly no business of yours," Mrs. Mac-Dougal said haughtily.

Behind her, Smoke could see the Mexican housekeeper appear in the kitchen door.

With a sigh, Smoke pulled his six-gun and said, "I'm sorry to disturb you, ladies, but I'm going to have to ask you to come out of the house."

"Oh, my God!" Mrs. MacDougal almost screamed, her hands going to her face. "He's going to kill us!"

Smoke sighed and shook his head. "No, I'm not, Mrs. MacDougal. I'm just going to send you away from here for a while."

As the two women filed out of the front door, glancing apprehensively over their shoulders at Smoke, he waved them out to the buckboard and helped them climb up onto the seat.

"Can either of you drive one of these?" he asked.

"I can, young man," the housekeeper said.

"Good," Smoke said, handing her the reins. As soon as she had them in her hands, he whacked the nearest horse on the rump and the wagon took off, both women screaming in terror.

Smoke walked back to the barn, got a can of kerosene and some rags, and made his way back to the house.

Sally and Louis and Cal and Pearlie rode as fast as they could down the road toward the MacDougal ranch, hoping they would get there in time to save Smoke's life.

Sheriff Tupper had finally broken down and told them of the twenty or so men Angus had out in the mountains going after Smoke. Sally and her friends hoped to find someone at the ranch who could show them which of the many mountains surrounding Pueblo was the one where the hunt was taking place.

As they rounded a corner, they were almost run down by a buckboard racing down the trail toward town. They jerked their horses' reins and barely got off the trail in time.

Pearlie scratched his head at the sight of two women in the racing wagon, both of whom were still screaming at the top of their lungs as the buckboard careened down the road.

"You think I should go and try and help them?" Cal asked Sally.

She shook her head. "No, they'll be all right. This is a smooth trail and shouldn't give them any problems. We need to get to the ranch and see if we can find Smoke."

Less than an hour later, they rode up to the ridge overlooking the MacDougal spread, and were astonished to see the main ranch house and the barn engulfed in flames.

"Holy smoke!" Cal whispered as the four sat on their horses staring at the burning ranch.

A voice called from a nearby clump of boulders as a head appeared on top of the largest rock. "You folks looking for me?"

They turned their eyes and saw Smoke sitting on top of the boulder watching the ranch burn.

Sally jumped down off her horse and ran as fast as she

could toward her husband, who'd also jumped down off the rock and was running toward her.

After they'd embraced and kissed—and kissed some more—Sally leaned her head back and said, "And just what is going on here, Smoke Jensen?"

He looked down at the burning buildings. "I'm just teaching a man a lesson, sweetheart. He lost his son, through no fault of his own, but then he went out seeking vengeance, and now he's lost his daughter, his best friend, and his home. I only hope the lesson sticks."

He put his arm around her and walked her back toward their horses. "Now, let's go home," he said, a smile on his face. "I don't believe I was quite through welcoming you back home when I was forced to leave."

WRATH OF THE
MOUNTAIN MAN

PROLOGUE

Sheriff Buck Tolliver set a bottle of whiskey in the middle of the rough-hewn table and took his seat. There were four other men sitting there, each as rough and weathered-looking as the old boards of the table.

Jerry Hogarth, known to friend and foe alike simply as Hog, both because of his great size and his rather slovenly personal hygiene, grabbed the bottle and splashed a generous amount into the tin cup in front of him. He also managed to pour about a third of a cup down the front of his already heavily stained shirt.

Bubba Barkley, sitting on Hog's left, gave him a rough elbow. "You gonna pass that bottle on over here or are you gonna try'n keep it all to yoreself, Hog?" Bubba was almost as big as Hog, but unfortunately had about the same mental ability—that is to say, very little.

Hog gave him a look, but shoved the bottle over with the back of a grimy hand as big as a ham.

Before Bubba was through pouring, Jimmy Akins, called the Kid by everyone because he favored fancy gunfighter attire and looked to be only about eighteen instead of his nearly twenty-three, shifted the toothpick around in his mouth and grunted, pointing at his own tin cup.

"You too lazy to pour yore own?" Bubba asked, but he poured anyway. "Or are you still trying to keep your gun hand free in case some desperado breaks in here and you have to fast-draw on him?" Bubba was referring to the Kid's rather irritating habit of trying to use his left hand for everything in order to keep his right hand hovering near the butt of his pistol. He'd read in a dime novel that it was something the real Kid named Billy used to do.

Buck ignored them and addressed himself to the remaining man at the table, Jeb Hardy, who, unlike the others, was well groomed and neatly dressed, and might almost have looked like an accountant, if you failed to notice his dead, cold, snakelike eyes, the way his pistol was tied down low on his right hip, and the way the wooden handle of the Colt was worn down from frequent use.

"How'd we do last week, Jeb?" Buck asked.

Jeb gave a half smile, reached into a leather case sitting on the floor next to him, and brought out a handful of papers. "We obtained the stake certificates to four new mines, and partnership agreements on three others," he said, his eyes smug.

"Any trouble?" Buck asked, meaning had they had to kill anyone to get the papers.

Jeb shrugged, his eyes again going flat, making it plain that he didn't appreciate being questioned like some lowly employee about how he'd done his job. "Not too much. A couple of miners fell and broke their arms, and one got a broken jaw, but we didn't have to plant any of them forked-end-up."

Buck nodded, pleased with the week's work. Before long, he and his band of men would own or control ninety percent of the best gold and silver mines in the county.

"I wanna know somethin', Buck," Hog growled, whiskey running down his chin, which he blotted with the tail of his shirt.

"Yeah, Hog?" Buck answered, turning to stare at the man and wondering how in the world one man could attract so much dirt and grime without actually lying down and wallowing in it.

"How come we do all the dirty work an' you an' Jeb git to keep most of the profits?" He glanced at Bubba and the Kid, but both of them just lowered their eyes and

pretended they hadn't heard the question. They, unlike
Hog, were smart enough to know it wasn't healthy to
question either Buck or Jeb about the split of their take.
Better to just take what they were offered and be thankful they weren't really having to work for a living.

Buck put out a hand when Jeb's eyes flashed. He'd
handle this, he signaled Jeb with a look.

"It's very simple, Hog, so even a dumb son of a bitch
like you ought to be able to understand it." When Hog's
eyes widened and his face turned beet red, Buck pointed
to the sheriff's badge on his shirt. "This badge and my job
as sheriff of this county is what is keeping all of our butts
out of jail, and Jeb's law degree is what enables him to fi-
nesse these claim stakes and partnership agreements
through the courthouse and, if they're ever challenged,
through the courts so that we'll get our money without
being hauled into jail and strung up for claim-jumping
and murder."

He leaned across the table and glared at Hog and the
others next to him. "All you bring to the table, Hog, is
your muscle, which I can hire on any street in any town in
this county for half what I'm paying you." He paused, not
wanting to talk too fast for Hog's slow-witted mind to keep
up. "Am I making myself clear?"

Hog pursed his lips and nodded reluctantly, the color
still high on his cheeks and sweat glistening on his forehead. "Yeah, I guess so."

"No, Hog," Jeb said, his dead snake eyes fixed on the
large man. "You'd better *know* so, because if you have any
doubts at all about the fairness of this arrangement, Buck
and I can change it in about two minutes flat, and you'll
be back shoveling horseshit in the livery so's you can eat."

The mention of the livery put fear in Hog's eyes. He'd
hated shoveling out the livery every day, but mucking
stalls had been the only job he could get until Buck and
Jeb had offered him this one. "No, no," he said, holding
up his hands. "What you're payin' me is jest fine."

The Kid looked at Hog disgustedly, shaking his head.
What a dumb ass, he thought. The Kid didn't particularly

think his pay was so hot, but the job had other compensations for him: He got to bully, beat up, and draw down on men just about every day, and this fed his soul much more than any money ever could. No, he'd keep his mouth shut. Things were going along just fine as far as he was concerned, and to be honest, he wasn't all that sure he could outdraw Jeb in a fair fight if it came down to it.

"Speaking of money," Buck said, drawing a wad of greenbacks out of his coat pocket and throwing it down on the table. "Weekend is coming up, so take that and go on into town and live it up a little bit."

He got up from the table. "But be careful not to flash around the whole wad and draw attention to yourselves; and you'd better not cause any trouble in my town," he warned, pointing his finger at the men. "Remember what I said. Save the rough stuff for work."

Buck walked out of the old, ramshackle mining cabin where he always met his men and pulled a long, black cheroot out of his shirt pocket. He fired up a lucifer and put the flame to the end of the stogie.

Jeb walked out and stood next to him, making sure he was upwind of the pungent tobacco smoke. "You think we need to worry about Hog?" he asked.

Buck blew out a stream of blue smoke and shook his head. "No, he's too dumb to try and go against us. Even he knows it'd be the end of a good thing for him."

"How about the others?"

Buck shrugged. "Same thing. Where else are they going to earn so much money for so little work?"

"That's for sure," Jeb said. "'Cause we are making a hell of a lot of money."

"And we're going to keep on making it, partner," Buck said, "as long as you keep any of the men we get the claims from too scared to go to the authorities."

Jeb's eyes again turned flat and hard and evil. "Any of them that do manage to grow the *cojones* to make a complaint won't live long enough to testify at a trial, that I'll guarantee you."

Buck shook his head. "Even so, I don't want any complaints

to come to the attention of the governor, so make sure you step on anyone who might even be thinking about shooting off their mouths."

Jeb leaned over and spit on the ground. "You let me worry about that, Buck. You just keep on keeping the law off our backs and we'll have enough money to retire to St. Louis within a year."

"St. Louis! Hell, I'm planning on going to New York City," Buck said. He grinned. "I hear beautiful women are thick as fleas on a hound dog up there."

Jeb looked at him out of the corner of his eye. "Yeah, but if you're planning on going up there, we might want to work an extra year. Those New York ladies are mighty expensive to maintain, especially for somebody as butt-ugly and downright crude as you, Buck."

When Buck started to bristle, Jeb laughed and slapped him on the shoulder. "Just teasing you a mite, partner. Don't take no offense now, you hear?"

Buck's eyes flashed. "Yeah, well if I did take offense at something you said, Jeb, you'd wake up with a bullet in your skull."

All of the amusement went out of Jeb's eyes in a flash and the grin faded from his lips. "Now don't let your mouth overload your ass, Buck, or someone might think you're good enough to take me down."

Buck smiled and tilted his head. "We may just have to find that out one of these days, Jeb."

"Any time, Buck, any time."

Buck rode back into what he liked to refer to as "his town" on his dun gelding, sitting high in the saddle, his chest thrown out, and a steely glint in his eye should anyone not know he was top dog in this kennel.

He'd come to the small mining camp known as Payday a few years back, when it was a typical lawless, anything-goes, wild and rowdy camp. Buck had seen his opportunity, and had bought himself a tin badge through a mail-order magazine and pinned it on. Anyone who had the temerity to question his authority found themselves looking down the barrel of his .45 Colt, or the twin barrels of the ten-gauge express gun he carried in a rifle boot on his saddle.

Buck was smart enough to not come down hard on the things the miners liked to do after working their claims all day, so he let the whores and the saloons and the gambling palaces stay in business, as long as they gave him a little cash on the side, "for security." He did, however, run off both the town's lawyers, not wanting anyone but himself deciding what was legal and what was illegal.

And when a drunk confided to all who would listen in a saloon one day that he was not only a good barber, but that he was a better than average dentist and doctor to boot, Buck managed to convince him the town needed him and that he could do worse than make Payday his home.

Dr. Hezekiah Bentley had settled in, and if the townspeople could manage to get injured before five in the afternoon when Bentley went off the wagon every day, they had a fair chance of getting fixed up and surviving the experience. If, on the other hand, they had the misfortune to get shot or stabbed or to break a bone after dark, they tried their best to survive on their own until Doc woke up the next day and was over his hangover before consulting him—it was much safer that way.

As Buck rode down the main street, he nodded and tipped his hat at some of the ladies of the evening as they passed, and waved and shouted hellos to some of the men, who waved back. Buck was pretty popular in town, having learned it was better to govern by giving the people what they wanted rather than enforcing a stricter interpretation of the law. So, in Payday, just about everything was legal, everything except making Buck Tolliver angry.

Every week, usually on Friday afternoons when most of the surrounding miners were in town to spend the dust they'd pried from the earth the previous week, Buck held court in the largest saloon in town. He would place a chair on top of the bar and any men with grievances against one another would come before him to argue their cases. Buck would nod sagely and then rule, usually for the man with the most money or the best mine, extracting his "fee" for legal advice later when no one was around to witness the transaction.

The few men who didn't appreciate Buck's wisdom or his judgments would often later be found shot or stabbed to death. It didn't take long for the people of Payday to get the hint: Buck Tolliver, for better or worse, was the law in their town, and if they didn't like it, they should just move on—it was healthier that way.

After a few years of this, making a good living but not getting what he considered rich, Buck decided to expand his horizons. Payday was growing larger every day, and more and more people were coming up into the mountains of northern Colorado to make their fortune by mining. He remembered a friend of his brother's, a man named Jeb Hardy, who'd managed to get a law degree through the mail and was working minor swindles on people back in the big city of Denver.

He took a vacation, made a run over to Denver, and looked Jeb up. Over drinks, after sharing a toast to Buck's dead brother, Buck put his proposition to Jeb. If he'd come back to Payday and take care of the legal matters, Buck had an idea how they could both get rich, without having to work overly hard doing it.

Soon, they had a thriving business. Jeb and the hard cases they'd hired would locate isolated mines and then threaten or beat the men into giving them part of their operations in exchange for "security" to keep other claim-jumpers away. The fact that Jeb and his men were the only claim-jumpers in the area mattered not at all. There was no one, other than Sheriff Buck Tolliver, to complain to, and for some strange reason, that never seemed to do any good.

Most of the miners just gritted their teeth and gave Jeb and his men their percentage and kept on working their mines. The few who refused soon found they couldn't mine much gold or silver with broken arms or wrecked equipment. Those that still weren't convinced soon found themselves dead, shortly after signing over their claims to Jeb.

It was a neat scheme with very little risk, as long as Buck Tolliver was sheriff and as long as Jeb could find men willing to do whatever he wanted to make the plan work.

So far, neither had been a problem, and Jeb and Buck just kept getting richer and richer.

1

The members of the Nez Percé tribe that made their home in far northern Colorado watched as the tall, broad-shouldered man with the salt and pepper hair walked among their young Palouse studs. He stood a bit over six feet tall, shoulders as wide as an ax handle, and even the loose cut of his buckskin shirt and trousers couldn't disguise the muscles that rippled and moved under the skins.

Some of the braves whispered among themselves, for they'd often heard their fathers sit around the campfire at night and sing songs of this man, a man known to them all as the Last Mountain Man. They sang of him and of his blood brother, a man who called himself Preacher, and how they'd stood alone against the High Lonesome itself and conquered it as no white men ever had before or since.

A few of the younger braves flexed their muscles and puffed out their chests and strutted around the camp as though the presence of this man, who was a legend even among people other than his own, did not impress them overly much. A couple even muttered derogatory comments, in their own language, of course, in the neighborhood of the big man to show him they weren't at all afraid of him or of the many guns on his belt or even the big knife in his belt.

A slight smile curled the lips of Smoke Jensen as he finished his examination of the young Palouse studs he'd come up here to barter for. He spoke the language of the

Nez Percé as well as the young braves, but he took no offense at their behavior, knowing it was a rite of passage among the Indians to show no fear when growing into manhood.

He ducked under the lariat rope that served the Indians as a makeshift corral and moved with long strides to stand next to the chief of the tribe, Gray Wolf.

As Smoke pulled two cigars from the breast pocket of his buckskin shirt and offered one to the chief, he said in a low voice, "You might tell Running Deer over there that even if by some miracle he was able to defeat me in battle and take my woman, she would break him over her knee as easily as I do this lucifer." Smoke demonstrated what he meant by snapping the match between his fingers after he'd lighted both their stogies.

The chief laughed, not at all embarrassed that Smoke not only overheard his braves, but that he spoke their language as well. The chief puffed out a large mouthful of smoke and said, "If I told him that, though it be true that you speak with straight tongue, for I remember your woman from last year, it would break Running Deer's spirit, which is high with the bravery of youth, my friend."

Smoke nodded, smiling, for the chief was correct; it would crush the young man to be confronted like that and be unable to defend his honor. "I know, old friend, so I'll handle it my own way," Smoke said.

He turned to face the group of young braves gathered near the fire and let his eyes seek out the one who'd said, just loudly enough for Smoke to hear, that if the chief would allow it he would whip the old man and take his woman into his teepee for the winter.

"Running Deer," Smoke called in perfect Nez Percé dialect, causing a surprised frown to appear on the young man's face and traces of fear on the faces of some of the others who had likewise spoken ill of the mountain man. "Would you show me how these young studs run? The chief tells me you are one of the best riders of green-broke horses in the tribe."

Running Deer's frown disappeared and was replaced by

a chagrined smile. "Chief Gray Wolf has told the Mountain Man the truth, and all of these horses can run like the wind," he said as he handed his bow to a friend and moved toward the remuda. "But there is one who is faster by far than the others. I call him Blizzard," he said in the Nez Percé language, "because he is like the strong wind from the north in winter as it races through the mountains—unstoppable."

Smoke nodded, deciding he would name the horse Storm if he proved to be as fast as Running Deer claimed.

Cal and Pearlie, Smoke's two hands who'd accompanied him on the trip up from Smoke's ranch in southern Colorado, stood nearby, their foreheads wrinkled as they tried to follow the conversation. During the two weeks it took them to drive the mares up into the mountains, Smoke had tried to teach them as much of the Nez Percé tongue as he could, but since they'd never heard it before, it'd been slow going for the two men, though they tried hard.

Cal, barely out of his teens and not much older than the young braves near the fire, leaned his head close to Pearlie, a grizzled veteran who was almost thirty, and asked, "What did that brave call the horse . . . Snowstorm?"

"Somethin' like that," Pearlie replied, being no more certain of what had been said than Cal was. "All I got was that he thinks the horse can run some."

"Let's see if he's right," Cal said, and he swung up into the saddle of his own Palouse stud, Dusty, while Pearlie climbed up onto his horse, Cold. Pearlie had named his horse Cold because he was cold-mouthed in the morning and would buck and snort and crow-hop for the first five minutes Pearlie was on his back.

Running Deer grabbed Storm's mane and swung up onto his back without bothering to put even a blanket on the mount. He kicked the horse's flanks and the stud reared up and raced across the corral, leaping up and over the lariat at the last moment.

As Cal and Pearlie spurred their broncs after the Indian, it was clear that Storm was indeed something special, for he left both Cal and Pearlie far behind as he raced at breakneck speed across the small plateau that contained the Indians' camp, weaving in and out of and through the many stands of small Ponderosa pine trees as if they weren't there.

Without even slowing down, Running Deer took Storm over the edge of the cliff and down the steep slope of the side of the plateau, and the stud never stumbled, but ran like he'd been born to do nothing else.

Cal and Pearlie, not wanting to break their necks, reined in at the edge of the cliff and watched in amazement as Running Deer and Storm made a wide sweep and raced back up the slope, just as fast as they'd gone down it. Man and horse were only slightly slower coming up the grade than they'd been going down it.

"Jimminy," Cal said, taking his hat off and sleeving sweat off his forehead with his arm. "That mount really *can* run like the wind."

"Wind, hell," Pearlie said, shaking his head, "more like a tornado!"

Cal waved his hat at the young brave as he raced by, and was rewarded with a show—Running Deer swung his leg up and over the horse's neck and whirled around to ride backward without the mount ever breaking stride. He gave a couple of loud yips in greeting, and then he reversed himself and was suddenly riding facing front again.

After Running Deer had returned Storm to the corral and joined Smoke and the others near the fire, Smoke grinned and shook his hand. "If you ever want a job as a wrangler, Running Deer," he said sincerely, "come on down to the Sugarloaf and you'll have a job for life."

Running Deer glanced at the chief out of the corner of his eyes and replied, "Though it would be a great honor to work with the man my people call the Last Mountain Man, I could never leave these mountains or my people, for to do so would be to make my heart small."

Cal stepped over and clapped Running Deer on the

shoulder, causing the young man to frown, as if such familiarity was unheard of among his people. "Golly, Running Deer," Cal said, his eyes wide, "I ain't never seen nobody ride like you do. It's like you was a part of that bronc."

Running Deer's expression softened somewhat at the compliment. "Thank you, Mr. Cal," he said formally. "We Nez Percé are taught to ride almost before we are taught to walk. It is something all of my brothers can do."

Pearlie nodded, his eyes twinkling. "Yeah, but I'll just bet you that they ain't none of them can do it near as good as you, Running Deer."

The young man ducked his head, unwilling to seem arrogant, but the chief chuckled. "You are right, Pearlie. Running Deer is the best of the young braves on horseback. They all wish to be like him."

Smoke winked at the chief and put his hand on Running Deer's shoulder, leading him over to the small remuda of studs that Smoke had brought from the Sugarloaf. "Tell me what you think of these studs, Running Deer. I've brought them up here to trade with your people for some studs of a different bloodline so that my remuda back home doesn't get too inbred."

Running Deer nodded, his eyes on the horses. He ducked under the lariat corral and walked among them, running his hands on their necks, whispering in a low voice to them, checking a few horses' teeth or withers or hooves. After a few moments, he smiled slightly, about as much a seal of approval as he could make. "They are very fine, Mountain Man. Are they too of the Nez Percé?"

Smoke nodded. "Not these directly, Running Deer, but their fathers and mothers were all acquired from some of your brother tribes a few years back."

"I thought so, for I can tell they are of the true Palouse blood, undiluted by your American quarter horses or thoroughbreds."

He looked at the chief and gave a slight nod. "These will make very fine breeders for our mares, Chief Gray Wolf."

Gray Wolf returned the nod and turned to Smoke,

holding out his hand. "It is, as you white-eyes say, a deal, Mountain Man."

After they shook hands, Gray Wolf clapped his hands together and yelled, "Now, it is time for a feast with our new friends! Have the squaws get the venison ready."

Smoke put his hand on the chief's shoulder and leaned down to whisper, "I've got a side of beef on one of those pack animals I've brought all the way up here from my ranch for you, if you'd like to have it instead of deer meat, Chief."

The chief's eyes lit up and he smiled broadly, revealing tobacco-stained teeth that were worn almost down to the gums. "It has been a long time since I've eaten beef, Mountain Man." He paused and then grinned wickedly again. "At least, beef that was freely given to us instead of that which wandered into our camp and accidentally fell upon a spear."

Smoke and Cal and Pearlie all laughed, for they had all heard many ranchers complain of the mountain Indians coming down and raiding their herds for beef to eat. Smoke sympathized with the Indians, for he remembered from his days in these same mountains how tiring a diet of only venison and moose and bear could become after several months.

Smoke nodded at Pearlie, who said, "Cal, grab that beef off the packhorse and let's eat. I'm so hungry my stomach thinks my throat's been cut!"

While the beefsteaks sizzled and spit on frying pans over the open fire, Running Deer and the other braves began to show Cal and Pearlie some of the games they played. They rode past a thick tree and threw spears while at full gallop; they shot arrows from horseback at bushes; they threw tomahawks end over end and tried to make them stick in the bark of the pine trees that surrounded the Nez Percé camp.

"It is good that your braves know how to be friends with white men," Smoke said as he and the chief smoked another cigar while the squaws got the meat and vegetables cooked.

Chief Gray Wolf nodded gravely, his eyes sad. "Yes, my friend, but not all white men are friends to us as you are. We must still be careful not to approach white men on the mountain unless we are invited, for some will still shoot to kill us on sight."

"It is still that bad?" Smoke asked, having hoped that things would have gotten better in the last few years.

"It has never changed," Gray Wolf said with a sigh.

2

When the squaws signaled the chief the food was ready, Cal and Pearlie and the braves all gathered around the fire to eat large slabs of beefsteak and vegetables. There were no women present, as they typically ate whatever was left over later while the men all napped after their meal. After the men and Smoke and the boys had finished most of the side of beef he'd brought, Cal and Pearlie and Running Deer and some of the younger braves went back to playing the Indian games the meal had interrupted. Pearlie, of course, said now that his mind was off of food for a while, he'd be able to do a lot better in the highly competitive games.

Smoke and Chief Gray Wolf sat in the shelter of a lean-to and smoked, the chief his pipe and Smoke his cigar. Smoke had given the chief a pound of real ground coffee, and the chief had directed one of the squaws near his tent to make them a pot of it.

When he took his first sip, the chief's lips curled in a wide smile. "Much better than piñon bean coffee," he said. He smacked his lips and added, "This is much too good for the braves. I believe I'll save this for my use alone."

Smoke nodded, having tasted the bitter brew made from piñon beans in the past. "Even the white man has some good things to offer your people, Chief."

The chief slowly inclined his head in agreement. "That

is true, Mountain Man, but even though my people live way up here in the High Lonesome, we have not escaped the corrupting ways of the white-eyes."

"Oh?" Smoke asked, trailing a stream of blue smoke from his nostrils.

"Yes. The yellow metal we take from the streams and mountain caves to make jewelry for our squaws is much sought after by the white-eyes from nearby towns. Some of my more . . . rebellious braves have learned that they can trade the yellow metal for firewater." He shook his head sadly. "It is a terrible thing what it does to these young men. They begin to act like a horse that has eaten . . ." and he gave the Nez Percé name for the bush white men called locoweed.

"I have seen the trouble that our whiskey can cause your people," Smoke agreed. "And there are some among us who think that men who trade liquor to you should be punished severely."

The chief's eyes were hard and as cold as the granite peaks of the mountains that surrounded them as he replied, "If I find out who has been doing this thing, you can be sure they will be punished"—he paused and turned his hard gaze on Smoke—"and punished to the death."

Smoke decided to change the subject before the chief became any more upset. He inclined his head toward the braves who were still playing their games off in the distant fields. "It appears that you have many fine young men in your tribe who still follow the old ways, Chief Gray Wolf."

For the first time in a while, the chief smiled. "Yes. My people are quite lucky that way. Some of the other tribes are having quite a problem keeping their young people in the mountains." He looked over at the remains of the beef they'd eaten earlier and held up his coffee cup. "Once they get a taste of the white man's food and drink, it is hard for them to live in the old manner." He grinned. "Dog just doesn't taste near as good as beef."

Smoke laughed. "You are not alone in that, my friend. Even in the land of the white man, we are having much the same problems. Our young people too are leaving the

farms and ranches and heading into the big cities, tired of
having to work hard from dawn to dusk and not having a
whole lot to show for it at the end of the day." He shook
his head. "I don't have a wrangler on my spread who is
under the age of twenty-five, except for Cal. All of the boys
in their teens want to go to Denver or even bigger towns
to make their way in the new world."

The chief chuckled and held up his coffee cup in a
toast. "To all the young ones who are not afraid to stay
with the old ways, Mountain Man."

Smoke grinned and returned the toast. "I'll drink to
that," he said.

Suddenly, from the distant field, Smoke heard a shout,
and looked up to see Cal waving his hands in the air. It
looked to Smoke like he was standing over a fallen body.
"Damn!" Smoke exclaimed when he recognized the form
of Pearlie lying still at Cal's feet.

When Cal pulled his pistol and fired three times in the
air, Smoke knew Pearlie was in serious trouble. He jumped
to his feet and bounded across the meadow, and was in his
saddle and spurring his mount forward within seconds.

He jumped off his horse and ran to where Cal was
bending over Pearlie, whose face was pale and waxen-
looking. The young man was clearly unconscious.

Smoke knelt next to him and looked at Cal. "What
happened?"

"We was playing fox and rabbit with the braves an'
Pearlie was the rabbit an' we was chasing him acrost the
field when his horse stumbled in a prairie dog hole.
Pearlie was thrown over there against that there log," Cal
said, breathless, as he pointed a few feet away.

Smoke glanced over and saw a dead Rocky Mountain
rattlesnake lying next to the log, Pearlie's knife pinning
its head to the ground.

"Shit!" he said, knowing exactly what had happened.
Pearlie had fallen against the log, moving it and disturbing
the rattlesnake that was curled up underneath it. The frightened reptile must have struck him before he even saw it.

Smoke leaned over and began to examine Pearlie's body

for the telltale twin punctures. "Where'd it get him?" he asked, his face knotted with worry. Mountain rattlers could be deadly if the bite was in a dangerous place.

"Before he passed out, Pearlie said it got him twice, once in the leg an' once in the neck," Cal said, pointing at the red marks on Pearlie's neck just over the blood vessel there.

"Damn," Smoke exclaimed, knowing there was little he could do about the neck wound. To cut it deep enough to get the poison out would also cut the big vessel in the neck and Pearlie would likely bleed to death.

He turned his attention to Pearlie's legs, quickly finding the bite mark there. He drew his big bowie knife from the scabbard on his belt and made crisscrossing cuts over the two puncture wounds. He lowered his head and began to suck the blood and poison out of the wound, turning his head to the side to spit the noxious liquid out between sucks.

After a few minutes, he stopped, sleeving blood off his mouth with his arm while Cal took his bandanna off and made a tight bandage over the wound, stopping the flow of blood.

"You think he's gonna make it, Smoke?" Cal asked, unshed tears in his eyes as he stared at his friend lying deathlike on the cold ground.

Smoke shook his head, knowing the chances weren't good. "I don't know, Cal. He's strong and he's a fighter, so he's got a better chance than most, and he's lucky that the snake struck him in the leg first. Most of its venom probably went into the leg and not into his neck."

Just then, Chief Gray Wolf came riding up on a Palouse pony. He dismounted and squatted next to Pearlie, his eyes narrow with concern.

"Mountain rattler," Smoke said, pointing to the twin bites on Pearlie's neck.

The chief's eyes widened for a moment, and then he shook his head slowly. "Such a bite always means trouble, and one in the neck is almost always deadly." He took a deep breath, not wanting to give his friend bad news. "I've only once seen a brave survive such a bite, and never a squaw or young one."

Smoke felt as if his heart was going to break. Aside from Cal, Pearlie was his best friend in the world. "Are there any towns near here that might have a doctor in them?" he asked, staring up into the old chief's eyes.

The chief looked at him, and Smoke could tell the old man didn't think it made much difference. He was sure Pearlie was going to die no matter what was done for him. He hesitated, figuring it wouldn't hurt to try to get the young white man to one of their doctors.

After a moment, the chief nodded. "There is such a town less than a day's ride from here. The white men call it Payday. It is full of men searching the mountains for the yellow and silver metals." He hesitated, and then he added, "It is a very tough town, Mountain Man, but I believe there is a medical man living there."

"Can you have your men make me a travois to carry Pearlie on while you tell me how to get there?" Smoke asked.

The chief barked an order in his native tongue to several young men standing nearby, and Running Deer nodded and beckoned them to follow him as he jumped on his pony and rode like the wind toward a strand of nearby pine trees.

"I will do better than that," Gray Wolf said. "I will have Running Deer lead you to the town, and I will have some of my braves accompany you as far as the town to keep you safe."

Smoke frowned. "Keep me safe?"

The old man shrugged. "There are many bad men in the area who would rather steal the yellow metal than work to dig it out of the ground. If they think you have money, they might attack you, which would slow you getting help for young Pearlie."

Smoke smiled and put his hand on the chief's shoulder. Even though his lips were smiling, his eyes were dark and dangerous. "God help any man who gets in the way of Pearlie's getting to a doctor," he said.

3

After Pearlie was placed on the travois and covered with blankets and furs against the cold, Chief Gray Wolf leaned down and placed a small leather pouch under the covers over Pearlie's heart. He looked up. "It is my medicine bag. It will help keep his heart strong and brave during his fight against the poison of the snake."

Smoke nodded his appreciation and shook the chief's hand, and then he and Cal began the long ride to the town called Payday. They had to go slow since the rarely used trail was so faint as to barely be visible, and it was bumpy with rocks and tufts of mountain grass.

As they rode, Running Deer looked at Smoke and saw his worried expression. He glanced back at the travois. "This man, Pearlie, he is like a brother to the Mountain Man?" he asked.

Smoke looked up, and then he too glanced back at Pearlie's pale, still body on the travois, watching it roll back and forth each time the travois hit a bump. "More like a son," he said slowly, realizing once again how much Pearlie and Cal meant to him and Sally.

He was thinking how devastated Sally would be if Pearlie didn't make it, when Running Deer spoke again. "He has been with you a long time?"

Smoke smiled, remembering how Pearlie came to work at the Sugarloaf. Pearlie had come into his and Sally's lives in a very roundabout way. He was hiring his gun out a few years back to a man named Tilden Franklin in a town named Fontana near Smoke's ranch when Franklin went crazy and tried to take over the Sugarloaf, Smoke and Sally's spread. After Franklin's men raped and killed a young girl in the fracas just to get Smoke's attention, Pearlie decided he'd had enough of Franklin and his lawless ways, and he sided with Smoke and the aging gunfighters he had called in to help put an end to Franklin's reign of terror.*

Smoke smiled, thinking of the night he'd braced the young gunman known only as Pearlie and asked him if he was happy working for a man like Franklin. When Pearlie had stared at him for a moment before answering, "Not 'specially," Smoke had told him there was always room on his payroll for a good worker. Pearlie had packed his war bag and quit Franklin the next day.

Smoke pulled a cigar from his buckskin coat pocket and struck a lucifer on his pants leg, sucking the harsh smoke deep into his lungs as he thought about what had happened next.

Franklin had been so pissed off at Pearlie that he'd sent a group of the men riding for his brand after Pearlie. They'd chased him down and shot him in the back, then tied him to his saddle and dragged him to hell and gone through miles of cactus and rocks until he was so bloody and battered he was hardly recognizable. They'd left him for dead out on the plains, not reckoning on the strength of his character.

Pearlie had walked almost ten miles with two bullets in his back and hardly any skin left on his carcass to get to Smoke's ranch. He'd stayed conscious long enough to knock on Smoke's door, and then he'd collapsed into unconsciousness so deep Smoke had feared he was dead when he answered the door and found Pearlie lying so still on the porch.

Smoke had had Doc Spalding take the lead peas out of

* *Trail of the Mountain Man*

Pearlie's back and fix him up as best he could, considering the damage that'd been done to the young man. When the doc had told Smoke it would be a miracle if Pearlie lived through the night, Smoke had just smiled and shaken his head. "This young'un's got too much sand to let post-suckers like Franklin's men kill him," Smoke had replied, though truth be told, he hadn't been all that sure that even a man as brave as Pearlie could survive the terrible damage that'd been done to him that night.

Pearlie was now honorary foreman of Smoke's ranch, and was in the midst of a fight every bit as tough as the one he'd been through when first he met Smoke.

"Yeah," Smoke said, answering Running Deer's question. "Pearlie's been with me for a spell, and I reckon no desert rattler's gonna succeed in putting him in the ground when a lot of hard men have failed."

Since they were moving so slowly, Smoke was able to push the horses closer and closer to Payday through the night. He stopped and made camp only after one of the young braves traveling with them fell asleep on the back of his horse and fell to the ground.

While Cal and Smoke made a campfire and pulled the travois with Pearlie on it close to the heat, Running Deer and his friends pulled salted, dried venison from their pouches and began to chew on the hard, jerky-type meat.

Smoke had the braves help him hobble the Palouse studs they had with them, while Cal started a large pot of coffee to brewing and began to heat some pinto beans with large chunks of fatback in it. While the coffee and beans were heating, Cal cut up some onions and peppers and fried them in a large cast-iron skillet with steaks cut off a side of beef on the packhorse.

By the time the studs were hobbled near some mountain meadow grass, Cal had supper ready.

Running Deer raised his eyebrows in question when Cal handed him a plate with a still-steaming steak and a pile of beans on it. "You'll like this a whole lot better'n that there jerky you been chewin' on," Cal said, bending and pouring Running Deer a cup of coffee in a tin cup.

"Now tell yore friends to dig in an' help themselves to the beans in the pot and the meat in the skillet. I ain't no waitress, you know."

Running Deer yelled something in his Nez Percé tongue, and his friends came over to the fire and began to fix themselves plates. Running Deer sliced a bite of steak with his skinning knife and shoved it into his mouth along with a generous portion of beans.

As he chewed, he rolled his eyes and grinned at Cal. "You are right, Cal," he said, bean juice running out of the corner of his mouth. "This much better than pemmican." He almost added that even a squaw from their village couldn't have done better, but he held his tongue, knowing white men had strange notions about the roles of men and women in life. A brave would rather starve than stoop so low as to cook a meal—that was woman's work. But this white man, who was as manly as any of the braves in Running Deer's tribe, had not hesitated to cook for all of them and then to joke about it. Running Deer shook his head as he stuffed the beef and beans into his mouth and drank the delicious coffee. He figured he'd just never understand white men.

Cal just nodded, but Smoke could tell Running Deer's compliment pleased him by the way a scarlet flush crept up from his collar to cover his entire face.

Smoke bent his head to keep the young man from seeing his smile, and as he shoveled food into his mouth using his big bowie knife as both knife and spoon, he thought about the day Sally had brought Cal home to the Sugarloaf to work for him just a few months after Pearlie. . . .

Calvin Woods had been just about fourteen when Smoke and Sally had taken him in as a hired hand. It was during the spring branding that year, and Sally was on her way back from Big Rock to the Sugarloaf. Her buckboard was piled high with supplies, because branding hundreds of calves made for hungry punchers who could just about eat their weight in grub at the end of the day.

As Sally slowed the team to take a bend in the trail, a rail-thin young man stepped from the bushes at the side of the road with a pistol in his hand.

"Hold it right there, miss."

Applying the brake with her right foot, Sally slipped her hand under a pile of gingham cloth on the seat. She grasped the handle of her short-barreled Colt .44 and eared back the hammer, letting the sound of the horse's hooves and the squealing of the brake pads on the wheels mask the sound.

"What can I do for you, young man?" she asked, her voice firm and without fear. She knew she could draw and drill the young highwayman before he could raise his pistol to fire if it came right down to it.

"Well, uh, you can throw some of those beans and a cut of that fatback over here, and maybe a portion of that Arbuckle's coffee too," the young ambusher said, his voice weak and quavering as if he hadn't eaten for some time.

Sally's eyebrows rose. "Don't you want my money?"

The boy frowned and shook his head, as if the question made no sense. "Why, no, ma'am. I ain't no thief, I'm just hungry."

"And if I don't give you my food, are you going to shoot me with that big Navy Colt?" Sally asked, trying to keep the humor from her voice.

He hesitated a moment, then grinned ruefully. "No, ma'am, I guess not."

He twirled the pistol around his finger and slipped it into his belt, turned, and began to walk down the road toward Big Rock.

Sally watched the youngster amble off, noting his tattered shirt, dirty pants with holes in the knees and torn pockets, and boots that looked as if they had been salvaged from a garbage dump. "Young man," she called, "come back here, please."

He turned, a smirk on his face, spreading his hands, "Look, lady, you don't have to worry. I don't even have any bullets." With a lightning-fast move he drew the gun from his pants, aimed away from Sally, and pulled the trigger.

There was a click but no explosion as the hammer fell on an empty cylinder.

Sally smiled. "Oh, I'm not worried." In a movement every bit as fast as his, she whipped her .44 out and fired, clipping a pine cone from a branch above him, causing it to fall and bounce off his head.

The boy's knees buckled and he ducked, saying, "Jiminy Christmas!"

Mimicking him, Sally twirled her Colt and stuck it in the waistband of her britches. "What's your name, boy?" she asked, a frown creasing her forehead.

The boy blushed and looked down at his feet, "Calvin, ma'am, Calvin Woods."

She leaned forward, elbows on knees, and stared into the boy's eyes. "Calvin, no one has to go hungry in this country, not if they're willing to work."

He looked up at her through narrowed eyes, as if he found life a little different than she described it. "I done tried that, ma'am," he said, a disgusted look on his face. "All the ranchers hereabouts said I'm too young to hire on to their spreads." He grimaced. "One said he'd have to have the cook fix me up a sugar tit to get me through a day of brandin'."

"If you're willing to put in an honest day's work, I'll see that you get an honest day's pay, and all the food you can eat," Sally said, trying to hide her smile. "After all, a man old enough to try and rob someone with that old gun you're carrying is old enough to earn his way on a ranch."

Calvin stood a little straighter, shoulders back and head held high. "Ma'am, I've got to be straight with you. I ain't no experienced cowhand. I come from a hard-scrabble farm and we only had us one milk cow and a couple of goats and chickens, and lots of dirt that weren't worth nothing for growin' things. My ma and pa and me never had nothin', but we never begged and we never stooped to takin' handouts."

Sally thought, *I like this boy. Proud, and not willing to take charity if he can help it.* "Calvin, if you're willing to work, and don't mind getting your hands dirty and your muscles sore, I've got some hands that'll have you punching beeves like you were born to it in no time at all." She hesitated, and then she added earnestly, "This is no handout, boy. If you come to work for my husband and me, you'll earn every dime we pay you, and then some."

A smile lit up his face, making him seem even younger than his years. "Even if I don't have no saddle, nor a horse to put it on?"

She laughed out loud. "Yes. We've got plenty of ponies and saddles." She glanced down at his raggedy boots. "We can probably even round up some boots and spurs that'll fit you."

He walked over and jumped in the back of the buckboard. "Ma'am, I don't know who you are, but you just hired you the hardest-workin' hand you've ever seen."

Back at the Sugarloaf, she sent him in to Cookie and told him to eat his fill. When Smoke and the other punchers rode into the cabin yard at the end of the day, she introduced Calvin around. As Cal was shaking hands with the men, Smoke looked over at her and winked. He knew she could never resist a stray dog or cat, and her heart was as large as the Big Lonesome itself.

Smoke walked up to Cal and cleared his throat, his eyes boring into Cal's. "Son, I hear you drew down on my wife today."

Cal gulped, "Yes, sir, Mr. Jensen. I did." He squared his shoulders and looked Smoke in the eye, not flinching, though he was obviously frightened of the tall man with the incredibly wide shoulders standing before him.

Smoke smiled and clapped the boy on the back. He appreciated a man who'd own up to his mistakes, and be willing to take punishment for them without whining about it. "Just wanted you to know you stared death in the eye, boy. Not many galoots are still walking upright who ever pulled a gun on Sally. She's a better shot than any man I've ever seen except me, and sometimes I wonder about me."

The boy laughed with relief as Smoke turned and called out, "Pearlie, get your lazy butt over here."

A tall, lanky cowboy ambled over to Smoke and Cal, munching on a biscuit stuffed with roast beef. His face was lined with wrinkles and tanned a dark brown from hours under the sun, but his eyes were sky-blue and twinkled with good-natured humor as he stared at the boy with Smoke.

"Yes, sir, Boss," he mumbled around a mouthful of food, his gaze moving up and down Cal as if he were mentally fitting him for clothes.

Smoke put his hand on Pearlie's shoulder. "Cal, this here chowhound is Pearlie. He eats more'n any two hands, and he's never been known to do a lick of work he could get out of, but he knows beeves and horses as well as any puncher I have. I want you to follow him around and let him teach you what you need to know."

Cal nodded. "Yes, sir, Mr. Smoke."

"Now let me see that iron you have in your pants."

Cal pulled out the ancient Navy Colt and handed it to Smoke. When Smoke opened the loading gate, the rusted cylinder fell to the ground, causing Pearlie and Smoke to laugh and Cal's face to flame red. "This is the piece you pulled on Sally?"

The boy nodded, looking at the ground.

Pearlie shook his head. "Cal, you're one lucky pup. Hell, if'n you'd tried to fire that thing it'd of blown your hand clean off."

Cal laughed. "It don't matter none, Pearlie. I didn't have no bullets for it nohow."

Smoke laughed again, shaking his head at Cal's actions, and inclined his head toward the bunkhouse. "Pearlie, take Cal over to the tack house and get him fixed up with what he needs, including a gun belt and a Colt that won't fall apart the first time he pulls it. You might also help pick him out a shavetail to ride. I'll expect him to start earning his keep tomorrow morning at first light."

"Yes, sir, Smoke." Pearlie put his arm around Cal's shoulders and led him off toward the bunkhouse. "Now the first thing you gotta learn, Cal, is how to get on Cookie's good side. A puncher rides on his belly, and it 'pears to me that you need some fattin' up 'fore you can begin think about punching cows."

Smoke glanced at Cal as he finished his meal, and he thought to himself that he truly couldn't love and care for a son any more than he did these two young men.

He took his last bite and started to get up as Cal walked over to him. "Give me that plate, Smoke, an' I'll clean 'em up 'fore we put 'em away."

"Thanks, Cal," Smoke said, handing him the plate. He settled back and lighted up a cigar to have with the last few sips of his coffee.

He glanced over at Pearlie, lying as still as death on the travois, and wished he'd raise his head up and say, "Is that food I smell?"

Smoke grinned at the thought, knowing Pearlie was as sick as he could be to miss a meal and not complain about it.

4

The next morning, Smoke woke to find a fine dusting of snow covering the camp. To his surprise, Cal was already awake and had a fire roaring and coffee boiling.

He chuckled to himself. Usually, Cal had to be forced out of bed with the toe of someone's boot, but Smoke figured the fears about his good friend Pearlie had kept the boy from sleeping very well, and he was probably as anxious as Smoke to get Pearlie to a town and under a doctor's care as soon as possible.

Cal glanced over at Smoke and grinned. "Glad to see you finally decided to crawl outta them blankets, Smoke. We been burnin' daylight for more'n half an hour now. I thought for a minute there I was gonna have to light a fire under you to git your eyes open."

Smoke looked around the camp and noticed there was no sign of the Indians. "Where'd Running Deer and his friends go?" he asked, gratefully accepting the steaming cup of coffee Cal handed him.

"They lit outta here just after daylight," Cal replied. "Said the town's right on up this trail 'bout half a day's ride an' they figured even a couple of white-eyes like us couldn't manage not to find it."

"What about the horses?" Smoke asked, noticing there were none in sight.

"They're gonna drive them on over to the south side of

the town and keep them there until we head back toward Big Rock. And Running Deer said not to worry or hurry, they'd stay with the studs as long as we needed them to an' make sure they had plenty of grass and water."

Smoke laughed. And he'd thought his being an old mountain man had impressed the young braves. Evidently not!

"You want me to scramble up a couple'a hens' eggs an' some fatback?" Cal asked.

Smoke glanced over at Pearlie, who lay still and pale as a corpse on his travois. "No," he answered, shaking his head and getting stiffly to his feet. "Since we're only a few hours from town, let's shag our mounts and see if we can get Pearlie there to see the doctor and worry about eating later."

"All right," Cal said, and he put his cup down and moved over to lay his palm on Pearlie's forehead. "He don't seem to have much fever. That's a good sign, ain't it?"

Smoke nodded, but he knew Pearlie was far from out of the woods yet. The only reason he was still alive at all was that the main portion of the snake's venom had gone into his leg and not into his neck. "Yeah, that's a good sign, Cal," he said, trying to keep the boy's spirits up. But it wasn't fever and infection Smoke was worried about. It was the effect the snake's venom was having on Pearlie's brain. It wouldn't do much good if the body survived but there was nobody home in the mind.

Cal sighed and moved to sit by the fire, taking a small canvas pouch out of his shirt pocket and beginning to build himself a cigarette.

Smoke noticed his hands were trembling so much that he could hardly keep the tobacco on the paper until he could lick it and seal it.

Cal looked up and saw Smoke watching him and grinned. "Kind'a cold this mornin', ain't it?"

Smoke nodded, knowing the trembling of Cal's hands was due more to his fear for his friend than to any cold in the air.

"Yeah, it is. So soon's you finish that cigarillo and your coffee, we'll get on our way."

Cal took a deep drag of the cigarette that was more paper than tobacco and then followed it with a deep draught of his coffee.

"Well, then, jingle them spurs, Smoke, 'cause I'm done," he said, jumping to his feet and stubbing out the worthless cigarette under his boot.

Smoke and Cal were about an hour down the trail when Smoke noticed two men ride out of the tree line on their right and begin to move toward them.

"Cal," he said in a low voice, nodding his head toward the men when Cal glanced at him. Both he and Cal let their hands drop to their thighs and they loosened the rawhide hammer thongs on their Colts. The men had made no threatening signs, but Smoke had survived a lot of years in the High Lonesome by being careful and not trusting anyone until they earned it. He smiled when he saw Cal's eyes as suspicious as his. Seems Cal was picking up his habits too.

As the men approached, Smoke saw that they were tough, hard-looking men and they wore their guns tied down low on their legs, as both he and Cal did.

"Howdy," the bigger of the two men called. Both were at least as wide as Smoke, though not as tall.

Smoke gave a half smile and inclined his head, his hand staying near the handle of his pistol.

"My name's Hog, an' this here is Bubba," Hog said, moving his horse around Smoke so he could get a closer look at Pearlie lying on the travois.

"Yore friend don't look so good," Hog said, taking his hat off and sleeving sweat off his forehead with his arm.

Smoke noticed this and figured it was too cold for the man to have worked up a sweat riding, so he must be nervous about something. Perhaps what he was about to do?

"He got snakebit," Cal said, kneeing his horse around

so he could keep an eye on Bubba, leaving Hog to Smoke without having to be told to.

"We're taking him to a town called Payday. You know it?" Cal added, still keeping his hand on his thigh next to his Colt.

"Yeah," Bubba growled, his eyes on Cal's hand. "It's on up the trail another couple'a hours."

Hog inclined his head toward Smoke's horse. "You men got any gold in them saddlebags?" he asked, trying to sound like it was just a friendly question.

"Well, what we have or haven't got in our saddlebags is none of your business, mister," Smoke said in a cold but even voice. His eyes were flat and dangerous looking, and if the men were smart, they'd take notice that he wasn't a man to be fooled around with.

Hog's eyes flashed with anger and he spurred his horse right up next to Smoke's, trying to intimidate him with his massive size. Smoke noted the man was almost as wide as he was tall, and his hands were big as hams, with scarred knuckles indicating he had been in lots of fights.

As the man got closer, Smoke took a pair of black, padded gloves out of his belt and slid his hands into them one at a time, his eyes never leaving Hog's.

"That ain't a real friendly comment, mister," Hog said, glowering at Smoke from under scarred eyebrows as if he were trying to scare Smoke to death.

"Maybe that's because you aren't my friend, mister," Smoke replied evenly, moving his shoulders a little to loosen them up for what he knew was about to happen. He could read the signs in the man's little pig eyes that he was about to attack.

Sure enough, Hog scowled and swung a haymaker right fist at Smoke's head, hoping to catch him off guard and end the fight before it got started.

Smoke leaned back in the saddle just enough for the fist to connect with nothing but air, and then he twisted in his seat as he sent a straight right hand into Hog's chest. Two of Hog's ribs snapped with a sound like dry twigs breaking when Smoke's knuckles plowed into them.

Hog squealed like his namesake and let out a loud whoosh and flew backward out of his saddle to hit the frozen ground with a thud. He lay there, stunned and trying to get his breath, making high-pitched wheezing sounds as he gulped through an open mouth, his eyes wide open and full of tears of pain and rage.

Bubba, seeing this, reached for his pistol, but found himself staring down the barrel of Cal's Navy Colt before he could clear leather. He slowly raised his hands out away from his gun butt and tried to lick his lips, but his mouth was too dry. "Don't . . . don't shoot me, mister," he pleaded.

Cal grinned. "I won't, lessen you try to grab that hogleg on your hip."

Smoke eased down out of his saddle and walked over to take Hog's pistol out of his belt and throw it into a nearby snowbank.

Hog got unsteadily to his feet, both hands massaging his chest as he continued to gasp for air. "Damn you, you son of a bitch," he yelled. "I ought to beat you to death."

Smoke, who'd had about enough of this loudmouth, just shook his head and motioned for Hog to come on with his hands.

"Did you say talk me to death or beat me to death?" Smoke taunted, knowing getting the big man angry would give him the advantage in the fight.

Hog growled something unintelligible and rushed at Smoke, his hands stretched out in front of him as if he was going to tear Smoke's head off.

Smoke leaned to the side and threw a hard left hook into Hog's right kidney as he stumbled past, causing the big man to let out another yelp and to grab his side with both hands.

He bent over, breathing heavily, both hands now on his knees as he groaned low in his throat. He knew from the pain in his side that he'd be pissing blood for a week.

"If you've had enough, I'd like to get on my way," Smoke said, standing there with his hands hanging at his sides. "My friend needs to get to a doctor and you're holding us up."

"Sure, go on, mister," Hog gasped, still leaning over and looking at the ground, wondering if he could keep from puking until the man and his friend had left.

When Smoke turned to get back up on his horse, Hog pulled a long, thin-bladed knife from a scabbard on the back of his belt and rushed at Smoke, holding the knife out in front of him.

Smoke heard him and whirled around. As Hog rushed at him, Smoke stepped to the side and lashed out with his left foot, catching the side of Hog's left knee with his boot. Hog's leg gave way with a loud snap as the knee bent at an impossible angle and the big man screamed as he fell to the ground, both hands clutching at his knee.

Smoke bent over and picked up the man's knife, shaking his head. He put the blade on the ground, put his boot on it, and raised the handle, snapping the blade into two pieces.

He flipped the handle down onto Hog's lap and walked away. "I don't think your leg is broken," Smoke said as he climbed up onto his saddle, "but I wouldn't put any weight on it until you see a doctor if I were you."

"Take that pistol out of your holster and hand it over," Cal said, pointing at Bubba's holster with the barrel of his Colt.

"What . . . what're you gonna do?" Bubba asked, fear thickening his voice as he glanced at his partner lying injured and helpless on the ground.

Cal took the pistol and stuck it in his belt. "I'm gonna leave this in the middle of the trail up ahead. If you're smart, which you sure as hell don't look like, you'll get it and ride in the opposite direction."

Bubba's eyes narrowed. "And if we don't?"

Cal shrugged and used a line he'd often heard Smoke utter. "Why, then, I suppose I'll just have to kill you next time I see you."

Smoke laughed out loud and winked at Cal as they spurred their horses on up the trail toward Payday.

"You think they'll follow us and give us any more trouble?" Cal asked.

Smoke shook his head. "No. They've had enough for one day, and the big one I put down is gonna have trouble walking for at least a day or two, so I don't think they'll come after us."

Cal took Bubba's pistol out of his belt and pitched it onto the ground. "I almost wish they would," he said, glancing back at Pearlie. "I'm so mad I'd kind'a like to take it out on somebody."

Smoke nodded, knowing the feeling. "Yeah, but let's get Pearlie to the doc first, and we can worry about that other thing later."

5

Smoke shook his head sadly as he and Cal passed a hand-lettered sign that read PAYDAY. The place could barely be called a town in his estimation. It consisted mainly of one long wide road with two smaller ones branching off it at right angles. There were very few buildings that were made entirely of wood and stone, most being large tents with a wooden front or perhaps at best a four-cornered open roof over the tent.

There were, however, some homes that were built in a more suitable manner, but they were few and far between.

It seemed every other tent along the main street was a saloon or gambling establishment, with only one general store and an assay office to break up the monotony of the bars. As he and Cal rode down the main street, they drew the stares of several of the townsfolk, who Smoke also considered unprepossessing. Most of the men in the town were hard-looking miner types wearing the canvas trousers made famous by Levi Strauss in recent years, and there were precious few females other than the occasional dance hall Gerties that walked up and down the street advertising their wares by wearing elaborately frilly, low-cut gowns and makeup caked so thick on their faces you could hardly tell their race, much less whether they were in fact pretty or not.

When Smoke passed the building that had a sign on it

reading SHERIFF'S OFFICE and the one next to it that read BANK, he knew they wouldn't likely find much help for Pearlie here.

"Jiminy, Smoke," Cal said, glancing from side to side as they walked their horses through town, "I don't see no signs for doctor or anything like that."

"This place is hardly more than a glorified mining camp, Cal. I only hope Chief Gray Wolf was right about there being a medical person here."

Smoke reined his horse in front of the sheriff's office and got out of the saddle. He walked up to the door to see if the sheriff could direct him to a doctor, but found the door locked.

"Sheriff ain't here, mister," an older man with a full gray beard said from his seat on a rough-hewn bench on the small boardwalk in front of the office.

"You have any idea when he'll be back?" Smoke asked.

The man got up from his bench and ambled over to stand next to the travois with Pearlie on it. He leaned to the side and spit a stream of brown tobacco juice into the dirt, and then he sleeved off the part that had run down his chin with his arm.

"Nope, can't say as I do."

Smoke sighed, and the man asked, "What's wrong with your friend? He shot or somethin'?"

"No," Cal said, swinging his leg over his saddle and jumping to the ground. "He's been snakebit real bad. We came here lookin' for a doctor."

The man nodded. "Nearest real doctor's up in Pueblo, 'bout fifty miles from here."

"Damn," Smoke said, glancing at Pearlie and knowing he'd never survive a fifty-mile trip on the travois.

"But," the old man continued, scratching his unruly hair, "we do got us a dentist, an' he takes care of most of our doctorin' when we need it . . . an' when he's sober."

Smoke whirled around and had to restrain himself from choking the old man for taking so long to tell them that. "Well, where is the dentist?" he asked.

"You take that first cross street there an' go left. His

office is 'bout a hundred yards down that road on the left.
You can't hardly miss it since it's a regular two-story house
an' he's got a big ol' barber pole in front painted red and
white."

Smoke and Cal swung up into their saddles and started
off toward the dentist's office. Even though it was just past
noon, Smoke hoped the man was sober, for if he wasn't
and it cost Pearlie his life, Smoke knew he'd make the
man regret his thirst for alcohol.

Ten minutes later, Smoke was knocking on the office
door. A man with red, bleary eyes and a two-day growth of
beard answered the door. "Yeah, whatta you want?" he
growled, his eyes squinting at the brightness of the sunlight.

"We have a man who's been badly snakebit," Smoke
said, turning and pointing at Pearlie, who lay as still as
death on the travois.

The dentist's eyes opened wider and he craned his neck
to peer around Smoke at Pearlie. "You cut it and suck the
poison out?" he asked.

"He had two bites," Smoke answered. "I cut and sucked
the one on his leg, but the one on his neck was right over
a blood vessel and I didn't dare cut into it."

"Neck bite, huh?" the man said, coming out into the
street and pulling his braces up over his shoulders as he
bent to take a closer look at Pearlie. "When did he get bit
and which one did he get first?"

"Yesterday, about noon, and he got the leg first," Cal
said, moving to squat next to Pearlie and wipe the sweat
off his forehead with his bandanna.

The dentist nodded and straightened up, yawning.
"Well, that's lucky," he said. "And it's a good sign he's
managed to stay alive this long."

"Can you help him?" Smoke asked. His voice was level
but his eyes were full of concern.

The dentist shrugged. "I don't rightly know, mister. I'll
take him in and feed him plenty of beef broth and try to

keep his wounds from festerin' up too bad, but that's about all I can do here."

He turned and opened the door all the way. "Bring him in here. I got a room where I keep patients who are recoverin' from one thing or another."

Smoke and Cal picked Pearlie up and carried him into the dentist's office, and on back into a room at the rear of the house that contained three double beds, each with a basin and towel on a nightstand next to it.

There weren't any other patients present, so Smoke picked the nearest bed and they laid Pearlie down on it gently. Smoke stripped Pearlie's pants and shirt off and pulled up the leg of his long underwear so the dentist could see the leg wound.

"My name's Hezekiah Bentley," the dentist said as he bent down and gently probed around the red, angry-looking bite mark on Pearlie's leg with his fingers. The edges of the wound were dark blue and there seemed to be a small crater in between the twin punctures.

"I'm Smoke Jensen and this is Calvin Woods," Smoke said. "The patient's name is Pearlie."

Bentley twisted his head to stare up at Smoke. "You *the* Smoke Jensen?" he asked.

Smoke gave a half shrug. "I don't know of any others. Why? Does it make a difference?"

Bentley shook his head and turned his attention back to Pearlie, now examining the neck wound, which was also starting to shed a little puss and was as colorful as the leg bite.

"Nope. It's just that we don't get too many visitors around here, an' the ones we do get are miners, not famous gunfighters."

"I'm no gunfighter," Smoke said. "I gave that up years ago. I'm just a rancher now."

"Uh-huh," Bentley grunted, as if he didn't believe a word of it.

Smoke sighed. Why wouldn't people let him forget his past and get on with his new life with Sally?

"Well, Dr. Bentley, what do you suggest we do?" Smoke asked.

Bentley went over to a nearby basin and washed his hands. As he was drying them, he said, "Like I said, leave Pearlie here with me for a while. I'll keep his wounds clean and try to get some nourishment into him. If he wakes up and is in pain, I'll give him some laudanum, but that's about all I can do."

"You need one of us to stay here and help you take care of him?"

"Naw," Bentley said, shaking his head. "I've got me a housekeeper who helps me out when someone's staying here, an' I expect you and your young friend would only be in the way anyhow."

"Well, Cal and I have a string of Palouse studs outside of town that we need to take back to my ranch in Big Rock, so if you think you won't be needing us, we'll do that and then come right back here."

He dug in his pocket, pulled out a wad of greenback bills, and put them in the dentist's hand. "This ought to take care of his board and medical care till we get back."

Bentley's eyes widened at the amount of money Smoke had given him. "Hell, Mr. Jensen, this'll take care of him for a year."

Smoke leaned down close to the man, and his eyes were flat and hard. "I don't plan on him being here a year, Dr. Bentley, but he'd damn sure better get your full attention while he is here, and he'd better be a whole lot better when we get back. You understand me?"

Bentley's face was suddenly covered with a fine sheen of sweat and he nodded his head vigorously. "Yes, sir, Mr. Jensen. You can count on me to do my best for the young man."

Smoke took a piece of paper and the stub of a pencil out of his pocket and wrote something on the paper. "Here's my name and the name of my town. I can be contacted by telegraph in care of Sheriff Monte Carson at that location." He paused. "You do have a telegraph here, don't you?"

"Oh, yes, sir. We just got it put in this last spring."

"Good, then I'll expect you to keep me informed, and if the news is good, there'll be plenty more of those greenbacks for you when I come back."

"That really ain't necessary, Mr. Jensen. I took an oath when I became a dentist an' I always take good care of my patients, payin' or otherwise."

"I wasn't trying to insult you, Doctor, but I expect to pay people who work for me, and I've always found that the better the pay, the better the job done."

Bentley grinned. "Well, now, I didn't say I wasn't gonna take the money, Mr. Jensen. I just wanted you to know I'll do my dead-level best to keep your friend alive."

Smoke returned Bentley's grin. "I know you will, Dr. Bentley, and I'll expect nothing less."

Smoke turned to go, and then he hesitated and turned back around. "Oh, one more thing, Doc," Smoke said, and his grin was gone and his face was dead serious.

"Yes, Mr. Jensen?"

"I've heard tell that you have a large thirst and you tend to slake it at the nearest saloon."

Bentley's face colored and he started to protest, "Why, that's outrageous. . . ."

Smoke held up his hand. "Now, Doc, I don't care what you do when you don't have a patient under your care, but as long as my friend is here, you will stay sober . . . or you will be dead. Do I make myself clear?"

"But . . . uh . . ." Bentley began, and Smoke stopped him with a shake of his finger. "Those are really your only two choices, Dr. Bentley," Smoke said firmly. "Sober and alive, drunk and dead—do you understand?"

"Yes . . . yes, sir," Bentley said, his eyes dropping and unable to meet Smoke's stare.

"Good. Then we'll see you when we get back, and Doc, we'd better see both you *and* Pearlie."

"But, Mr. Jensen," Bentley protested, "I've already told you, your friend is powerful sick. He could die at any time, whether I'm drunk or sober!"

"Well, if he does die, you'd better be damned sure

you're sober when it happens and you'd better stay that way until I get back here or there will be hell to pay," Smoke admonished, and he turned and walked out of the room.

The doctor took a handkerchief out of his pocket, wiped the fear-sweat off his forehead, and then bent over Pearlie and began to check his vital signs. He'd never been more concerned about a patient's welfare in his entire professional career.

One good thing, he thought. He wasn't a bit thirsty!

6

Smoke and Cal got on their horses and rode out of town to the south to meet up with Running Deer and the braves holding their studs for them. Cal, who was leading Pearlie's horse on a dally rope, slowed his horse when they came abreast of a large wooden barn with a sign on it that read LIVERY STABLE and called to Smoke, "Hold on, Smoke. I'm gonna leave Pearlie's hoss here just in case he gets well and wants to go for a ride 'fore we get back."

Smoke smiled and nodded, though he thought it would be a miracle if Pearlie got well that fast. "Sure thing, Cal. Heck, he may even beat us home since we're gonna be herding those broncs."

Cal tied his horse to a hitching rail out front and walked Pearlie's mount into the large barn. He was out ten minutes later and was smiling. "I told the boy to let the doc know he was holdin' Pearlie's hoss just in case," he said as he climbed up into the saddle. "I also told the boy to exercise him every day and to make sure he gets plenty of grain."

Smoke grinned. "You tell that boy how Cold got his name?" Smoke asked, thinking if he hadn't, the livery boy was going to get the ride of his life the first time he climbed up on Pearlie's horse in the morning.

Cal nodded, returning the grin. "Yep, only I maybe

didn't tell him just how little Cold likes to be ridden in the morning. I figure he'll find out soon enough."

As they rode out of town, Smoke had an idea. "Say, Cal, it's less than half as far to Pueblo as it is back to Big Rock, isn't it?"

Cal pursed his lips, thinking on it for a moment, and then he nodded. "Yep, I reckon that's about right. Why?"

"Well," Smoke said, "it'd take us a couple of weeks or more to drive those ponies all the way to Big Rock and then get back here to see how Pearlie's doing."

"Uh-huh," Cal said. "And that's if we don't take a day or two to let our butts recover from all that time in the saddle."

"Why don't we take them on up to Pueblo instead? We can put them on a railroad car and have them taken to Big Rock. I can wire Monte Carson to have Louis or someone else meet the train and take the horses out to the ranch." He grinned. "That'd save us a passel of time and we wouldn't be so worn out from the long trip."

"Yeah, an' we'd be able to get back here twice as fast to watch over Pearlie too."

"Good, then that's what we'll do."

"Hey, Smoke," Cal said, looking back over his shoulder at the town. "I seen some train tracks outside of town here an' a small station platform. Why don't we just load the hosses here? That'd save us the ride to Pueblo."

Smoke shook his head. "I considered that, Cal, but this is just a quick stop on the train's way. They won't allow loading of livestock at such a place, just people."

As they spurred their horses forward, Cal said, "Whew, Smoke. I'm sure glad you thought of that. I really wasn't lookin' forward to spending the next three or four weeks living in this here saddle."

Smoke laughed. "Me neither, Cal, me neither. These old bones just won't take that kind of punishment anymore."

Cal laughed, though he knew that even though Smoke had over twenty years on him, he could ride Cal into the dirt any time he wanted to.

* * *

When they met up with Running Deer, the young brave's first question was how was Pearlie doing. Smoke shook his head and shrugged. "The doctor thinks it is a good sign that he lived this long after the bite. He's hopeful Pearlie will wake up soon, but he really doesn't know what's going to happen over the next few days."

As Running Deer handed the dally ropes to Cal and Smoke, he grew serious. "I will have our tribe do a healing dance around the campfires every night until the Great Spirit tells us that our new friend is well."

"Thank you, Running Deer. I'm sure that the Great Spirit will hear and listen to your people, for the Nez Percé are much favored by the Great Spirit."

Running Deer gave a half smile. "That is true, Mountain Man." He glanced around at the mountain peaks on all sides of them. "For look at the wonderful home He has given us to live in."

"And tell Chief Gray Wolf that when this is over, before we head back home, I will see that another side of beef is delivered to your village in thanks for all that you have done to help us."

Running Deer's smile widened. "I would like to say there is no need, Mountain Man, but my belly will not let me deny it the chance to once again feast on something other than venison or bear or dog."

Smoke gave the young brave a salute and turned his horse's head around to the northwest to head for Pueblo and the railroad yards.

As they rode away, Cal looked at Smoke and grimaced. "Did he say they ate bear and dog?"

Smoke nodded.

"I remember last year when you took Pearlie and me up into the High Lonesome to teach us something about living out in the wild and you fixed us bear one night."

"Uh-huh," Smoke said.

"I never ate anything that tasted worse in my entire born days," Cal said, shuddering as he remembered the pungent, wild taste of the bear meat. "However, I'd have to say I'd rather have two helpings of bear than one helping of dog."

"Oh, bear isn't so bad if all you got to compare it to is venison," Smoke said, his eyes far away as he remembered his days in the mountains with Preacher. He even remembered a couple of times during extended winter storms when he would've given all he owned to even have dog to eat.

"That's the problem," Cal said. "I ain't never been hungry enough to eat bear and I hope to never let myself get that hard up."

Smoke laughed. "Hell, Cal, when I was a little younger than you and I was traipsing around these mountains with Preacher, he made me eat things that would make a billy goat puke."

"Why'd you put up with that?" Cal asked.

Smoke's face sobered as he thought back to just how difficult things could get in the mountains in the dead of winter. "Sometimes we'd have blizzards that would last for ten days to two weeks and that would leave the snow so deep a horse couldn't walk in it. We'd put on our snowshoes and go and look for food. If we were lucky, we'd find a rabbit or two, but usually all we'd be able to dig outta the snow would be field mice or maybe muskrats if we got really lucky."

"You ate muskrats and mice?" Cal asked, a look of horror on his face.

Smoke smiled grimly, remembering. "I said if we were *lucky* that's what we'd find. If we weren't lucky, many times we survived by chewing on bark and leaves, and one really bad winter we ended up eating one of our pack mules."

Cal swallowed and turned pale. "I wish you hadn't told me that, Smoke."

"Hey, Cal, mule isn't all that bad. In fact, Indians consider mule meat a delicacy. It's sweeter than beef and not nearly as tough as horse."

"That's enough!" Cal called, "I don't want to hear any more about it."

"Sure, after all," Smoke said with a smile, "I wouldn't want to spoil your appetite."

"Speaking of that, isn't it about time we stopped for lunch?"

Smoke reached into his saddlebag and pulled out a paper sack with grease stains on it. He pulled out a long, stringy piece of meat and tossed it to Cal.

"I think we should just stop once a day, for supper, so we can make better time. For our nooning, we'll have to get by on this jerky I got from the Indians."

Cal took a bite of the meat and began to chew, a sour look on his face. "If there's anything that tastes worse than beef jerky, it's venison jerky," he moaned.

"I know, it doesn't go down very well, but not stopping for lunch will save us a day and a half and get us back to Pearlie that much sooner."

"In that case, I guess I'll just have to make the best of it," Cal said.

"I'll tell you what, Cal. Since you're being so brave about all this, tonight I'll cook up some extra biscuits and a little more beef than we need for supper. We can put the beef between two halves of the biscuits and have that for lunch tomorrow."

Cal grinned around the lump of jerky in his cheek. "How about breakfast? Are we gonna do without that too?"

"Naw, we'll just get up a little earlier, that's all. After all, the horses can't go all day without stopping to graze and water themselves."

"Then when we fix breakfast, maybe we can cook a couple of extra pieces of fatback too. That'd go mighty good with biscuits later in the day."

"You get up early and get the fire going, and I'll take care of fixing us something to last until supper," Smoke said, all the talk of food making his stomach growl.

"That's a deal," Cal said, and then he winced and grabbed his jaw. "Ow, I think I almost broke a tooth on this here jerky."

"Want me to see if I can find us some field mice or nice juicy muskrats to chew on instead?" Smoke asked, a glint in his eye.

"No . . . no, that's all right," Cal said hastily. "I'll just chew this jerky a little more carefully from now on."

7

Sheriff Buck Tolliver rode down the main street of Payday slowly, so everyone could see he was leading two horses behind him, each with a man folded facedown across the saddle.

He wanted the townspeople to see just how tough he was so they'd never even think of going against him, no matter what the provocation. As he rode, he nodded solemnly to the citizens who stared at the bodies riding silently behind him. One nice thing about being sheriff, even if it was in a little shitty town like Payday, he thought, was that few men had the temerity to question you about anything you did—even if it involved killing two men.

He planned to tell anyone who asked that the two men were claim-jumpers and that he'd had to kill them to protect the men whose claim they were trying to steal, but that was just a lie he'd cooked up on the way back to town.

In truth, the men were two miners he'd come upon who were dancing around a campfire just outside of their mine. Tolliver had ridden up and dismounted, a wide smile on his face. When they heard him, the men stopped dancing and pulled pistols and pointed them at Tolliver, until he opened his coat and showed them the star on his chest. The two relaxed and even kidded each other about being so scared about somebody finding out about their good fortune. Tolliver continued to smile and nod as the men offered him a drink from their bottle of whiskey, which was already almost half empty.

He accepted the bottle and took a deep swig, sleeving off his mouth as he asked, "What's the big occasion, gents?"

"We done struck the biggest vein of gold you ever seen, Sheriff," one of the men said, slapping Tolliver on the shoulder.

"We're gonna be the richest doggone miners in this here territory," the other one added, doing a little jig and turning in a circle while trying to drink from his bottle, but spilling more than he swallowed.

"Is that so?" Tolliver asked.

"Damn right!" the first man said.

Tolliver smiled gently, shaking his head. "I sure hope you've already filed on this land with the territorial land office over in Pueblo," he said.

Both men suddenly stopped their dancing. "Whatta you mean by that, Sheriff?" one asked.

"Well, if you haven't filed a claim and you let some scoundrel know you've hit a big vein, someone else is liable to rush on over to Pueblo and file on your mine and take it away from you."

"Damn, Joe, he's right," the man said, suddenly as sober as a judge.

"Don't tell me you haven't filed on this land yet," Tolliver said, as if he couldn't believe it.

"Well, not exactly," Joe said. "We filed on some land all right, but it was about a mile over to the east. When that place didn't produce nothin', we come on over here and started digging without botherin' to go to town and file."

"Yeah," the first man said, a worried look on his face. "We figured if we struck somethin' worthwhile, we'd have plenty of time to file on it later."

"Well, now, you see, gentlemen, that was your first mistake," Tolliver said, handing the bottle back to the man standing next to him.

"Our *first* mistake?" Joe asked from over near the campfire.

"Yeah," Tolliver answered, drawing his pistol. "Your second mistake was telling me about your gold strike," he added, firing point-blank into one man's chest and then taking careful aim as Joe turned and began to run toward the mine.

He slowly squeezed off two more shots, grinning as Joe was flung forward to fall and skid in the gravel on his face.

Without bothering to check and see if they were still alive, Buck moved to his horse, took some stakes with his name carved in them, and walked around the mine, driving the stakes into all four corners of the property. Then he looked around and wrote down some distinguishing landmarks to add to his quick claim when he got back to town.

On the way around the property, he noticed that the bottle of whiskey had landed right side up in the snow next to where the first man he'd shot had fallen. Not one to waste good whiskey, or bad for that matter, Tolliver bent and picked up the bottle. He raised it and said, "To your very good luck, gentlemen." Then he took a deep swig and gasped. It was good whiskey and tasted just fine.

Once he was finished, he went into the men's cabin, searched for and found four small canvas bags of gold dust and flakes they'd mined from the mine and small stream nearby, and stuck them in his saddlebags.

With a sigh, he saddled their horses and tied them together with a dally rope. Once that was done, he heaved the two bodies up on the horses and started his long ride back to Payday, thinking what a profitable day it'd turned out to be.

And the best part of it was, this fortune he wouldn't have to share with his partners in crime. It was to be his and his alone. None of his partners would ever have to know about this mine and how he'd obtained it. It would be his little secret, his and his banker's, of course.

He tied his horse up in front of the tent housing the local undertaker and stuck his head inside, interrupting

Jonas Slackmeyer as he was planing the edges of a coffin down smooth and round.

"Hey, Jonas," Tolliver called, to get the man's attention.

Slackmeyer straightened up and wiped sawdust from his forehead with a dirty rag in his back pocket. "Yes, Sheriff?" he answered.

"I got you two new customers out here on a pair of horses. Give 'em the cheapest coffin you got and bury 'em over in boot hill."

"And who will pay for their burial, Sheriff? The city?" Slackmeyer asked.

"Yeah," Tolliver said, flipping him a two-dollar gold piece. He figured it was the least he could do. "And when you're done, take the horses over to the livery and tell the boy to take 'em out to my spread and add 'em to my remuda."

"What about the saddles and such?"

Tolliver thought about it. The saddles were pretty much junk and not worth bothering with. Besides, he had plenty of saddles and tack already. Any more would just clutter up his barn. "You can sell 'em and keep whatever you get for your trouble," he said, figuring giving Slackmeyer a little bit extra would encourage him to keep his mouth shut about one of the men being shot in the back.

Slackmeyer grinned, dipping his head. "Why, thank you, Sheriff. I'll get right on it."

"And Jonas," he added, his face stern.

"Yes, Sheriff?"

"This is city business, so there's no need speaking about it to any of the townspeople. Understand?"

Slackmeyer grinned. "Of course, Sheriff, you can count on my discretion."

As Tolliver left, Slackmeyer took a deep breath. The man scared him half to death. If the townspeople knew half the shit about their sheriff that *he* did, they wouldn't sleep a wink at night.

Tolliver rode his horse to the livery to have the boy brush him down and give him some grain and to tell the boy Slackmeyer would be bringing a couple of horses for his remuda.

As he dismounted, he saw a strange horse in one of the stables. It was a striking animal—gray with a series of spots on its rump, and it was heavily muscled and sleek-looking as it stood munching on a bucket of oats in its stall.

Tolliver gave the boy his message, and then he nonchalantly asked who the new bronc belonged to.

"Oh, that hoss belongs to some man over at the doc's office," the boy said. "His friends left him here in case he got well enough to ride 'fore they get back."

"What do you mean before they get back?" Tolliver asked.

"They had a herd of hosses to take home, an' then they was gonna come back here to see how their friend was doin'," the boy answered as he unbuckled Tolliver's saddle and pulled it off his horse with a grunt.

"What were these men's names?"

The boy shrugged. "I don't know. They told me the horse belongs to a man named Pearlie, but they didn't give me their names."

Tolliver nodded and started to walk off.

"I'll tell you one thing, though," the boy added as he grabbed a brush and began to brush Tolliver's horse.

Tolliver stopped and looked back over his shoulder. "What's that?"

"The man riding with the one who gave me the money to pay for the hoss's care is one of the biggest men I ever seen, an' he was dressed all in buckskins like some of those ol' mountain men who used to come through here."

Tolliver felt a chill go down his spine, and he turned and walked back to the livery boy.

"What did this hombre look like?" he asked, his voice low and hard.

The boy looked up, alarmed at the change in Tolliver's face from friendly to harsh. "Uh, I dunno."

Tolliver grabbed the boy by the front of his shirt. "Think, damnit!"

"Uh, he was 'bout six feet or a little more, wide shoulders, lots of muscles, and he had yeller-gray hair and no beard nor mustache."

Tolliver shuddered. "Anything else?" he croaked through a suddenly dry throat, letting go of the boy's shirt. "Was he heeled?"

The boy stepped back. "Yeah, now that you mention it. He carried two pistols. The one on his left hip was butt-first and the one on his right was tied down low on his thigh. He also had a big knife stuck in the back of his belt." The boy managed a halfhearted grin, still scared at the way Tolliver was acting. "He looked about as dangerous a man as I've ever seen, an' I sure as hell wouldn't want to do anything to make him mad at me."

"Damn it to hell," Tolliver muttered, whirling around and walking as fast as he could without actually running toward the doctor's office.

"It can't be," he said to himself, wiping at his brow to remove the sweat that suddenly broke out on his forehead. "It just can't be after all these years!"

His heart was beating so fast he thought it was going to jump out of his chest before he got to the doc's house.

Suddenly, he had a fearsome thought. He hadn't asked the livery boy how long ago the man had been there. Maybe he was still in town right now.

Tolliver slowed and let his hand drop to hang next to his pistol butt. *Hell, he might even have seen me ride up and be waiting for me this very instant.*

As he walked, Tolliver turned around and around, looking on all sides for the mysterious man dressed all in buckskins and carrying two pistols and a knife on his belt.

Jesus, he told himself, take ahold of yourself, Buck. It's been more'n twenty years since he's seen you. He couldn't possibly recognize you after all this time.

Still, he couldn't shake the bone-deep fear that coursed through his body at the very thought that Smoke Jensen might be in his town.

Because he knew if that was the case, one of them wasn't going to leave the town alive. . . .

8

Buck Tolliver's heart had slowed down a little by the time he got to Doc Bentley's office without seeing Smoke Jensen anywhere around. He couldn't imagine what circumstances might have occurred that would bring the famous gunfighter to his little town out in the middle of nowhere, but if the man the boy in the livery was describing was Jensen, then Tolliver's prayers of more than twenty years had finally been answered.

Just thinking about what he was going to do to Jensen if he was in town caused his heart to hammer again and a fine sheen of sweat to break out on his forehead. He found himself clenching his teeth so hard his jaw actually creaked.

When he raised his hand to open the doc's door, he noticed his hand was shaking. This just won't do, he thought. Forcing himself to calm down, he paused and took a few deep breaths. It wouldn't do to let the doc see just how interested he was in the identity of the man in buckskins who'd visited while he was gone. No. That would mess up any plans Tolliver had for the man he hated more than anyone else in the world.

Finally, he was able to control himself enough to be able to talk to Bentley without arousing the man's suspicions, so he opened the door and strolled inside as if he didn't have a thing on his mind.

Bentley was straddling a chair in his main examining room, his elbows out and his foot up on a footrest attached to the chair. A pair of trousers could be seen moving back and forth between the doc's legs, and Tolliver heard Bentley saying, "Just hold on a minute there, Clem. I've almost got the son of a bitch."

The patient addressed as Clem jumped and moaned loudly as Bentley's right arm flew back, and Tolliver could see his hand was holding a pair of dental forceps with a bloody tooth in them.

"There," Bentley said, climbing down off the poor patient, who was sweating profusely and whose face was pale and drawn-looking. He had a river of bloody drool running down his chin as if he'd been poked in the mouth.

Clem gently put his hand up to his swollen jaw and probed the tissues, a look of relief finally appearing on his face. "Damn, Doc, I thought you'd never get the bugger out. It's been painin' me for nigh on two weeks now."

Bentley held up the tooth and looked at it. "Yep, this is what was causing you all that pain, Clem. See how it's all black and rotted out inside." He shook his head. "You been eating too many of those peppermint sticks over at the general store and it's rotting all your teeth out. If you don't cut back, Clem, you're going to be seeing me again real soon to have some more work done."

Clem shook his head and climbed unsteadily out of the dental chair. "No, thanks, Doc. I'd just as soon not look if'n you don't mind, and I promise to give up peppermint for good. What do I owe you?"

Bentley pursed his lips as he dropped the tooth in a nearby wastebasket. "Oh, I suspect ten cents ought to about do it," he said, and he handed Clem a small piece of gauze and motioned for him to wipe the blood off his chin.

Clem took the cloth and wiped his mouth and threw the pad in the wastebasket without looking at the bloodstains on it. Then he dug in his pocket and pulled out a coin. "Here you go, Doc, an' much obliged."

Clem grabbed his hat off a peg and turned toward the

door, seeing Tolliver for the first time. "Oh, howdy, Buck," he said, nodding as he passed on his way out the door.

"Howdy, Clem," Tolliver said, touching the brim of his hat in greeting. He could hardly restrain himself. He was busting at the gut to ask the doc about the man in buckskins and everybody wanted to jaw all morning.

"Good morning, Sheriff," Bentley said, moving to wash his hands in a basin on a small stand against the wall. As he turned around, still wiping them on a towel, he asked, "You having some tooth problems this morning, Buck?"

"No, thank the Lord," Tolliver said with a small shiver. He remembered the last time he'd had to have Bentley pull a tooth. The doc was lucky Tolliver had taken his gun off before climbing in his chair or Bentley would most probably have been shot during the extraction.

He looked more closely at the doc now, thinking something was different. The doc was clean-shaven for one thing, and his eyes were unnaturally clear for this time of day. Usually by now he would've had a few shots of whiskey and would be already slurring his words. As he stared at the man, Tolliver noticed his hands had a fine tremor, but not the heavy shaking too much alcohol caused.

"Something the matter, Doc?" Tolliver asked.

"Why . . . uh . . . no, Buck. It's just that I've decided to give up drinking for a while," he answered with a sickly grin. "I think the alcohol was impairing my treatment of my patients and so I'm trying to stay away from it." He shook his head and looked down at his trembling hands. "It is tough, but I reckon after a couple of days I won't even notice it."

Tolliver nodded as he wondered what in the world could make a drunk give up booze.

"That's mighty nice, Doc," Tolliver said. "I'm sure your patients will appreciate the fact that you're sober when you work on them, but why did you suddenly decide to give it up now?"

"Oh, I just thought it was about time. Now, you said you didn't have any tooth problems, Buck?" Bentley asked, wondering why the sheriff was here if he didn't have a medical problem.

"I was just over at the livery and the boy there said you had a new patient. Someone from out of town." Tolliver faked a yawn and covered his mouth with his hand as he added, "So I thought I'd just mosey on over and see what the story was." He smiled disarmingly. "You know how I like to keep up with any newcomers to town, especially if they suddenly come up in need of medical attention."

Bentley smiled back and threw the towel on a pile of similarly stained ones on the floor. "Oh, it's nothing for you to be concerned with, Buck. The man wasn't shot or stabbed nor nothing like that."

Tolliver didn't speak, just raised his eyebrows, knowing the doc wouldn't be able to resist telling him what was ailing his patient.

"Man got snakebit out in the foothills of the mountains. Hit him twice, once in the leg and once in the neck." Bentley shook his head as he walked over to a coffeepot steaming on a potbellied stove in the corner. "Wonder the poor man is still alive."

He picked up the pot and glanced at Tolliver. "You want a cup of coffee, Sheriff?"

Tolliver didn't, having had several cups already that morning, but he knew if he didn't take a cup he wouldn't have an excuse to stand around jawing with the dentist, so he nodded his head and took off his hat.

He hung his hat up on the peg by the door and accepted a cup of steaming coffee from Bentley. "So, how's the gent doing?" he asked.

Bentley took his own cup and sat down at the table in his dining room, motioning Tolliver to join him. "Can't rightly tell, Buck. He's been in a coma ever since he arrived. Hasn't stirred one little bit, 'cepting to moan in his sleep a couple of times."

"You got a name for this feller?"

Bentley smiled at Tolliver over the rim of his cup. "Why, Buck? You think he might be on one of them wanted posters you got hung up in your office?"

Tolliver shrugged. "Never can tell, Doc. Being on the run or planning on digging up some gold are about the only two reasons anybody'd want to come all the way up here in the mountains to Payday. Anyway, it's my job to check out any newcomers to the town."

"Well, you can rest easy," Bentley said, leaning back in his chair. "This man's a cowboy, up here herding some horses he and his friends bought from the Nez Percé."

Tolliver took a deep breath and had to restrain himself from reaching across the table and strangling the doc until he answered his questions and told him what he really came here to find out. "I didn't ask you what he did for a living, Doc," Tolliver snapped, a little more angrily than he meant to. Once again, he took a deep breath and tried to calm himself, knowing the doc would give him the information he needed sooner or later if he could just keep from aggravating the man. In a more gentle, conversational voice, he added, "I asked if you knew his name so I can wire it over to Pueblo an' see if he's wanted or anything like that."

Bentley's eyes narrowed, and Tolliver realized he had made him suspicious with his earlier outburst, so he forced himself to relax and lean back with a disinterested look on his face. "But it's all right if you don't know," he said, as if it didn't matter in the least to him.

"His name's Pearlie," Bentley said. "Don't know his last name."

"Did the men who brung him in give you their names?" Tolliver asked, still trying to mask his excitement and make the question seem ordinary.

Bentley grinned. "Yeah, an' you'll never guess who it was, Buck. First time I know of anyone famous ever set foot in Payday, leastways since I've been here anyway."

Tolliver sighed heavily, trying to keep his temper under control. "I didn't come here to play guessing games, Doc," he said as evenly as he could.

"Fellow who brought Pearlie in was named Jensen," Bentley said, his eyebrows raised to see if Tolliver would make the connection.

"Would that be Smoke Jensen?" Tolliver asked, hoping the doc couldn't hear his thudding heart.

Bentley slapped his hand on his thigh and grinned. "Yes, it was Smoke Jensen. Can you believe it, Buck? One of the most famous gunfighters in history, right up there with Wyatt Earp and Bat Masterson, right here in my little office bringing his friend in to see me for treatment."

"I know of him," Tolliver said, keeping his voice flat. "You don't have to tell me how famous he is. Fact is, Doc, he *was* a famous gunfighter a few years back, but that was a long time ago, and I haven't heard much about him in the last four or five years."

Bentley's eyes widened. "Buck, you don't think he's wanted by the law anywhere, do you?" he asked. "I didn't think of that when he told me who he was or I would've let you know he was here."

Tolliver shrugged. "Not to my knowledge, but I might just wire Pueblo or Denver an' see if there's any warrants out on him just to be sure. I do know that in his day it was said he killed over two hundred men in various gunfights."

Bentley nodded slowly, his eyes far away as he thought back to the day his patient had arrived. "You know something funny, Buck? I remember the day Jensen and another man brought his friend in to see me. Both Jensen and the young man with him had their guns tied down low on their thighs in the manner of gunslicks. I didn't think anything of it at the time, but it isn't the usual way cowboys around here wear their irons." He gave a short laugh. "Hell, it wasn't till he told me his name I even thought much about it."

Tolliver drained his cup and stood up. "Mind if I take a look at this patient of yours, Doc? Just in case I got a picture of him over at the office."

"No, you go right ahead, Buck," Bentley said, also getting to his feet.

Tolliver went into the room where Bentley kept his bedridden patients and stood next to the bed with Pearlie in it. He stared down at him as he slept and realized he didn't recognize him. The man who'd been with Jensen the last time Tolliver had seen him had been elderly twenty years ago and was most likely dead by now. This man was much too young to have ridden with Jensen when he was up in the mountains, or even later when he was on the owl hoot trail.

"All right, Doc," Tolliver said, putting his hat on and walking toward the door. "I'll let you know if I find out anything about Jensen or his traveling companions."

"You do that, Sheriff, an' I'll be sure and call you if I hear back from them or if this Pearlie fellow wakes up." He paused and looked worried. "At least I hope he's gonna wake up. I sure as hell don't want to lose a friend of a man like Jensen if he's as dangerous as you say he is."

"Oh, I suspect he's still dangerous, Doc, even though he's getting up in age for a gunfighter."

Tolliver stopped and suddenly realized why the doc had quit the drinking. He narrowed his eyes and stared at him. "That man in there being Jensen's friend wouldn't have anything to do with why you stopped drinking, would it, Doc?"

Bentley's eyes dropped and he hung his head. "Well, Jensen may have mentioned it'd be better if I stayed sober until Pearlie got well, but I was planning on doing it sooner or later anyway, Buck."

"Did he threaten you, Doc?" Tolliver asked, hoping the man would swear out a complaint against Jensen. It would give him an excuse to draw down on him and if he killed him, no one could ever say he wasn't just doing his duty.

"Uh, why, no, Buck. Jensen didn't threaten me. He just reminded me it'd be better for me not to drink while taking care of a patient."

"All right, Doc," Tolliver said, disappointed, "but if that boy in there comes awake, you give me a holler, 'cause I may just have a few questions to ask Mr. Pearlie."

9

Tolliver was so engrossed in his thoughts when he left Doctor Bentley's office that he stepped out into the street right in front of an ore wagon.

The driver jerked the reins to the right and kicked his foot down on the wagon wheel brake, yelling at Tolliver to watch out as he did so.

The screeching of the metal brake pad got Tolliver's attention and saved his life. He glanced up and dove back, hitting the ground and rolling to the side so that the wheels of the wagon and the hooves of the big draft horses missed him by mere inches.

Bentley, standing at the window of his office, shook his head and scratched his chin. He'd known there was something strange about the way the sheriff had been so interested in his patient and in Smoke Jensen. Tolliver'd never before come asking about newcomers the doc had treated. He spent a moment wondering why before turning and walking toward the room where Pearlie lay.

Maybe when the young man woke up, if he woke up, he could shed some light on why Buck was so interested in him and his friends.

Bentley stood over Pearlie's bed for a moment looking down at the wan, pale face. One thing was for sure—this young man was no hardened criminal. The doc could tell that just by looking at his hands. They were callused and hardened the way only hard cowboy work could make them, and his fingernails had dirt under them. Bentley had seen his share of gunnies and hard cases in his younger days when he practiced in Denver, and not one of them had hands like these.

He shook his head and took a washrag out of the basin next to the bed, wrung it out, and gently wiped the sweat off Pearlie's forehead. Nope. Whatever the sheriff wanted with this boy and his friends, it sure as hell wasn't due to his job—it was personal.

Of course, if there was one thing Bentley had learned in his years of practicing medicine out West, it was that personal business was just that—personal. And it was always better to stay the hell out of other people's personal business, lest you be caught up in it more than you'd like. Yep, he thought, he'd just keep his mouth shut, treat his patient, and stay away from the booze. If he did all that, he might just come out of this with his skin intact.

That is, if Pearlie survived. Everything depended on that fact first and foremost.

Tolliver got up and dusted himself off, glaring at the wagon driver, who was staring back at him like he was crazy. The driver didn't dare say anything, though, for everyone in town knew all about Buck Tolliver's hair-trigger temper. After a few more moments staring, the driver just shook his head, leaned to the side and spit a stream of brown tobacco juice into the street, and slapped his reins against the horses' rumps. As the heavy wagon rumbled off down the street, the driver glanced back over his shoulder and shook his head again, showing Tolliver just what he thought of idiots who walked out in front of an ore wagon that weighed several tons.

Tolliver looked both ways this time before he crossed Main Street and headed back to his office. He needed to think about what he was going to do when Jensen came back to town. Even if Jensen was twenty years older than he had been the last time Tolliver had seen him, that didn't mean the man wasn't as dangerous as a grizzly bear in heat. Even old gunfighters could still manage a quick draw once in a while, and Tolliver didn't want to make the mistake of underestimating Jensen, not when his life depended on it.

He hung his hat on the door peg and sat at his desk, putting his feet up on the corner and leaning back in his chair, his hands crossed behind his neck.

He closed his eyes, but instead of making plans for Jensen's return, he thought about the last time he'd seen the man. . . .

Buck had been just over twelve years old that day back in his hometown of Homestead, Colorado Territory. It was the first time his older brother had let him ride into town with him and the other hands on his daddy's ranch.

After he'd helped them load up the buckboard with wire and nails and lumber, Jack Tolliver had given Buck a nickel and told him to buy him some peppermint candy sticks or maybe some licorice while he and the men stopped by the saloon for a couple of drinks.

Buck waited for nearly an hour, moving around the general store and looking at all the fine merchandise the owner had brought in by big freight wagons from Denver and Pueblo. Finally, he started getting antsy, wondering why his brother and the other men were taking so long. He'd spent all of his money and the candy was just about all gone, and the owner of the store was looking at him funny, wondering why the skinny kid was hanging around so long and not buying anything else.

He stuck his last peppermint stick in his mouth and walked out of the general store toward the saloon. Jack would box his ears for interrupting his drinking, but Buck knew his daddy had already had to warn Jack several times about his drinking and he didn't want Jack to get in trouble.

He worshiped his brother and if he could help keep him out of trouble, then some sore ears was a small price to pay.

He looked ahead and saw two men dressed all in buckskins come out of the saloon and climb up on what looked like Indian ponies, the ones with the spotted rumps. Buck smiled. They were about the dirtiest men he'd ever seen in town. He figured they must be mountain men, 'cause his daddy had told him about them once. He'd said they were misfits who couldn't hold down regular jobs so they lived up in the mountains, eating berries and wild animals like the Indians did.

In fact, Buck thought, these men looked like wild animals themselves, with their dirty clothes, wildly disarranged hair and heavy beards, and Indian moccasins on their feet instead of leather boots.

As the two men jerked their horses' heads around, the saloon batwings flew open and Jack and a few of the men from the ranch came bursting out. Buck started to yell hello, until he saw that Jack and the others were so drunk that they were almost staggering as they pushed their way out onto the boardwalk, elbowing other citizens aside.

Buck stopped, his eyes opened wide when he saw that Jack and the other men had their guns in their hands and were pointing them at the backs of the two mountain men who were riding slowly down the street.

Jack fired first, snapping off several shots that evidently went wild since neither of the men on horseback were hit.

Quicker than a rattlesnake striking, the younger man with the sandy yellow-colored hair twisted in his saddle as he filled his hand with iron and fired back.

His first shot took Jack in the chest, knocking him back with outspread hands. Buck screamed at the sight of his brother being blown off his feet to land spread-eagled on his back on the boardwalk.

Buck raced forward, ignoring the smoke and loud explosions of gunfire up ahead of him. He raced to kneel next to his brother and took his face in his hands.

"Jack . . . Jack . . . !" he screamed at the open, staring eyes.

Finally, there was silence, and Buck glanced around to see Joe and Sam and Larry all lying on the ground with blood pumping from bullet holes in their bodies. None of the men from the ranch were left alive.

Buck screamed again and grabbed the pistol from Jack's lifeless hand. He stood up and whirled around, holding the big Walker Colt in both hands and prying the hammer back with his right thumb. He had no idea how many bullets were left in the chamber, but he didn't care. He just wanted to kill the men who'd shot his brother down.

The man with the yellow hair aimed his pistol at Buck, but pulled it up when he saw he was just a boy—a boy who still had a peppermint stick in the corner of his mouth.

Buck took aim, blinking away his tears, and fired, grinning fiercely when he saw blood spurt from the man's left shoulder as the force of the slug turned him half around in his saddle.

The older man, a man with a face full of gray whiskers and a stink on him Buck could smell from ten feet away, leveled a long, Sharps fifty-caliber buffalo gun at Buck.

To Buck, the hole in the barrel of that rifle looked to be big enough to put his fist in. He didn't care; let the son of a bitch shoot. He lowered his pistol between his knees and again used both hands to pry the hammer back, hoping to get one more shot off before the old man killed him.

He glanced up and saw the man with yellow hair hold up his hand and yell *no!* at the old man.

The old man just shook his head as he lowered his rifle barrel. Good, Buck thought, and he again raised his pistol and aimed it at the man with yellow hair.

The old man spurred his horse forward between Buck and the man who'd shot his brother, and he swung his rifle like he was swinging an ax.

The barrel hit Buck on the temple and put his lights out. It was the last thing he remembered until he woke up a day later out at the ranch with his daddy leaning over him.

* * *

Tolliver came back to the present and unconsciously fingered the scar on his left temple that still remained as a souvenir of that day. His father had told him the man who'd killed his brother was named Smoke Jensen, and that the sheriff had cleared the two men of all charges, since Jack and the other men from the ranch had fired first and had fired at the other men's backs without giving them any warning.

He explained to Buck that Jack and the others had gotten stinking drunk and had begun to make fun of the two mountain men and the way they looked and the way they smelled. When the old man had grabbed Jack by the front of his shirt and slapped him back and forth with his open hand and then thrown him to the ground like a child, it had started a full-scale fight between the two strangers and the men from the ranch.

In spite of being outnumbered two to one, the two mountain men had kicked the ranchers' butts, leaving them bruised and bleeding on the floor when they walked out of the saloon. But, his daddy said, shaking his head, Jack wouldn't let it go. He had a snootful of whiskey and it made him liquor-brave, as his daddy put it.

He and the others had tried to back-shoot the two mountain men, and had paid for their foolishness with their lives. Buck's daddy added he didn't ever want Buck to mention Jack's name to him again, and he hadn't. But Buck had never forgotten the vacant stare in his brother's eyes on that fateful day. He'd vowed then to someday make things right and to make that Jensen fellow pay for shooting his brother down like a stray dog in the street.

It didn't matter to Buck Tolliver how much time had passed. For the past twenty years he'd prayed that someday he would come face-to-face with the bastard that killed his brother, and now his prayers were about to be answered.

Of course, he wasn't going to make the same mistake his brother did and go up against Jensen while he was drunk. No, sir. He would make careful plans and make sure that when he faced Jensen down and killed him, he would have the edge and not the gunfighter.

As he thought on it, he realized that Jensen had one weakness he probably hadn't considered. The man he'd dropped off at the doctor's was obviously a good friend. Maybe Tolliver could use that fact against the mountain man. It certainly deserved some serious consideration.

10

Cal was just finishing his breakfast in the dining room of the Palace Hotel in Pueblo when Smoke Jensen walked into the room.

Cal wiped syrup off his lips and raised his hand to signal his position to Smoke. When Smoke started toward him, Cal got the waitress's attention and made a drinking motion with his hand so she would bring some fresh coffee for the mountain man. From the somber look on his face, Smoke was going to need it, Cal thought. He looked skyward and gave a silent prayer that Smoke hadn't gotten any bad news about Pearlie's condition. Cal didn't know what he'd do if Pearlie didn't make it through all of this. The man was like an older brother to him and his life just wouldn't be the same without Pearlie in it.

By the time Smoke threaded his way through the crowded room and took his seat, their waitress was pouring steaming coffee into a tall mug in front of him.

"You have any luck?" Cal asked, dreading the answer. Smoke had left him almost two hours earlier to go to the telegraph office so he could wire Big Rock and have Sheriff Monte Carson be on the lookout for the horses they were going to ship by rail car later in the day, and also to wire the town of Payday and see if there had been any change in Pearlie's condition.

Smoke picked up the coffee mug, took a deep swallow,

and shook his head. "Not much. I got an answer back from Big Rock. Monte said he'd take care of the horses and wished us luck with Pearlie. Said the entire town would be praying for his recovery."

Cal nodded slowly. "I suspect they will. Pearlie's a right popular feller in Big Rock. He don't have an enemy in the world far as I know."

For the first time that morning, Smoke smiled, though it was a small smile. "You're right there, Cal. I've never heard anyone speak a word against Pearlie in all the time I've known him, and that's something to say about a man who's lived here as long as Pearlie has."

"Did you manage to get a message to the dentist and did you hear back from him 'bout Pearlie's condition?" Cal asked, hoping the news would be good, or at least not bad.

The smile faded from Smoke's face. "Yeah. The doc sent a wire saying Pearlie was no better, but the good news is he isn't any worse either. He said about all we could hope for was that every day Pearlie lives makes him a little stronger and gives him a better chance to survive the bites."

The waitress moved to stand next to Smoke with a pad and pencil in her hand. "You gonna want something to eat this mornin', sweetie?" she asked in a gravelly voice.

Smoke smiled. He hadn't been called sweetie since he was a little shaver. When Smoke hesitated, Cal said, "You might as well eat something, Smoke. We can't head back to Payday till this afternoon 'cause we still got to get those hosses loaded and on their way."

Smoke sighed. "You're right, Cal. It's just that worrying about Pearlie has about ruined my appetite."

The waitress, who'd overheard part of their earlier conversation, laid a meaty hand on Smoke's shoulder. In a kind voice, she said, "I know you're worried 'bout your sick friend, mister, but some of our flapjacks and scrambled hens' eggs will make you feel better. I guarantee you can face whatever comes your way better with a full stomach, no matter what it is."

Smoke looked up at her, touched by her concern. He smiled. "Might as well fry me up a side of bacon to go with 'em," he said. "And a touch more coffee would go down nicely too."

She smiled and winked as she put her pencil behind her ear. "I'll be right back with that coffee."

That evening, just before dusk, Sheriff Buck Tolliver was sitting in his office staring out of his window as he had been for most of the day. He kept turning things over in his mind, trying to figure out the best way to cause Smoke Jensen the same pain and suffering he'd gone through all these years whenever he thought of his dead brother and the terrible way he'd died—choking on his own blood in the dirt of the street of his hometown.

He knew that he could shoot the man when he came back to see about his sick friend, catching him unaware, but that somehow seemed too easy. The bastard wouldn't suffer near enough, no matter how long it took him to die. No, Tolliver would have to figure something else out for the gunman, something that would make him have the same sort of nightmares Buck had been living with for almost twenty years. If only he could do something that would hurt the gunman to the soul as his brother's death had *him*, Tolliver thought he'd be satisfied.

When Tolliver saw Hezekiah Bentley leave his office and make his way toward the Dog Hole Saloon to have his dinner, he had an idea. He knew how he could make Jensen suffer as he had, and even better, he'd do it so he could be there to taunt him with it and the man wouldn't be able to do anything about it no matter how much he suspected Tolliver might be behind it.

Tolliver grabbed his hat and followed Bentley into the saloon. He wondered if the doc was going to go back to his drinking, but noticed he shook his head when one of the girls approached his table and offered him a drink. I'll be damned, Tolliver thought, a wry smile on his lips, the doc is ordering water with his food.

Tolliver looked around the saloon, hunting for the reason he'd come into the place. Sure enough, Tolliver's cousin, Blackie Johnson, was at his usual place at the bar. Tolliver caught his eye and motioned him to come outside and talk. As he waited outside the batwings for Johnson, Tolliver gave a silent prayer that the man wouldn't be too drunk to do what he was going to ask him to do.

The sheriff uttered a low curse when Blackie stumbled through the batwings. Blackie grinned stupidly at Tolliver and held up his hand in greeting. "Yo, Buck, was-s-s goin' on?" he slurred.

Damn, Tolliver thought angrily, almost reaching out and slapping the shit out of his cousin. He was drunk as a skunk. Well, Tolliver figured, thinking rapidly, even a drunk man ought to be able to handle a man as sick as Jensen's friend was.

"Come over here, Blackie, we need to talk. I got a job for you to do."

"Aw, Buck, it's the middle of the night an' I'm busy with some friends in the saloon."

"First off, it's not the middle of the night, you fool, it's barely dusk; an' second of all, you ain't got no friends in the saloon nor nowhere else unless you're the one doin' the buyin'."

Johnson's face screwed up in anger, which turned to fear when Tolliver grabbed the front of his shirt and jerked him into the darkness of the alleyway next to the saloon. "Now here's what I want you to do," he said. "There's a gent over at Doc Bentley's who's sleepin' in one of his patient rooms."

Johnson gave a half grin. "Oh, you mean the man who got hisself snakebit?"

"Yeah. I want you to go over there and sneak in and put his lights out for good."

"You mean, kill him?" Johnson asked, his eyebrows raised. "Why? He ain't never done nothin' to me."

Tolliver took a deep breath. Blackie had always been as dumb as a post, and when he'd been drinking, he was even dumber. "You remember my brother Jack?" he asked, hating that he had to explain himself to Blackie, after all he'd done for him over the years. Hell, he thought, if he hadn't been sheriff, Blackie would've been sent to jail a dozen times at least.

Startled and somewhat confused at the change of subject, Johnson hung his mouth open for a moment before he answered. "Uh, sure, Buck. He was always nice to us when we was young'uns. He hardly ever beat up on us . . . at least not in no serious way."

Tolliver grabbed the front of Johnson's shirt again and pointed at Bentley's house. "That man lyin' in there is a close friend of the bastard who shot my brother down like a dog, Blackie. An' I want you to go in there and kill him to send that man a message for me."

Blackie cut his eyes toward Bentley's house, following Tolliver's pointing finger. "Well, sure, Buck, since you put it that way. Don't make no never mind to me." He hitched up his pants and took a step toward Bentley's before he turned back around, a puzzled look on his face. "But Buck, why don't you do it yourself since it was your brother he kilt?"

Tolliver took a deep breath to keep from slamming his fist into Blackie's dumb-ass face. "'Cause I'm gonna be in the saloon having a drink with Doc Bentley so no one will suspect I had anything to do with it, Blackie. Now, you gonna do what I ask or you gonna stand out here jawin' the night away?"

Blackie nodded and turned and took another step, stopped, and turned back around.

"Now what?" Tolliver asked hurriedly, worried that Bentley was going to finish his meal before Blackie ever got around to killing the man in his office. Since Bentley wasn't drinking anymore, there wouldn't be any reason for the doc to stick around the saloon after he'd finished his dinner.

"How do you want me to do it?" Blackie asked. "Gun, knife, or just strangle him?"

Tolliver sighed again. The man was a complete idiot. "I need you to shoot him, Blackie, so everyone can hear when it happens, and they'll know I was in the saloon and couldn't have been involved."

When Blackie raised his eyebrows and nodded in comprehension, Tolliver added, "So just go over there and put a gun between the man's eyes, blow his head off, and then hightail it out of the house and down the back alley until you're a couple of streets away from the doc's."

Blackie turned, and Tolliver stopped him with a hand on his arm. "And Blackie, make sure you don't get his brains an' blood splattered all over you, all right? Put a pillow over his head or something 'fore you shoot him."

"All right, Buck, but I ain't no idiot. You didn't have to tell me that."

"And just head on home when you're done, an' I'll check in with you tomorrow."

Blackie nodded and stumbled as he turned to walk toward the doc's house. Tolliver just shook his head and hurried through the batwings, his eyes searching for Bentley so he could join him for a drink or two until they heard the gunshot. He'd have the perfect alibi for the killing. He'd make sure to give Jensen enough hints that he'd be able to figure out who did it and why, but he wouldn't be able to do anything about it. At least not legally.

And if the old gunman made the mistake of drawing down on an officer of the law, it wouldn't matter who won the gunfight. If he manages to kill me, Tolliver thought, then he'll be back on the run for the rest of his life. But if he's lost some of his speed after all these years, then I get the pleasure of not only killing his friend, but of planting him forked-end-up in boot hill.

All in all, not a bad plan if I do say so myself, Tolliver told himself as he spied Bentley and raised his hand in greeting as he moved over toward his table.

11

Blackie looked back over his shoulder to make sure Buck was gone and wasn't looking, and then he pulled a small pint bottle of whiskey from his hip pocket. It wasn't that he was afraid of his cousin . . . not exactly. There was just no need to stir up Buck's temper unnecessarily, that's all. He pulled the cork and upended the bottle, drinking until it was completely empty.

He sleeved his mouth off and chucked the bottle into an alley as he walked toward the doc's house. He only weaved a little as he moved back and forth from side to side of the small street. Damn that Buck, he thought. Just when I was gittin' a good snort on he has to come and tell me to go to work killin' a feller, even though he don't mean nothin' to me.

He chuckled and looked again to see if Buck was still gone, as if the man could read his mind. Hell, he thought, I don't care if'n the gent kilt his brother Jack or not. Jack wasn't all that good to me anyhow—always tellin' me an' Buck what to do as if he was our pappy 'stead of Buck's brother. Served the asshole right to git hisself all shot up 'cause he couldn't mind his own business an' went an' picked on a man tougher than he was. Buck should'a realized that, 'cause his daddy shore did.

Course, Buck has been pretty nice to me, all considered, Blackie thought, even if he is bein' inconsiderate makin' me go to work in the middle of the night like this. Might as well do as he asks or there'll be hell to pay next time he has to stop somebody from pressin' charges on me or somethin'.

Well, Blackie figured as he walked up the stoop to Doc Bentley's back door, time to get this over with. Ol' Buck'll never let me forget it if'n I don't kill this stump-sucker for him, and what's worse, he won't give me no more of that gold money he's been takin' from the miners round here.

Blackie stumbled on the top step and fell against the back door, banging his head and making quite a bit of noise when the bell the doc'd hung there commenced to ringing.

"Sh-h-h!" he said to himself, holding a finger up against his lips as he used the other hand to stop the swinging of the bell. "Mustn't make so much noise, Blackie, or you'll wake the dead," he mumbled, chuckling at his own joke. "Oops, I forgot, he's not dead yet."

He reached down and opened the door, thanking the doc silently for never locking his doors. The door screeched on its hinges as he opened it and again he shushed himself, laughing softly as he tiptoed into the doc's kitchen, which was just off the back door.

Now, he thought, slipping his six-gun from its holster. Just which way is that bedroom?

He fumbled around in the semidarkness, banging into a table and knocking a lamp over on its side. Luckily, the bell holding the kerosene didn't break, so he just righted it and went on searching.

Up ahead, in the bedroom, Pearlie stirred, the noise bringing him almost awake. He moaned softly and tried to open his eyes, but the lids were stuck shut with dried tears.

He sighed, figuring he'd wait a few more minutes before climbing out of his bedroll and helping Cal and Smoke to get breakfast ready.

Blackie finally found the door to the bedroom and pulled the door open, holding his six-shooter out in front of him. As a cloud passed from in front of the moon, soft light filtered in the window and he could see a man sleeping soundly on the bed in front of him.

That must be the galoot Buck was talkin' about, he told himself. He laughed again softly to himself when he saw there was no one else in the room. That's good, he told himself, chuckling again. Wouldn't want to kill the wrong galoot, now would we, Blackie ol' man?

He tiptoed over to stand next to the bed and eared the hammer back on his Colt. Then, he hesitated as the moonlight struck a pocket watch and some silver and a wallet on the bedside table off to the side, along with a holster and rig with a knife in a scabbard.

Hey, looky there, he thought. The gent may have some real money in that wallet, an' that watch has got to be worth four or five dollars over in Pueblo. I'd better get it 'fore I shoot him 'cause afterwards I won't have time.

He turned, letting his gun point away from Pearlie, and took a step toward the bedside table, reaching out with his left hand to grab the money and watch.

Pearlie's eyes finally opened at the metallic sound of a pistol being cocked, and in the moonlight he could see a tall, lanky man standing over him with a gun in his hand.

"Son of a bitch!" Pearlie croaked, but his throat was dry and he barely made a sound.

When the man heard him and whirled around, Pearlie reached up and grabbed the pistol with both his hands, surprised at just how weak he felt.

Blackie jerked at his gun, trying to free it from the sick man's grasp, but as he did so he stumbled over his own feet and fell backward against the side table, dragging the half-awake Pearlie with him.

As they tumbled to the floor, Pearlie's holster and rig fell off the table and banged him in the head, causing stars to blossom and shine behind his eyelids. "Jesus," he grunted hoarsely, shaking his head to try and clear it, but only making himself more dizzy.

Blackie grunted, and Pearlie could feel the barrel of the Colt turning toward him and he was too weak to stop it. He knew with a sudden crystal clarity that he was going to be dead in a very few seconds if he didn't do something about it.

His eyes fell on the knife in his scabbard, lying next to him on the floor. As quick as a wink, Pearlie let go of the pistol with one hand and grabbed the hilt of the knife, jerking it out of its scabbard.

As Blackie grinned, his teeth glinted in the moonlight and the barrel turned the last few inches toward Pearlie's face. Pearlie could see in the man's eyes he intended to pull the trigger and put his lights out.

In a last spasm of what little strength he had left, Pearlie jabbed out and upward with the knife, gasping when it hit Blackie under the chin and cut his carotid artery.

A great spout of blood spurted out as Blackie grunted and his eyes opened wide in surprise. Then he moaned and gurgled as he choked on his own blood, dropping his gun and trying to staunch the pulsating flow with both hands to his neck. His eyes found Pearlie's and looked surprised and helpless as he fell over backward, dead as a stone.

Pearlie sleeved the blood out of his eyes and struggled to his feet. Suddenly, his head felt light and his vision darkened and he fell into a dark pool at his feet, unconscious again.

When an hour passed and Tolliver didn't hear a gunshot, he began to get worried. *Hell, with my luck,* he thought, *Blackie's passed out next to the bed with the sick man in it.* He shook his head, and was startled when a very alert Doc Bentley asked, "Something wrong, Buck? You look like you swallowed a frog or something."

Tolliver forced a smile and shook his head. He wasn't used to Doc being this observant in the evenings. By now he was usually well on his way to passing out for the night.

"Naw, I just gotta get to making my rounds 'fore it gets too late," he said, wondering what in the hell was keeping Blackie from finishing the pilgrim off like he told him to.

Doc Bentley covered a wide yawn with the back of his

hand and he pulled out a pocket watch. "I guess you're right, Buck. Hell, it's getting late and I got a couple of teeth to pull in the morning."

Bentley and Tolliver got to their feet. "Uh, I'll just walk along with you to make sure you get home all right," Tolliver said, ignoring the look Bentley shot at him.

"All right, but I really don't need a chaperon, Buck," Bentley said irritably. "Since I ain't drunk any whiskey at all and only one beer all night, I think I can make it the two blocks to my house by myself."

Tolliver shrugged. "Well, I got to go that way anyhow, so I might as well walk along with you as by myself."

Bentley nodded. "So long as you don't think I need it," he said, irritated that he still craved a drink of whiskey and even more irritated that he was too cowardly to get one.

The street the saloon was on went right by Bentley's back door, and when the doc and Tolliver got there, Tolliver noticed the back door was ajar.

"Uh-oh," he said, putting out his arm to hold Bentley back as he drew his pistol. "Someone's left your back door open, Doc."

Bentley snorted. "Naw, the wind just probably blew it open. Nobody'd try and rob me. Hell, everyone knows I don't have a pot to piss in, Buck."

"Nevertheless," Tolliver said, earing back the hammer of his pistol. "Let me take a look around before you come in."

"Oh, all right," Bentley said irritably. He sat down on the rear steps and leaned back against the wall of the house. "Just don't take all night. I'm tired and I want to get in my bed."

Tolliver eased the back door open and slipped inside. He moved through the house, keeping his gun pointed out in front of him. When he was near the bedroom door, he called softly, "Blackie, you there?"

When he heard no response, he moved slowly into the bedroom, and gasped when he saw the two men lying on the floor in a spreading pool of blood.

"Jesus," he whispered to himself. He holstered his pistol and knelt next to Blackie, making sure to keep his boots out of the blood.

Blackie's eyes stared sightlessly up at Buck in silent accusation with Pearlie's knife still embedded in his throat, and Tolliver knew he was dead as yesterday's news. Damn, he thought, now he had two deaths of family members he could blame on Smoke Jensen.

"You dumb son of a bitch," he whispered, shaking his head. "You couldn't even kill a man who was already half dead."

Tolliver looked over at Pearlie, and could see his chest moving slowly up and down as he breathed.

He stood up, trying to think of a way out of this mess. After a few moments, he grinned sourly. There was only one thing he could do to salvage this.

He moved quickly to the bureau by a sidewall and took out Pearlie's trousers. He pulled Pearlie up into the bed and slipped his pants on, pulling them up under the nightshirt and fastening the belt, making sure not to get any of the already clotted blood that covered the sleeping man on him.

Looking around to make sure he hadn't forgotten anything, he walked out into the kitchen and called for the doc to come on in.

"You find anybody hiding under the beds?" Bentley asked, grinning sleepily.

"You'd better take a look at this," Tolliver said, keeping his hand with his pistol in it by his side and leading the doc back into the bedroom.

When Bentley saw Blackie's body on the floor lying in a pool of blood, and Pearlie lying on the bed with his pants on and his nightshirt smeared with blood, he gasped, "What the hell is going on here?"

Tolliver slowly raised his pistol. "I'm sorry about this, Doc, but you just got in the wrong place at the wrong time."

"What do you mean?" Bentley asked, his eyes wide. "Why are you doing this?"

"To repay an old debt, Doc." Tolliver shrugged. "It's really nothing personal."

He slammed the pistol down on top of Bentley's head, watching as the man folded and fell to the floor as if he'd been poleaxed.

He quickly holstered his pistol and bent down and pulled the doc's watch and money and wallet out of his pockets and stuffed them into Pearlie's pockets, along with his belongings from the bedside table. Then he picked up Pearlie's gun belt and holster and strapped them around Pearlie's waist, rolling the unconscious man back and forth to do it.

He grunted as he picked Pearlie up and slung him over his shoulder. Moving as quickly as he could, he took Pearlie out the back door and went about fifty yards down the alley, dumping him in a strand of high weeds in a vacant lot.

Hurrying back into Bentley's house, he pulled his pistol out and aimed it at Bentley's chest. Taking a deep breath and feeling really bad about what he had to do, he squeezed the trigger.

The gun exploded and blew a fist-sized hole in the doctor's chest, killing him immediately where he lay.

Tolliver holstered his gun and sprinted out the back door and down the alley toward where he had laid Pearlie in the weeds.

As he ran out of the door, he never noticed the elderly lady at the top of the stairs in Bentley's house, or the horrified expression on her face as she watched what he'd done.

Tolliver squatted down next to Pearlie in the weeds, and waited until a sizable crowd had gathered around the doc's house, and then he stood up and yelled, "Stop! You, there, stop!" He waited a moment and then he slapped Pearlie on the head with the barrel of his pistol, laying his scalp open and snapping his head back.

He stood up and yelled, "Help me! I've caught the thief over here!"

Moments later, when some townsmen came up to them,

Tolliver was bending over with his hands on his knees breathing heavily.

"I got the son of a bitch who shot the doc," he said breathlessly.

"What happened?" one of the men asked as they stared down at Pearlie lying unconscious with his head leaking blood all down his face to pool in the sandy soil under him.

"Me an' my deputy, Blackie Johnson, heard the gunshot in the doc's house. When we ran inside to check it out, we found this hombre standing over the doc's body. 'Fore we could react, he knifed Blackie and ran out the back door."

"Why'd he shoot the doc?" the man asked.

Tolliver shrugged. "I dunno. I think the doc caught him trying to steal his money and they must've had a fight an' the doc lost." He reached down and pulled the bills and the doc's watch that he'd stashed there earlier out of Pearlie's pockets, and held them up for the men to see.

Tolliver glanced down at Pearlie. "Now, pick this rotten bastard up and carry him over to the jail, before I shoot him down like the mangy dog he is."

"What about Blackie, Buck?" one of the men asked, looking toward the doc's house.

Tolliver shook his head. "He ain't gonna make it, Sam. The knife cut his throat almost clean through and he was bleeding like a stuck pig and already dead on his feet when I went out the door after this son of a bitch."

While Tolliver and the townspeople were all out back, watching Pearlie being carried to the jail, Doc Bentley's aunt, Janet Rule, gathered her bags together and snuck out of his house by the front door and walked to the hotel. She'd come to visit her only nephew the week before, but Tolliver hadn't known about it because he was out of town hunting down prospectors to rob.

Janet rang the bell on the desk until a sleepy-eyed desk clerk came out and let her book a room. He was too sleepy to ask what a respectable woman like her was doing booking a room in the middle of the night.

He just handed her a key and turned and went back to his room to get some sleep. He didn't even look at the name she signed on the hotel register.

12

The next morning, Sheriff Tolliver stepped out of his jail to find an angry crowd of citizens milling around in the street and on the boardwalk.

Trying to hide his grin at how things were playing out just as he'd planned, he held up his hands and tried to look authoritative and stern as he addressed the mob in a loud voice. "What's going on here?" he asked, though he knew full well what was happening.

George Orwell, the president of the bank and one of Payday's leading citizens, held up his right hand with a coiled rope in it. "We're here to see justice is done, Buck. That son of a bitch in there killed our doctor and one of your deputies. For that, he's going to hang!"

Tolliver puffed out his chest and hooked his thumbs in his belt. "Now, George. You know I can't let you do that, leastways not till there's been a trial."

Bubba Barkley, who was standing in the rear of the crowd, shouted out just as Tolliver had told him to the night before. "Hey, Buck, why don't you just go on over to the saloon and get yourself some breakfast. Me an' the good citizens here will watch your jail for you." He glanced at his friend, Hog Hogarth, who was standing next to him all bent over to one side, most of his weight still on his right foot from the injuries Smoke had inflicted on him the previous week.

When Tolliver and the others had asked how he came to get hurt, Hog had told them a rattlesnake spooked his horse and he got thrown into some boulders. He was too ashamed to admit a man had kicked the shit out of him, and he'd sworn Bubba to silence with threats of a severe beating if he told anyone the truth. Thus, Bubba and Hog had no idea the very man their boss was going after was the one who'd beaten the crap out of Hog.

Tolliver grinned as several of the men in the crowd shouted their agreement with Bubba's plan for him to make himself scarce so they could get on with the hanging. He shook his head, trying to look regretful. "Sorry, boys. I know you'd be sure an' do a real good job of lookin' after my prisoner, but I done told you, he ain't gonna be hanged till we've had us a real trial."

"But Buck," Mayor Sam Hemmings said, "it'll take at least two or three weeks to get a circuit judge up here, and that's only if there's one in the county. Hell, it might even take longer if he's over on the other side of the mountains."

Tolliver nodded slowly, as if he was thinking about what could be done, though that too was in his plans all along. "That's true, Sam, but as mayor, you could call a special trial an' appoint some . . . uh . . . impartial citizens to be on the jury an' we could go on and get on with it right away."

"But who'd serve as judge?" Hemmings asked.

Tolliver scratched his jaw, and then he smiled broadly. "Say, didn't that feller, Joshua Banks, that just came into town a few weeks back from Denver to try his hand at prospecting on Culver Creek, say he was a lawyer 'fore he decided to come out here?"

Orwell nodded rapidly. "That's right, Buck. He told me that when he took out a loan on his prospecting equipment."

Bubba snorted and said, "Couldn't have been too good a lawyer if'n he had to take out a loan to buy some picks and shovels."

This remark caused the crowd to break out in laughter, all except Tolliver, who scowled at his friend. "There's no need for that kind'a talk, Bubba," he said. "Especially when we're talkin' 'bout the town's new judge."

The crowd laughed again, until Sam Hemmings asked, "All right, Buck, now we got our judge. What about the defense attorney and the prosecutor?"

"Well, of course I'll do the prosecutin', since it's my job to keep law and order here in Payday, an' I suppose since you're 'bout the most fair-minded man I know, you can defend the murderin' scum, Mayor."

Hemmings frowned. "I don't know as that'd be right, Buck, since I don't exactly believe in this man's innocence. I don't know how good a job I'd be able to do."

Tolliver shrugged. "Makes no never mind to me, Mayor. If you don't want to do it, I guess we can wait two weeks or maybe a few months to get the circuit judge here an' do it all up nice and proper."

When Hemmings heard the crowd of citizens behind him, men who he'd be counting on for their votes in the next election, set up a roar of disapproval, he knew he had no choice. Not if he wanted to keep his job—which he did.

He turned to the crowd and held up his hands. "All right, friends," he said in his best campaign voice, "I'll do it. I'll take the job."

"Don't worry, Mayor," Bubba shouted from the rear of the crowd, trying to redeem himself with Tolliver. "It'll be a short trial and a quick hangin'."

Hemmings, who really was a fair-minded man, held up his hands again. "Now, folks, I really must protest this sort of talk. We got to remember the man hasn't been found guilty yet, so let's try to keep neutral until we've heard all the evidence. At least, that's the way things are going to be if you want me to be a part of this trial. Otherwise, like Buck said, we can wait for a few weeks or months for a circuit judge to come up here."

George Orwell held up his hands and addressed the crowd. "Now, folks, simmer down. You all know Sam is right, and I for one wouldn't want him to have to do anything that went against his grain, even if it did mean his getting reelected."

This last comment sent up a roar of laughter from the crowd and caused Hemmings's face to burn a bright red.

"How about setting the trial for tomorrow, Mayor, assuming we can send somebody out to Banks's claim and get him back here in time to preside?" Tolliver asked, trying to sound reasonable and yet ignoring the fact that this gave Hemmings almost no time to mount a credible defense.

Hemmings thought for a moment, and then he nodded reluctantly. "That should be enough time for me to confer with the accused, though it won't give me much time to—"

"So be it then," Tolliver said, interrupting Hemmings before he could plead for more time. He grinned, unable, now that he'd gotten what he wanted, to keep the smug look of satisfaction off his face. "We'll have the trial in the saloon tomorrow morning at eight o'clock."

As the crowd cheered, he held up a warning finger. "But there'll be no liquor nor beer served until after the guilty verdict is in."

When the crowd moaned in disappointment, Hemmings started to protest at the sheriff's choice of words, but he was drowned out by Tolliver adding, "And then we'll have time for a couple of quick rounds on the town before we all have to get back to work."

This earned another cheer from the crowd, causing Tolliver to marvel not for the first time at how easily men could be manipulated—and it seemed the more of them there were in a group, the easier the manipulation. In a mob, it was usually the man with the loudest voice who swayed them rather than the man with the best argument.

As the crowd began to disperse, Tolliver noticed Robert Jacobson, the man who ran the general store and also minded the town's telegraph office, standing on the periphery.

"Hey, Bobby," Tolliver called, raising his hand to get the man's attention, "hold up a minute."

"Looks like the town's gonna have a hanging before too long," Jacobson said after Tolliver made his way through the milling crowd to stand next to him. "Course, it's a real shame 'bout Doc gettin' killed and all."

Tolliver's grin faded when Jacobson failed to mention

his cousin Blackie Johnson's death. "Yeah, shame about Blackie too, Bobby."

Jacobson's face flushed and he nodded when he realized his mistake. "Course it was, Buck. I didn't mean no disrespect. It's just that Blackie was. . . ." He hesitated, trying to figure out something to say that wouldn't set the sheriff off. People out West were sometimes peculiar about their relatives, no matter how dumb or no-account they were.

Tolliver rescued him by putting his hand on Jacobson's shoulder. "I know, Bobby. Blackie wasn't exactly the town's most respectable citizen." He sighed as Jacobson nodded. "Still and all, he was my cousin and he didn't deserve to have some asshole stranger put a knife in his gizzard."

"No, no, of course not!" Jacobson hastily agreed, shuddering at the mental picture Tolliver's words evoked.

Tolliver walked alongside Jacobson as he moved toward the store. "You hear anything on your telegraph from those friends of his, Bobby?"

Jacobson's brow knit as he thought about it. "Yeah, but it was yesterday. Got a wire from Pueblo to the doc about how the man was doing. I ran it over to his office and he had me wire back the man was still unconscious."

"Did they wire back an answer?"

Jacobson scratched his head. "Seems I recollect the party in Pueblo wired back he'd be here within the week to see how his friend was doing, Sheriff."

Tolliver nodded. He was going to have to work fast if he wanted to have the trial over and done with by the time Jensen returned from Pueblo. Of course, he reasoned as he thanked Jacobson and ambled over toward his office, he didn't want things to move too fast. He certainly didn't want the man called Pearlie to have already been hanged when Jensen got here. No, sir. That would make things too easy on the gunman. Nope. Tolliver wanted Jensen to have to face his friend and tell him there was nothing he could do to prevent his being hanged—and to make it worse, Jensen would almost certainly believe Pearlie when he told him he didn't kill the doc.

Tolliver rubbed his hands together and grinned as he thought about how frustrated and anguished Jensen was going to be when faced with the imminent death of his good friend. Tolliver would, of course, have to make certain the hanging was scheduled soon enough that Jensen wouldn't have time to get to any U.S. marshals or the governor or anyone else who might put off the hanging long enough for a real trial. That was going to be the tricky part, but Tolliver was certain he was up to it.

He stopped grinning and stood in the middle of the street, unmindful of the wagons and horses having to change course and go around him, when he realized the only course of action open to Jensen would be to use his guns. What if the man went crazy and started shooting up the town? Maybe I'd better take some precautions in that matter, he thought.

He changed course and walked over to the mayor's office.

"Howdy, Buck," Mayor Sam Hemmings said when he entered the office. "What can I do for you?"

Tolliver hitched his hip on the corner of Hemmings's desk and crossed his arms. "I been thinking, Mayor," he began. "This here Pearlie feller was brought into town a few days back by some pretty tough-looking hombres. The boy at the livery even said they looked to him to be gunfighters or some such thing." He didn't tell the mayor that the doc had told him it was Smoke Jensen who was Pearlie's friend. The fewer people who knew that, the better it would be all around. Couldn't have anyone on the jury afraid to render a guilty verdict knowing that the famous gunfighter Smoke Jensen might resent their vote.

Hemmings leaned back in his chair and looked worried. "Are you saying this Pearlie man might also be a gunfighter, Buck?"

Tolliver nodded. "Yeah, but that's not what's got me worried, Sam. I'm more concerned about what's going to happen if his friends on the owl hoot trail hear he's about to be hung in some small town out in the middle of nowhere." Tolliver paused to let the mayor think about that for a moment.

"Just what do you suppose they might do, Sam?" he asked.

Hemmings took a deep breath and turned in his chair to look out his window. "You think they might try and tree the town?" he asked, worrying about what would happen to all of his friends in the town if a bunch of gunmen rode in with their six-shooters blazing.

Tolliver shrugged. "It's a thought."

Hemmings turned his chair back around to face the sheriff. "What do you think we ought to do about it?"

"How about if you give me permission to hire me a couple of deputies, men who are good with guns."

"What do you think that'll cost the town, Buck?" Hemmings asked.

"A whole lot less than burying half the town if a bunch of gunslicks come in here with murder and mayhem on their minds and try and break their friend out of jail."

Hemmings nodded, his face suddenly pale. "All right, Buck. I'll have to clear it with the other members of the town council, of course, but I'm sure they'll see it the same way we do. Who do you have in mind to hire?"

"Well, I haven't really thought about it yet," Tolliver lied, "But, I figure Jerry Hogarth and Bubba Barkley would be good choices, an' maybe even Jimmy Akins and Jeb Hardy."

"You really think you'll need four more men?"

"Sam, we got to guard that jail twenty-four hours a day. Just how many men do you think that'll take?" Tolliver sighed. "I could work double shifts, but if I'm gonna maybe be in a gunfight, I'd hate to be too tired to think or shoot straight if it came to it."

Hemmings nodded, his lips tight, thinking about what this was going to cost the town. "All right, Buck, but you make it clear to them that the job is just until the trial is over."

Tolliver grinned. "You mean until the trial and the hanging is over."

Hemmings held up his hand. "Now, Buck, I warned you

about that. Since I'm gonna be defending this man, I want the trial to be on the up and up, and I'm not going to be planning any hanging until the verdict is in."

"All right, Sam," Tolliver said, laughing good-naturedly. "I won't start building a scaffold until the jury has spoken."

"By the way," Hemmings said, "When would be a good time for me to interview Pearlie? I need to get his side of the story if I'm going to be able to do a good job of defending him."

Tolliver pursed his lips. "Oh, any time is all right with me, Mayor. But remember, the man is a killer so it's probably pretty safe to assume he's a liar as well."

"Nevertheless, he deserves to get the chance to give his account of what happened that night," the mayor said, inwardly cursing the fate that had put him on the side of the most hated man in Payday.

13

When Tolliver opened the jail door and let Hemmings into Pearlie's cell, the mayor sucked in a deep breath and turned with angry eyes on the sheriff.

"Why haven't you seen to this man's injuries, Buck?"

Tolliver glanced at Pearlie, who was lying half propped up against the wall in his cot with dried, crusted blood covering the right side of his head and face. His skin was pale and his eyes were unfocused, as if he didn't quite know where he was or how he'd gotten here.

"I ain't no doc, Mayor, an' in case you forgot, this bastard killed the only doctor we had in town. What'd you want me to do, drag Bentley's corpse over here and ask him if he'd clean the son of a bitch up?"

Hemmings shook his head; Tolliver was impossible. The mayor went to sit on the edge of Pearlie's bunk. He gently shook Pearlie's shoulder. "How are you feeling, young man?" he asked, his voice kind, but his eyes were probing deep within Pearlie's as if he could somehow tell if the man were a murderer or simply a cowboy who'd been in the wrong place and at the wrong time.

Pearlie's eyes focused and he seemed to come out of a trance. He looked at Hemmings and then at the sheriff. "What am I doing in jail?" he asked, his voice a hoarse croak. He winced when his movement caused one of the scabs on the side of his face to break open and fresh blood began to ooze out of the wound and run down his cheek. "And what happened to my head? It feels like I been hit with an ax handle."

Hemmings glanced over his shoulder at Tolliver. "Buck, bring us a pail of water and a dipper, and then I want you to go on over to the saloon and see if Hattie Monroe is up yet."

"What do you want Hattie for?" Tolliver asked, a leer on his face as if the mayor was going to provide prostitutes for the prisoner. "I really don't think the man is up to a roll in the hay this morning, Mayor."

Hemmings sighed, getting tired of Tolliver's smart mouth. "Hattie worked as a nurse at an army hospital back in the Civil War, Buck. I want her to take a look at this man's injuries and see if she can help him."

"How'd you know that about Hattie, Sam?" Tolliver asked. "You two good friends?"

Hemmings blushed a bright red. "We talked about it, Buck. Now, go and do what I asked, please."

Tolliver scowled and backed out of the cell. "All right, but I'm gonna have to lock you in while I'm gone, Sam. Wouldn't want the prisoner to try and escape."

Hemmings looked at Tolliver like he was crazy. "Escape? Why, the man can barely talk, let alone overpower me and run off into the mountains on foot and escape. Don't be a fool, Buck."

Tolliver blushed and scowled deeper and slammed the cell door anyway, locking it with a loud metallic click.

Hattie took one look at Pearlie and went into the sheriff's office and put some water on the Franklin stove to boil. "I'm gonna need some clean cloths, some alcohol—the rubbing kind, not the drinkin' kind—and a needle and thread," she told Hemmings and Tolliver.

"What do you think is wrong with him?" Hemmings asked.

"For one thing," she said, looking at Tolliver with anger in her eyes, "he got hit pretty good by the sheriff here, and that was on top of just recovering from what I've been told was a couple of pretty nasty snakebites. And if that's not enough for you," she said, looking back at Hemmings now, "he's got a gash in his scalp that's gonna need to be sewn up, and I can only guess if his brains is scrambled or not."

When she'd finished, she began to dig in a small black valise like doctors carry. When Tolliver had gone to her at the saloon and told her they needed some nursing done, she'd brought her bag with her—the same one she'd carried in the Civil War when she'd treated hundreds of men in the field.

"Is he gonna be able to stand trial?" Tolliver asked, worried that any delay might put a crimp in his plans for vengeance on Smoke Jensen.

"He will be if you two get outta here an' get me what I asked for an' let me get to work fixin' him up," she said with hands on her ample hips.

Half an hour later, after she'd shooed the mayor and sheriff out of the cell and had cleansed the dried blood and dirt out of his head wound, Hattie bent over Pearlie with needle and thread in hand.

"I'm sorry, mister, but I can't give you no alcohol to numb the pain, not with a head injury like you got."

"Pearlie," he croaked up at her from where he lay on the cot.

"What?" she asked, leaning back with eyebrows raised.

"Pearlie. My name's Pearlie, miss."

She clucked. "My, aren't you the polite one, tryin' to be a gentleman after all you've been through."

Pearlie gave her a lopsided grin, wincing again when the movement caused his wound to open. "My mother always told me being polite didn't depend on the circumstances, it was just something you did or you didn't do, and she preferred me to do it all the time." He paused, and added, "An' I think I still got the back-strap bruises on my hide from when I forgot what she told me."

"Well," Hattie said, pleased but trying hard not to show

it, "this ain't no social date, Pearlie, so you just lie back and grit your teeth, 'cause this is gonna smart a mite."

"Just a minute, miss," Pearlie said. He rolled on his side and reached down and unbuckled his belt, causing Hattie to raise her eyebrows. Pearlie just smiled wanly as he pulled his belt out and folded it over. "This is something Smoke Jensen taught me once when he had to remove a bullet from my carcass." And then he stuck the leather between his teeth and clamped down on it. His eyes closed as he laid his head back and nodded, signaling he was ready for her to begin.

"Well, I swan," she muttered under her breath, wondering how a man as brave and resourceful as this one could have done the awful things they were accusing him of. I guess one never knows, she thought as she leaned forward and began to sew Pearlie's wound shut. Of course, him knowing Smoke Jensen well enough to speak of him might just explain it. Hattie had been working in a saloon in a small town on the southern border of Colorado Territory some years back when Jensen had walked in and stood in the doorway, his hands at his side, his eyes roving back and forth around the room like he was searching for someone.

After a minute, he'd called out, "I'm looking for the three men who just rode into town about five minutes ago. Their horses are outside and I know they came in here."

When no one spoke up, Hattie saw him turn his eyes to her. She was standing off to one side of the room, next to a table with one of her regulars sitting at it. When she saw his eyes on her, she involuntarily looked at the three men standing at the bar who'd just burst in through the batwings like their tails were on fire.

Jensen had smiled, and it changed his whole face. Suddenly he wasn't a fearsome gunfighter, but one of the most handsome and masculine men she'd ever seen.

His smile faded when he turned his body slightly to face the men at the bar and called out, "What kind of low-life, mother-grubbing bastards attack a woman living alone outside of town and shoot her and her two kids just to rob a few dollars she had hidden in her kitchen?"

One of the men blushed a bright scarlet and blurted out, "She didn't need no money livin' out there with her kids like that an' we did. If she would've given it to us nice-like, we wouldn't have had to shoot her kids to get her to tell us where it was."

Smoke's face had now turned as hard as granite, and Hattie had never seen anyone look so mean and dangerous.

"You'd better fill your hands, gents, or I'm going to come over there and beat you to death with my bare hands!" he growled.

All three men put their drinks down, turned to face Smoke, and went for their pistols.

In a shorter time than it takes to tell it, both Smoke's hands were filled with iron and he was blazing away before any of the men even cleared leather.

The smoke and cordite billowing through the room made Hattie's eyes burn and water, but a few minutes later, she saw the three men sprawled out on the wooden floor, covered with blood and dead as stones.

Smoke then had holstered his pistols and addressed the crowd in the saloon. "There's a lady in a cabin about five miles south of town who's been wounded pretty badly. Her two children are dead, but she may make it if some-one will go out there and tend to her wounds." He paused and looked down at the dead men. "When I found her, she told me these men did it after she was kind enough to offer them water for their horses and a fresh-cooked meal." He shrugged. "It's your town, do what you want."

After he'd left, Hattie had taken this same medical kit she was using now on one of Smoke Jensen's friends and gone out to tend to the Widow McKay. After that, when-ever she saw something in a newspaper or magazine about Smoke Jensen, she'd taken the trouble to read it. She'd found he'd killed a lot of men, but she'd never read once that anyone he'd killed hadn't provoked it or deserved it.

* * *

Later, after she'd finished sewing up Pearlie's head and done the best she could with his other wounds, she stuck her head into Tolliver's office and called out, "I'm done in here, Mayor Hemmings." She pointedly didn't speak to Tolliver or acknowledge his presence. There was something about the man she just couldn't stand—even before she'd seen how he treated his prisoners, she'd always felt there was something wrong about him, something evil.

Hemmings got up from his chair in front of Tolliver's desk and walked back into the room holding Pearlie's cell. As he paused to thank Hattie, she whispered, "I hear you're going to be defending him in court." She paused and blushed a mite as she added, "He sure don't seem like a man capable of cold-blooded murder, Mayor."

Hemmings's eyes narrowed. "What do you mean, Hattie?" he asked.

Her blush deepened and spread all the way down to her bosom, and she dropped her gaze. "Over the past few years, working in saloons like I have been doing, Mayor, I've gotten so I can read men pretty good." She looked up at him to see if he understood what she was saying. "You have to learn that in my profession or you can get pretty badly hurt."

Hemmings nodded. He knew what she meant. Though most men out West treated women with respect and kindness, men full of liquor in the presence of a prostitute often acted like swine, or worse.

"Anyway," Hattie went on, "that man in there has a gentle soul, and he is a gentleman. I think he could kill, if he thought the person he was up against deserved it or he was pushed into it, but I don't for a minute believe he'd kill someone like Dr. Bentley, who'd helped him out, for a few dollars and a gold watch."

"But Hattie," Hemmings said, glancing over his shoulder to make sure Tolliver wasn't nearby, "the sheriff said he saw him do it."

Hattie sneered, following Hemmings's glance toward the door to Tolliver's office. "Oh, and you think Buck Tolliver is so high-and-mighty he ain't never lied?" she asked.

When Hemmings didn't answer, she leaned close and whispered in his ear, "You come see me, Sam, where we can talk private-like, an' I'll tell you some things about Buck that'll curl your toes."

She jerked back, her eyes wide with fright, when Tolliver strolled through the door and eyed her suspiciously. "You 'bout done in here, Hattie?" he asked, moving a toothpick around in his thick lips. "'Cause if you are, I'm sure they have need of you over to the saloon."

Without looking at Hemmings again, Hattie ducked her head and moved past Tolliver, shrugging to the side as she passed him in the doorway so their bodies wouldn't touch.

After she'd left, Tolliver snorted. "Whores," he said derisively. "If it wasn't for what they carry between their legs, there'd be a hunting season on 'em."

Disgusted by Tolliver's crudity, Hemmings walked down the hall to Pearlie's cell. When he opened the door, he looked over his shoulder at Tolliver. "I need to talk to this man alone, Sheriff."

Tolliver looked dubious. "I don't know, Mayor. He might be dangerous now that Hattie's fixed him up and he's feeling better."

Hemmings sneered, "I think I can handle a man who's had his head half-caved in and can barely sit up in bed, Buck."

"All right, Sam, don't get your dander up," Tolliver said defensively.

"And you might see about rustling up some grub and water for the prisoner, Buck, 'less you're planning on starving him to death before the trial."

Tolliver just shook his head as he turned and walked down the corridor toward his office, thinking they'd be wanting him to get lace curtains for the bastard's cell next.

Hemmings looked around the cell, and since there was no other place to sit, he eased down on the edge of Pearlie's bunk bed down by his feet.

"Now, Pearlie," he began, "there are some things you need to know. Dr. Bentley and another man named

Blackie Johnson were killed the other night at the doc's house. The sheriff says he saw you standing over the doctor's dead body and when he and Blackie walked in, you stabbed Blackie and hightailed it out and back down the alley until the sheriff ran you down and knocked you out." Hemmings hesitated, noticing the blank look on Pearlie's face, as if he were hearing this for the first time. "I need you to tell me what you say happened that night."

Pearlie winced at the sudden pain as he turned his head to look up at Hemmings. "You mean when I caught that man going through my things?" he asked.

Hemmings's brow knit in surprise. "You mean Dr. Bentley was going through your things?"

Pearlie shrugged. "I don't know any Dr. Bentley. The last thing I remember 'fore waking up to find a tall man with booze on his breath riflin' my things was being bitten by a snake up in the mountains."

Hemmings realized that was the truth, that Pearlie would have no way of knowing the doc had been taking care of him since he'd been unconscious the entire time. Maybe he'd woken up like he said, found himself in a strange house, and decided to steal himself some money and a watch. When the doc woke up and caught him at it, he must've killed him without knowing who he was.

"So," Hemmings said after working this out in his mind, "your story is when you found this man in your room, you shot him to keep him from stealing your things?"

Pearlie shook his head, wincing again when the movement brought on a stabbing jolt of pain. "No, I didn't shoot no one," he said, putting his hand up to the side of his head. "The hombre pointed his gun at me an' I grabbed it. We struggled and fell on the floor. I was able to get my knife outta my gun belt and stab the son of a bitch just 'fore he could shoot me in the head. Last I remember, he was lying next to my bed with blood everywhere, and then I must've passed out. When I come to, I was lying right here where you see me an' a nice lady was fixin' to sew my head back together."

"But that doesn't make any sense, young man," Hemmings protested. "The doc was shot and *then* Blackie Johnson was stabbed."

Pearlie frowned. "I done told you, mister, I didn't shoot nobody, an' I sure as hell didn't hear no gunshot before I woke up."

He closed his eyes and tried to remember all he could about that night. After a moment, he opened them and said, "The man I stabbed had the beginnings of a beard, like he hadn't shaved in a few days, an' he stunk of sweat like he hadn't bathed in a month, an' he smelled of alcohol like he'd been drinkin' a lot that night." Pearlie grinned. "Funny how 'bout all I remember 'bout him is the godawful stench on him." Pearlie paused and laid his head back, exhausted. "Now, that's all I can tell you, 'cept to say again, I didn't shoot nobody. I done the stabbin', but it 'twas in self-defense. I could see it in his eyes, Mr. Hemmings, that man meant to kill me as sure as I'm laying here in this here jail."

Hemmings told Pearlie to get some sleep and that the sheriff should be back in a while with some food.

Pearlie had grinned. "You know, Mr. Hemmings," he said looking around at the cell and the bars on the windows, "for 'bout the first time in my life I can honestly say I ain't a bit hungry."

Hemmings smiled and told him he had to eat to get his strength back so he could heal, and then the mayor went into Buck's office, sat at Buck's desk, and pulled his tobacco pouch out of his pocket and built himself a cigarette. After he lighted it, he sat there smoking and thinking about Pearlie's story. It didn't make any sense according to what Tolliver had said. He'd said that Pearlie shot the doc and then stabbed Blackie when they ran into the house.

He shook his head. It just didn't add up, unless maybe Pearlie had blacked out and shot the doc and not been able to remember it. Hemmings knew men who'd drunk until they passed out and then didn't remember a thing they'd done the night before.

But, he thought, if that were so, how come he could remember killing Blackie so clearly? Nope, it just didn't make sense. Someone was lying about what had happened that night. But if Pearlie was telling the truth, that meant it must have been the sheriff that killed the doc, and what possible reason could Tolliver have to kill Dr. Bentley, and why would Blackie have been going through Pearlie's belongings? Blackie was dumb as a stump, but he'd never been known to be a thief as far as Hemmings knew.

Damn, he thought, how did I ever get mixed up in this mess? He grinned ruefully to himself as he inhaled a lungful of acrid smoke. Maybe being mayor in Payday isn't worth all this grief after all. But then he smiled and shook his head. "Yep, I guess it is," he muttered, struck with that most powerful urge among politicians, the urge to stay in office as long as possible.

14

Janet Rule eased down the stairs in the hotel, going slowly and making sure that she didn't see any sign of the sheriff looking for her.

Maybe she'd get lucky and be able to get out of town before he realized she'd been staying with her nephew. She knew she didn't have long before some busybody told him she'd been there, so she had to make tracks. She knew she didn't dare go back home to her house in Pueblo, because once Tolliver realized she'd been in the house that night and might have seen him, he'd either come for her or send someone to Pueblo to make sure she wasn't able to testify against him.

She didn't understand why someone would want to kill her nephew. He was such a kind man who only cared about helping people. Sure, he'd had his trouble with the bottle, but in the last couple of days of his life he'd seemed to be getting that under control. What a shame, to be cut down in the prime of life like that for no good reason that she could think of.

In her seventies, she knew she could never ride a horse all the way to some other town, and the thought of trying to drive a buckboard or surrey that far didn't appeal to her either. And, if she tried to buy a ticket on the next train, the stationmaster would be sure to remember her if

Tolliver came asking, which he was sure to do once he found out she'd been Hezekiah's houseguest at the time he killed him.

At the foot of the stairs, she glanced around and, seeing no one who seemed overly interested in her movements, she slipped into the dining room. It was still very early and the place was almost deserted except for her and a young boy in his teens who was mopping the floors.

That's it, she thought. She sat at a table near where he was working and opened her purse, extracting a handful of bills. When she got a chance, she motioned him over to her.

"Yes, ma'am?" he asked. "The waitress is out back helping the cook with the mornin's biscuits. She'll be here in a few minutes."

"Young man," Janet said, "how would you like to make five dollars?"

The boy's eyes opened wide. Five dollars was more than he made in two weeks sweeping out the place. "Yes, ma'am!" he said, wondering just what it was he was going to have to do to earn so much money.

Janet handed him the bills and said, "Take this money on over to the train station and buy me a ticket on the next train out."

"Uh, where do you want to go?" the boy asked as he took the money and stuffed it in his jeans pocket.

"It doesn't matter," she said, lowering her voice, "just get me a seat on the very next train leaving, but you've got to do it without raising any suspicions or getting the attention of the stationmaster."

The boy looked around to make sure no one was near enough to hear him, and then he leaned down and whispered back at her, "Are you in trouble, ma'am?"

Janet thought furiously for a moment, and then she took out her hanky and wiped at her eyes as if she'd been crying. "Yes, son. There's a man who is threatening to hurt me because I owe him some money. If I don't get out of town fast and without anyone knowing where I've gone, I'm afraid he's going to beat me."

The boy looked horrified that anyone would pick on a nice old lady like this. Heck, she reminded him of his own granny. "You can count on me, ma'am. I'll run right over there and get your ticket for you."

"Thank you, sonny. Thank you so much," Janet said, patting his arm in a grandmotherly way.

After he'd left, Janet raised her hand to signal the waitress that she was ready to order. "I'll just have a cup of tea and perhaps a biscuit and a little gravy if you don't mind," she said.

After the waitress left, the table next to Janet filled with what appeared to be local businessmen.

Without meaning to, Janet overheard them talking excitedly about the upcoming trial of the man the sheriff said had killed Dr. Bentley and Blackie Johnson.

"That blackguard," she muttered to herself. "He's going to try and hang some poor innocent for what he himself did." She began to shake her head back and forth. "That just won't do—it won't do at all!"

"What did you say, dear?" the waitress asked, having heard the old lady muttering to herself.

"Oh, nothing," Janet said, picking up her biscuit and slathering gravy on it. "Nothing at all."

Smoke and Cal were just finishing loading up the last of the Palouse studs into a railroad stock car when Smoke heard a man laughing behind him.

He shut the loading gate, dusted his gloved hands off, and turned to see what was so funny. Four men were leaning on the stockyard fence, their arms crossed on the top rail as they watched Smoke and Cal work.

Smoke nodded and touched the brim of his hat. "Howdy, gents," he said amiably, thinking it was about time for some coffee.

One of the men, who had a face that had seen lots of wear and tear, sneered and inclined his head toward the stock car. "What you boys gonna do with them there Injun ponies? Try and join a tribe?" He threw back his head and laughed heartily at his own lame joke.

Before Smoke could answer, he snorted and added, "Maybe you two oughta grind 'em up an' feed 'em to your dogs, 'cause that's all that Injun hosses are good for."

As he and his cronies laughed at this bit of wit, Smoke's lips got tight. He ambled over to stand in front of the men and said in a good-natured tone of voice, "You seem to have an awfully big mouth, mister." When the men all stopped laughing and stared at Smoke as if he were crazy to speak like that to the man, who was a little under six feet tall and weighed well over two hundred pounds, Smoke added, "Care to put your money where your big mouth is?"

The man bristled as one of his friends said, "You gonna let him talk to you like that, Axel?"

Axel's eyes narrowed. "Whatta you mean about my money, mister?"

Smoke glanced over at his and Cal's Palouse horses where they were tied up at a hitching rail near the entrance to the stockyard. He'd sent the horse he rode up onto the cattle car and was now riding the one called Storm. "My friend and I are both riding those 'Injun' ponies as you called them. I'm willing to bet any amount of money you want to wager that either one of our horses can beat any horse you bring in a race—short or long, it doesn't matter."

Axel glanced at the Palouse studs Smoke had indicated. Both were sleek and well muscled and both just stared back at the man.

"You say I can bring any hoss an' you'll bet on the race without even seein' him run?"

Smoke nodded. "That's right, Axel," Smoke said sarcastically, "unless you were just speaking out of your hat a while ago and want to admit to these friends of yours that you don't know shit about horses or that you're just too cowardly to bet on your judgment of horseflesh."

Smoke watched the big man's muscles bunch under the

skintight shirt he wore as his mouth opened and closed twice without him being able to think of any suitable retort. "It's your call, Axel," Smoke continued, grinning widely. "Put up or shut up."

"How about I just kick your ass all around this here stockyard instead?" Axel asked, sticking out his chest as if he might frighten Smoke with his size.

Smoke shrugged. "You're even stupider than you look, Axel, and that's going a ways," Smoke said. "I was hoping to earn some money from you, but if you want to dance around a little and get those stubs you call teeth knocked out, it's fine with me."

Cal glanced at Smoke. He knew the mountain man didn't usually respond to ignorant people like Axel, but he guessed Smoke was in a foul mood because he was worried about Pearlie.

Cal shook his head and whispered in a loud manner to Axel's friends, "You better tell your friend there to just shut up and go on about his business while he can still eat solid food. Otherwise, in about ten minutes he's gonna be drinkin' his food for the next few weeks."

The man next to Axel laughed. "Your friend said he wanted to make some money . . . how about you, kid?"

Cal grinned. "Sure, I can always use some extra. What did you have in mind?"

The man pulled a crumpled-up wad of bills from his jeans pocket and counted them slowly. "I got eight dollars here says Axel cleans your friend's plow and doesn't even break a sweat doing it."

The other two men quickly reached into their pockets and pulled out money also. After conferring among themselves for a moment, the first man held up a handful of greenbacks. "All told, we got thirty-three dollars here. You can bet it all or any part."

"Oh, I'll definitely take it all," Cal said. He reached into his pocket and brought out his wallet. After a minute, he blushed and glanced at Smoke, who grinned and handed

Cal a wad of money so thick it made the other men's eyes widen in surprise.

Cal peeled off thirty-two one-dollar bills, added one of his own, and handed them to the man. "That'll cover your bet," he said, and climbed up on the fence railing to watch.

Axel pulled a soiled pair of gloves out of his rear pocket and slipped them on as he climbed up and over the fence, grinning at Smoke as if he were going to eat him for breakfast in the next few minutes.

Smoke pulled his own gloves tight and tilted his head as he looked at Axel's scarred eyebrows, cauliflower ears, and bent and misshapen nose. "I usually try not to mess up my opponent's faces when I fight, out of courtesy," Smoke said easily as he and Axel walked in small circles around each other, sizing each other up. "But I can see from yours that you like to fight, and that you usually lead with your nose, so I guess I don't have to worry overly much about what you're going to look like when we're done."

"All you got to worry about, stranger, is who's gonna pick up your pieces when I'm through with you," Axel growled, and he quickly stepped forward and swung a haymaker right cross at Smoke's jaw, obviously hoping to catch the mountain man unawares and end the fight quickly.

Smoke barely leaned his head back and let Axel's fist breeze by, missing his chin by inches.

While Axel was off balance and leaning forward, Smoke reached out and slapped him with an open palm, back and forth, snapping Axel's face to and fro but not hurting him, only his pride.

"This is going to be easier than I thought," Smoke said, grinning widely as Axel's face reddened with fury and embarrassment at the way Smoke had slapped him like a girl.

"You're not only dumber than a post, you can't fight either," Smoke said as he shifted slowly from one foot to the other, keeping his balance.

Axel yelled incoherently at the insults, lowered his head and spread his arms and rushed at Smoke, intending to get him in a bear hug and break his spine.

Smoke danced lightly to the side, stuck out his foot, and tripped the big man, tapping him smartly on the back of the head as he sprawled on his face.

Cal grinned at Axel's friends. "Any more bets, gentlemen?" Cal taunted. "I'm now giving two-to-one odds."

He was met with stunned silence, as Axel's friends watched a man who'd beaten up any and all challengers in Pueblo get his clock wound.

Axel screamed and jumped to his feet, whirling around with his fists up. Smoke danced forward and shot out three lightning-fast jabs with his left hand, smashing Axel's nose and snapping his head back.

When Axel's eyes clouded and went unfocused, Smoke decided to take mercy on him and end it quickly. He twisted his shoulders to the right, and then swung his right hand with all of his might in a mighty uppercut that hit Axel just under the sternum, lifting him off his feet and sending him sprawling backward to land spread-eagled on the dirt, vomit erupting from his bloody mouth.

Smoke rolled him over with the toe of his boot so he wouldn't drown in his own vomit, and then he turned to the men still hanging on the fence. "I believe you're holding our bet money," he said, not even breathing heavily and definitely not sweating.

One of the men jumped down from the fence and grabbed at the six-gun hanging on his hip. Before he could clear leather, Cal drew and backhanded him in the face with his pistol, sending shattered teeth flying and splitting his lips and knocking the man out cold.

Smoke just shook his head. "When will men like you learn it's always easier to just pay your debts than to get stupid and maybe dead?" He cut his eyes at the other men and let his right hand rest on the butt of his pistol, an ominous warning that he would tolerate no further nonsense.

"Here, mister," the man holding the money said in a quavering voice, glancing at his friend's bloody and battered face and at Axel lying motionless on the ground, snoring softly through his ruined nose.

Smoke handed Cal the money and Cal casually stuck it in his pocket. "You ready to hit the trail, Smoke?" he asked.

Smoke smiled and held out his hand. "Sure, as soon as you give me back the money I gave you to cover your bet."

"Oh, yeah," Cal said, grinning as he counted off thirty-two bills and handed them to Smoke. "I almost forgot."

"Uh-huh," Smoke said, taking the money and walking off with his arm around Cal's shoulders. "I was born at night, Cal, but not last night," Smoke said, laughing, "and I didn't come into town on a turnip wagon neither."

15

Robert Jacobson knocked twice and then walked into Sheriff Tolliver's office. "Hey, Buck," he said, stopping short when he saw that Tolliver was deep in conversation with some other men.

Tolliver looked up, annoyance written on his face. "Yeah, Bobby? What is it?"

Jacobson looked pointedly at the other men and cleared his throat. "Uh," he said hesitantly, holding up a yellow piece of paper, "I got another wire from that fellow we were talking about the other day."

Tolliver glanced at Hog Hogarth, Bubba Barkley, Kid Akins, and Jeb Hardy, who were all sitting around his desk. "Oh, don't worry about these men, Bobby. They know all about how I'm looking into that matter."

Relieved, Jacobson handed the sheriff the wire, even though it was addressed to Doc Bentley and wasn't supposed to be given to anyone else, according to the rules of the telegraph company. Jacobson told himself it was all right since the Doc was dead and the sheriff was in charge of prosecuting the man who killed him. "Here it is, Buck. Man said he was leaving Pueblo and headin' this way immediately and for Doc to do whatever he could to keep his friend alive until he got here."

Tolliver smiled sourly. Jensen sounded very concerned about the man named Pearlie. That was good.

It meant Pearlie was more than just a casual friend or riding partner—it was almost as if he was family. Having Smoke care deeply about the man would suit Tolliver's plans nicely.

Tolliver looked up. "Did the wire say if the man who sent it was waiting for a reply?"

"Uh, yeah. Now that you mention it, he is."

"Good. Just send back that nothing has changed and the man is still unconscious . . . and sign the doc's name."

Jacobson's brow wrinkled and he began to sweat as he looked around at the other men present. Ordinarily, it wouldn't bother him overly much to go against the rules of the company, especially for a good cause, but there were far too many witnesses here for comfort. If any one of them talked and the company found out about it, Jacobson knew he'd be fired immediately. "Well, now, Buck. I can't hardly do that. It's not only against the law, it's against the rules of the company I work for. I could get fired if they find out," he finished lamely, his voice rising in pitch until it was an irritating whine.

Buck got to his feet and reached into his pocket and pulled out a five-dollar bill. He folded it over into a small square and stuck it in Jacobson's shirt pocket. He patted his chest, none too lightly. "And you could get a lot worse than fired if you don't do what I tell you too, Bobby. You understand me?" Tolliver asked, his voice harsh and hard. "This here is a murder investigation, and I expect my orders to be carried out to the letter, and without question. Is there anything about that you do not understand?"

"Sure, Buck, sure. I didn't mean nothin' by it. I'll go and get that wire right off," Jacobson said hurriedly, his eyes no longer on the men at the table but on Tolliver, as if he expected the man to reach out and slap him.

"Good, 'cause I wouldn't want Mr. Smoke Jensen to have to wait on word of what's going on with his dear friend," Tolliver said gruffly.

After Jacobson left, Tolliver went back to his desk and sat down, leaning back and putting his feet up on the corner and his hands behind his head. The trial was supposed to start the next day, and it was at least a three-day ride to Payday from Pueblo, if you pushed it.

Hog Hogarth's eyes opened wide and he coughed as if he were choking on something he ate that didn't go down right. "Uh, Buck. You say that galoot that brought that snakebit man into town is Smoke Jensen? Smoke Jensen the famous gunfighter that's killed over two hundred men?"

"That's right, Hog," Tolliver said, realizing this was the first time he'd told his men who they were going to be going up against. "Why? Does it matter to you one way or the other?"

Hog sat back in his seat, his left hand going unconsciously to the sore ribs and flank that still ached from where he'd been beaten. "Uh, not really, Buck."

Bubba shook his head. "The hell it doesn't," he exclaimed. He looked at Hog and said regretfully, "I got to tell him now, Hog, considering who it is we went up against."

"Tell me what?" Tolliver said irritably.

"You remember when Hog an' me came in from being out on the trail and Hog was all crippled up?" Bubba asked, leaning forward in his excitement.

"Yeah, you said he fell off his horse," Tolliver answered.

"Well, that weren't actually the entire truth of the matter," Bubba continued, ignoring the angry look Hog was giving him. "In point of fact, Hog and me braced the two men bringing that sick man into town. Words were said and Hog got into a fistfight with the big man wearing buckskins, the man you now tell us was Smoke Jensen."

Tolliver's eyebrows rose. "You mean to tell me Smoke Jensen beat the shit outta Hog and it was a fair fight? Jensen didn't cheat or anything?"

Bubba shook his head and Hog let his gaze drop to the table, ashamed of everyone finding out he'd been beaten in a fair fight. "Hell, no, Buck. That Jensen is one mean son of a bitch."

"But he's older than dirt," Tolliver said. "Hell, he must be pushing forty-five or fifty."

"I don't give a shit if he's a hundred and fifty, the man is built like an ox and fights like a grizzly bear," Bubba said, rolling his eyes around to make sure the others were listening. "And I for one don't have any intention of ever tangling with that man, leastways not in a fair fight."

Jeb Hardy took a cigar out of his jacket pocket, licked the length of it, and then he put it in his mouth and chewed on it without lighting it. His cold, hard eyes fixed on Tolliver. "How long you gonna let this Jensen thing distract you, Buck? Every day you sit around here messing around with this Pearlie character trying to get to Jensen, we're losing money."

Tolliver stared back. "I'm gonna do whatever it takes to first make Jensen's life a living hell, Jeb, an' then I'm gonna kill him." He paused, his face going flat. "And if you don't like it, there ain't nothing you can do about it."

Hardy's eyes flashed and he straightened in his chair, his right hand automatically pulling back the right edge of his jacket to expose his Peacemaker Colt hanging on his hip. "Oh, you don't think so?" he growled.

Tolliver felt a stab of fear course though his chest and he thought his heart skipped a beat. Hardy was the fastest man with a gun he'd ever seen, and he certainly wasn't afraid to use it, having killed at least fifteen men that Tolliver knew about, and no telling how many others he didn't know about.

He let his feet drop to the floor and he sat up straight, his hands out toward Hardy. "Now, Jeb, don't get your dander up," Tolliver said reasonably. "You know I've got a heavy score to settle with Jensen, and I've been waiting plumb near all my life to do it."

The rigidity went out of Hardy's shoulders and he seemed to relax. "That's so, Buck, but it don't give you call to talk to me like some hired hand neither."

"No offense meant, Jeb. We been friends too long to let something like this come between us."

"Hell with friendship," Hardy said, but his lips were grinning. "I'm talkin' about business and when we're gonna get back down to it."

Tolliver took a deep breath, relieved that the tension was over. "Well, the trial starts tomorrow and it shouldn't last more'n a day . . . two at the most. Jensen should get here about three days from now, about when I'm ready to hang his friend. I might let him stew for another day, and then I'm gonna hang his friend right in front of him and kill him right after that."

Kid Akins snorted. He'd seen Buck draw, and while he was faster than the average man, he was no match for him, or for Jeb Hardy for that matter. "You sure you gonna be able to take Jensen, Buck?" he asked, smiling to show Buck there was no malice nor disrespect in his question.

Tolliver pursed his lips. "Hell, I reckon I can. Jensen was full growed when he shot my brother, an' that was more'n twenty years ago. I'd guess he must be close to forty-five by now, and years piled up on a man who's lived as rough a life as Jensen will tend to make him a mite slower than he was when he was young and full of piss and vinegar."

Akins laughed again and inclined his head toward Hog. "From what I seen that old man do to Hog with his bare hands, Buck, I wouldn't be too sure about him slowing down a whole hell of a lot."

"I don't know either, Buck," Hardy said, shaking his head. "From what I hear when I talk to some of my friends from back when I used to hire my gun out, even though Jensen is retired, word is, he is still pretty damn fast." He stared at Tolliver through his cigar smoke. "Hell, I heard tell he killed a whole passel of men up in Canada a year or so back, and that don't sound like the work of a slow, old man to me."

"Well," Tolliver said, his face dark and flushed from what he was hearing, "if Jensen kills me, I guess I'm just gonna have to depend on my friends here around this table to take him out for me."

Hardy glanced at the others and gave a half smile. "Now, why would we risk going up again' a man as fast as Jensen just to avenge your death, Buck? It sure as hell wouldn't bring you back to life, now would it?"

Tolliver mulled this over for a minute, and then he took pen and paper out of his desk. He bent over and spent another couple of minutes writing, and then he held up the paper for all the men to see. "Here's a good reason, Jeb. I've just written out my will leaving all of my assets to the man who kills Smoke Jensen, and I guess you all know that I've managed to put away quite a nice bundle over the past few years we've been stealing claims."

Hog Hogarth's eyes narrowed. "Just how much we talkin' 'bout, Buck?" he asked. "Not that I think Jensen is gonna kill you nor nothin', but just in case I happen to go up against him again, I'd kind'a like to know what I'm gonna gain by killing the bastard."

"I'd guess what with the land and gold claims and all, it'd be close to a half-a-million dollars, Hog. And it'll all go to the man who plants Smoke Jensen in the ground."

"You know, of course, a will like that ain't exactly legal, Buck," Hardy said.

"Oh, I'll have my lawyer in Pueblo write it up all nice and legal-like, and since he'll be the executor of my will, he'll know exactly what I want him to do."

Hardy smiled slow and easy, but his eyes stayed as dark as a snake's eyes. "I could write that will up for you, Buck, seeing as how I've still got my license to practice law."

Tolliver grinned. "No offense, Jeb, but I'd just as soon not everyone know about what I got stashed away and where, leastways not while I'm still alive."

"Well, not to wish anyone bad luck, Buck, I will say that if Jensen does somehow get the best of you, I will take the son of a bitch down myself."

Kid Akins laughed. "You'll have to stand in line for that kind of money, Jeb ol' son."

"The hell with shooting him," Hog said, holding up two hands as big as hams. "I'll just wring the bastard's neck."

Akins laughed. "Yeah, just like you did last time you went up against him, huh, Hog?"

Hog stuck out his lower lip like a child pouting. "He tricked me, that's all. He tripped me when I wasn't looking."

Bubba didn't say anything, but just sat there staring at Tolliver. He didn't know exactly how much half-a-million dollars was, but he barely had two dimes to rub together, and he'd been in the game with Tolliver since the very start. He wondered how the sheriff had gotten so rich while *he'd* done all the dirty work and was as poor as a church mouse.

He sighed. He'd need to work it over in his mind, but he didn't intend for Buck to retire rich and him have to go back to mucking out stalls for a living. No, sir!

In the Pueblo telegraph office, Smoke took the wire from the telegraph operator and frowned as he read it.

"Bad news?" Cal asked, his face going pale, thinking that maybe the wire said Pearlie was already dead.

"Yeah, but not as bad as it could be," Smoke said, handing the wire to Cal. "Pearlie's not awake yet, and the doctor says there's been no change in his condition."

"So, at least he's not getting any worse," Cal said, trying to sound optimistic.

"That's right, Cal," Smoke said, smiling slightly. "Let's keep our hopes up as we ride, and remember, Pearlie's a fighter. He won't go down easily."

"Damn right," Cal said, hitching up his pants and taking long strides trying to keep up with Smoke as they strode toward their horses.

"How long you reckon it'll take us to get back to Payday without running a string of horses?" Cal asked.

"Three days by the trail, but we can cut a full day off that by cutting through a couple of mountain passes I remember from my days up in these parts with Preacher."

Cal glanced up at the surrounding peaks that were still covered with snow. "You think those passes will be open this early?" Cal asked.

Smoke grinned. "They will be after we go through them."

16

Joshua Banks, wearing a dress suit for the first time in over two months since he gave up practicing law to run his claim and try to find his fortune in the hills around Payday, slapped his hand down flat on the desk behind which he sat looking out at just about everyone who lived within ten miles of the town. He winced as his hand stung and burned, wishing yet again he had a gavel like a real judge and vowing for the tenth time to bring a wooden hammer with him if the trial lasted more than one day—which he doubted it would since the evidence stacked against this Pearlie was so overwhelming.

The trial was being held in the Golden Nugget Saloon and Poker Emporium, the largest structure in the town. The oldest and best of the many saloons and bars in the area, it was made entirely of wood instead of being a wooden front with a tent in the rear like most of the buildings in Payday.

Banks glanced over the crowd, most of whom were staring at Pearlie with undisguised hatred or talking to their neighbors with fire in their eyes. These people had all at one time or another availed themselves of Dr. Bentley's services and all had an interest in seeing his killer hanged by the neck until dead.

Banks shook his head. He was sure that most of the good citizens of Payday thought this entire trial was a waste of time and that the murdering scum should just be hanged so they could go on about their business of pulling gold and silver out of the ground. He had no idea how in the world he would be able to convene a jury that was even remotely fair and impartial, but he was damn sure going to try. One of the reasons he'd elected to give up the practice of law was the corruptness of most of his fellow practitioners. Banks was a rarity among lawyers, and even among men: he was an idealist who felt the guilty should be punished and the innocent freed. Unfortunately, in the few years he'd actively practiced law, he'd found the opposite was often the case, with guilt or innocence more often being a function of the amount of money the accused had rather than his guilt or innocence.

He pointed at the first two rows of chairs that had been hastily arranged in front of his desk. "You men get up and go sit in those jury chairs over there," he said.

A couple of the men gave Pearlie, who was sitting in a chair across the room next to his defender, Sam Hemmings, a withering look that showed they'd be happy to be the ones who sentenced him to die.

Once the men had all taken their seats, Banks began to ask each of them a question. "Josh, I'll start with you," he said. "Have you formed any opinion as to the innocence or guilt of the accused?"

Josh Pringle grinned and looked around at the crowd. "Sure have, Joshua. He's guilty as sin!"

When the crowd erupted with laughter and a few catcalls, Banks banged his hand down on the desk with a resounding smack. "Josh, call me Your Honor whenever I'm in this chair, and you are excused from jury duty."

Pringle's mouth dropped open and he started to reply when Banks pointed a finger at him. "I fully intend to run this trial like it should be run, and anyone in this room who doesn't believe me is welcome to spend a few nights in our jail and a few dollars in fines. As long as you good people elected me to do the dirty work of being a judge on this case, I will be a judge and that means I can fine you, imprison you, or do both as I see fit! Do I make myself clear?" he asked, staring around at the suddenly quiet crowd.

When no one said anything in reply, he added, "The only thing that makes us a town instead of a lynch mob is this court and how we conduct ourselves. If you can't handle that, then you might as well get a rope and go find the nearest tree . . . but you'd better bring two ropes, 'cause you'll have to kill me first to do it!" His eyes flashed as he went on. "I don't intend to be a rubber stamp for a lynching. This will be a fair trial and we will abide by all the rules of jurisprudence."

As he continued with his questioning of the potential jurors, Banks found that they'd learned from his quick dismissal of earlier men how to answer his questions. Suddenly, it appeared that practically every potential juror was supremely fair-minded and impartial, and of course they didn't think Pearlie was guilty yet—they were all going to wait and judge him after all the evidence was in. In a pig's eye, Banks thought. They've just learned to say the right things to get on the jury and probably not one of them was telling the truth.

But, since he could find no real reason to throw them out of the jury pool, and since it was evident that he wasn't going to find twelve men who were really ready to listen, he finally shrugged and seated the twelve men he thought would at least give Hemmings a chance to argue his case, for whatever good it would do the poor bastard named Pearlie.

Banks looked out over the crowd and said, "Now, we're gonna start this here trial, and if anybody in here gets the notion he can disrupt these proceedings by opening his big mouth, then he'll find himself on the outside looking in, and his wallet will be lighter by twenty-five dollars. Is that clear to everyone?"

His question greeted by silence, Banks turned to Sheriff Buck Tolliver, who was sitting at a table on the opposite side of the room from Pearlie's.

"You may begin your prosecution, Sheriff."

Tolliver stood up and cleared his throat. "I'll begin by calling Jonas Slackmeyer to the stand."

The town's undertaker rose ponderously in his characteristic black coat and trousers and boiled white shirt and made his way to the front of the room, where he took a seat in the witness's chair next to Banks's desk.

"Now, Jonas," Tolliver began, "did you examine the bodies of Dr. Hezekiah Bentley and Blackie Johnson on the night of their deaths?"

"I did," Slackmeyer said in his deep, gravelly voice. His demeanor was solemn and grave, as befitted his profession and his duty as medical examiner.

"And what did you find?"

"Well," Slackmeyer said, rubbing his chin and looking upward as he recalled the night, "Blackie was stabbed once in the throat. Looked like the knife entered just below the chin and sliced through the Adam's apple and cut the main artery to the head. He bled out like a stuck pig," Slackmeyer added indelicately. "There wasn't a teaspoon of blood left in the man's entire body."

Tolliver winced at the crudity, and then he nodded and turned and picked up a large knife from his table. The blade was still stained with dried, crusted blood. "Was this the knife you found sticking out of poor Blackie's neck?" Tolliver asked.

"I object to the prosecutor calling Mr. Johnson 'poor Blackie,' Your Honor," Hemmings said. "Blackie wasn't poor, he just elected not to work for a living."

This statement caused Banks and Tolliver to frown, but almost everyone else in the room broke into laughter, for they all knew Blackie had been pretty much of a deadbeat.

"We'll strike the word 'poor' from the question," Banks intoned, glancing down at one of the girls from the saloon who was taking notes of the proceedings.

Slackmeyer waited until the judge was finished and then he nodded and grunted, "Yeah."

Tolliver then picked up Pearlie's gun belt with its holster and pistol still in it and its empty knife scabbard on the rear of the belt. "And does this rig belong to the defendant, Pearlie, as far as you know?"

"Yes, I was told it was his by you, Sheriff," Slackmeyer answered, drawing another laugh from the crowd.

Tolliver held up the belt and holster and theatrically slid the knife into the scabbard on Pearlie's belt, showing it was a perfect fit.

When there was an angry murmur from the crowd, Banks banged his hand down on his desk again, glaring at the offenders with narrowed eyes until they quieted.

Tolliver dropped Pearlie's rig on his table and turned back to Slackmeyer. "Now, what about Dr. Bentley?"

"Doc was shot once in the chest. Appeared to be at close range as his shirt was all burned and stained with gunpowder."

"When you examined Doc's body, was he wearing a side arm?" Tolliver asked.

Slackmeyer shook his head. "Hell, no. Everybody knows Doc never went heeled." He grinned sadly as he looked out at the crowded courtroom. "He even told me once he didn't hold with guns. Said they was only good for two things—killing people and cracking walnuts, an' he wasn't partial to walnuts."

A few men in the room laughed quietly at this remembrance of a man they all liked, and almost everyone glared angrily at Pearlie once again.

"That's all," Tolliver said, and took his seat.

When Slackmeyer started to get up, Sam Hemmings called, "Just a minute, Jonas. I have a couple of questions for you."

Slackmeyer sat back down, a puzzled expression on his face as if he couldn't think of anything else he had to say.

Hemmings stood up and moved to stand in front of the witness stand. "Did you notice anything else about Blackie Johnson when you examined him?"

Slackmeyer thought for a moment, and then shook his head again. "Nope."

Pearlie had told Hemmings when he gave his rendition of the occurrences that night that the man he'd fought with and stabbed had smelled strongly of alcohol, as if he'd been drinking heavily.

"What I'm getting at, Jonas, is the smell. Did you smell anything unusual about Blackie?"

Slackmeyer grinned widely. "No, nothing unusual. Blackie smelled like he always did, like he hadn't bathed in a month of Sundays and like he'd drunk up half the liquor in the saloon that day."

As the crowd stirred, Banks silenced them with another glare.

Hemmings pursed his lips, thinking. So far, what Pearlie had told him checked out, and the newcomer would have no way of knowing Blackie was a habitual drunkard.

"So, you'd say Blackie was drunk at the time he was stabbed to death?"

Slackmeyer nodded, sobering a little. "Hell, Sam, you know Blackie was always drunk if he'd been awake more'n a hour, so I guess I'd have to say he was pretty well lit at the time of his death."

"All right," Hemmings said. "Now, how about the doc? Anything unusual there?"

"He didn't stink, if that's what you mean?" Slackmeyer said, his eyes turning a bit angry, as if Hemmings was trying to sully the doc's reputation.

"No, Jonas, that's not what I mean. Was there anything unusual about the body's position or anything else?" Hemmings asked, not really knowing what he was looking for, since Pearlie had told him he remembered nothing after his scuffle with the man who was trying to rob him.

"No . . ." Slackmeyer began, and then he hesitated, his eyes going unfocused for a moment as he thought back to that night. "Well, yes, there was one thing."

"Oh?"

"Yeah. The doc had a large bump and a gash on the top of his head, like he'd been pistol-whipped or something before he was shot."

Hemmings was suddenly interested. "You don't think

his head injury could have come from falling down and hitting his head after he was shot?"

"Naw, couldn't have been that. There was blood in his hair from the cut, from where it'd bled. The doc had a hole in his chest right through his heart from the bullet. He died instantly, so if he'd hit his head while falling, the wound wouldn't have bled 'cause the heart would've already stopped pumping."

"Was the head wound serious enough to cause the doc to be knocked unconscious?" Hemmings asked.

Slackmeyer scratched his chin. "Yeah, I 'spect so, though it's awfully hard to tell with head wounds. They tend to bleed heavily, so even a small wound can look real bad if all you have to go by is the amount of blood."

"So whoever did this knocked the doc out and then stood over him and placed his pistol against his chest and shot him to death?"

"Oh, I wouldn't go that far, Sam, though it certainly could've happened that way," Slackmeyer said, but his eyes now had a flicker of doubt in them. He knew what the sheriff had told everyone the night of the killing, and it didn't jibe with what he'd just testified to. He took a deep breath. He was going to have to give this some thought.

"That's all I have," Hemmings said, and sat down next to Pearlie.

Tolliver stood up. "I guess I'll have to call myself as the next witness, since I'm the only other one who was there that night and really saw what happened," he said, giving Slackmeyer a withering glare for daring to say the doctor might not have died as he'd testified to.

Banks nodded. "All right, Buck. Just get up there in the witness chair and tell us what you saw."

Tolliver took his seat facing the room. "Well, I was out making my rounds, and Blackie Johnson joined up with me. Like Jonas said, he'd been drinking some over to the saloon and he said he wanted to take a walk to get some fresh air."

Some men in the room snickered at this, knowing that Blackie would never willingly leave a saloon once he'd started drinking until he was thrown out or the place closed for the night. Tolliver glared at them and then he continued. "When we walked down the alleyway behind the doc's house, we noticed the door was open but there weren't any lights burning."

He paused, as if he were trying to recall the exact events of the night. "Suddenly we heard a shot and we both pulled our pistols and ran into the house. When we ran into the parlor, we saw a figure in the dark standing over the doc. Quick as a wink, that man over there," he said, pointing at Pearlie, "stuck a knife in Blackie's throat and shoved his body against me, knocking my gun out of my hand as he ran out of the door. By the time I picked it up and chased him, he was a good ten feet ahead of me and running like hell. I finally caught him at the end of the street and slapped him in the head with my gun and knocked him out." He took a deep breath, and then he added, "When I caught my breath, I looked in his pockets and found the doc's watch and ring and some cash money in them. I figure he was robbing the doc's house when the doc came home and caught him. They must have struggled, and he must have hit the doc over the head with his pistol before he shot him."

He leaned back in his chair. "And that's about it," he said.

"Sam," Banks said, "you got any questions for the sheriff about his testimony?"

Hemmings got to his feet. He'd never particularly liked Buck Tolliver personally, but had always worked fairly well with him on town business. "Buck, that story doesn't make a whole lot of sense to me."

Tolliver's face turned red and he sat forward in his chair, his muscles bunching under his shirt. "What do you mean by that, Sam?" he asked ominously, as if he were ready to jump out of the chair and hit Hemmings in the mouth.

"Well, first off, why'd you let a man as drunk as Blackie was go into a house with you to investigate a gunshot? That's not typical of the way you patrol our streets after dark, is it? In the company of a drunk?"

Tolliver took a deep breath and leaned back, knowing he was going to have to keep his wits about him when he answered these questions or the people in the town might start wondering just what he'd been up to that night. "I didn't exactly *let* him go with me, Sam. You know Blackie. When he asked to walk along with me, I wasn't exactly expecting a double murder. Far as I knew, we were just taking a walk in the evening air. And then when we heard the shot, we just both drew our guns and ran into the house without thinking much about it. There wasn't a lot of time for discussion on the matter."

Hemmings nodded. "And secondly, if my client had just shot the doc and was standing over him with his gun in his hand, why did he take the time to draw his knife and stab Blackie instead of just shooting him and you?"

Tolliver panicked. He hadn't thought of that when he'd made up his story. "Uh . . . I'm damned if I know, Sam. Why don't you ask him?" he said, grinning at the crowd to mask his confusion.

Hemmings didn't return the smile. "I did, Buck. He says he didn't do it, so why don't you make a guess as to what would make a man pull a knife when he has a perfectly good gun in his hand?"

"I told you, Sam, it was dark in there. Maybe . . . maybe he had a gun in one hand and his knife in the other and he just struck out with the hand closest to Blackie."

"So, let me get this straight," Hemmings said. "Pearlie is robbing the doc's house, the doc comes home and catches him, and they have a fight. Pearlie pulls out his gun and his knife during this fight, hits the doc over the head and knocks him out, and then he stands over the body with his knife and gun in his hands and shoots the doc in the chest, making enough noise to wake the entire town instead of just reaching down and cutting his throat if he wanted to kill him. Is that what you think happened?"

Hemmings was getting excited. Suddenly, he believed Pearlie, or at least he knew that things hadn't happened like the sheriff said they did. He could see it in Tolliver's eyes, the way panic hit them when he questioned him.

The man was lying through his teeth. He didn't know why Buck was lying, but he was certain he wasn't telling the entire truth.

Tolliver's jaws clenched and his face turned beet red. "How the hell do I know what happened 'fore we got there, Sam? All I know is we heard a shot and ran in to see what was going on. Blackie got stabbed and that son of a bitch over there ran out of the room and down the alley until I knocked him out and found a bunch of Doc's things in his pockets."

He took a deep breath and leaned back in his chair, forcing himself to calm down. "What went through his mind or why he shot the doc instead of knifing him, I don't know."

Hemmings gave him a flat look and said, "I have no further questions of this witness, Your Honor."

There was a murmur among the men in the crowded room, and more than a few sets of eyes were watching Tolliver, wondering just what was going on between him and Hemmings.

Banks pursed his lips. The tension in the room was thick enough to cut with a knife. He knew he'd better defuse the situation or Tolliver and Hemmings were going to come to blows. "I think we'll adjourn for lunch," he said, glancing at his pocket watch. It was a quarter to twelve—close enough. "Everyone back here at two o'clock, and I don't want anyone to talk to the jury during the break," he said, and he glanced over at the bartender standing behind the bar to his left. "And I don't want any liquor or beer served in this room until after the jury verdict is in."

17

When the trial resumed after lunch, Banks noted the crowd seemed to be in a much better humor, making him surmise a lot of them had drunk their lunch rather than chewed it.

He started to smack his hand down on his desk to call the court to order, stopped, and looked at his red, raw palm. He looked over at the bar. "Curly, bring me that wooden hammer you use to open beer kegs, if you would, please?" he asked.

Once he had the hammer, he banged it down a couple of times, smiling to himself, and said, "This court is now in order." He inclined his head toward Hemmings. "Are you ready to begin, Sam?"

Hemmings got to his feet, and Banks could see the resignation of defeat on his face. "Yes, Joshua . . . uh, I mean Your Honor," he replied. "The defense is ready."

Banks looked at Tolliver, who was sitting at his table with a smug, self-satisfied expression on his face that made Banks angry. It was all right to win a case, but you didn't have to look so all-fired happy about sending a man to his death, even a murderer. "Is the prosecution ready?" he asked archly.

Tolliver gave him a nod and a wink. Asshole, Banks thought. He looked at Hemmings and nodded for him to go ahead with whatever defense he could mount.

Hemmings turned to Pearlie. "Pearlie, would you take the stand, please?"

Pearlie got up and walked to the witness chair, his stride long and confident with no evidence of shame or embarrassment in his manner. He still had a thick cloth bandage on his head where Tolliver had hit him, and the wounds and bruises on his face were still colorful, but his expression was one of quiet confidence that he was in the right and nothing bad could happen to him.

Banks shook his head slightly, and wanted to call out to the young man to not be so sure. It wasn't important to know you were right. You had to prove it to twelve people who had absolutely no reason to believe a word you were saying.

"Now," Hemmings began, "would you tell us what happened in your own words?"

Pearlie nodded. "The last thing I remember before waking up the other night was being up in the mountains with my friends. We were buying some horses from the Nez Percé and I was out in a meadow when I fell off my horse and ended up getting snakebit in the leg and neck. After I killed the snake with my knife," he said, his eyes involuntarily going to the evidence table where his knife lay covered with a dead man's blood, "I must've passed out."

He looked directly into Hemmings's eyes. "I've been told by you, Mr. Hemmings, that after I passed out and became unconscious, my friends brought me here to see the doctor, but I was asleep during all that time. The next thing I remember is waking up the other night in the dark and finding a man standing over me with a gun in his hand. At the time, he was going through my things that were laid out on a nightstand next to my bed. Of course, I didn't know where I was and right then I didn't remember 'bout bein' snakebit—all I saw was that big six-killer the man was holding as the moon glinted off its barrel."

Pearlie paused and cleared his throat, which was becoming hoarse and raspy. Hemmings poured him a glass of water and waited patiently while he drank it down.

When Pearlie continued, he sounded better. "Well, sir,

the man evidently heard me wake up and he turned and pointed his gun at me. I grabbed the barrel and we wrestled around a bit until he fell backward and pulled me out of bed onto him. When we hit the floor, my belt and holster fell off the bedside table and I saw the handle of my knife. I didn't know why, but I was weak as a newborn kitten, so knowing I couldn't hold the barrel of that Colt away from me forever, I grabbed the knife and jammed it in his throat." Pearlie paused, his face becoming pale when he remembered how much blood had spurted out of the man's neck. "I . . . uh . . . managed to hit him in the neck and he jerked back and fell down and died. When I tried to get up, everything went black, and the next thing I remember is waking up in jail with a real bad headache and a pretty woman fussing over a cut on my face and head."

Hemmings, who'd been watching the jury and the crowd out of the corner of his eyes, noted that the men were interested in what Pearlie was saying, but he also knew that that didn't mean they believed him.

"And that is all that you remember of the night the two men were killed?" he asked.

Pearlie nodded. "Yeah, like I say, I did kill the one man with my knife, but only 'cause he was aiming to kill me. I never even saw the doctor that was trying to help me, and I ain't the kind to steal from someone bent on doin' me a good turn." He hesitated and his face filled with color as he added, "Or steal from anyone, for that matter."

"So you have no idea who might have come in and killed Dr. Bentley?"

Pearlie hung his head. "Mr. Hemmings, I don't even know how I got my pants on. Last I remember, I was in some kind of nightshirt in a strange bedroom and lying in another man's blood."

"That's all I have, Pearlie," Hemmings said. He turned to the sheriff. "Buck, your witness."

Tolliver stood up at his table and fixed Pearlie with a hard, flat look. "I have no questions for this lying son of a bitch," he said.

He ignored Hemmings when he jumped up and hollered, "I object, Your Honor!"

Tolliver didn't wait for the court's ruling but continued. "I know what I saw and I saw the bastard standing over the doc's dead body and I saw him stick his knife in Blackie's throat right in front of me."

"I won't have any name-calling in this court," Banks said, slapping his hammer down on his desk and glaring at Tolliver. "Now if you're through with this witness, and if Sam has no further witnesses," he said, looking at Hemmings, who shook his head, "then I'll give the case to the jury."

"Hey, Joshua," a voice called from the back of the room.

Banks looked up, irritation on his face. "What is it, Bob?" he asked.

Robert Jacobson, the owner of the general store, stood up. "Why ain't you all calling Miss Rule to testify? Maybe she could tell you what she saw that night."

"Miss who?" Banks asked, raising his eyebrows.

"Janet Rule," Jacobson answered. "She's the doc's aunt and she was staying with him for a few days 'fore he got kilt." He looked around the room. "I know 'cause the doc bought some special bathing salts for her when she got in the week 'fore he got killed."

Tolliver turned pale as all the blood ran from his face. Damn, he thought, I didn't see nobody else in the house that night. He had a sudden urge to run from the room, get on his horse, and ride like hell out of town.

Banks looked around the room. "Well, has anyone here seen or heard from this Miss Rule since the night of the murders?" he asked.

Joe Samuelson raised his hand and said, "I saw an older lady that night, Joshua. She woke me up and took a room in my hotel."

"Why would she go to a hotel the same night her nephew was killed?" Banks asked.

Samuelson shrugged. "I dunno. Maybe she didn't want to stay in a house with two dead men in it."

As the crowd gave a low laugh at this bit of humor, Banks frowned and asked, "Is she still there?"

Samuelson shook his head. "Nope. She paid her bill the next morning and took off. I ain't seen hide nor hair of her since."

"She happen to say where she was going?" Tolliver asked, trying to hide his excitement at this new development. Maybe if he found out where she was first, he could make sure she never gets to tell anyone her story, if she did in fact see him kill the doctor.

"Nope. She just walked out of the lobby and disappeared," Samuelson answered.

Tolliver turned back to Banks. "Joshua, I'll try and find this lady, but evidently she don't have nothing to add or she'd be here to tell it. Why don't you let the jury be thinking on what they want to do while I go look for her? If she has something to say about that night that'll be helpful, then I'll bring her in."

"I object, Your Honor," Hemmings said. "The defendant should have the benefit of this woman's testimony before the jury is released to deliberate."

"I agree, Sam," Banks said gravely, "but it's like Buck says. If she's in town, she's sure as hell heard about the trial, and if she's not here, then she evidently doesn't have anything to add. On the other hand, if she's left town, there isn't anything we can do about it since she could be just about anywhere by now. If Buck can find her before the jury comes in with a verdict, then I'll allow her to speak. Otherwise, we go with what we have."

"But—"

"I've spoken," Banks said, and then in a more kindly tone of voice he added to Hemmings, "My hands are tied, Sam. There's nothing else I can do." He looked up and addressed the crowd of spectators. "Court's adjourned while the jury deliberates." He glanced at the jury. "You men go on over to the livery and you can have your meeting there while you decide if this man is guilty and if he is, what sentence you'd like to impose."

"Uh, Joshua, it's almost dinnertime," one of the men on the jury said. "Can we go home an' eat an' then do our deliberatin'?"

Banks smiled. "No, George, you can't. I'll have something sent over from the hotel dining room to tide you over until you've made your decision."

Sheriff Buck Tolliver didn't waste any time hanging around the courtroom after Banks sent the case to the jury. He practically ran out of the saloon and over to his office. His cronies Jeb Hardy and Kid Akins followed him at a discreet distance. Bubba Barkley and Hog Hogarth headed instead for the nearest bar, Hog still limping badly on his injured leg, telling Hardy and Akins to let them know if Tolliver needed anything.

"Damn, damn, and double damn!" Tolliver ranted, pacing around his office like a wild man, kicking at the stove and throwing the empty coffeepot against a wall.

Hardy and Akins walked in just in time to see the coffeepot carom off the wall. "My, my," Hardy said, grinning at Akins, "the sheriff seems to have a burr under his saddle this afternoon."

Tolliver whirled around, panting, his hair askew, looking like he was in the midst of a fit of apoplexy. "Why the hell didn't you tell me the doc had some old-maid aunt visiting him?" he asked. "You knew I'd been out of town for over a week when she came."

Hardy shrugged. "You didn't ask, Buck," he said in an even tone, though his eyes were flat and hard at the way Tolliver was talking to him. "Besides, how were we to know you were going to hatch some harebrained scheme to kill that fellow that was lying unconscious over at the doc's place?" He paused, and then he added, "You didn't exactly share your plans ahead of time with us, Buck ol' man, and after it was over and all hell broke loose, I plumb forgot about the old lady being there visiting."

Tolliver began to calm down, realizing Hardy was right. He hadn't told his friends what had really happened at the doc's until well after everything had gone horribly wrong and Blackie was dead.

He took a seat behind his desk, but was so agitated he

couldn't sit still, and fidgeted in his seat like a schoolboy with a full bladder. "Well, we have to find her and make sure she didn't see anything that night."

Hardy leaned back in his chair and shifted the toothpick he was chewing on from one side of his mouth to the other as he stared speculatively at Tolliver. "What do you mean we, Buck? Far as I remember, the boys and me didn't have nothing to do with that little fuck-up you engineered at the doc's." He glanced at Kid Akins. "All we're being paid by the city to do is to guard the town in case some of the defendant's hardcase friends try to shoot it up."

Tolliver's face went flat and he tried without much success to hide the anger in his eyes. "No, you're not on the hook for that, Jeb, but we've been making a pretty good living with our little operation against the miners in the area." He too sat back and crossed his legs at the ankle as he put them up on the corner of his desk, trying to appear in control and unafraid, though it was difficult. "It would seem to me that if I get arrested for murder and hanged, it might just put a crimp in your plans to retire within the next year with enough money to live out the rest of your days without ever having to work again."

Hardy pursed his lips and glanced at Akins, who merely shrugged. They could see Tolliver had a point, and a good one. They'd all been living high on the hog the way things were, and Buck was right, losing him and the protection he offered them by being sheriff would be a major blow.

Before he could answer, Tolliver added, "And if that's not enough of a reason for you to help me, you might want to consider that if I'm in jail, then the extent of my holdings and bank accounts are sure to come out." He looked from Akins to Hardy, his eyes becoming dark. "And if people around here start to investigate just how I accumulated all that money and all those claims, they might just stumble upon some other men in the town who have a lot more than they should in the bank and whose names are on some of the same mining claims as mine."

Hardy's face flushed. "You're not threatening to spill the beans on our little arrangement, are you, Buck?" he asked, his voice silky smooth with danger. "'Cause if you are, the simple way for the boys and me to protect ourselves from hanging would be to put a lead pill in your skull."

Buck's eyes widened and his hand moved to his thigh just above his pistol. "That might not be as easy as you think, Jeb; and it might keep you out of jail and your neck out of a noose, but it sure as hell wouldn't make you any money in the future."

Hardy sighed and sat back, relaxing as he realized Tolliver was correct. "You're right, Buck," he said in a more normal voice. "Why should we mess up a good thing, a scheme that's going to make us all rich?"

Tolliver let his feet flop to the floor and he leaned forward on his desk. "I'm glad you see it that way, Jeb. Now, what you and the boys can do for me is to ask around town about this Rule lady. She's either staying here hiding out with someone, or she's left town, an' the only way she could've left town is by train or by stagecoach."

Kid Akins leaned against the stove, which was cold and unlit since Tolliver had been in the saloon/court all morning. "Why do you need us to do the askin', Buck? After all, you're the sheriff around here."

"Oh, I'll do some light snooping, Kid, but I can't seem too anxious about it or it might seem suspicious." He grinned. "And if she did see me kill the doc and she finds out I'm asking around about her, she's sure to hightail it outta here first chance she gets."

Akins frowned, "Well, just what reason can I give for askin' 'bout some old lady's whereabouts?"

"Just tell them you owe the doc some money for a past treatment and you want to make sure his family gets what's coming to them," Tolliver said, exasperated that he had to do all the thinking for his band of thieves.

Hardy gave a lopsided grin. "Or you could just tell them you're looking for a date to the next Sunday picnic."

Tolliver and Hardy both laughed at that, for they all knew Akins had a reputation for jumping just about anything that walked on two legs and was female, and they weren't too sure about *two* legs.

18

As the jurors pulled up square bales of hay to sit on in the livery, Danny Boyd, a miner from the foothills near town, groused, "I don't know why in the hell we're even bothering to sit down. It's a clear as the nose on your face that the son of a bitch is guilty."

Royce Peterson, a rancher from the lowlands south of town, cocked his head and disagreed. "I don't know, Danny. The boy don't look like no killer to me."

Jack Dunhill, a man who did odd jobs around town to earn drinking money, broke in. "Well, now, Royce, anybody can be a killer if the situation is right."

"Yeah," Peterson said. "Anyone can kill on the spur of the moment or if they're frightened enough, but to knock a man out and stand over him and shoot him while he's unconscious, and then to stab another man in the throat, takes someone who's a lot more cold-blooded than that Pearlie fellow appears to be." He looked around at the others. "Did you see the way he looked right in Sam's eyes while he was telling his story? Hell, I'd bet my last dollar that boy didn't have nothing to hide and he was telling the whole truth."

"Hang on here a minute," Boyd said heatedly. "The sheriff says he saw him standing over the doc's body and saw him stab Blackie Johnson in the neck. Now, either Pearlie killed the two men, or the sheriff is lying about what happened that night." He paused and glared around at the other eleven men in the livery stable. "And I can't for the life of me think of why the sheriff'd be doing that."

Willie Baker, a cook at the hotel dining room, agreed. "I think Danny hit the nail on the head. Either Pearlie killed 'em, or the sheriff did. Now, I don't think Buck Tolliver is above lying about some things, but I can't see him killing the doc for no reason at all, and Pearlie did admit he killed Blackie."

"But he said he did that in self-defense," Peterson argued back. "And I know Blackie Johnson was not above pilfering someone else's belongings if the occasion presented itself. Why, just last year, the Widow Paulson said she hired Blackie to do some odd jobs around her ranch and she said half her milk money was missing after he left."

Wally Broadman, a driver who drove the wagons loaded with gold and silver ore to Pueblo, spoke up. "I can see that we have some disagreement among the troops," he said good-naturedly. "And we haven't even talked about the doc's aunt and what she might have to say yet."

"Yeah, how about that?" Peterson said, sticking his chin out like he was ready for a good argument.

Wally held up his hand. "I have an idea that might just get us outta here 'fore the cows come home."

When everyone looked expectantly at him, he said, "Now it all boils down to this: Either the boy is lying and he done it, or the sheriff is lying and he done it. Since we don't have no evidence or even any reason the sheriff would do something like that unless Miss Rule can tell us different, we got to figure it's the boy that's lying. How about we vote guilty on the charges of murder and sentence the young man to hang, but add in our verdict that the hanging is not to be carried out for at least two weeks to give the sheriff time to track down Miss Rule and see just what she has to say, if anything. That way, if she clears the boy, he can be released, and if she don't, he gets to dance on the air."

After some more desultory discussion, the men all

agreed to do as Wally suggested, and the verdict was delivered to Joshua Banks at the office in the bank he had been using during the trial.

When he read the verdict, Banks shook his head sadly. He knew it was the correct verdict considering the evidence, but damnit all, sometimes you just got a gut feeling something was wrong. That was the way it was for him in this case. Everything pointed at Pearlie as guilty, but Banks just couldn't bring himself to believe the boy was a stone-cold killer like he'd have to be to do what had been done.

Banks put on his coat and hat and sent a boy who worked in the bank to go and get the sheriff so he could give him the verdict personally. He knew the sheriff wasn't going to like the part about the hanging being delayed until Miss Rule could be found, but Banks agreed with the reasoning behind it. If there was another witness to the crime, it was only fair to the defendant for her to be found and questioned before he was hung by the neck until dead.

Sheriff Buck Tolliver tried to hide his anger at having his hands tied when Banks summoned him and gave him the news of the verdict and its prohibition against staging the hanging until after Miss Rule had been found and questioned.

He nodded, doing his best to keep his clenched jaws shut tight and not to rail against the stupidity of the jury for having the effrontery not to fully believe his testimony.

"All right, Joshua," he said stiffly. "I'll send a wire to the sheriffs in Pueblo and Denver to be on the lookout for someone fitting Rule's description."

Banks sighed. He could sense Tolliver's anger. "Don't take this as an insult to your word, Buck. It's just that the jury didn't seem to feel Pearlie was the sort of violent man who could do such cold-blooded murders."

Tolliver snorted and slapped his hand against his thigh. "And what am I, Joshua? A man who'd lie about something as serious as the doc's murder?" He almost growled when he added, "A man I been friends with for several years?"

Banks shook his head. "Come on, Buck. You know you

haven't exactly gone out of your way to be a friend to the people of this town. Hell, half of them cross the street when they see you coming down the boardwalk 'cause they know you got a bad temper and they're half-afraid you'll explode at them over some minor infraction."

"That's the trouble with people, Joshua," Tolliver spit. "They want someone tough enough to keep the peace and keep the desperados from overrunning their town, but then when they hire someone like that, they don't want him coming into their nice neat houses and stinking them up with the scent of his dangerousness."

"You're right, Buck," Banks said, shrugging. "It's not fair, but it *is* the way people are, and you were aware of that when you took the office—and the job."

"Yeah, well, after this is all over, the good citizens of Payday might just be looking for someone else to keep their fat out of the fire," Tolliver said, whirling on his heels and storming out of the office.

Banks took a deep breath and smiled slightly, muttering, "And perhaps that would be a good thing, Buck, a good thing for this town and everyone in it."

He got slowly to his feet, grabbed his hat, and prepared to reconvene court and read the verdict to the defendant and the rest of the townspeople. All in all, he figured it was a fair and just verdict, especially given that it required Miss Rule to corroborate the sheriff's story about what happened before the young man could be hung.

Two days later, a trail-weary Smoke Jensen and Cal Woods road their horses down the main street of Payday. They were about frozen clear through from their journey through the mountain passes between Pueblo and Payday, where they'd slogged through snow that was clear up to their horses' withers.

"You want to get something to eat first or head straight to the doctor's office?" Cal asked.

"Let's take a quick look in on Pearlie and make sure nothing's changed before we go to the hotel," Smoke suggested, though every weary muscle in his body cried out for rest and a hot bath.

When they reined up in front of the doctor's office, they found the door locked and a black wreath of dead flowers nailed to the door.

Smoke shook his head. "I don't like the looks of this, Cal."

"Me neither, Smoke, but Pearlie's just a patient of the doctor's. If he'd died, there wouldn't be no wreath on the door."

Smoke stood on the porch and looked around the town, wondering just what had happened in his absence. There was a sense of something going on, something that had changed the town and made its citizens seem more somber, less friendly. Finally, he crossed the street and stopped a man walking toward the general store.

"Say, mister," he said, "excuse me, but could you tell me why the doctor's office is locked up in the middle of the day and why there is a wreath on the door?"

The man glanced at Smoke and Cal's trail-soiled clothes and their lathered horses and said, "You just got into town, didn't you?"

Smoke and Cal nodded.

The man looked over their shoulder at the doctor's office and crossed himself. "Well, the doc was shot down and killed a week or so ago, along with a sheriff's deputy who was knifed to death when he came to investigate the shooting."

Smoke's heart began to race and he felt a cold sweat break out on his forehead. "What about the man who was staying with the doctor? The man who was unconscious from a snakebite?"

The townsman's eyes widened a bit and he looked over at the jail. "Why, that's the fellow that did the killing. He's in jail, convicted of two murders and scheduled to hang in the next week."

"That's a lie!" Cal almost shouted, taking a step toward the man as if it were all his doing.

Smoke stretched out an arm and held Cal back. "Take

it easy, Cal. We'll get to the bottom of this later, after we've had a chance to talk to Pearlie."

He turned back to the man. "Sorry about my friend, mister, he's a mite excitable. Now, did you say the accused man is in the jail?"

The man slowly edged away from Smoke and Cal as if he were afraid they might attack him at any moment. "That's right, mister." And then he hurried away, glancing back over his shoulder a time or two to make sure the two crazy men weren't following him.

Cal turned and headed toward the jail, until Smoke again stopped him with a hand on his shoulder. "Hold on, Cal, don't go off half-cocked."

"But ain't we gonna go see about Pearlie?" Cal asked, almost jumping up and down in his anxiety to get to his friend and help him.

Smoke nodded. "Yeah, but not looking like saddle tramps. The man said he wasn't scheduled to hang until next week, so we've got time to kind'a scout out the situation before we go blundering into something without knowing exactly what we're facing." Smoke looked around again at the surrounding town. "I don't like the mood the town is in. It's as if they're all heated up about something. The whole town feels like a powder keg about to blow, and I don't want us to get caught in the explosion."

Cal took a deep breath. "You're right, Smoke. Something fishy is going on here 'cause Pearlie wouldn't shoot nobody, not unless they was gonna shoot him first."

Smoke walked back across the street to the rail in front of the doctor's office, grabbed his horse's reins, and swung up into the saddle. "Let's get our horses taken care of and then get rooms in the hotel and get cleaned up. After we've had a bite or two to eat and had time to ask some questions around town, we'll mosey on over to the sheriff's office and see what we can find out from Pearlie."

Cal brightened up marginally. "You think they might have a hot bath over there?" he asked.

"They'd better or I'm gonna shoot somebody myself," Smoke said, grinning.

19

Smoke and Cal walked into the hotel and placed their saddlebags on the floor in front of the desk.

The desk clerk took one look at their road-weary look, dirty and dusty buckskins, and unshaven faces, and turned up his nose. "I'm afraid this is a quality hotel, gentlemen," he said in a snooty voice, "and very expensive. If you desire . . . uh . . . less luxurious accommodations, you might try Barstow's tent around the corner."

Smoke took a deep breath, and he curbed his anger, realizing he really couldn't blame the man because they did rather look like itinerant saddle tramps. Instead, he took a wad of greenbacks out of his pocket that was large enough to choke a horse, and held them in his hand ready to count out what he needed. "And just how much would two rooms, a hot bath, someone to do our laundry, and a visit from a good barber cost in this town, sir?" he asked amiably.

The clerk's Adam's apple bobbed up and down in his skinny neck as he swallowed twice. "Uh . . . that ought to cover it," he said, reaching out and taking a twenty-dollar bill off the top of Smoke's stack of money.

Smoke grinned. "I just want to rent a couple of rooms, not buy them," he said in a light voice.

The clerk gave a polite laugh, turned the register around, and handed Smoke a pen. While Smoke signed the register, the clerk picked two keys out off the wall behind the desk and handed them to Cal.

"Now, about that bath and the barber," Smoke said.

"It'll take me at least an hour to heat up enough water for two baths, unless you want to share the water?"

"Not hardly," Smoke said grimly.

"All right then, I'll have a boy take your things up to your rooms if you want to get a bite to eat while you wait . . . Mr. . . . uh . . ." The clerk whirled the register around and read the name. "Smoke Jensen?" he asked, almost choking on his tongue.

"That's right," Smoke said easily.

"Is that *the* Smoke Jensen?" the clerk asked, turning pale when he realized how he'd talked to one of the most famous gunfighters and most dangerous men in the country just a few short moments before.

"I'm the only one with that name I've ever come across," Smoke said, having to bite his lip to keep from laughing at the terrified expression on the clerk's face.

"You hankering to eat?" Smoke asked Cal, who just shrugged. "Aw, the hell with it," Smoke said. "Let's go see Pearlie while they heat up our water."

He turned to the clerk. "Have those baths ready in an hour and have the barber standing by a half hour after that," he said, flipping a five-dollar gold piece on the counter. "That's for your trouble," Smoke said as the clerk magically made the gold piece disappear without seeming to look at it.

Smoke didn't bother to knock on the sheriff's office door, but just jerked it open and strode inside, almost giving Tolliver a heart attack when he looked up and saw his greatest enemy walk in.

Tolliver cleared his throat and reached down under the desk to unhook his rawhide hammer thong in case Jensen caused any trouble.

"Yeah?" Tolliver croaked through a dry mouth, and

then he cleared his throat and tried again. "Can I help you gentlemen with something?"

"We hear you got a friend of ours locked up here," Smoke said quickly, his eyes narrowing as he saw something vaguely familiar about the sheriff's face.

"Would that be a man named Pearlie?" Tolliver asked, leaning back in his chair and starting to enjoy the look of discomfiture on Jensen's face.

"It would."

Tolliver got slowly to his feet, picking a ring of keys up off a nail in the wall behind his desk. "I'm gonna have to ask you to leave your weapons out here," he said, inclining his head at the several pistols and knives on Smoke's and Cal's belts.

Smoke just stared at him. "I don't think so," he said, his voice low and hard. "Nobody gets my guns while I'm still alive, Sheriff, and that includes you."

When Tolliver's face turned red and his cheeks puffed out, Cal said, "Look, Sheriff, if we wanted to start trouble we'd have come in here with our guns in our hands and you wouldn't have stood a chance. We just want to talk to our friend for a few minutes to find out his side of the story."

Tolliver cooled down at the reasonable tone of Cal's voice. He snorted. "The jury has already heard his side of the story an' they didn't believe a word of it, but I guess it won't hurt to let you have a few words with him."

When Smoke turned to enter the door into the cell block, the sheriff added, "But I'm gonna be watching from the door and I'm gonna have an express gun in my hands. You try to slip that boy a weapon, an' it'll be the last thing you ever do."

As Smoke walked through the door and the sheriff took a short-barreled Greener off the wall rack, Smoke muttered loud enough for Tolliver to hear, "And if you point that shotgun at me, it'll be the last thing *you* ever do."

Tolliver's face paled at the threat, but he opened the door and pointed them toward the last cell on the row. As they walked down the short corridor, Tolliver leaned back against the doorjamb, the express gun cradled in his arms, but he was careful not to point it in Smoke's direction.

When Pearlie heard the cell-block door open, he sat up on his bunk and blinked his eyes against the sudden light from the doorway. His cell had no window in it and it was almost as dark as night.

"Who is that?" he asked, his voice weak and thready from lack of water and disuse.

"It's me and Cal," Smoke said, making sure to keep a few steps back from the bars on Pearlie's cell door.

"Smoke . . . Cal . . ." Pearlie cried with relief. "I thought you'd forgotten all about me."

"Not a chance," Cal said. It almost broke his heart to see the way Pearlie looked. He appeared to have lost ten or fifteen pounds, his skin was pale and shrunken-looking, and his eyes were lackluster. It just wasn't the same old Pearlie he'd come to know. "It just took us a while to get the hosses on the way to Big Rock and to get back here to see you."

"Pearlie," Smoke said, "it's real good to see you awake and doing better, but what the hell happened to get you arrested for murder?"

Cal's eyes narrowed when he noticed the black-and-blue swelling and gash on Pearlie's head. "And what the hell happened to your head?" he asked.

Pearlie leaned up against the bars, his hands clinging to them as if he were drowning. He cut his eyes toward the sheriff down the corridor. "That was a gift from the sheriff, though I don't remember it much."

Smoke took out his fixings and built two cigarettes, using the routine to get his temper in check. He felt like running back down the corridor and beating the shit out of the sheriff for what he'd done to his friend. He handed one to Pearlie, who looked as if he needed it, and he lit it and then the one he screwed in the corner of his mouth.

"Why don't you tell us about it?" he asked, leaning back against the wall, crossing his feet at the ankles, and smoking slowly as he watched Pearlie.

Pearlie told them how he'd awakened to find a strange man with a gun in his hand going through his things and how they'd struggled and how he'd ended up stabbing the man to death.

"And was that the doctor?" Cal asked.

"No, evidently not," Pearlie said. "It was some man named Blackie Johnson, the sheriff's cousin and part-time deputy."

"What happened then?" Smoke asked.

Pearlie shrugged. "I don't rightly know, Smoke. I got up off the floor and things started to go kind'a crazy. I blacked out and when I woke up, I was in jail with this gash on my head and a pretty woman fixin' it up."

Cal grinned. "Leave it to Pearlie to fall into a bucket of shit and come out with a girl."

"And that's all you remember?" Smoke asked, trying to stay focused on his story.

Pearlie nodded, and then his knees buckled and he almost fell to the floor. He caught himself and stumbled back over to his cot and sat on it, leaning back against the wall and holding his head.

"What's the matter?" Cal asked, alarmed at how pale Pearlie looked all of a sudden.

"All I been getting to eat is bread and a little soup that's more water than meat," Pearlie said.

"The doctor said you needed lots of heavy beef stew to help you get over the snakebite," Smoke said.

Pearlie gave a half grin. "Well, since they claim I killed that doctor, they ain't exactly been trying to follow his advice about my welfare."

"We'll see about that," Smoke said grimly. "We'll sniff around town and see what we can come up with, Pearlie. You sit tight."

"Do I have a choice?" he asked, gamely trying to keep his spirits up.

Smoke smiled gently and handed him the bag of tobacco and some papers and matches. "You do like I said, Pearlie. Leave the worrying to us."

As Smoke and Cal walked down the corridor, Pearlie called out, "Say, Smoke."

"Yeah?" Smoke asked, stepping back to his cell door.

"There was something about the doc's aunt, a Miss Janet Rule, who was supposed to be in the house that night. She's disappeared, but she might know something about what really happened if you can find her."

Smoke nodded. "We'll see what we can do, pal."

When they got back into the sheriff's office and he'd relocked the door to the cell block, Smoke asked, "What's this I hear about there being a possible witness to the doctor's murder?"

Tolliver almost choked and his mouth went dry. "Uh, where'd you hear that?"

"Never mind. Is there?"

"Yeah, I guess so. The doctor's aunt was visiting and she might've seen something, but I've got wires out to Denver and Pueblo and I'm sure we'll find her and she'll tell us your friend in there killed the two men."

"Well, I hope you don't mind if we do some looking for her too, Sheriff."

Tolliver felt sick at the thought of Jensen finding Rule before he did, but he forced a smile on his lips. "Of course not. The more the merrier."

"And just what is this I hear about the prisoner not getting anything but bread and water to eat?"

Tolliver shrugged and had to struggle not to grin. He loved seeing Jensen so worried about his friend, and his worrying was just starting. "The county don't have a lot of money to be spending on food for a man due to hang in a week," Tolliver answered smugly.

"Well, I'm going to pay to have the cook over at the hotel fix him three square meals a day and deliver them over here. Is that all right with you?"

Tolliver did grin this time. "Sure it is. Course I might have to sample them meals to make sure they're all right for the prisoner."

Smoke took a step toward the sheriff, who backed up and laid his hand on the butt of his pistol. Smoke grinned, his face only inches from Tolliver's. "I'd be very careful how you treat my friend, Sheriff. Very careful indeed, 'cause if he tells me you as much as touched him, or if I see any more evidence he's been pistol-whipped, then you'd better never cross my path again."

"Is that a threat, Jensen?" Tolliver asked, becoming angry when his voice quavered and broke a bit. " 'Cause if it is, I could arrest you and put you in jail right now."

Smoke stepped back and regarded Tolliver with a speculative look. "I see you know my name, Sheriff. How is that?"

Tolliver could have kicked himself for making such a blunder. He wasn't quite ready to let Jensen know they'd crossed paths before. "Uh . . . I've seen your face on some old wanted posters."

Smoke pursed his lips and stared into Tolliver's eyes. "My face hasn't been on a wanted poster in over ten years, Sheriff."

Tolliver smirked, trying to regain the high ground he'd lost. "I've got a long memory, Jensen."

Smoke reached out and poked Tolliver in the chest with a stiff finger. "Good, then you won't forget what I said about treating my friend right, will you?" When Tolliver failed to respond, Smoke added, "And I am going to have a talk with the mayor of this hole-in-the-wall and find out just why the town can't afford to feed its prisoners."

Tolliver didn't bother to answer as Smoke and Cal walked out of the door and moved down the street. He went to his window and watched them walk directly into the hotel.

Damn, he thought. This is getting out of hand. If Jensen finds Rule before I do and he talks to her, he might just be able to figure out what really happened.

He slammed his hand down on his desk. Damn that jury for tying his hands and setting the hanging date so far away. It would give Jensen far too much time to fool around trying to find out what really happened that night.

As he was thinking on how he might prevent that, he saw Bubba Barkley enter the saloon across the street. That was it. He'd send Barkley over to the hotel and see if the big man might be able to stop Jensen from finding the old lady. Hell, he'd offer the man a hundred dollars and Bubba would jump at the chance to prove himself tougher than the gunfighter, especially after the way the gunfighter had humiliated him and Hog in their first meeting.

It wouldn't be nearly as satisfying as killing Jensen himself, but he couldn't afford the luxury of that sort of vengeance now that the mountain man was looking for Miss Rule. Better to end it quickly and get on with making money.

Besides, as long as Jensen got planted and it was him that caused it to happen, it didn't really matter who actually pulled the trigger, he reasoned.

20

Tolliver locked up the jail and walked across and down the street to the saloon he'd seen Bubba enter. Sure enough, the big asshole was already sitting at a table with one of the ugliest saloon girls in town on his lap and a bottle of whiskey in his hand.

Bubba sure as hell wasn't no prize in the looks department, Tolliver thought, but as long as he was spending good money, he damn sure ought to make sure he got a better-looking woman to spend it on.

Tolliver shook his head as he saw Bubba not bothering with a glass as he tried to pour the whiskey down the woman's throat. She was laughing, but her eyes were cold and dead as he managed to get most of it on the front of her dress. She was obviously pretending to be having a good time, and Tolliver wondered why Bubba couldn't see that.

As ugly as she is, he'd do better pouring the rotgut down his own throat so he could manage to sleep with her without tying a feed bag to the nag's face, Tolliver mused as he made his way through the crowded room toward his friend.

Bubba glanced up through eyes that were either already red from a morning's drinking, or still red from the night before's drinking. Either way, the man was pretty well lit and Tolliver hesitated, not wanting to make the same mistake of sending a drunken man to do a delicate job of assassination as he had with Blackie.

Bubba looked up and noticed Tolliver approaching, and his little pig eyes cleared and stared with a surprising sharpness at the sheriff when he came up to the table. Maybe he's not as drunk as I thought, Tolliver figured.

"Hey, Buck ol' buddy," Bubba said, squeezing the whore's right breast with his right hand, which was draped over her shoulders, hard enough to make her wince. "Sit down an' have a little nip to take the chill off."

He moved his hand until his fingers were inside the top of her dress, and he moved them back and forth as he added, "I'm sure Molly won't mind an extra man at the table."

Tolliver frowned and jerked his head to the side. "Beat it, Molly. Bubba and I have some business to discuss and we need some privacy."

Molly made a pout and stuck out her lip, but when Tolliver raised his hand and stepped toward her, she jumped up off Bubba's lap and hurried away, looking back over her shoulder with a frightened expression.

Bubba looked after her and then up at Tolliver. "Well, now, Buck, you done run off my mornin's entertainment, so you might as well set and tell me what's on your mind."

Tolliver realized the slur had left Bubba's words and that the man wasn't nearly as drunk as he'd pretended to be. That thought made Tolliver wonder just how much of Bubba's apparent dumbness was put on and how much the man really knew about their business dealings together. It wasn't a comforting thought to start the day off with.

As Bubba raised the whiskey bottle to take another drink, Tolliver reached out and stopped him. "You might want to hold off on that stuff until you've heard what I have to say," he said, lowering his voice so the men at nearby tables couldn't hear him.

Now Bubba's eyes looked really interested. He sensed there might be some profit for him in Tolliver's strange actions. He set the bottle down, put his elbows on the table, and hunched forward so his face was close to Tolliver's over the table. "So, what's so damned important that you not only take away my slash, you mess with my drinkin' too?"

"I got a job for you, Bubba, and you can earn nice money if you can do it right now."

Bubba cocked his head to the side, and his eyes were sharp as tacks as they bored into Tolliver's. "Uh-huh, now that usually means you got some dirty work you want done but you want to keep your hands clean."

Tolliver sighed. He was right. Bubba was far from drunk, and probably not nearly as dumb as he let on most of the time. "Smoke Jensen and a friend of his just showed up over at the jail," he said.

Bubba nodded, remembering the way the man had humiliated him in their first encounter a while back. "Yeah, I heard. Nearly everybody in town knows that the famous gunfighter Smoke Jensen is in town, thanks to that little snot Samuelson from the hotel. But you was expectin' that, weren't you?"

"Yes, I was expecting him to show up, but Jensen's suddenly talking about looking for the Rule lady and finding out what she has to say about how the doc got killed."

Bubba's lips curled in a sly grin. "An' I'll bet you're afraid he'll find her 'fore you do an' she'll spill the beans 'bout how things really went down that night," Bubba said, his voice slightly mocking. Seemed his skin wasn't the only one that bastard Jensen was getting under, Bubba thought. Well, it was about time the high-and-mighty Sheriff Buck Tolliver got a taste of a little humility himself.

Tolliver frowned. This wasn't like Bubba. Something must've upset him to make his so ornery. "That's right, Bubba. Now he and his pal are staying over at the hotel. From the looks of them, they just came off a long trail ride, so I suspect they'll be cleaning up or taking a siesta for the next little while."

"So?" Bubba asked, raising his eyebrows and playing with Tolliver. He'd already figured out what Tolliver wanted him to do. Now he just had to make him say it and find out just how much it was going to be worth to him to get it done. "What's that got to do with me? He sure as hell didn't come to town to find out if I killed somebody and blamed it on a friend of his in order to get him hanged."

Tolliver glanced hurriedly around to make sure no one was watching or listening to Bubba shooting his mouth off. He figured he'd better get on with it before the whole town heard what Bubba was spouting off. "I'll pay you a hundred dollars to go over there, sneak up the back stairs, and put bullets in their heads."

Bubba broke out in laughter so loud it made everyone in the vicinity glance in their direction. "Shut up, you fool!" Tolliver hissed. "What's the matter with you this morning?"

Bubba's face sobered and he leaned forward. "You want me to sneak into the hotel and kill one of the most feared gunfighters in the country and another man for a measly hundred dollars? You, the man with half-a-million greenbacks in the bank, and me with not two dimes to rub together?" Bubba snorted, picked up the whiskey bottle, and took a large swig. "Uh-uh, I don't think so Mr. Sheriff."

So that was it, Tolliver thought. The idiot is pissed because I've made so much money in the past couple of years and he hasn't. Tolliver sighed and leaned back in his chair, knowing it was going to be a little more costly to get rid of Jensen than he'd figured. "All right, Bubba. Just what do you think the job is worth?"

Bubba pursed his lips, picked up the whiskey bottle again and took a small sip, and wiped his lips with the back of his hand before he answered. "A thousand dollars."

Tolliver snorted. "You must be joking! That's more'n most men make in two years."

Bubba shrugged. "I figure you can afford it, Buck, after all the money you made off my work the past year. An' if'n it's too much for you, then you can just mosey on over there an' do the job yourself." He smirked and leaned forward, whispering, "After all, it was your brother Jensen put in the ground, not mine."

"That's still a lot of money for a couple of minutes' work, Bubba."

Bubba grinned. "That's a lot of hombre you want kilt, Buck. And it ain't like it ain't been tried before, and nobody's managed to plant the man yet, so I think for a risk like that I ought to get paid big money."

When Buck didn't answer, Bubba shrugged again and looked across the room. "Molly," he yelled, motioning her back to him.

Tolliver reached out and pulled his hand down. "All right, you son of a bitch! A thousand dollars it is, but you'd better do a good job of it and not let anyone see you."

When Molly took two tentative steps toward them, Bubba shook his head at her and mouthed the word "later." Then he turned back to Tolliver. "I been sneakin' in an' outta that hotel for years, Buck ol' man. You just sit here and have a drink or two of my whiskey an' I'll be right back."

"No, that's too obvious," Tolliver said, worried that if Bubba screwed up the plan people would remember they'd been talking together. "I'll wait for you over at the jail."

"Whatever you say, Buck. Just have my money ready and waitin' for me."

"You do this right, Bubba, and I'll see that you get made a full partner in Hardy's and my dealings. That'll mean more money than you've ever seen in your entire life."

Bubba's eyes glittered with greed. "I'll hold you to that, Buck." As he got up, he thought to himself, "This is great. Not only do I get to pay that son of a bitch Jensen back what I owe him, I get to get rich doing it."

As Tolliver got up to head for the jail, he thought about the new way Bubba was acting, and he didn't like it. Not one bit of it. No, it was clear to him that once Bubba finished off Jensen, *he* would have to do the same thing to Bubba. He'd just have to make sure to get him out of town first, and then kill him and bury him where he'd never be found. Bubba was such a no-account type of person, people would just figure he'd gone on down the road to find another town to get drunk in.

* * *

Smoke and Cal walked into the hotel lobby, and Joe Samuelson immediately raised his hand. "Oh, Mr. Jensen, your baths are ready, and I've told the barber I will send for him the minute you're finished."

Smoke walked up to the desk. "What is your name?"

"Uh . . . Joe Samuelson," the clerk replied, afraid that he'd offended the gunfighter somehow.

Smoke smiled. "Well, Mr. Samuelson, you've done a good job, and I'll be sure and tell your boss how helpful you've been."

"Yes, sir, thank you, sir," Samuelson said. "The bathroom is on the second floor, just down at the end of the corridor. There are two bathtubs there and a stove with hot water in a bucket on it. I've instructed a boy to check in on you periodically to make sure there's nothing else you need."

Smoke nodded. "I'll tell you what, Joe," he said. "It's worth another five dollars to you if you'll get our horses taken down to the livery and rubbed down and fed plenty of grain for us while we take our baths."

Samuelson nodded and smiled. "Consider it done, sir."

Smoke smiled back, and he and Cal climbed the stairs toward the second floor. "Why were you so nice to that man?" Cal asked.

"Because he did a good job for us, Cal, and because hotel clerks tend to be gossips and he'll probably know as much about what goes on in this town as anyone. It won't hurt to be on his good side when we question him about this Rule lady and anything else he might know about Dr. Bentley's business."

Cal glanced at Smoke. "You think the real killer might be someone who had a grudge against the doctor?"

Smoke shrugged. "I don't know, but I'm betting that Samuelson will know if anyone in town had reason to want the doc dead." He looked at Cal. "There are only a few reasons a man is killed in cold blood, Cal: strong emotion like hate or love, for money or profit, or revenge for some past wrong done to the killer. We just have to figure out which one applies in this case and we'll be halfway to finding out who really killed the doctor."

When they entered the bathroom, they were pleased to find it full of steam from the heated water in their tubs. A young black man was busy heating more water on a large, potbellied stove in the corner, and he grinned at them when they entered. "Mr. Samuelson tol' me to git you men anything you need," he said.

Smoke looked around the room. There was a coffeepot on one of the burners of the stove, and a bottle of whiskey and two glasses on a chair in the corner right next to a box of cigars. He grinned. Samuelson had spared no effort to make them feel at home. He realized he might have to give the man a bigger tip since he was so good at his job.

Smoke and Cal shrugged out of their trail clothes, and they handed them to the young man. "Get these cleaned at the nearest laundry and have them sent back to our rooms at the hotel," Smoke said.

"Yes, suh," the young man said, gathering the pile of dirty buckskins and shirts in his arms.

"I think that'll be all," Smoke said, flipping the young man a fifty-cent piece, which he managed to catch without dropping any of the clothes.

"Thank you, suh," he said, and left with a wide grin on his face. Most customers of the hotel didn't bother to tip him, so he'd make sure the gentlemen's clothes were done just right.

Smoke tested the water with his hand, and then he grabbed the bathtub and eased it around until it faced the doorway. He slipped his Colt from its holster, laid it on the floor next to the tub, covered it with a small towel out of sight of the doorway, and eased into the water with a contented sigh.

Cal, without watching Smoke, did about the same thing, having learned from Smoke that safety is all about preparing for the unexpected. Once he had his tub also facing the door and his gun on the floor next to it, he poured them both cups of coffee, adding just a dollop of whiskey to each cup, and handed one to Smoke. Then, he took two cigars out of the box, lighted both of them, and handed one to Smoke before he climbed into his own tub.

"You know, Cal," Smoke said after he'd taken a drink of his coffee and a deep drag on the cigar, "one of the great pleasures in life is relaxing in a steaming-hot bathtub with a cup of good coffee and a fine cigar."

Cal laughed, exhaling a cloud of blue smoke and then taking a sip of his own coffee. "For you old fellas, maybe. As far as us young guns are concerned, most of the great pleasures in life involve a female with long hair and a pretty face and a trim figure to top it all off."

Smoke chuckled. "I may be 'old' as you say, Cal, but I'm not dead. And I do remember those days, believe it or not." He smiled, thinking to himself, "And that's just what I've got waiting for me back at the Sugarloaf."

Cal was about to reply when the door opened and a large, heavyset man with a cloth mask made out of an old flour sack over his face burst into the room. He had Colt pistols in each hand and his eyes were flashing with malevolence.

Smoke could see the man's teeth flash through the mouth-hole in the mask when he saw Smoke and Cal sitting defenseless in their tubs, drinking coffee and smoking cigars.

The man chuckled. "So this is how the great Smoke Jensen ends his days, huh? Soaking his sorry ass in a bathtub with a cup of coffee in one hand and a cigar in the other."

Smoke slowly raised his left hand with the coffee cup in it while he stuck the cigar in his mouth and laid his right hand over the edge of the tub. "You mind telling me who it is that's going to kill me and why?" he asked around the cigar, hoping to keep the man's attention off Cal, whose right hand had also moved over the edge of his tub.

"As for who, the name's Bubba Barkley, and as for why, it's 'cause you keep stickin' your nose in other people's business. You messed with me once before, Jensen, an' now I'm paying you back in spades!"

"What about me?" Cal asked, raising his eyebrows. "Why are you gonna kill me?"

When the man's eyes shifted toward Cal, both Smoke and Cal made their moves. Their pistols were up and fired in less time than it takes to tell it. Neither man bothered to aim, and Smoke's gun exploded only a scant fraction of a second before Cal's did.

Red blossoms of death bloomed on the man's chest as their slugs tore through his body and flung him backward against the wall.

Through the eyeholes in the mask, Smoke saw surprise flicker in the man's eyes just before they softened and took the long stare into eternity.

The head drooped and his body slithered down the wall, ending up sitting there with his legs splayed out and his arms hanging limp at his sides, streaks of his blood trailing down the wall to end behind his back.

Cal took a deep breath. He was still young enough that sudden death unnerved him a bit. "You think he's got friends outside?" he asked.

Smoke shook his head and laid his pistol back down on the floor. He leaned back in his tub and took a sip of his coffee, of which he hadn't spilled a drop, and then a drag on his cigar. "No, if there were more of them, they'd've come in here with him. They wouldn't've wanted to miss seeing us killed."

Cal glanced down at his now empty coffee cup and the sodden cigar he'd dropped into his bathwater in the excitement of the battle. He shook his head. "Damn, now I'm gonna have to get out of the tub an' get more coffee an' another cigar."

Smoke laughed. The boy was certainly growing up fast in the wilds of Colorado Territory.

"While you're up, son, I could use a warming myself," Smoke said, holding out his cup.

21

Even above the chatter and the plunking of the piano in the corner, Tolliver thought he heard the sound of gunshots from the direction of the hotel. He decided to pretend not to hear them and to wait for someone to come and get him. That would give Bubba more time to get away and would solidify Tolliver's claim to not know anything about what was happening.

He smiled, thinking of how much he was going to enjoy seeing Jensen's bullet-riddled, dead body lying on the floor of the hotel. It would almost make all these years of waiting worthwhile. The only thing better would be if he could have watched Jensen's eyes when he first realized he was fixing to die.

Suddenly, Joe Samuelson burst through the batwings, his face white and pale. "Sheriff, Sheriff, there's been a shooting at the hotel!" he almost screamed, his voice going up a full octave in his excitement.

Tolliver tried to look surprised. "Anybody hurt?" he asked, getting to his feet and adjusting his gun belt, loosening the rawhide hammer thong as if he was afraid there might be more gunplay.

"Uh . . . I don't rightly know," Samuelson stammered. "I didn't go upstairs to look. I'd just gotten back from the livery taking Mr. Jensen's horses over there and I heard this godawful commotion upstairs with what seemed like dozens of gunshots all happening at once." He hesitated, and then he added in a whisper, "And then it got awful quiet, Sheriff, not nary a sound."

Tolliver made a show of bravado. "Well, come on then, Joe. I'll go have a look and see what's going on." As they left the saloon, he asked, "And you say the shots came from Smoke Jensen's room?"

"Oh, no, sir."

Tolliver felt a stab of fear. "The shots didn't come from Jensen's room? Then where did they come from?"

"Mr. Jensen and Mr. Woods weren't in their rooms. They were in the bathing room taking hot baths. It sounded like that's where the shots came from."

"Oh," Tolliver said, feeling relief wash over him like a flood. Bubba must've found them in the bathtubs and killed 'em right where they sat, soaking, he thought with satisfaction. Even better. He could just see it in his mind's eye. There they sat, all cozy and warm and feeling safe, when suddenly Bubba burst in and started blazing away with his six-killer. He hoped Bubba had waited a few minutes to give them both time to realize their days were over, that Jensen's luck had finally run out for good.

With Samuelson so close behind him he could smell the man's aftershave, Tolliver eased up the hotel stairs, his pistol in his hands for show. He really didn't expect to find a gunman there, knowing Bubba would be long gone by now.

The hallway was still full of gun smoke and the heavy, acrid smell of cordite when the sheriff and the desk clerk eased their way down the hall toward the bathroom.

"It must've come from in there," Samuelson said. "Like I said, Mr. Jensen and Mr. Woods were in there bathing at the time."

"You think they could've shot each other in an argument or something?" Tolliver asked, already thinking that might be a good cover story for the killings.

"Oh, no, sir. They were very good friends," Samuelson

answered. "And the boy that works in the bathing room said they'd already gotten in their tubs, so they wouldn't have had their guns close at hand if there'd been an argument or something like that."

"Where was the bath boy at the time of the shooting?" Tolliver asked, hoping the young black man hadn't been a witness to the shooting. That might complicate matters if he could recognize Bubba.

"Oh, he'd gone for more hot water," Samuelson said. "He was down in the lobby with me when the shooting started, and he took off like a scared rabbit." He shook his head. "I doubt he'll be back to work anytime soon."

"Well, you never know. . . ." Tolliver began as he stepped into the smoke- and steam-filled room.

"Howdy, Sheriff," Smoke Jensen said, holding up his coffee cup in a mock salute to the sheriff.

Tolliver's eyes opened wide when he saw Cal and Smoke sitting in their bathtubs as calm as you please, drinking coffee and smoking cigars as if nothing had happened.

"Uh . . . the clerk here says he heard gunshots," Tolliver began, and then he saw Bubba's body sprawled against the wall, blood still seeping from five or six holes in his chest, and holes in the wall where the bullets had gone through, with bloodstains trailing down the wall from the holes to his body.

"That would've been us, I suspect," Smoke said calmly. He indicated Bubba with a nod of his head. "That gentleman burst in here with guns in his hands and said he was going to kill us." Smoke grinned. "Obviously, he was wrong."

Tolliver didn't know what to say. His chest felt like someone was sitting on it, and he could hardly catch his breath. "Uh . . . um . . . he say anything else?" he asked, hoping against hope Bubba hadn't had time to shoot his mouth off too much before he'd been killed.

Smoke glanced at Cal. "Did you hear him say anything else, Cal?"

Cal pursed his lips, and then he grinned. "I think I might've heard him say ouch when my first slug hit him in the chest."

Smoke laughed. "I don't think so. I got off the first shot."

Cal shook his head. "No, I think it was me, Smoke, shot him first."

Samuelson glanced at the two men in the tubs arguing over who'd drilled the man first, and then at the dead body lying in a pool of blood, and then he fainted dead away, his body hitting the floor with a thud.

Tolliver reached down and pulled the black cloth mask off Bubba's head. He sat back on his haunches and glanced at Smoke and Cal. "Either of you know this man?"

Smoke looked at Cal and nodded. "Yeah. The first time we were coming into town this man and a friend of his braced us and tried to steal our saddlebags."

Tolliver frowned. Damn that Bubba. It seemed the man just couldn't do anything right. "What happened?" Tolliver asked, though he knew the story full well.

Cal grinned. "Smoke beat the shit outta his friend, and then he and his friend decided they had better things to do than to mess with us."

"Sheriff," Smoke said, interrupting the talk.

"Yes?"

"Would you mind handing me that towel over there? Both my water and my coffee are getting cold."

Tolliver grunted and shook his head. He'd never seen anyone so cool in the face of an attempted murder. He hoped he hadn't underestimated the gunfighter.

He grabbed a pair of towels from a stack in the corner of the room and flipped one each to Cal and Smoke.

"By the way," he asked as Smoke and Cal stood up and began to towel off. "If he burst in here like you say with his guns out and you two were in the tubs, how is it you had time to get your guns from over there before he shot you?" He looked over at the chairs on the other side of the room, where Smoke and Cal's gun belts were lying.

"Our guns weren't over there, Sheriff," Smoke said easily. "Whenever I'm bathing, I always keep my Colt next to the tub on the floor, covered with a towel, just in case of events like this."

Tolliver arched an eyebrow. "You get attacked often while bathing, Mr. Jensen?"

Smoke shrugged, but Cal replied, "Why, I do believe this is at least the third time, isn't it, Smoke?"

Smoke grinned. "Third or fourth, I tend to lose count."

Tolliver couldn't believe the men weren't the least bit rattled by the attempt on their lives. As he stepped over the prone body of Samuelson on his way out of the room, he looked back over his shoulder. "Come see me in my office when you're done getting dressed," he said, "an' you can tell me more about what happened here."

Smoke and Cal took their time with the barber, and it was over an hour later when they appeared in Tolliver's office, cleanly shaven and with hair neatly trimmed and clothes that were neat and pressed.

Tolliver took a long look at the Regulator Clock on the wall and said sarcastically, "I'm glad you could finally make it."

Smoke's face went flat and his eyes bored into the sheriff's. "I wasn't aware there was a time limit, Sheriff. Besides, we told you all we know over at the hotel, and since you're so concerned, Mr. Samuelson is fine."

Tolliver blushed. He hadn't even slowed to make sure the clerk was all right after he'd fainted. He'd been too deep in his thoughts about how to handle this monumental fuck-up by Bubba. He knew Jensen was bound to find out Bubba and the sheriff were at least well acquainted, even if the fact that they were partners wasn't widely known.

He decided to be open about his association with Bubba and try to minimize the damage. "Have either of you seen or had any dealings with the murdered man since the fight earlier?" Tolliver asked, moving a sheet of paper and a pencil to the center of his desk in order to take notes.

Smoke's face colored slightly and his eyes flashed, turning dangerously dark. "The man wasn't murdered, as you say, Sheriff. He was killed while trying to commit a crime.

That doesn't make it murder, which, if I'm not mistaken, is a crime itself."

Tolliver sighed. "All right then, have you seen the *dead* man since your first altercation with him?"

Both Smoke and Cal shook their heads. "We don't even know his name," Cal volunteered, "and we haven't seen hide nor hair of him or his friend since the fight."

Tolliver pursed his lips, as if considering whether to give them that information or not. Finally, after a few moments, he said, "The man's name was Bubba Barkley, a well-known figure around Payday."

"Do you have any idea why he braced us?" Smoke asked as he pulled out his makings and began to build a cigarette. "It seems a rather extreme act just because his friend got his butt kicked a little and Cal took his gun away from him."

Tolliver shook his head. "No, none at all. The man had no known employment, living on odd jobs like mucking out stables at the livery and sweeping out the saloon to pay his bar bills." He hesitated. "In fact, I knew him fairly well, and to my knowledge he'd never before broken the law or robbed anyone that I'm aware of."

Smoke stared at Tolliver through the flame of a match as he lighted his cigarette. He tipped smoke out of his nostrils, and said, "Is that so? Were you close friends, Sheriff?"

A scarlet flush appeared on Tolliver's neck and moved steadily up his face to his forehead. "I didn't say we was friends, Jensen, I said I knew the man. That's an entirely different thing. However, I did just the other day offer him employment as a sheriff's deputy to help guard the town during your friend's trial."

When Jensen didn't reply but just sat there smoking and staring into Tolliver's eyes as if he could read his mind, Tolliver cleared his throat and broke his gaze. "So, Barkley didn't say anything about why he was trying to kill you two?" he asked, his voice sounding rough and coarse coming out of a dry throat.

"No, he didn't, Sheriff," Smoke answered, omitting to tell the lawman what Barkley had said about Smoke sticking his nose in other people's business, "but I'm sure we'll get some idea what was on his mind when we talk to people that knew him."

Tolliver's eyes opened wide and he leaned forward pointing his finger at Smoke like a gun. "Now you listen to me, Jensen. This is my town, and if there's any investigating to do about this, I'll be the one to do it."

Smoke got to his feet, dropped his butt on the floor and ground it out under his boot, and said, "Last time I looked, Sheriff, there isn't any law against talking to people, not even in a Podunk like this one. So now, if you're through asking us questions, we'd like to talk to our friend again."

Tolliver started to object, and then he saw the gunfighter's eyes go from pale to dark and dangerous, and figured it really wouldn't hurt anything to let them talk to the condemned man—hell, it might even make the mountain man suffer a little bit more, and that was fine with him.

"Sure, go right on in, the door's open," he said, smiling a little to show he was being generous by not making them take their guns off.

Smoke stared at him for a moment more, and then when they walked out of the room and closed the cellblock door behind them, Tolliver wiped sweat off his forehead. "Damn that Bubba," he muttered, "now the fat's really in the fire."

The only good thing out of all this is that now I won't have to kill the stupid son of a bitch, Tolliver thought.

When Pearlie saw Smoke and Cal, he jumped to his feet. He finally looked like the old Pearlie they knew, so both men were relieved to see he'd recovered from his earlier injuries.

"Hey, Pearlie, how you doin'?" Cal asked, sticking his hand through the bars to clasp Pearlie's.

Pearlie cocked his head to the side and gave Cal one of his old grins. "How the hell do you think I'm doin', young'un? They only serve three meals a day in this joint."

Smoke laughed. "Aside from that, how is the food?"

Pearlie looked at him and smiled. "Thanks for what you did, Smoke. The lady who delivers the food said you'd forced the sheriff to get it from the hotel dining room, and it sure as hell beats what I was getting before." He chuckled. "I even got her to promise to bring in extra helpings of dessert."

He paused for a moment, and then he asked, "You got any news 'bout who might've done in the doc?"

Smoke shook his head. "No, but we've found out there may have been a witness there that night, a lady name of Rule. Did you see anyone else in the house that night?"

Pearlie frowned and shook his head. "No, not that I can recall. Course, I was kind'a busy fighting for my life, and then I passed out, so she could've been standing right there in the room and I wouldn't've seen her."

Smoke reached through the bars and put his hand on Pearlie's shoulder. "Don't worry, ol' pal, we'll see that you're cleared of this and we'll have you back in Big Rock before you know it."

Pearlie glanced over his shoulder at the one window in the cell block down the corridor, and listened to the hammer blows of the men building the scaffold to hang him from. "I sure hope so, Smoke, 'cause I ain't exactly anxious to test those boys' work."

Smoke and Cal laughed, glad to see their friend still maintaining his sense of wry humor.

Cal couldn't resist a gibe. "I tell you what, Pearlie, if'n I was you, I think I'd give up on those second helpings of dessert from the hotel dining room."

"Why?" Pearlie asked, looking down at his waist to see if he was gaining weight.

"'Cause if'n you get any fatter, your hoss Cold ain't gonna be able to carry your fat butt all the way back to Big Rock."

Tears brimmed in Pearlie's eyes at the thought that he might be going home soon and he just nodded, unable to speak.

22

As Smoke and Cal walked out of the corridor after talking with Pearlie, Sheriff Tolliver said with a smirk, "You find out anything from your friend, Jensen?"

Smoke just looked at him. "We found out enough to know he didn't kill the doctor, and the man he did kill was trying to kill him."

Tolliver forced a laugh. "Now just why would someone want to kill a complete stranger to the town?"

"That's what I intend to find out, Sheriff," Smoke said, his eyes boring into Tolliver's. "You wouldn't happen to have any ideas on the subject, would you?"

Tolliver turned beet red. "What? That's preposterous! Why would I possibly know anything about that?"

Smoke grinned and continued to stare into Tolliver's eyes, which were now tinged with fear. "Well, the man Pearlie killed was not only a relative of yours, but it seems he occasionally worked as your deputy. That's a pretty close connection, wouldn't you say?"

Tolliver's mouth opened and closed, but he didn't have anything further to say. When his eyes dropped, unable to meet Smoke's gaze, Smoke tipped his hat and headed for the door. "We'll be seeing you again, Sheriff, you can count on it."

After they left the sheriff's office, Smoke told Cal they were headed over to see Sam Hemmings.

"Why are we going there?" Cal asked.

"I need to get a feel for what was said at the trial," Smoke said. "It may give us a hint about who really did the killing of the doctor, and why a man who was not only a relative of the sheriff but who also worked as a deputy might have been trying to rob Pearlie."

"You mean you don't think it was just 'cause the man was a footpad?"

Smoke shrugged. "I doubt it, Cal. If Pearlie was the sort to flash around a big wad of greenbacks or sport some fancy watch fobs or diamond stickpins, maybe. But Pearlie's just a cowboy, and not a particularly rich one at that." He shook his head. "I just can't figure why the man Pearlie stabbed would have taken such a chance of breaking into a popular town doctor's house to steal the few dollars and old pocket watch Pearlie had."

Even though the job of mayor of a small town like Payday wasn't a full-time job, Mayor Hemmings happened to be in his office when Smoke and Cal arrived.

He answered the door himself. "Yes?" he asked politely.

"Hello, Mayor," Smoke said. "I'm Smoke Jensen and this is my friend Calvin Woods. We're friends of Pearlie's and we're the ones who brought him to town."

"Oh, yes," Hemmings said, "I've heard of you, Mr. Jensen." He motioned them inside.

Smoke smiled. He heard that all the time when he introduced himself. It was the price of being famous, or rather, infamous. Sometimes it was said with a smile and sometimes with a frown; just about everyone had heard of Smoke in some way or other, and it was often a toss-up which way they felt about him.

"Come in, gentlemen," Hemmings said, showing them to a pair of well-worn chairs in front of his desk.

He sat down, put his elbows on the desk, and rested his chin in his hands. "Now, first let me say that I'm very sorry I didn't get your friend acquitted of the charges against him." He sighed. "The evidence against him was just too strong, I'm afraid."

"That's one of the things we came to talk to you about, Mayor," Smoke said.

Hemmings held up his hand. "Please, call me Sam," he said with a deprecating grin. "The job isn't all that important in a town this size."

"All right, Sam. First off, I would like to know something about this Blackie Johnson that Pearlie says he killed because he caught him robbing Pearlie. Pearlie also says he got the feeling that Johnson was going to kill him and that the theft of his things was just an afterthought."

Hemmings leaned back in his chair. "You know, I wondered about that myself. Blackie Johnson, though certainly not one of the town's leading citizens, has never really been in trouble before; at least not jail-type trouble. He was pretty much a drunkard, but he usually sobered up enough to hold down a job doing menial labor, and as far as I know, was never charged with stealing anything before." He elected not to mention the widow's egg money Hattie had told him about since it was only hearsay.

"So, you can't think of any reason he might have to try and kill Pearlie?"

Hemmings smiled sadly. "Mr. Jensen, you brought your friend into town less than a week before all this happened, and he was unconscious and lying in bed the entire time he was here. No one in town had ever heard of Pearlie before this, and no one could possibly have had any reason to want him dead that I can think of." The smile faded from his face. "Hell, far as I know, no one in town even knew anything about him until the killing. Doc wasn't one to shoot his mouth off about his patients." Hemmings hesitated. "In fact, that was one of the things that worked against Pearlie with the jury—there was just no motive to kill him that I could come up with."

Smoke nodded slowly. "That's right, Sam. I hadn't thought of that until you mentioned it. Just how would anyone have known Pearlie was in town if the doctor didn't talk about it?"

"That's what I'm trying to tell you, Smoke. Johnson would have had no reason to try and kill your friend. Even if he'd met him before and had some sort of grudge against him, which is highly unlikely, he wouldn't have known he was in town."

Smoke snapped his fingers. "What about the telegraph operator?" he asked. "Dr. Bentley and I kept in touch by sending telegrams back and forth. The operator would have had to know about Pearlie, and that it was me who brought him into town."

Hemmings shrugged. "Well, that'd be Bob Jacobson," he said. "He also owns the general store, but that don't help you much, Smoke. That means there were two men who knew Pearlie was in town, and Jacobson didn't have anything to do with the killings."

Smoke leaned forward in his chair. "Maybe not, Sam, but maybe Mr. Jacobson wasn't as closemouthed about the doctor's business as the doctor was."

Hemmings frowned. "Well, you may be right there, Smoke. Ol' Bob does like to gossip a bit, like all general store owners I've ever known. But so what? From what Pearlie tells me, he's just a cowhand on a ranch down in the southern part of the state. Unless he's got a past that's a lot more exciting than that, I still don't see where anyone would care if he was in town or not."

Smoke leaned back. "Pearlie does have a past, Sam. He used to hire his gun out to ranchers a long time ago, but I doubt that has anything to do with his present predicament. I think that just might have to do with the fact that he's my friend and employee."

"What do you mean?"

Smoke smiled grimly. "Sam, I'm sure you know I *do* have a past, quite a long and involved one, and I've made more than my share of enemies in that past. Now, I'm starting to wonder if one of them isn't behind all of this."

"Now wait a minute, Smoke," Hemmings said, his face skeptical. "Surely you don't think someone killed the doctor just to get Pearlie hung to hurt you? Isn't that rather . . . well, complicated?"

Smoke shook his head and his face too was puzzled. "You're right, Sam. On the face of it, that doesn't make a whole hell of a lot of sense, but it makes more sense than for me to believe that a man I know as well as Pearlie would kill two people to steal a few dollars worth of bills and jewelry, especially when he's just waking up from a serious illness."

"Maybe we ought to talk to Bob Jacobson after all," Hemmings said.

Smoke shook his head. "No, Sam. I think I'll do better talking to Mr. Jacobson by myself."

"You won't, uh, do anything rash, will you Smoke?" Hemmings asked, his face now worried. He *had* heard of Smoke Jensen and from what he'd heard, Smoke was not the sort of man to use half measures, especially where a friend's life was involved.

Smoke smiled. "Of course not, Sam. You have my word I won't lay a finger on Mr. Jacobson."

After he got up and shook Sam's hand, he added with a smile, "I won't promise not to scare him just a bit, though."

After they were out of Hemmings's office, Smoke stopped on the boardwalk to build himself a cigarette. Cal took the opportunity to do the same. As he was lighting his cigarette, Smoke glanced over at Cal. "I need for you to do me a favor, Cal."

"Sure," Cal said, squinting as smoke from his own cigarette irritated his eyes.

"I want you to mosey on over to the livery and have a talk with the boy that works there."

Cal frowned. "What about?"

"I got to thinking when we were talking to the mayor that there was someone else who knew we brought Pearlie into town."

Cal's eyes widened. "Of course, the boy at the livery who took care of our horses. You gave him money to take care of Pearlie's horse until he got well, an' you even told him Pearlie was over at the doc's."

"That's right, and we need to find out just who these

two might have talked to that might have a reason to go after either Pearlie or me," Smoke said.

Cal let smoke trickle out of his nostrils as he said, "You can count on me, Smoke. If'n that boy told anyone about us, I'll find out."

"I know you will, Cal. I'm counting on it."

Smoke spent some time browsing in the general store until all of the other customers had left and he was alone with the proprietor. After a few minutes, the man walked over to stand behind Smoke while he fingered some fancy holsters.

"Can I help you, sir?"

Smoke put the holster down and turned around. "Are you Mr. Jacobson?" he asked.

"Sure am. Robert Jacobson, but everybody calls me Bob." He stuck out his hand. "Pleased to meet ya'. Are you new to town . . . Mr. . . . ?"

Smoke took his hand. "Jensen, Smoke Jensen," Smoke replied. "And no, I haven't moved to town." He noticed Jacobson's face drain of blood and go as pale as the cotton sheets he had in aisle two.

Smoke cocked his head. "Something wrong, Mr. Jacobson?" he asked.

"Uh, no, why, nothing's wrong."

"Good," Smoke said, dropping his easy smile and moving to the door. He reached up and pulled the shade down, turning the cardboard sign in the door's window from OPEN to CLOSED.

"Here now," Jacobson said, holding up his hand and taking a step toward Smoke, until he saw the look in Smoke's eyes when he turned around to face him.

Jacobson stopped short and sweat suddenly appeared on his forehead. He turned as if to run toward the back door, but Smoke said harshly, "I wouldn't do that, Bob. You wouldn't get ten feet 'fore I dropped you like a bad habit."

Jacobson turned back around, raising his hands in the air. "Is this a holdup?"

"Oh, put your hands down, Bob," Smoke said, smiling grimly. "I just want to talk to you without any interruptions for a few minutes."

"What about?" Jacobson asked, slowly lowering his arms, his eyes fixed on the gun in Smoke's holster.

"I think you know what about, Bob. You were the one sending messages back and forth between Dr. Bentley and me about my friend Pearlie."

Jacobson's head bobbed up and down. "That's right. So what?"

Smoke eased his hip up on the counter and sat. "Well, I think you got to shooting your mouth off about those messages and told someone here in town I had a friend at the doc's place."

"No . . . no . . . I would never talk about any of my messages. The company would fire me for that."

Smoke cocked his head. "So, you never gossiped about me to any of your friends?"

"Certainly not!"

Smoke sighed. Maybe he was wrong. Maybe Jacobson didn't have anything to do with Pearlie's problems after all. He glanced back at the man and noticed his eyes wouldn't meet his. No. The man was definitely nervous about something.

Smoke thought back over the messages he'd sent and received, and then he had it. His eyes narrowed. "You know, Bob, just before I left Pueblo for here, I got a message from Dr. Bentley telling me there'd been no change in Pearlie's condition. Do you remember that message?"

Now the sweat fairly poured from Jacobson's face, and his shirt had dark spots under his arms that reached almost all the way down to his belt. "Uh, no. Why should I?"

Smoke eased off the counter and moved until he was less than a foot from Jacobson's face. "Because the doctor was already dead when that message was sent, and Pearlie had already been arrested for his killing."

Jacobson sobbed and hung his head. "You're right, Mr. Jensen, you're right."

"Now, what I need to know, Bob, is why would you do something like that?"

Jacobson looked up into Smoke's eyes. "The sheriff, Mr. Jensen, the sheriff made me do it. He told me he'd hurt me if I told anyone about it, even though I told him it was wrong and that I could lose my job over it."

"You mean Sheriff Buck Tolliver ordered you to send that wire telling me that Pearlie was still unconscious so I'd hurry and come back to Payday?"

Jacobson nodded, his face flaming red with humiliation and shame.

"Now why would . . ." Smoke began, and a faint tickling at the back of his mind reminded him that Tolliver had looked somehow familiar when they'd first met.

He put his finger on Jacobson's chest. "We're going to forget this talk ever took place, aren't we, Mr. Jacobson?"

"Yes, sir!" Jacobson said, his head nodding up and down rapidly.

"And you're especially not going to tell the sheriff we talked, are you?"

"No . . . no."

"Good," Smoke said, reaching up to pat the man's shoulder. "Then I'll see you later, Bob."

"Uh, Mr. Jensen?"

"Yes, Bob?"

"You're not going to mention anything about that message I sent you to the company, are you? I really need that job. This store doesn't do all that well."

"Don't worry, Bob," Smoke assured him. "Like I said, this conversation is going to be our little secret."

After he left the store, Smoke decided to head on over to the saloon and have a beer and a smoke. Sometimes you could find out a whole lot about someone by simply asking about him in his local watering hole, and he fully intended to find out everything he could about Sheriff Buck Tolliver.

He knew there was something about the man; either his face or his name was familiar, but he just couldn't put his finger on it. If he could only remember, it might give him the reason Pearlie was in such deep shit.

23

Cal walked into the livery and over to where the boy had put his and Smoke's horses, right next to the stall that held Pearlie's mount.

Cal busied himself with running a currycomb over his horse Dusty until the stable was empty of any other customers. He put the currycomb down and ambled over to where the boy was mucking out a stall with a pitchfork that looked as big as he was.

"Howdy," Cal said, forcing a friendly smile.

The boy looked up and leaned against the pitchfork handle, obviously glad of any excuse to stop work for a moment. "Howdy," he said.

"My name's Cal Woods," Cal said, sticking out his hand.

The boy looked startled, as if no one had ever been friendly before. He glanced at his own hand, wiped it on his trouser leg, which was only marginally cleaner than the floor of the stalls he was mucking out, and then took Cal's hand.

"I'm Jerome Stone, but ever'body calls me Jerry."

"Well, Jerry," Cal began, glancing over his shoulder at his horse. "I see you have a good memory for faces."

Jerry looked puzzled. "Huh?"

"Yeah, my friend and I were here 'bout two weeks ago and left another friend's horse with you, an' this time when we come back I noticed you knew to put our horses next to our friend's bronc without us having to tell you which one it was."

"Oh, yeah," Jerry said, smiling and looking at the horses. "Well, it weren't so much. After all, ain't that many fellers come in here ridin' full-blooded Palouse studs." He scratched his head for a moment, and then he grinned widely. "Matter of fact, you three are the first ones I've seen ridin' that particular kind'a hoss."

Cal gave a small laugh. "Oh, is that all there was to it?" He leaned forward and lowered his voice as if he were going to tell Jerry a secret. "I thought maybe it was 'cause you recognized the fellow I rode in here with. He's kind'a famous most places."

"Well, no, not really," Jerry said, lowering his voice and looking around to make sure no one else could hear. "Actually, your big friend in the buckskins is kind'a hard to forget. He's probably the first real true-to-life gunslinger I ever seen."

Now Cal frowned. "What makes you think he's a gunslinger, Jerry, if you didn't recognize who he was?"

Jerry grinned and nudged Cal with his elbow. "Aw, come on, Cal." His eyes dropped to Cal's pistol, slung low on his hip and tied down to his leg. "Both of you wear your irons like gunslingers." He chuckled. "And don't try an' tell me I'm wrong neither, 'cause I read all of Ned Buntline's penny dreadfuls and he's pretty clear on that particular point."

"What point is that, Jerry?" Cal asked.

"'Bout the way gunslicks tie their pistols down low on their leg whereas regular cowboys wear 'em up high so they won't get hung up on brush and such."

Cal returned Jerry's smile. "Oh, you're not wrong really. It's just that Smoke gave up his gunslinging days a long time ago. He's just a rancher now, like me."

"Smoke?" Jerry asked, his eyes wide and his freckles standing out against his skin, which had suddenly turned as pale white as a newly washed sheet. "Don't tell me that man was Smoke Jensen!"

Cal nodded. "Yep, but don't tell nobody, Jerry. He don't

exactly like to advertise when he's in a town 'cause of all the men gunnin' for him."

"Jumpin' Jehosaphat!" Jerry whispered, his face turning even paler. "I can't believe I curried the horse of the famous Smoke Jensen." He reached into his pocket and took out the money Smoke had given him as a tip. "I'm gonna keep this here money and never spend it an' I'm gonna tell ever'body my friend, the famous Smoke Jensen, gave it to me."

Cal began to grin when Jerry looked up from the money in his hand and added, "No wonder the sheriff almost fainted when I described your friend to him."

Cal reached out and grabbed Jerry's shoulder. "What did you say about the sheriff?"

Jerry stepped back, alarmed at the change in Cal's demeanor. "Nothin', I didn't say nothin'." Tears of fear brimmed in his eyes. "Don't hit me, mister, please."

"Oh, don't be silly, Jerry. I'm not going to hit you, but you did say something about the sheriff," Cal persisted, trying to soften his voice and not be so harsh.

"Well, after you was here a couple weeks ago, the sheriff came by and saw that Palouse you left for your friend. He asked me about it an' I told him 'bout you and Smoke, though course I didn't know his name at the time. Well, when I described Smoke to him, the sheriff turned as white as my mamma's sheets and dang near passed out right there in the street." Jerry chuckled now that he saw that Cal wasn't mad at him. "Heck, I thought I was going to have to throw a bucket of water on him to wake him up."

"Did he say anything else?" Cal asked, pleased to have found out so much, and pleased that he might have found out how people knew that Pearlie and Smoke were connected in some way and that Pearlie was in town.

Jerry shrugged. "Not really. He asked what y'all were doing in town, an' I told him 'bout you leavin' your sick friend over at the doc's an' all."

"So the sheriff seemed interested in what Smoke and I were doing in town, huh?"

"Heck, yes," Jerry said. "After I told him what I knew, he turned and wandered off like his mind was off somewheres else. Dang near got runned over by a couple of hosses on his way to the doc's too."

"You mean he left here and went directly to the doctor's office?" Cal asked.

Jerry nodded. "Sure did. An' he was mumblin' somethin' 'bout he couldn't believe it, not after all these years, or somethin' like that."

Cal reached into his pocket and pulled out a dollar bill. "Here, Jerry. Thanks for taking the time to talk to me. See that our mounts get a little extra grain if you would."

"Jesus . . . uh, I mean, hey, thanks a lot, Cal," Jerry said when he saw Cal was tipping him more than he made in a whole day of mucking out stalls. "Oh, and Cal . . ."

"Yeah, Jerry?" Cal called back over his shoulder.

"You tell Smoke I said hello, would ya?"

"Sure thing, Jerry," Cal said, laughing as he hurried to find Smoke and tell him what he'd found out.

Cal didn't know exactly where to find Smoke, so he decided to wait for him in the saloon. Besides, all that talking and excitement had made him thirsty for a cool beer.

When he walked through the batwings, he immediately stepped to the side with his back to the wall like Smoke had taught him, and waited for his eyes to adjust to the gloom. Not that Cal had all that many people interested in gunning him down like Smoke did, but since he rode with the man and was known to be his friend, Smoke had told him to take the same precautions he did and he'd live long enough to grow whiskers.

As soon as his eyes were adjusted, Cal saw Smoke standing at the bar, his elbows planted around a shot glass of whiskey, and he started to walk toward him.

Smoke saw him coming and gave a minute shake of his head, cutting his eyes toward a nearby table that was empty.

Cal took the hint and altered his course to the table and took a seat, pretending not to look at Smoke. When one of the girls came over and asked him if he'd like some company, Cal shook his head. "No, but if you'll get the bartender to send over a glass of beer, I'll buy you a shot too."

She leaned down close to him and whispered in his ear. "I don't really like liquor all that much, but I'll take the money instead and get you your beer if you don't let on to the bartender about it."

Cal grinned, enjoying the view down the front of her dress, and said, "Sure thing, ma'am."

She noticed where his gaze was locked on and winked at him. "You sure you don't want some company? We got some awfully nice rooms upstairs where we could go and be alone while you drink your beer."

Cal blushed from the top of his head all the way down to his boots. "Uh . . . no, thank you anyway, ma'am." When she made a face and stuck out her lip in a pout like her feelings were hurt, he explained, "I'm just here waiting on a friend of mine. As soon as he gets here, we got to leave. Otherwise, I'd be right honored to go upstairs with you."

She smiled and tousled his hair. "All right, cowboy, it's your loss." And she strutted off to get his beer, looking back over her shoulder to see if he was enjoying the view of her hips as they swayed back and forth—which he most definitely was.

Cal was on his second beer when he saw Smoke pat the man next to him at the bar on the shoulder, throw some money down, and walk over toward Cal's table.

Smoke pulled up a chair and leaned back, building himself a cigarette as his eyes roamed the room as they did every few moments, checking for familiar faces or for danger. "Did you learn anything from our friend at the livery?"

Cal nodded and filled Smoke in on what Jerry had told him about the sheriff, his obvious interest in their business, and how he'd acted when he recognized Smoke from Jerry's description.

"What did you find out?" he asked Smoke.

Smoke tipped smoke out of his nostrils and said, "Pretty much the same as you. The sheriff seemed to show a lot of interest in our comings and goings, more than would be usual for a sheriff in a small town like this, especially since he didn't have any paper on me."

"Yeah, an' Jerry said he went right off to talk to the doc about what Pearlie was doing there an' to find out what he could 'bout us."

"You know, Cal," Smoke said, dropping the butt to the floor and squashing it with his boot, "I'm inclined to think the sheriff is hip-deep in this affair, and what worries me is, I don't know why."

"Jerry seemed to think the sheriff knew you, or at least recognized who you were from your description," Cal said. "Does that mean anything to you?"

Smoke frowned. "Not really, but I've crossed paths with more than my share of hard men in the past, Cal, and it could be that Sheriff Tolliver is one of them." He inclined his head toward the bar and the man he'd been talking to. "Word around town is that the sheriff always has a pocketful of money and has a hell of a nice spread out of town stocked with some fine livestock, much better than what he makes as sheriff would account for."

"Where do they think he gets it?"

Smoke shrugged. "There's been rumors of miners turning up missing and friends of the sheriff turning up with signed bills of sale for their claims, but nothing definite anyone wants to get involved with. I get the idea everyone is pretty much afraid of Tolliver and his friends and no one wants to stand up to them."

"And they told you all this?" Cal asked, amazed that Smoke could get so much information being a stranger in town.

Smoke grinned. "Give these miners enough whiskey and before you know it, they're telling you their life stories and anything else you want to hear." He grinned.

"But, like I said, most of it is just miners' gossip, so a lot of it can be discounted."

Cal laughed. "That's still strange that they would repeat all that to you since they don't know you."

"Not when you think about it," Smoke said. "Mining is a pretty lonely business. After working for months alone out in the mountains, when you come to town and someone buys you whiskey and offers a sympathetic ear, it's only natural to want to talk more than you should."

When Cal shook his head, Smoke added, "The two best places to pick up on gossip are a women's quilting circle and the most popular bar in town, 'cause the only person who gossips more than women is a man who's drunk more than he can handle."

24

Robert Jacobson's eyes widened when he translated the dots and dashes of the telegram that came in over his wire that afternoon. He sleeved at the sweat that suddenly appeared on his forehead as he sat and reread the wire.

"To Mayor Samuel Hemmings, Payday: Mr. Hemmings, please meet the five o'clock train at the station in Payday tomorrow afternoon. I will be in the last car, but I refuse to exit the train. I have important information about the killing of my nephew Dr. Bentley. Please tell no one of this wire, as my life will be in danger if news of my arrival gets out." It was signed *Janet Rule*.

Holy shit! thought Jacobson. The wire is addressed to Mayor Hemmings, but the sheriff told me to keep him informed of any information about Missus Rule that came in over the telegraph. Jesus, now what do I do? And then there's Smoke Jensen. Holy shit, maybe this job isn't worth all this aggravation after all!

Finally, he decided it wouldn't hurt to let the sheriff have a peek at the wire after he showed it to Hemmings. After all, the sheriff was the one investigating the murders, not the mayor. Besides, he reasoned, all Hemmings could do if he found out was get him fired. The sheriff, on the other hand, could and probably would do much worse if he ignored his orders to keep him informed, and he didn't even want to think about what Jensen might do—

so he just vowed to make sure Jensen never learned of the contents of the wire or that he intended to let the sheriff know about it.

After discussing it for a while, Smoke and Cal decided about the only person in town they dared to trust with their new information about the sheriff was the mayor, Sam Hemmings, and only because he seemed to genuinely believe in Pearlie's innocence.

They met him in his office just after lunch. "What can I do for you boys?" he asked. "You come up with any evidence that might help clear Pearlie?"

Smoke and Cal looked at each other. "Well, it's not exactly evidence, Sam, but we've been talking to some people around town and we've come up with some rather strange behavior on the sheriff's part. We'd like to see what you think about it," Smoke said.

Hemmings shrugged. "I don't see what that has to do with the case, but go ahead. I'm willing to listen to anything at this point," he said, glancing out of his window and shuddering at the hanging scaffold that was almost completed. He certainly didn't want someone to go to the gallows because he hadn't done his job well enough.

Smoke began by telling Hemmings what Jacobson had said about how the sheriff had told him to send the fake wire to get Smoke and Cal back to town, and then Cal finished by detailing what the livery boy Jerry had told him about the sheriff's strange reaction to his description of Smoke and how he'd immediately gone to the doc's to investigate Pearlie.

Hemmings rocked back in his chair, stroking his chin and glancing longingly at a box of cigars on his desk. "Go ahead and light one up," Smoke said, grinning. "It won't bother us if you smoke."

"Are you sure?" Hemmings asked, looking relieved. "It's a small office and the smoke can get pretty thick, but I think better when I'm chewing on a stogie."

Cal got up and opened the mayor's office window. "There, now the smoke can get out."

Hemmings struck a match on his trousers leg and held it under the tip of a long, black cigar until it was smoking like a train engine.

He flicked the match out of the window and leaned back in his chair, staring at the ceiling. "Now," he said contentedly, "I agree, Sheriff Tolliver's actions seem a bit out of the ordinary, but they don't necessarily mean he had something to do with Dr. Bentley's death. It might just be that you two have crossed paths in the past, Smoke, and that as sheriff he was worried about having a . . . no offense . . . rather famous gunfighter in his town."

Smoke, who'd been thinking of the sheriff's actions for some time now, said, "Let me say something, Sam, and give me a little leeway on it until you hear all of it."

Hemmings looked at him. "All right."

"Let's assume, for the sake of argument, that the sheriff has a longtime, very strong grudge against me for some reason that I'm unaware of."

"Go on."

"And then, he comes into town one day and sees a strange horse. When he inquires of the livery boy, he's given a description of me, and it shakes him up so much that even the livery boy notices it."

"But how could he recognize you from a description that could fit dozens of men?" Hemmings asked, playing the devil's advocate.

Smoke smiled. "Sam, how many men do you suppose run around in this day and time in buckskins, are over six feet tall, and have two guns and a knife on their holster tied down low on their legs? I agree, there are lots of big men with light-colored hair, but when you put that with the buckskins and the guns"—he shrugged—"it may have struck enough of a chord with Tolliver that he wanted to see the doctor and check it out to see if it really was me."

"All right, I'll grant you that you do present a rather unique appearance. Go on."

"Now, once he's determined that I might be in town, what is he to do? He has to go immediately to the doctor's house to see if it really is me and find out what the hell I'm doing in his town after all these years."

Hemmings nodded slowly. "I can see that. And I suppose that the doctor fills him in that it is indeed Smoke Jensen and that you've left your very good friend in his care."

Smoke agreed. "And not only that, but he probably tells Tolliver that we've been keeping in touch by telegraph from Pueblo, so his next stop is to see Jacobson and find out what else he can."

Hemmings leaned forward to tap his ash into his trash can, and then he said, "All right. Even granting all of that, how would you get from there to the killing of the doctor? Like I said, each and every one of his actions could just as easily be explained by the fact that he's sheriff here and it's his job to keep the peace. Maybe he just wanted to keep an eye on a notorious gunman, and that is all."

"Just suppose, again for the sake of argument," Smoke said, "that Tolliver decided to have Pearlie killed. That would do two things. One, it would cause me great grief and pain, and two, it would bring me running back to town."

"And that's where Pearlie's story starts to make sense," Cal said. "He says he woke up to find that Blackie man—the sheriff's cousin, remember—standing over him with a gun. It makes sense that the sheriff would have sent someone he trusted to do the dirty work, someone who'd never tell anyone that the sheriff had ordered him to commit cold-blooded murder."

Smoke held up a finger. "According to his testimony, the sheriff was having drinks and dinner with the doctor when he and Blackie decided to make their rounds. What if in fact it was just Tolliver that walked the doctor back home, intending to be there when he found Pearlie dead, but instead he found Blackie dead and Pearlie lying unconscious near the body?"

Hemmings nodded, beginning to see how Smoke's story might explain some things about the case that had been bothering him. "That would put him in a devilish position, trying to explain what Blackie was doing in the doc's house and how he happened to get himself killed by a man in a coma."

"Exactly," Smoke said, leaning back and spreading his

arms out wide. "His only way out would be to do what I think he did. Kill the doctor and try and put the blame on Pearlie."

"That would also work to get Smoke back to town, once we found out about Pearlie's arrest," Cal said. "And then he'd have him right where he wanted him if he intended to do him some harm."

"And what better way to hurt me than to make me watch my good friend being hanged for something I would be sure he hadn't done?" Smoke asked.

Hemmings smiled and held up his hands. "All right. You two have at least given one way things could have happened that would explain the sheriff's actions, but you still have not one shred of proof or evidence to back up your claim." He shrugged. "It could just as easily have happened just as the sheriff said it did, if we assume Pearlie is guilty."

Smoke's face fell. "You're right, Sam. But we're going to work on that. We just wanted someone in this town to know what we're doing and why."

Hemmings was about to reply when the door burst open and Robert Jacobson burst in. "Say, Mayor," he began, and then stopped, his face flushing bright red when he saw Smoke and Cal sitting there.

"Oh . . . uh . . . I didn't know you had someone here," he stammered, at a loss for words. "I'll come back. . . ."

"No, don't be silly, Bob. You can talk in front of these men. What is it?" Hemmings asked.

"I . . . uh . . . this wire came for you just now. I thought you might ought to see it right away." As he held out the wire, Jacobson said while keeping his eyes away from Smoke. "The wire specifically asks that the contents be kept strictly confidential, Mayor."

Hemmings took the wire and read it, being careful not to hold it where anyone else in the room might be able to read it. When he was finished, he immediately glanced at Smoke and Cal. "All right, Bob. Thank you. I'll take care of it." He folded the wire and put it in his pocket until Jacobson had left.

Once the door closed behind him, he said, "This may solve all of our problems, one way or another." He stubbed out his cigar. "The doctor's aunt, Janet Rule, was staying at his house at the time of the murders. She probably saw everything."

Smoke nodded. "We know, Sam. Our next step is to try and find her to get the evidence we need to clear Pearlie."

Hemmings grinned. "You won't need to find her. She's going to come here and she says she has some information for me to hear about the killings."

"Great news!" Smoke said. "When is she going to get here?" he asked.

Hemmings's face turned serious. "I don't think I should divulge that information, Smoke. After all, if I'm wrong and Pearlie is guilty and you are trying to protect him, then you might be inclined to prevent Miss Rule from testifying, by fair means or foul."

"But . . ." Smoke started to argue, and then he saw Hemmings's point and nodded. "Of course. You can't be one-hundred-percent sure we're on the up and up, and you have to protect your witness. I can see that." He hesitated. "But don't you think it's strange that she sent that wire to you, and not to the sheriff? After all, he is the law in town, and I can think of only one reason she wouldn't feel safe in confiding her account of the murder to him."

Hemmings's face became thoughtful. "I agree, it is strange for her to send the wire to me, but I guess we'll just have to wait until she gets here for her to tell us her reasons for doing so."

When Smoke nodded, Hemmings smiled again. "Thank you, Smoke, for being so understanding of my need for secrecy, and I assure you, you'll be the first to hear what she's told me after we talk."

Smoke got up and held out his hand. "That's all we can ask, Sam. Thank you."

Hemmings rose and took Smoke's hand. "For me, my money's on her telling me that Pearlie had nothing to do with the doctor's death," he said.

"You and us both," Cal said enthusiastically, "and I'll also bet she tells you that the sheriff is up to his eyeballs in this mess."

25

As soon as he left Mayor Hemmings's office, Robert Jacobson walked straight to Sheriff Tolliver's office, checking back over his shoulder occasionally to make sure Hemmings and Jensen didn't see him heading that way. Jensen hadn't *specifically* ordered him not to tell the sheriff anything about a *new* message, just not to discuss that he and Jensen had talked about a previous message, so he didn't think Jensen had any gripe coming, but with a man like Jensen, you didn't want to take chances.

When he entered Tolliver's office, he found the sheriff sitting at his desk staring off into space as if he were deep in thought. Uh-oh, he thought, maybe this isn't the best time to bother the man, what with all he's got on his mind and all.

"What do you want, Bob?" Tolliver asked irritably without looking at him.

"Uh . . . I got this wire from Pueblo a while ago, Buck. I thought you ought to know about it."

For the first time, Tolliver showed some animation. He sat up in his chair and leaned forward, his eyes now boring into Jacobson's. "What is it? Has the sheriff there located that Rule lady?" he asked, thinking it was too much to hope for that she'd died of old age or apoplexy or something suitable for a meddling old bitch.

Jacobson smiled slightly. "Better than that, Buck," he

said, sure now that he'd done right in coming to see the sheriff. Now the sheriff would owe him, and he'd just have to try and think of some way to collect on the debt.

"Well, what is it? Don't just stand there grinning like a cat with a bird in its mouth."

"Oh, this is much better than a bird, Buck. But first you got to promise you won't tell nobody I told you about the wire. It wasn't addressed to you and if anyone finds out," he said, an image of an irate Smoke Jensen playing in his mind, "I could get fired."

Now Tolliver looked puzzled as well as irritated. "Well, who the hell was the damn thing addressed to?"

"Mayor Hemmings."

"Hemmings?" Uh-oh, he thought, that doesn't sound too good. "Who was it from?"

"It was from that Miss Rule herself you been looking for and it was sent to Mayor Hemmings. She said she's gonna be on the afternoon train tomorrow from Pueblo, but that she ain't gonna get off. She wants Hemmings to meet her on the last car in the train while it's stopped and she's gonna tell him something important about the killing of Doc Bentley, but she didn't say what it was she was gonna tell him."

Oh, shit, thought Tolliver. Please tell me you didn't already give the message to Hemmings. "Bob, am I the only one you've told this to?" he asked out loud.

"Why, no, Buck," Jacobson answered, surprised that he would ask such a question. "I gave the written message to Mayor Hemmings like it was addressed, but I thought you ought to know about her being in town 'cause you're the one investigating the crime."

Tolliver figured it was time he tried to disavow any interest in the matter. "No, that's not true, Bob," he said, leaning back in his chair and putting his hands behind his head. "I already got the killer in jail, and he's already been convicted, so nothing Miss Rule or anyone else has to say on the matter makes any difference to me."

"Then, you ain't gonna go and talk to her?" Jacobson asked incredulously.

"Naw, I don't think so, Bob. But, hey, thanks for filling me in. I'm sure the mayor will tell me all about what the old lady had to say next time I see him."

Disappointed that his news hadn't been received with more enthusiasm, Jacobson nodded. So much for Tolliver owing him one, he thought. "Sure thing, Sheriff, glad to be of help."

"Oh, and Bob. One more thing," Tolliver said as Jacobson moved toward the door.

He stopped and turned around. "Yeah?"

"I wouldn't go around telling anyone you told me about the wire from Miss Rule. After all, it wasn't addressed to me, and if the company found out you were giving me confidential messages, they'd not only fire you, but they'd probably prosecute you and put you in jail."

Jacobson's face paled. "Now, Sheriff, you asked me to. . . ." he stammered.

Tolliver held up a hand. "Yes, I did, Bob, and I appreciate the way you're cooperating with the law, so I won't tell anyone about it either. It's just that the company might not be so understanding, if you get my drift."

Jacobson shook his head and jerked the door open. "You can bet I won't tell nobody, Sheriff," he said, thinking if Hemmings or Jensen found out he'd talked to Buck, they'd probably do a lot worse than put him in jail.

After he left, Tolliver put his hat on and walked down the street to the livery, forcing himself to walk slow and easy and not seem to be in any hurry in spite of the fact he felt like running the entire way.

This entire matter was getting out of hand, and he knew he'd better put a stop to it before it went any further. Jensen was proving too hard to kill, so he figured he'd end the investigation another way.

Jerry Stone looked up from his usual job of mucking stables and smiled nervously when he saw it was the sheriff. He hoped that Cal feller hadn't said nothing to the sheriff about what he'd told him. If it was one thing Jerry didn't need, it was John Law on his back.

"Howdy, Sheriff. What can I do for you? You need your

horse saddled?" he asked, knowing he was talking too fast but unable to control his mouth. He was also sweating like a pig, but that wasn't unusual when he was mucking stalls.

"Yeah," Tolliver said, flipping him a nickel. "And I need it quick."

"Sure thing, Sheriff," Jerry said, putting the nickel in his pocket and wondering why it was that gunfighters and outlaws always tipped better than lawmen did. That sure said something about the way of the world, all right.

Tolliver turned the head of his dun gelding down the trail that led to the mining cabin where his men spent their time between jobs when they weren't in town. It was one of the first mines he and his men had "liberated" from its previous owners, now dead and forgotten, and it was still their best producer of gold ore. Except, of course, for his new acquisition, but they didn't know anything about that and if he played his cards right, they never would.

"Yo, the cabin," he called, not wanting to surprise the boys or they might just shoot him before they realized who it was.

"Yo yourself," Jeb Hardy called back from the corner of the cabin, where he stood with a rifle in his hands.

Tolliver grinned. "You heard me coming, huh?" he asked as he stepped down off his mount and tied it up at the rail in front of the cabin.

"I heard that old horse of yours puffing and farting for the last quarter mile. He wouldn't be so windy if you'd give him a little grain instead of all that hay."

Tolliver snorted. How's that for a lawyer giving a rancher advice about how to take care of his horse! "The boys inside? I got some business to discuss."

"All but Bubba," Hardy said. "He ain't been here for two, three days. We figure he's staying with that Molly girl over at the saloon spending all his loot from the last job." Hardy shook his head and grinned. "I can't understand that boy, and that's a fact. If he wanted to lie down with a horse-faced female, we got plenty of horses up here at the cabin."

Tolliver stopped Hardy with a hand on his chest. "That ain't it, Jeb. Bubba's dead," he said, wanting to tell him before they got inside so the others wouldn't hear.

"Dead? Whatta you mean dead?"

"Dead, as in not breathing anymore. That kind of dead."

"What the hell happened?"

"You remember how he told us 'bout him and Hog bracing Jensen and his friend a couple of weeks ago and how Jensen took his gun away and dropped it in the dirt down the trail a ways?"

"Yeah, what of it?"

Tolliver shrugged. "I guess he nursed a grudge and he tried to settle it last night with his pistol, and Jensen ventilated him."

"He manage to put a lead pill in Jensen?" Hardy asked, his eyes hard. He'd never particularly liked Bubba; after all, the man was dumb as a rope. But he was a sort of partner, and Hardy didn't like the fact that some out-of-town hard case could come into his town and kill one of his friends. Men just didn't let things like that pass without doing something about it, usually something deadly.

Tolliver shook his head. "Nope. Far as I could tell, Bubba never got off a shot."

"Please don't tell me the son of a bitch was dumb enough to draw against a man like Jensen?"

Tolliver smiled. "No, he walked into the bathroom over at the hotel and surprised Jensen and his friend while they were taking baths."

"And Jensen still managed to kill him?"

Tolliver nodded. "Nobody ever accused Bubba of being smart, or fast with a gun." He hesitated. "Let's not tell the others just yet, all right?"

Hardy shrugged. "Sure. All right by me, but I got to tell you, Buck. I ain't plannin' on letting Jensen get away with this. Bubba wasn't no prize, but he was still one of us, and Jensen has got to be made to pay."

"Count on it, Jeb," Tolliver said, and he went on into the cabin and greeted Kid Akins and Hog Hogarth. "Howdy, boys," he said.

"I see Jeb didn't shoot a hole in your ass with that big Henry of his," Kid said, laughing and putting his cards down on the table.

"Hey," Hog said, looking at the cards and the small pile of money in the middle of the table. "Let's finish this hand. I got a good one this time."

Kid inclined his head. "Take it, Hog. I was bluffin' anyway."

While Hog grinned and raked in the pile of bills, Kid looked at Hardy and then at Tolliver. "What brings you out to our happy home, Buck? You got some more miners lined up for us to skin?"

"Not this time, Kid. It's more important than that."

Akins gave a short laugh. "What could be more important than making a few bucks the easy way?"

Hardy pulled out a chair, and the three men sat and listened while Tolliver told them about the wire from Janet Rule and how she was supposed to meet Hemmings in the last car of the train while it was stopped in Payday. He also told them about how Jensen and Cal were going around asking a lot of questions about him and the night the doc and Blackie were killed.

Hardy grinned. "So, I assume you're here 'cause you sure as hell don't want the lady talking to Mayor Hemmings about what she saw that night."

"Or anybody else," Tolliver added grimly. "She needs to be eliminated from my life before that train gets to Payday, or I'm gonna be in deep shit."

"That might be difficult to manage, Buck," Kid said, leaning back in his chair with his hands behind his head. "That train goes over some pretty rough country 'tween here and Pueblo. There ain't hardly no place where it can easily be stopped." He looked around. "Especially by three or four men. Maybe if we had a dozen or more . . ."

"I got that figured out," Tolliver said, leaning down with his hands on the table. "You all know the train don't actually come into Payday, but just stops outside the town to let people on and off."

The men all nodded.

"Well, there's a grove of oak trees just before the train gets to its stop. I figure someone could hide in those trees and pitch a couple of sticks of dynamite into that car the lady's riding in, and that'd be the end of our problem once and for all."

Hog squinted his little pig eyes. "What do you mean 'our' problem, Buck? Seems to me this lady is your problem, not ours."

Tolliver straightened up, frowning. "I already told you once, Hog. Any problem I got is a problem for all of us, unless you got an aversion to keeping on getting rich off me."

Hardy glared at Hog and held up his hands. "We already agreed to help you, Buck, but dynamiting the whole train to kill one little old lady seems a mite . . . extreme, don't you think?" He stared at Tolliver. "A job like that would bring the federal marshals swarming down on Payday like locusts, and I for one can do without that sort of grief."

"You got a better idea, Jeb?" Tolliver asked. "Like the Kid said, there just ain't no good place to ambush that train and make it stop between here and Pueblo unless we had a dozen or so men, and I only count four here."

Hardy shook his head. "Don't need to make it stop," he said. "Since the lady was kind enough to tell us which car she was going to be in, it should be an easy matter to wait by that big clump of boulders right at the base of that last incline 'fore the train gets to Payday. When it starts up that hill, the train slows to almost a walk. It should be easy enough to ride up next to the windows in that last car and put a couple of slugs into one little old lady."

"Yeah, but we won't know which side of the car she'll be on," Kid said.

Hardy sighed. "That's why there's gonna be two of us, Kid. One on each side." He looked back at Tolliver. "Now, killing one little old lady, or even maybe a couple of others in that car, ain't gonna be big enough news to bring no marshals down here. So, since we got the local sheriff on our side, the investigation into the killings ought to pass on by easy enough without anyone getting fingered for it."

"What about me?" Hog said.

"You're gonna stay here, Hog," Hardy said. "Your fat ass is too distinct, even with a mask on. The other people on the train are liable to recognize you."

"Besides," Kid said laughing, "your horse would probably have a stroke if it tried to haul your lard ass up that hill to catch the train."

Hog gave Kid a flat look. "Keep it up, Kid, and this lard ass is gonna be sitting on your face 'fore you know it."

26

After Smoke and Cal left Hemmings's office, they went to the hotel. "I want you to pack an overnight bag, Cal, and then we're going to put you on today's train to Pueblo."

"Why?" Cal asked. "I thought we were gonna look into the sheriff's dealings an' see what he's been up to."

"That's exactly what you're going to be doing in Pueblo, Cal. If the sheriff has been stealing claims around here, he's sure not going to file them in the local claims office where everyone knows who he is. They'd all know he doesn't have time to be out prospecting for gold with his job here in town as sheriff."

Cal nodded. "I see. You want me to check the claims office in Pueblo for any claims listed under Buck Tolliver's name."

"Not only claims listed under his name, Cal, but any claims he might be a partner in. I'm sure he's not working alone, but he's probably too smart and too cautious to let his partners have the claims in their names alone, so he could be listed as partners with them in the claims with his name second on the recorded deed."

"What about askin' around at the bank?" Cal asked. "If he's makin' all this money he's got to be stashing it somewhere, and like you said, it sure as hell wouldn't be here in Payday."

Smoke nodded. "That's a good idea, Cal, but I don't think the bankers in Pueblo would talk to you about one of their customers, especially if he's got as much money as I think he has."

"Oh," Cal said, disappointed his idea hadn't panned out.

"But," Smoke said, clapping him on the shoulder, "there's another way to get the information we need. As soon as you get to Pueblo, wire Monte Carson at our bank there and have him get the president to wire the bank in Pueblo for a credit report on Buck Tolliver. Have them say he's down there wanting to invest in some ranches and they need to know if he's good for the money."

"Why not just wire Big Rock from here?" Cal asked. "It'd be a whole lot quicker."

Smoke glanced toward the general store down the street. "I don't think Robert Jacobson is a man we can trust, Cal. I think the sheriff probably has him in his pocket, and the less Buck Tolliver knows about our business, the better I'll feel."

Cal's eyes widened. "Smoke, that reminds me. You don't think he might've told the sheriff about when Miss Rule is coming into town, do you?"

Smoke nodded, his mouth grim. "It wouldn't surprise me a bit, Cal, but I don't think bracing him about it would do any good. He's probably more scared of Tolliver than he is of me, so he'd probably just deny it and we couldn't prove a thing. But if he did, and if the sheriff is as dirty as we think he is, then he won't be able to allow her to talk to Hemmings. He'll have to try and do something to keep her from talking."

"What are you gonna do?"

"I'm going to stick close to the sheriff without him knowing it. If he does go after her, maybe I can stop him before he gets to her and prevents her from clearing Pearlie's name."

"You watch your back and ride with your pistols loose, Smoke. The sheriff is almost certain to suspect we're on to him, so the chances are pretty good he'll come after you too," Cal advised.

"Don't worry, Cal. I never turn my back on a snake, especially one as slippery as Buck Tolliver." He grinned. "Course, if he were to try something, it sure might solve all of our problems, 'cause he'd be planted six feet under boot hill."

"Come on, then, Smoke. Let's go get me packed and on that train."

As soon as Cal was safely on the train, Smoke went to the livery and asked Jerry to saddle up his horse. He wanted to be able to ride on a moment's notice if the sheriff decided to leave town.

Jerry just stood there, his mouth hanging open slightly with a dazed look in his eyes.

"Are you all right, son?" Smoke asked, wondering if the boy had eaten something that disagreed with him.

"It's just that I never met a famous gunfighter before, sir," Jerry said, his eyes wide.

Smoke laughed. "Well, we're just like everyone else, Jerry. We put our pants on one leg at a time just like you do."

"Uh, do you think you could sort'a sign your name on my hat, Mr. Jensen?"

Smoke shook his head. It was the first time he'd ever been asked to give his autograph. "Sure, if you'll get Storm saddled before it gets dark."

While Jerry was saddling his horse, Smoke casually asked him, "Which horse belongs to Sheriff Tolliver?"

"Oh," Jerry said over his shoulder as he tightened the cinch strap on Smoke's horse, "it ain't here now. The sheriff took him out about an hour ago."

"Is that so?" Smoke asked, handing him his hat with his name written on it. "You see which way he rode out of town?"

Jerry straightened up, a puzzled look on his face as he took the hat and stared at the name Smoke Jensen had written on it. "Why you askin', Mr. Jensen?"

Smoke shrugged. "Don't worry, Jerry. I'm not gonna shoot him or anything like that. It's just that he's got my friend in jail, and I owe him for some extra food I had him order from the hotel dining room. I thought if he was around I'd pay him now and settle the bill."

"Oh, well, in that case, he took the north road up into the mountains like he usually does when he goes riding."

"He have a place up that way?" Smoke asked, trying to sound casual.

"Naw, his ranch is off to the south where the land is flat. Ain't no good ranch land up north, it's too hilly up in the mountains. Nothing up there but gold mines an' such."

"I see," Smoke said, realizing the sheriff probably had a camp up there that he used to meet with his accomplices.

He gave Jerry a gold two-dollar piece and climbed up into the saddle. "Thanks, Jerry."

Jerry's eyes shined as he turned the gold coin over and over in his fingers, thinking what a cheapskate the sheriff was. "If I see the sheriff, I'll tell him you're looking for him."

Smoke shook his head. He didn't want Jerry warning the sheriff that he'd been asking around about him. He wanted the man off guard as much as possible. "Don't bother. I think I'll just leave the money in his desk at the jail where he'll be sure to find it. See ya' later, young man."

Smoke took the north road out of town and rode slowly, keeping a sharp lookout up ahead. He didn't want to run into the sheriff on his way back to town and have to explain what he was doing on the same road.

He figured he was pretty safe from being bushwhacked since the sheriff didn't know Smoke was tailing him, but he rode with his eyes searching both sides of the trail just in case.

There were too many tracks on the road, which was actually little more than a trail where the horses and wagons had worn down the grass, to determine which ones were the sheriff's. Smoke figured he'd have to check each trail or path that turned off the road and hope that sooner rather than later he'd find the one the sheriff took.

He'd gone up and down six or seven trails with no luck by the time the sun began to set. This was no job to attempt in the dark, and so he reluctantly turned his horse around and headed back toward town, hoping the sheriff wasn't already on the way to do harm to Miss Rule.

He considered trying to warn Hemmings that the sheriff might well know about Rule's plans, but finally decided against it. Hemmings just wasn't quite ready to think the sheriff was behind the killings, and Smoke didn't want to alienate him by pushing too hard. He'd just have to hope that Cal came up with something before Rule came to town and put herself in harm's way.

He decided if the sheriff wasn't in town when he got back, he'd get up early the next morning and check out the rest of the trails to the north of town and try to find his hideout.

He was just coming into town when he saw the sheriff leaving the livery. Smoke breathed a sigh of relief, and pulled his horse in and told Jerry to give it some extra oats and grain before bedding it down for the night.

When he left the livery, he saw Tolliver entering the batwings of the saloon down the street. Smoke loosened the rawhide thong on his Colt and decided to follow him in. No telling what he might learn, he thought, and after his long trail ride, he was more than ready for a cold beer and a couple of hard-boiled eggs.

Smoke timed his entrance to coincide with the entrance of several miners who were in town to spend some of the dust they'd dug out of the mountains. Ducking down so the other men hid him, he broke off, moved into a corner, and took a seat at a table where the lantern light didn't quite reach.

He pulled his hat down low on his head and slumped in his chair as he looked around the crowded room. After a moment, when his eyes adjusted to the relative gloom and smoke, he saw Tolliver sitting at a table across the room with three men.

Smoke grinned slightly when he saw that one of the men was the gent he'd beaten up who'd been with the man who'd later tried to kill him and Cal. "I see you're keeping bad company, Sheriff Tolliver," Smoke mumbled to himself.

The men had their heads down and close and were talking earnestly, evidently in low voices so they couldn't be heard above the clink of glasses and the rowdy laughter that was normal in saloons after dark.

"I'll just bet those are your partners, Buck ol' man," Smoke said, nodding to himself and giving the men a good long look so he'd be sure and recognize them the next time he saw them.

Smoke ordered a beer and a plate of hard-boiled eggs when one of the waitresses came by, and drank and ate slowly, keeping his head down and watching to see what happened across the room.

In less than an hour, the sheriff and his men had finished their business and all four got up and walked outside. Smoke noticed the bottle of whiskey they'd had at the table was still over half full, so the talk must've been about something important for them to forgo drinking while they talked. He bet they were planning on how they could get to Miss Rule and keep her from talking.

Smoke quickly got up, left through the back door, and peeked around the corner of the building to see what they did. He was disappointed when the men waved good-bye to the sheriff and made their way toward the hotel instead of the livery stable. Evidently, they were going to spend the night in town since they didn't seem to be in any hurry to get their horses out of the stable.

Smoke wished Cal was with him. If the men separated in the morning, there was no way he could follow or watch all of them, and he figured the sheriff was probably enlisting their help in silencing the Rule lady.

Once they were all out of sight, Smoke made his way to the hotel and went up the rear stairs to his own room. He'd need to be on watch first thing in the morning in case the men decided to get on the move early.

Of course, he mused as he got undressed and flopped down on the bed, they might try to sneak out in the middle of the night, but there was nothing he could do about that. He had to sleep sometime, and since Miss Rule was an elderly lady, she most likely wouldn't be traveling at night.

If he couldn't find the men in the morning, he'd have no choice but to go to Hemmings and demand to know Rule's schedule so he could try to protect her. That was his last thought before he dropped into a deep, dreamless sleep.

27

As soon as Cal got off the train in Pueblo, he went straight to the telegraph office. He sent the telegram to Sheriff Monte Carson in Big Rock as per Smoke's instructions, and even added a request that the sheriff inform everyone that Pearlie was all right physically and they were going to make sure he stayed that way.

"I'll check back in an hour or so for any reply," Cal said. "I've gotta go by the land claims office."

He could see the eyes of the man behind the counter light up with gold fever. "You struck it rich, mister?" he asked, his eyes measuring Cal to see if there was some way he could get some of Cal's new riches. The telegraph operator had been known to make a few extra dollars by tipping off some rough friends of his when men sent wires back home that they'd struck it rich. His friends would then waylay the men and rob them of their dust with no one making the connection to the telegraph man.

Cal grinned and shook his head. "Nope. Sorry, but I'm just gonna check on somebody else's claims. I'm not a prospector, I'm a cowhand."

"Oh," the man said, getting back to his work and ignoring Cal as if he didn't exist any longer now that he wasn't going to be rich. He'd never seen a cowhand with two nickels to rub together, much less enough to rob him for.

Cal chuckled to himself and wondered why so many

men were eaten up with the prospect of getting rich. It was as if their own lives were meaningless unless they happened to find gold. He further mused that for most of the men who did strike it rich, their newfound wealth was probably more of a curse than a blessing. Smoke and Sally were about the only rich people he'd ever known who were completely happy, but of course, they didn't act like rich folks either.

Cal opened the door to the claims office and went inside. His heart fell when he saw stacks and stacks of folders arranged along both side walls and even all the way across the back wall. "Jimminy, I ain't never gonna get through all those files," he muttered to himself, taking off his hat and scratching his head.

A gray-haired, older lady who was puttering behind the counter must have heard him, for she gave a low laugh and cleared her throat to get his attention. "Excuse me, young man. I couldn't help overhearing you. Are you looking for a particular file or information on a particular mine?"

Cal walked up to the counter and leaned on it, his eyes still roving across the thousands and thousands of files. "Well, ma'am, I was going to, but seein' as how you got more claims in here than the number of people in the whole world, I'm sort'a rethinking my options. I need to find out if a certain man has filed any claims for mines and such here, and if he has, who his partners in the ventures are."

The lady chuckled. "Well, sonny, you look so cute standing there with your eyes big as melons that I'm going to take mercy on you and show you the easiest way through our little maze here."

"Gosh, ma'am," Cal said, "that'd be great. I'm in kind of a big hurry, and if I don't find out what I need to know, a very nice lady might be hurt."

"Oh," the lady said, her eyes big and round. "That sounds very serious. All right, first off, let's get the formalities out of the way. If I'm going to slog through all those dusty files for you, I should at least know your name. Mine's Martha Jameson."

"Oh, excuse my manners, Missus Jameson. I'm Calvin Woods," Cal said, quickly taking off his hat and holding out his hand to her.

"I'll bet they call you Cal, right?" she asked, taking his hand and giving it a firm shake.

"Yes, ma'am, ever since I was a shavetail."

"And there ain't no Mr. Jameson, so just call me Martha instead of Missus."

"Yes, ma'am," Cal said, blushing scarlet.

She took a small pad of paper off the desk behind her and handed it to Cal with a pencil. "Now you just write down the names of all the men you're interested in and we'll get to work." She hesitated, still holding the pencil. "You can read and write, can't you?" she asked, not unkindly.

"Oh, yes, ma'am," he said. "I graduated high school and everything, and my boss's wife used to be a schoolteacher, so she's been helping me with some college courses during the winter at the ranch."

"You must be very lucky to have such a good friend and boss," Martha said, handing him the pencil.

"Yes, ma'am," Cal said, and he wrote "Buck Tolliver" on the paper and smiled ruefully. "This is the name I know, but I just don't know who else may be involved with him. I'd assume the mines would be in the vicinity of the town of Payday."

Her brows knit. "Involved? What do you mean involved?" she asked, opening the countertop to let Cal walk through and back toward the file shelves.

Cal began to tell her what he and Smoke suspected about the sheriff's nefarious activities, and she stopped and stared at him with wide-open eyes. "Why, it's like a great mystery, isn't it?"

"Uh . . . what do you mean, ma'am?" he asked, not understanding what she meant by "mystery."

She took his arm and leaned in close. "I've been reading the most delightful series of mystery stories by a British author, Conan Doyle, about a detective named Sherlock Holmes. They're all about how he uses deductive reasoning to solve crimes."

Since the only detectives he'd ever heard of were the Pinkertons, and since he had no idea whatsoever what the words "deductive reasoning" meant, Cal just smiled and nodded his head and hoped she'd drop the subject.

Within minutes, she was climbing up on a small three-step ladder and snatching various files off the shelves and flinging them at him.

By the time his arms were full, Cal was covered with dust and was sneezing fitfully from the dust that'd gone up his nose and clogged his mouth.

"Most of these claims are filed alphabetically by first letter of the last name and then filed by county, so we should be able to find some with your fellow's name on it if they're here."

Within ten minutes, they'd struck pay dirt. After that, it was relatively easy to follow Tolliver's trail through the maze of file folders. After they'd noted the names of men on the claims that had Tolliver listed first, they then went through the stacks and found lots of other claims with those other men's names listed first, though Tolliver's was always there someplace.

An hour and a half later, Cal folded up the paper on which he'd written the information they'd gathered and stuck it in his pocket.

"Can I offer you some money for helping me out, ma'am?" he offered.

"Of course not, young man," she said indignantly. "I did this to help you solve your mystery and free your friend from this sheriff's evil clutches."

Thinking Martha sure did talk funny, Cal thanked her again and left, hurrying toward the bank to see if the wire from the bank in Big Rock had done any good.

When he gave one of the tellers his name, he was immediately shown into an opulent office in the rear of the building.

A portly man wearing a full suit, vest, and a carnation in his buttonhole grinned at Cal like he was an old friend and got up from behind his desk to come around and shake Cal's hand. Cal didn't know what the bank president at Big

Rock had written about him, but whatever it was, it sure as hell had impressed this man.

"Howdy, Mr. Woods. I'm Gerald McManus, the president of this bank," the man said, showing Cal to a plush armchair in front of his desk.

After he'd taken his seat, McManus stared at him from under bushy eyebrows. "My, but you look awfully young to have such impressive credentials."

"Credentials?" Cal asked, bewildered.

McManus's head bobbed up and down. "Yes. The president of your bank back in Big Rock tells me you're out here to purchase some large tracts of land and that you're interested in the financial status of one of the men you're going into partnership with, a Mr. Buck Tolliver."

So that was it, Cal thought. McManus thinks I'm some rich investor out here to spend a lot of money.

"Of course, we'll be glad to be of any assistance to you that we can here at my bank," McManus said, leaning over to offer Cal a cigar from a wooden humidor on his desk. As Cal took the cigar and struck a match on the bottom of his boot, the man frowned and asked, "Would you care for a snifter of brandy or a cognac, Mr. Woods?"

"No, thank you kindly," Cal said, not having the faintest idea what a cognac was. As he exhaled a thick blue cloud of smoke, he thought, this is the best cigar I've ever had.

McManus hooked his thumbs in the armholes of his vest and leaned back in his chair until Cal thought he was in imminent danger of tipping over. "Do you plan on keeping any of your investment capital in this town, Mr. Woods, or will you use your bank back in Big Rock?"

"Well," Cal said, thinking like crazy. "I'm sure Mr. Tolliver and I'll need a local bank to handle some of our money," he said, not knowing if he was making any sense at all. "That is, if Mr. Tolliver is as well heeled as he tells me he is."

McManus took a sheet off the top of his desk and handed it to Cal. "Here is a current financial statement on Mr. Tolliver's holdings in our establishment, which I'm sure will be more than adequate for almost any investment you two would care to make."

When Cal's eyes almost bugged out as he glanced over the paper, McManus leaned forward and whispered conspiratorially. "And I understand that Mr. Tolliver also has dealings with both of the other banks in town, though I can't imagine why he doesn't just put all of his money in one place. It would be so much more convenient for him."

And it'd mean a hell of a lot more money for you too, Cal thought. "Can I take this with me?" he asked.

"Certainly," McManus said expansively. "We here at the First Territorial Bank of Colorado intend to please."

After he left the bank, Cal saw that if he hurried, he had time to get a wire off to Smoke and still be able to make the afternoon train back to Payday.

He kept the wire short and simple, not wanting to put too much in it for Robert Jacobson to read. It read, "Smoke, got what I came for and it's going to knock your eyes out. Cal."

He paid the man for the wire and took off at a dead run for the train terminal, hoping he'd make it in time.

The train was already pulling out of the station, so he didn't have time to stop and buy a ticket. He ran down the tracks after the last car, and just managed to grab the rail and pull himself up, panting and sweating, as the train picked up speed.

"Golly, that was close," he muttered as he dusted himself off and entered the rear door of the last car.

"It certainly was, young man," an elderly, white-haired woman said from the next to last seat in the car. "I was afraid for a moment you weren't going to make it and that you might trip and fall under the wheels."

"Oh, no danger of that, ma'am," Cal said, wondering what it was about his face that made little old ladies want to adopt him and take him under their wings. "The train weren't going all that fast yet."

"Wasn't," the lady corrected him.

"Uh, yes, ma'am. Wasn't," Cal repeated, taking the seat across the aisle from her and leaning his head back to hopefully catch a few winks of sleep on the trip. If his luck continued to hold, the lady across the aisle wouldn't chatter the entire way to Payday.

28

Smoke was waiting outside the hotel, standing well back in the alley so he wouldn't be seen, when the three men Tolliver had been talking to the previous night in the saloon walked out of the door.

Smoke had been there since just before dawn, and yawned widely as he watched the men walk down the street and enter a small café named Mom's. Glancing at his watch and seeing it was almost eleven o'clock in the morning, Smoke decided to stir up some action by following the men into the place and having himself some breakfast. Truth was, he was bored; he'd been standing in that alley for almost six hours and he wanted to make something happen.

As he entered, he chuckled to himself. Long ago he'd promised himself he'd never again eat at any place named Mom's. The food in such establishments was invariably terrible, bordering on inedible. However, present circumstances dictated that he give Tolliver and his men a push, so he guessed he'd have to make do.

He walked through the door and took a table in the rear of the rather small room, sitting so his back was to a wall and he had a clear view of the front door and the inhabitants of the place. The three men he'd followed had taken a seat near the front window, and were just giving their orders to a plump, matronly woman wearing a flour-stained apron and a kerchief tied on her head.

They hadn't seen him as yet, and he was interested to see what their reaction would be when they did. It could be that they were just friends of Tolliver's and not involved in his schemes or in the murders, but he didn't think so. The way they'd sat last night with their heads close together and their voices low bespoke of nefarious dealings—he'd bet his ranch on it.

After the waitress left their table, she stopped by his on the way to the kitchen and asked quickly, "Coffee?"

Smoke nodded, but kept his eyes on the men across the room. After a few moments, the youngest one of them happened to turn his gaze onto Smoke. Smoke almost grinned when the young man froze and his mouth dropped open and his eyes went wide.

He hurriedly lowered his head and leaned in close to his companions, speaking rapidly, and then all of their heads turned and all of their eyes were on Smoke.

Smoke grinned and dipped his head in greeting, as if he were just being polite to strangers whose eyes happen to meet across a room.

The young man's face turned beet red, his right hand went to the gun on his hip, and he started to stand up, until the oldest man at the table reached over and grabbed his arm, whispering something under his breath that made the young man sit back down.

Just as the waitress was setting Smoke's coffee on his table, Sheriff Buck Tolliver walked into the room. He started toward the table with the three men, until one of them gave a quick shake of his head and looked over at Smoke.

Tolliver followed his gaze, and quickly altered his course and walked over to stand before Smoke's table. He tipped his hat. "Howdy, Mr. Jensen," he said. His voice was light, but his eyes were dark and suspicious.

"Hello, Sheriff," Smoke replied. "Care to join me for some breakfast? I know it's a bit late in the day, but I've been busy this morning talking to people about how things are here in Payday."

Tolliver started to look over his shoulder, then caught himself just in time, but not before Smoke saw the movement. "Sure. I don't normally eat breakfast this late, but since it's a bit early for lunch, I'll have a cup of coffee with you." He wondered what the mountain man was up to. Had he been following Hardy and the others, and if he had, how had he known they were partners with him?

He pulled out a chair and took a seat, setting his hat on a chair next to him. He glanced up at the waitress, who was still standing patiently waiting for Smoke's order. "Hey, Mom," he said, "bring me a cup of coffee, will ya'?"

She nodded and looked down at Smoke. "You gonna eat, mister?"

Smoke said, without taking his eyes off of Tolliver, "Three hen's eggs, scrambled, half a pound of bacon, crispy, fried potatoes, sliced tomatoes if you have 'em fresh, and biscuits and gravy."

Mom grinned. "That all for you, mister, or are you expectin' a wagon load of miners in here to eat with you?"

Smoke smiled and looked up at her. "It's all for me, Mom. I'm still a growing boy."

"Huh," she said, blushing down to the roots of her hair as she gave him a wink. "Growing, maybe; boy, definitely not!"

After she brought the sheriff his coffee, Tolliver leaned back in his chair and shook his head. "Now just what am I going to do with you, Mr. Jensen? I can't have you running all over town sticking your nose in where it don't belong. It won't look right to the citizens of this town that elected me to do that very thing."

Smoke shrugged and sipped his coffee, staring at Tolliver over the rim but keeping the men behind the sheriff in his peripheral vision at the same time. "First off, Sheriff, there's not a damned thing you *can* do about it, and I think you know it. But what I'm wondering is why it bothers you so much that I'm looking into the killings, unless it's the fact that you railroaded my friend into jail for something you or your friends over there did."

Tolliver's face flushed and his jaw clenched so hard his

jaw muscles bulged and his teeth creaked. "I don't allow nobody to talk to me like that, Jensen!"

Smoke grinned and leaned back in his chair. This was what he'd been waiting for. Get a man mad enough and he'll often say things he'd later wished he hadn't. He said in an even voice, with no trace of anger or hostility, "Then fill your hand or shut your mouth, Sheriff, 'cause I'm going to say and do what I please."

Tolliver stared at him for a moment, and then he forced himself to take a deep breath and relax, an insolent grin on his face. "Naw, I don't think I'll kill you right now, Jensen. I'd rather wait until I see the look on your face when your friend dances on the air at the end of a rope. Maybe then I'll put you out of your misery."

Smoke knew then that he'd been right. Everything that had happened to Pearlie had been because of Tolliver. For some reason that Smoke still couldn't remember, Tolliver had a gutful of rage at *him* and he was using Pearlie to get his revenge.

"That's not going to happen, Sheriff," Smoke said, his voice low and hard and the smile gone from his face.

"Oh, and why not?" Tolliver said, his grin showing he was enjoying making Smoke sweat.

Smoke leaned forward, his elbows on the table, and talked in a low voice that only Tolliver could hear. "Because you and I both know you're dirty, Sheriff. You've disgraced that badge you're wearing dozens of time over—and I'm going to prove it. And when I do, not only will Pearlie go free, but unless I miss my guess, you and your friends over there will be taking his place on that scaffold they're building down the street, only there'll be four ropes dangling from it, not one."

"Why you . . ." Tolliver said, half-rising from his chair and reaching for his gun.

His eyes widened and his mouth dropped open when he found himself staring down the barrel of Smoke's Colt before his hand had even touched the butt of his own pistol.

Across the room, Kid Akins was watching and exclaimed,

"Holy shit!" He'd never seen anyone draw so fast in his entire life and vowed then and there that if he ever went after Jensen, it was going to be from the back, not the front.

Hardy, who'd also seen Smoke's lightning-fast draw, just nodded. His friends had been right when they'd told him Jensen was the fastest they'd ever seen with a short gun. He knew *he* was fast too, and the only question he had in his mind right now was whether Jensen was faster.

Sheriff Tolliver froze, his hand trembling over the butt of his pistol, but no longer making a move to draw. "Sit down, Sheriff," Smoke ordered, and he holstered his gun.

When Tolliver was in his seat, beads of sweat pooling on his forehead, Smoke said, "I don't know what you have against me, Tolliver, or why you've gone to so much trouble to hurt my friend, but I'll find out sooner or later and we'll have a reckoning, you and me." Smoke took a drink of his now-cold coffee, made a face, and set it back down. He looked into Tolliver's eyes. "You do know, don't you, Buck, that only one of us is leaving this town alive?"

Tolliver tried to speak, but his throat was too dry, so he picked up his coffee cup and drank, spilling a little with his shaking hand. "You can bet on it, Jensen," he croaked. "And I'll make sure and tell you why you're going to die before I plant you in the dirt."

Smoke threw back his head and laughed out loud. "Well, from what I've seen so far, Sheriff, you'd better bring plenty of help, 'cause if you're not any faster than I've seen so far, you'll be dead and lying on your back in the dirt before you ever clear leather."

"Now, if you gentlemen are finished with your discussion, I'd kind'a like to put this food down on the table 'fore it gets cold," Mom said, her eyes moving back and forth between the sheriff and the stranger.

Smoke looked over and saw she'd been standing there during the entire incident with the gun.

He leaned back, still keeping his eyes on Tolliver and his friends. "Sure, Mom, put it down. I'm done with this snake for a while."

Tolliver flushed again, nodded once at Mom, and then

he got up and walked quickly out of the café, followed close behind by the men at the table across the room.

As they walked down the street toward Tolliver's office, Jeb Hardy whistled. "Jesus, Buck, I been around and I've seen some of the best in the business handle iron, but I'll tell you true—I ain't never seen nobody as fast as Smoke Jensen."

Tolliver stopped and turned his reddened eyes on Hardy. "You telling me you're afraid of him, Jeb?"

Jeb shrugged. "Let's just say I've got a newfound respect for the man, that's all. But what I do want to say is that if you expect *me* to go up against someone like that for you, then you're going to have to come up with a lot more money than we've talked about up till now." He grinned. "I still think I can take Jensen, but it'd be close and I'd probably take some lead in the deal, so I'm gonna need a pretty good incentive to even try."

"That goes for me too, Buck," Kid Akins said, moving a toothpick around in his mouth and looking back over his shoulder to make sure Jensen hadn't followed them out. "That man is snake-quick with a six-killer and I'd love to be the one that gets famous for putting him down, but like Jeb says, it'd be a mighty tall risk."

"Don't you worry none, Buck," Hog Hogarth said, sticking his thumb against his chest. "I ain't afraid of that bastard Jensen."

Hardy laughed. "That's 'cause you're an idiot, Hog. Jensen already chewed you up and spit you out once and the word is he didn't even break a sweat doing it."

Hog's face turned bright red and he squeezed his right hand into a fist and stuck it under Hardy's nose. "What'd you call me, Jeb?"

Before he could blink, Hardy had his pistol out and the barrel was punching up under Hog's chin, raising it until Hog was staring at the sky. "I said you're an idiot, Hog. Do you want to do something about it?" He eared back the hammer with a loud metallic click, making Hog blink and start to sweat.

"Uh . . . no, Jeb. That's all right," Hog said, his eyes

rolling as he tried to look down at Hardy's gun. "Like you said, Jensen done took me once."

"Oh, for God's sake," Tolliver said, whirling around and heading for his office. He looked at the sky. "Why did you saddle me with such idiots for partners?" he asked in a plaintive voice.

The others followed him in and he closed the door behind him. After they'd all taken a seat and Tolliver had poured whiskey all around, he sat on the edge of his desk and said, "Now, you boys saw what Jensen did and you know what you got to do or he's gonna be on us from now on like a duck on a june bug.

"Hog, you're gonna head on back to the cabin, and Jeb, you and the Kid are gonna get your mounts and head on over to the hill coming into town and take out that meddling old lady in the last car of the train."

"Aw, why can't I go with them?" Hog asked.

"Because you're pretty near worthless with a short gun, Hog, and that express gun you carry won't go through the windows and walls of the train car. Besides, I want Jensen to follow you out of town so Jeb and the Kid can do their jobs."

"What makes you think Jensen will follow Hog to the cabin?" Hardy asked.

Tolliver smiled and drained his glass. "Because I'm gonna go with him. Jensen can't afford to let me out of his sight. My guess is that Hemmings hasn't told him when the Rule lady is arriving, so he'll have to follow me thinking I'm gonna be going to take her out. And so when the news comes that Rule was killed by two gunmen, Smoke Jensen is going to be my alibi: that I was up in the mountains and nowhere near the train line when she was killed."

Jeb Hardy grinned and also drained his glass. "Good, now that we've got the plan outta the way, we need to do some more talking about money."

"What do you mean?" Tolliver asked. "We've already discussed the fact that since we're partners, you need to help me to keep the money coming in."

"Yeah," Jeb said, "but we ain't exactly equal partners,

Buck. And since we're gonna be pulling your fat outta your fire, I figure it's only fair that from now on all of the money we manage to liberate from the miners is split up into equal shares."

"But . . ." Tolliver began.

Hardy held up his hand. "And don't give us that 'I'm the sheriff' business, because if we don't help you, you ain't gonna be the sheriff for too much longer." He looked around the desk at the other men. "Far as I'm concerned, everything we take in from now on gets cut into equal shares. You boys agree with that?"

Akins and Hog both nodded, their eyes on Tolliver to see if he would agree.

Tolliver sighed. "All right, all right. Equal shares, but only after Miss Rule *and* Smoke Jensen are both dead."

29

Smoke figured something was going to happen and probably happen fast after his confrontation with the sheriff in the café, so he got his horse from the livery stable and stationed himself at the end of an alley just down the street from the sheriff's office so he could see what went on.

About an hour after they entered, two of the men left the office and walked directly back to the hotel and entered. Smoke saw that it was the older man and the younger one, who dressed like he fancied himself a gunfighter, who went into the hotel.

Five minutes later, the sheriff and the big, wide man that Smoke had beaten up left the office and walked down to the livery stable. Smoke moved down the street and waited behind a large tent building where he could see the entrance to the livery. After about ten minutes, the two men rode out the door and turned left onto the main street of Payday.

The sheriff led the way and headed his horse north out of town the way he'd gone the night before when Smoke had trailed him up into the mountains.

Smoke hesitated. If the sheriff was heading up into the mountains, it probably meant Miss Rule wasn't arriving today for her talk with Hemmings, because she sure as hell wasn't coming into town over the mountain passes between Pueblo and Payday.

He knew he couldn't watch both sets of men, but he figured the most important one to keep an eye on was the sheriff, since he was almost certainly the leader of the gang.

As they moved on up the trail, Smoke let them get just out of sight, and then he walked his horse after them. The sheriff was sure to know Smoke would be tailing him, and so he reached down and loosened the rawhide hammer thong on both of his Colts, knowing that it wasn't unlikely that the sheriff might try to lead him into an ambush. Smoke grinned to himself at the thought. Men a lot more dangerous than Tolliver had tracked him and he was still alive. Besides, as soon as they got out of town, Smoke planned to ride his horse off to the side of the road and trail the men by moving along with them, not behind them, so an ambush would be impossible.

Hardy and Akins watched through the second-story window of their hotel room, and saw Smoke follow the sheriff and Hog as they rode out of town.

Hardy nodded as he peered through the binoculars in his hand. "I'll give Tolliver one thing," he said.

"What's that?" Akins asked.

"He knows his men. He was right about Jensen following him and Hog and leaving us alone to do what we got to do."

"You know," Akins said, looking back out of the window at Jensen as he rode down the street, "if I had my rifle up here, I could end all of this right now." He aimed with his finger and made a motion of pulling a trigger.

Hardy snorted. "Now you're sounding as dumb as Hog, Kid."

Akins glared around at him. "Why do you say that?"

Hardy shook his head. "Just what would you do after you shot Jensen? Walk out of the hotel with your smoking

Winchester in your hand and say, 'Here I am, arrest me for murder'?"

Akins laughed a little, but his eyes were flat and his voice was hard. "Nope. I'd hightail it down the stairs and out the back door. By the time the crowd started looking for the killer, I'd be on my horse and headed out of town with no one the wiser."

"Bullshit, Kid," Hardy argued. "Our names are on the register downstairs along with our room number. You think none of those people on the street down there are gonna see where the shot came from?"

Akins started to reply, and then he just shut his mouth and looked back out of the window. "Well, it was just a thought anyhow."

"You let me and Tolliver do the thinking, and you'll live a lot longer," Hardy said, a mocking tone in his voice that went right through the Kid.

Akins whirled around and his right hand dropped to the butt of his pistol, his eyes flashing.

Hardy grinned and stepped back, his right hand also near his gun. "You sure you want to test me, Kid?" he asked. "You may be a tad faster, I don't know. But at this distance, I'll get off at least one shot and you'll eat some lead no matter who fires first."

Akins took a deep breath and moved his hand out away from his side. "What are we arguing for, Jeb?" he asked, grinning slightly. "After all, we're on the same side here."

"Glad you see it that way, Kid. Now, let's get our mounts and head on out to the hill where we're gonna ambush that train."

Akins pulled out a pocket watch and frowned. "But we got several hours yet 'fore the train's due in."

Hardy sighed, thinking the Kid really was dumb as a stump. "I know, Kid, but I'd kind'a like to look around the area before we have to take down the train. We might have to clear some brush from alongside the track where we're gonna be riding, and that might take some time. Besides, it's better if the people in town don't see us riding off toward the ambush site right before the ambush occurs, all right?"

"Yeah, sure, Jeb. But if we're gonna hang around out there in the wilds all day, you mind if I get a bottle to kind'a keep my throat from getting dry?"

"As long as it's a short bottle, Kid," Hardy said with a laugh, trying to ease the tension between them. "It wouldn't do to get drunk an' fall off our horses when we're trying to kill somebody."

Mercifully, the little old lady across the aisle from Cal spent most of the trip knitting instead of talking, though Cal couldn't for the life of him figure out how she managed to make those tiny knots with the railroad car swaying and bouncing the way it did.

Anyway, by the time the train was nearing Payday, he was sound asleep and snoring like an engine himself. Smoke had always marveled at how Cal could fall asleep on the back of a horse while they were riding the trail and not fall off, and the train ride wasn't much smoother.

"Well, I swan, would you look at that?" the lady next to him exclaimed, bringing him out of a deep sleep.

"Wha . . . what is it?" he asked groggily, wiping at his eyes and trying to force himself awake.

The lady smiled at him and pointed out the window. "Looky there. Those men are trying to race the train up this hill," she said gaily, as if intrigued by the actions she was seeing.

"Race the train?" Cal asked, leaning forward and glancing out the window across from her. Sure enough, a man with his hat pulled down low was leaning over his saddle horn and riding hell-bent for leather alongside the car as the train struggled up the incline and began to slow down.

"That's funny," Cal said, and he glanced out his own window and saw a different man doing exactly the same thing, only this man had a gun in his hand and his eyes were on the window Cal was looking out of.

"Shit!" Cal exclaimed, realizing what was about to happen. He drew his own pistol and hunkered down between the seats for cover.

"What did you say, young man?" the woman asked harshly, looking up from her knitting and glaring at him as if she'd never heard a man curse before.

"Ever'body get down, now!" Cal hollered, trying to get the other people in the car to take cover.

When they just turned and looked at him like he was crazy, and when he saw the man outside the car raise his pistol, Cal aimed his gun at the roof and fired off two shots.

Men shouted and women screamed, but all of them dove out of their seats and hit the floor, some covering their heads with their hands. All except the old lady across the aisle from Cal, who just continued to glare at him as if he'd committed some terrible faux pas like farting at the dinner table.

Just as he was reaching for her to drag her down with him, both men opened fire. Bullets crashed through windows on both sides of the car sending shards of glass flying and showering sparks as the slugs ricocheted off metal struts.

The lady grunted once and her eyes opened wide in surprise as a bright flower of blood blossomed on her blouse just over her right shoulder.

Cal grabbed her, and her eyes rolled back and she fainted and fell into his arms. He pulled her down and laid her gently on her back on the floor under the seats as more bullets thudded into the car.

Really pissed off now, Cal raised his head and aimed out the window and fired off shots as fast as he could pull the trigger until his gun was empty. He was rewarded by seeing the horse of the man on his side of the train swallow his head and somersault forward, sending the outlaw tumbling through the air to land hard in a sycamore bush.

Cal quickly began to reload, but by the time he'd filled the chambers, the other bandit had pulled up his horse and was riding across the tracks to help his friend.

It didn't matter anyway as the train had reached the top

of the hill and was picking up speed and would soon be at the Payday stop.

Cal holstered his pistol, reached down, and slid the old lady out from under the seat into the middle of the aisle. He leaned over and ripped the lady's blouse open at the shoulder.

"Here now, young man," a woman from several rows ahead shouted indignantly, pointing her parasol at him like it was a rifle. "Just what do you think you're doing to that poor, unfortunate woman?"

Cal didn't answer until he'd taken his bandanna off and tied it tightly around the lady's shoulder, slowing the steady stream of blood pouring from her wound.

Then he looked up and said calmly, "I'm tryin' to keep this woman from bleedin' to death. Do you mind?"

The woman's husband, who was evidently much smarter than her, or at least had maybe seen gunshot wounds before, shushed her and came back to kneel next to Cal.

"You need any help, son?" he asked.

"Help me get her up on the seat. She'll be more comfortable there," Cal said. "We're gonna need to keep some pressure on that wound to slow the bleeding down as much as possible."

After they'd picked her up and laid her on the seat crosswise, the man helping said, "Sounds like you've seen a few gunshot wounds before, son."

Cal thought of the many scars on his body from similar wounds he'd suffered helping Smoke, and grinned. "A few, mister, so I know what we got to do."

He eased down on the edge of the seat next to the lady and said, "I'll stay here with her and as soon as the train stops, someone needs to get a wagon from Payday and we need to get her to a bed where someone can try and get that bullet outta her shoulder 'fore it festers up."

The man shook his head. "I don't know who that'd be," he said. "I'm from Payday and our only doctor was killed a few weeks back."

Cal grinned sourly. "I know," he said, hoping Smoke was still in town. He knew the mountain man had plenty of experience removing slugs from people's bodies, and to him it looked like this lady wasn't going to make it unless someone worked on her sooner rather than later. "I guess we'll just have to find somebody else to do it."

He glanced up at the man's wife, who was hovering over them, watching to make sure Cal didn't do anything inappropriate. "Ma'am, do you know this lady?" he asked.

She shook her head. "Why, no, I don't."

Cal inclined his head toward the lady's handbag, which was lying next to her knitting she'd dropped when she got shot. "Maybe there's something in her bag that'll tell us who she is. We need to notify her family she's been hurt."

The lady picked up the bag and opened it. She took a yellow piece of paper out of the bag. "Here's a telegraph receipt," she said, reading it. "It's a message to the mayor of Payday and it's signed *Janet Rule*."

Jiminy, Cal thought, this is the lady we've all been looking so hard for and she's right here on the train with me.

He looked down at the lady, struggling for her life. "She's got to survive," he said to the man leaning over her with him. "She's got some important news for the mayor, so we've got to get that bullet out of her and keep her alive."

The man shrugged. "Well, we got a sheriff here in Payday. He's had some experience with gunshot wounds. Maybe he can take the bullet outta her."

Cal glanced up at him. He knew the sheriff was probably the reason she had a bullet in her in the first place. "Over my dead body," he said, causing the man to look at him strangely.

Just then the train jerked to a stop and the conductor stuck his head in the door. "Is everyone all right back here?" he asked.

Cal looked up. "We need a wagon from town and some blankets and we need 'em fast!

30

Jeb Hardy watched the train disappear in the distance and shook his head. What a colossal fuck-up this was, he thought sourly. He took his Stetson off and looked at the bullet hole punched neatly in the crown, about one and a half inches above where his head had been. He didn't know who the yahoo was who'd started shooting back at them from the train, but he was damned good.

He jerked his horse's head around and rode it across the tracks. He grinned for a moment at the sight of the very proud and self-important Kid Akins lying ass over teakettle in a sycamore bush, but he was careful not to let the Kid see his amusement.

He walked his horse over to the bush. "Hey, Kid. You all right?" he called.

"Hell, no, I ain't all right, you asshole," the Kid yelled back from among broken branches and limbs of the bush. Evidently, the fall hadn't improved his disposition any, Hardy thought wryly.

"What's wrong?"

"I think I broke my damned arm," the Kid called back, struggling to free himself from the limbs and branches he'd broken in his fall that were entwined all around him.

When he finally emerged from the tangled mess, Hardy whistled softly. "Whew, that looks like a nasty break," he said sympathetically.

The Kid glanced down at where his left arm hung limply at his side. Between the elbow and the wrist, the arm took a bend that wasn't at all natural and was swollen to almost twice its size. The Kid's face was scratched and bleeding and screwed up in pain, and he just shook his head. "I hope I get my hands on the son of a bitch who was doing all that shooting," he groused, his voice harsh and almost a croak from the pain.

"Well," Hardy said, climbing down off his horse and pulling a large-bladed knife from the scabbard on his belt. "You can't hardly blame him none, Kid. After all, we started the shooting and he was just shooting back."

The Kid turned flat, dangerous eyes on him. "That don't matter none at all. If I ever find out who it was, he's a dead man."

When Hardy moved toward him, his knife extended, the Kid slapped at his empty holster with his right hand, and then he looked around wildly for his pistol, which had evidently fallen from his hand when he was somersaulting over his horse's head. "What are you doin' with that blade?" he asked, backing away until he was almost back in the sycamore bush.

Hardy grinned, pleased to see the Kid was frightened of him. It was a fact worth savoring, and remembering. "Hey, don't worry, Kid. I'm not going to hurt you. But I figure we're gonna need to cut some limbs off that there sycamore bush to make you a splint for that arm, 'less you want to ride back to town with it bouncing and flopping around all over the place."

After he cut four limbs about twenty-four inches in length, Hardy turned to the Kid, who was sitting on a rock cradling his left arm with his right, his face pale and covered with sweat and dried blood from all the scratches.

"Now for the fun part," Hardy said, laying the sticks at the Kid's feet.

"Whatta ya' mean?" he asked, his eyes widening in fear and pain.

"I'm gonna have to set that wrist, Kid, or you're gonna

have to go the rest of your life with an arm as crooked as a dog's hind leg."

"Wait a minute," Kid said, looking around as if he might find someone to tell him he didn't have to go through with it.

Hardy took the Kid's arm. "No use fighting it, Kid. We done drank all the whiskey while we was waiting to shoot up the train. Now, just bite on this and I'll fix you right up." He handed Kid his leather knife scabbard.

Kid put it between his teeth and closed his eyes, and Hardy took his wrist in his hands and gave it a quick jerk.

When the bone snapped into place, Kid screamed once and then he leaned over and vomited into the dirt. When Hardy shifted his grip, the Kid looked at the arm, swallowed once, and fainted dead away.

Hardy looked down at him and shook his head. What a baby, he thought as he bent over and tied the four sticks to Kid's arm, holding the bone straight until they could get to town and put a proper splint on it.

While the train was stopped at the small platform that served as the Payday station, Cal waited by the old lady's side until someone had fetched a buckboard from the town, and then he climbed in next to her for the trip back to town.

Once there, Mayor Sam Hemmings directed the driver of the wagon to park it in front of Dr. Bentley's house.

"But Mayor," the man argued, "the doc's dead. He ain't there no more."

"I know that, you fool," Hemmings said irritably, "but he's got the only place set up for someone to be treated for a gunshot wound in."

Once the lady was lying on one of the doctor's beds, still unconscious, the mayor got a good look at her. "Well, I'll be damned," he said, shaking his head.

"I see you know who she is," Cal said from the other side of the bed.

"Sure I do. That's Janet Rule, Dr. Bentley's aunt," the

mayor said. "I was supposed to meet her when the train came in this afternoon so she could give me some information about the doc's murder."

Cal nodded. "I know. We looked in her bag on the train and found the telegram she'd sent you with her name on it," Cal said, still astonished at the tricks fate can play on man. Here was the very lady Smoke and he had been trying to find ever since they found out about Pearlie's arrest and her maybe having knowledge that would clear him.

"Jesus, what a mess," Hemmings said. He took his hat off and scratched his head. "I just hope she comes around so she can tell me whatever it was she wanted to." He looked at Cal. "Otherwise, your friend is gonna hang."

"Speaking of friends," Cal said, "have you seen Smoke around this afternoon?"

Hemmings shook his head. "No, but when I went to get my horse out of the stable to come up here to meet the train, Jerry Stone said Smoke got his horse and rode out of town this morning and hasn't come back since."

"Damn," Cal said. "Isn't there someone in this town who can take that bullet outta her shoulder?" Cal asked worriedly. He knew that time was critical in gunshot wounds. If the bullet stayed in the flesh too long, suppuration was almost sure to set in and the patient would have little chance of surviving.

Hemmings shook his head. "No, I'm afraid not, son. Since we had the doc here for so long, none of us ever had to learn to take bullets outta people."

"Shit!" Cal said, rolling up his sleeves. "Get me a basin of water, boiled and hot, and some towels."

Hemmings's eyebrows shot up. "You gonna try to get that lead outta her?"

Cal nodded, his stomach doing flip-flops. "I will if you'll show me where the doctor kept his instruments. The last time I did this, I did it with a skinning knife heated in a campfire, but the doctor's probably got something better suited for it than that."

"You sure you know what you're doing?" Hemmings

asked after he told one of the men standing nearby to get the water and the doc's bag of instruments.

Cal grinned sourly. "No, but I've at least done it a time or two before, and I've seen Smoke do it on me four or five times. You got any better ideas?"

"We could send someone to Pueblo. . . ." Hemmings started to say, until Cal cut him off.

"She'd be dead before he got there, much less before anyone could get back here. If we're gonna do this, it's got to be done now."

After a pan of steaming-hot water was placed next to the bed and Cal had the doc's instruments laid out on a side table next to him, he closed his eyes and whispered a silent prayer before he began. When he opened his eyes, he noticed Mayor Sam Hemmings doing the same thing, and chuckled. He was going to need all the help he could get, and a little divine intervention would be more than welcome.

Taking a long, slim knife off the table, he glanced up at Hemmings, who was standing behind him. "If you want to help, you can stand next to her and make sure she don't move."

Hemmings nodded and sleeved sweat off his brow. It was obvious that he'd had no experience with such matters in the past.

Cal took the knife in one hand and a pair of slim tongs in the other. He used the tip of the knife to open the wound a bit, and then he probed down deep with the tongs, trying to feel with the metal like it was his fingers. Immediately, blood began to ooze up out of the wound, but since it wasn't spurting, Cal tried to ignore it.

After a few moments, he felt a slight click as the tip of the metal tongs touched lead. Spreading the tong tips slowly, he gently pushed deeper, and then closed them around the butt end of the slug.

As easy as he could, he withdrew the tongs and sure

enough, lying there between the tips was a slightly bent and crumpled lead bullet.

"Good God Almighty," Hemmings exclaimed, grinning as sweat continued to pour off his face, "you did it!"

Cal dropped the slug into a metal basin and put the knife and the tongs down. "It ain't over yet, Mayor."

He took a clean cloth, rolled it into a small cylinder, and dipped it in the hot water, and then, after wringing it out, he gently pushed it down into the wound, which was oozing blood a little faster now that he'd stirred things up inside her.

Once the flow of blood was stopped, he took a larger piece of cloth and asked Hemmings to hold her shoulder up off the bed while he wrapped the cloth around it in a figure eight, making it tight enough to keep pressure on the wound.

When he was done, Cal got to his feet and sighed deeply. "Now, it's up to her and how bad she wants to live," he said, feeling as bone tired as if he'd run several miles.

Hemmings glanced down at the sleeping lady. "Well, at least her color looks a mite better."

"Yeah," Cal replied, "but I'm worried that she didn't even move when I was probing her wound. She's still pretty deep asleep, an' that ain't exactly a good sign."

Hemmings put his hand on Cal's shoulder. "Well, at least she's got a chance now, son, thanks to you."

Cal nodded quickly and moved over to take a seat in a chair next to the wall. He leaned back against the back of the chair, loosened the rawhide thong on his pistol, and laid his head back and closed his eyes.

"Uh, what are you doing?" the mayor asked.

Cal opened one eye. "This lady's got some information that's gonna put some galoot's neck in a noose, Mayor. He's already tried to kill her once, and if he finds out she's still alive, it's my guess he's gonna try again." He closed his eye. "I aim to prevent that from happening."

"I was planning on asking the sheriff to stand watch over her until she woke up, Cal," Hemmings said.

Cal snorted without opening his eyes. "That'd be like askin' the fox to guard the henhouse, Mr. Hemmings."

"Oh, I don't. . . ."

Now Cal opened his eyes. "You're welcome to stay here if you want, or have some lady from the town stay here with us, but I'm not leaving this lady's side until she tells us who really killed the doctor."

Hemmings pursed his lips. "And what if she says your friend did it?"

Cal grinned. "That ain't gonna happen, Mayor."

"And just how are you so sure?"

Cal sighed. "Think about it, Mr. Hemmings. The trial was over and done with, and Pearlie'd been sentenced to hang. If this lady knew he was the one that done it, why would she come all the way down here to tell you about it? Hell, he was done for. All she had to do was keep her mouth shut an' he was gonna hang."

Hemmings narrowed his eyes and stroked his chin, thinking about what Cal said.

Cal smiled. "See? The only thing that makes sense is that she knew an innocent man was gonna die for something somebody else did unless she spoke up. That's the only thing I can think of that would make her come all this way to talk to you. And the fact that she wanted you to keep it a secret means the man she was going to accuse was still running around loose and might do her hurt if he found out she was going to talk."

Hemmings finally nodded. "By gum, you're right, Cal." He hesitated. "And like you and Smoke said earlier, the only reason she'd have to wire me instead of Sheriff Tolliver with her offer to testify is if she was going to accuse him."

Now it was Cal who nodded. "Now you're catching on, Mayor. As you know, my partner, Smoke Jensen, and I think it's definitely the sheriff that is somehow mixed up in all this. That's why I don't intend to let him near Miss Rule until she's had a chance to talk."

Hemmings shook his head. "I just can't believe that

Sheriff Tolliver is a murderer, but what you say does make a lot of sense."

Cal measured the mayor with his eyes for a moment. He didn't know if he was mixed up with the sheriff or not, but he decided to trust him. "That ain't all either," Cal said. "What would you say if I told you that the sheriff and some other men named Hardy, Akins, Hogarth, an' Barkley are partners in over twenty mining claims in this county, and that the sheriff has over three hundred thousand dollars in one Pueblo bank and no telling how much in other banks in the city?"

Hemmings's eyes nearly bugged out of his head. "What? That . . . that's just not possible," he finally managed to say. "Why, the sheriff only makes a hundred dollars a month salary, and he hasn't spent any time prospecting or mining that I know about."

Cal closed his eyes and leaned his head back again. "Something to think about, huh, Mayor?"

Hemmings sat down across the room from Cal and did just that, turning things over and over in his mind until he was certain that Cal and Smoke had called it correctly— Sheriff Buck Tolliver was in this up to his eyebrows.

31

The next day, Smoke was up at dawn after sleeping only fitfully in the woods near the cabin Sheriff Tolliver and his companion stayed in. Smoke had made a cold camp, not daring to light a fire lest he give his location away. He felt sure the sheriff knew he was out there following him, but he didn't want to make it too easy in case the man decided to do something about it and came looking for him after dark. The thought made him grin in anticipation, for the dark and the woods and the mountains were Smoke's elements, not the sheriff's.

When the sun rose and there was no sign the two men in the cabin were even awake yet, Smoke said "to hell with it" and made himself a hat-sized fire. He used only small, very dry sticks so there'd be little or no smoke, and he cooked bacon and beans and used the grease to make the rock-hard biscuits in his saddlebags soft enough to eat without the danger of breaking a tooth.

By the time Smoke was on his last cup of boiled coffee and his second cigarette of the day, he saw signs of life in the cabin. Tolliver walked out the door and into the old outhouse out back.

Smoke used the time to pack up his breakfast fixings, and was ready to go when Tolliver and his companion finally got onto their horses and headed back toward town. He hadn't seen any smoke coming out of the small stovepipe on the roof, so he knew the men hadn't cooked themselves any breakfast or made any hot coffee.

After a while, Smoke decided to have some fun, so he walked his horse out of the thick brush alongside the trail and got into line a hundred yards or so behind the sheriff, only keeping pace with the two men and not catching up, but making sure they knew he'd been following them.

Other than glancing over his shoulder and grinning a few times, Tolliver didn't look like Smoke's being there bothered him at all.

Smoke began to wonder if he hadn't been suckered; if the sheriff hadn't guessed he'd be following him and sent the other two men off to do his dirty work. If that were true, then Miss Rule had probably already been sent on to her reward in the afterlife and he was going to have to find some other way to prove Pearlie's innocence. Oh, well, Smoke thought, shrugging, there wasn't anything he could do about it. He could only follow one of them, and the sheriff had been the logical one to keep an eye on.

After years of living in the High Lonesome with Preacher when he was younger, Smoke had developed the ability to live in the present while preparing for the future, and all without dwelling on the past. What was done was done, and there was no changing it, so there was rarely the need to worry excessively over it. If mistakes had been made, he just tried harder not to make them again. It was a good philosophy to live by, but it was small comfort when a friend's life depended on you making the right choice the first time, because you weren't going to get another chance.

When they got to town, the sheriff and his fat friend walked their horses straight to the café they'd eaten at the previous day. The men had obviously been too lazy to make themselves breakfast, so they were going for an early lunch, Smoke figured.

No need to follow them there. He'd do better checking in with the mayor to find out if he'd heard anything from Miss Rule since Smoke had last talked with him. It was about time for Smoke to put his foot down and make the man divulge when and where she was going to show up so that he and Cal could make sure she lived long enough to testify.

When he got to the mayor's office, Smoke found a note tacked to the door saying the mayor was over at Dr. Bentley's house.

"That's strange," Smoke said to himself. "What would he be doing at a dead man's house?"

Smoke tied his horse to the hitching rail out front and knocked on the doctor's door. A haggard-looking mayor answered; his hair was askew, his face was unshaven, and his eyes were bleary and bloodshot.

"Oh, hello, Mr. Jensen," he said, stepping to the side and ushering Smoke inside.

"Good morning, Mayor Hemmings," Smoke said, taking his hat off and hanging it on a peg near the door. "You look like the north end of a southbound mule."

The mayor grunted and nodded. "Yeah, it comes from staying up all night jumping at every sound 'cause you're sure someone's gonna shoot you in the head while you're asleep."

Smoke raised his eyebrows, and was just about to ask what Hemmings meant when Cal walked into the room. "Hey, Smoke," he said. Cal looked considerably fresher than the mayor, as if he hadn't had any trouble sleeping at all. In fact, Smoke thought, he looked quite chipper.

"Hey, Cal. Now just what have you two been up to?" Smoke asked, looking from one to the other.

"You tell him," Hemmings said to Cal, waving a limp hand. "I'm going to shave while you make us some fresh coffee."

He turned and shuffled into the doctor's bedroom, looking for a razor and shaving soap and water to scrape his beard off with.

"Come on in the kitchen and I'll make us all some coffee while I tell you what's been happening," Cal said.

* * *

Half an hour later, the mayor had shaved, the coffee'd been made and drunk, and the men were standing in the clinic room looking down at Janet Rule.

Smoke leaned over and put his palm on her forehead. "If she's got a fever, it's very slight," he said. He peeked under the bandages on her shoulder, and then he glanced at Cal and smiled. "You did a good job getting that slug out of her, Cal. You probably saved her life. There is absolutely no sign of festering or suppuration around the wound."

Cal frowned. "Yeah, maybe. I just wish she'd wake up and tell us what she knows that might help Pearlie. That way no one would have any reason to kill her and we could relax a little bit."

"So, you two sat up with her all night?" Smoke asked, an appraising glint in his eye.

The mayor nodded, glancing at Cal. "Yes. Your friend here thought her life might be in danger, so we both elected to guard her during the night."

"He was obviously correct, Mayor," Smoke said. "From what Cal said, the outlaws who attacked the train only fired into the last car. That means they weren't trying to rob the train, and it also means they knew beforehand when Miss Rule was arriving and exactly where she was going to be seated."

Hemmings snapped his fingers. "Of course, I hadn't thought of that." He shook his head. "I was so busy worrying about whether she was going to live or not, I plumb forgot to think through what her attack meant."

"Who else besides yourself knew of Miss Rule's plans?" Smoke asked.

The mayor thought for a second. "Only myself and Robert Jacobson, the man who took the telegraph message."

Cal snorted. "Huh. We already know Jacobson's got a big mouth and that he's pretty friendly with the sheriff."

Smoke looked at Hemmings. "What do you think about what Cal found out in Pueblo, Mayor?"

The mayor shrugged, looking uncomfortable. "It doesn't sound too good for the sheriff," he said. "It probably means he's been stealing claims from miners for some time, but it does not necessarily mean that he had anything to do with Dr. Bentley's death. The two things may not be connected, and while it certainly puts him on the hook for a lot of crimes, it won't help clear Pearlie unless the sheriff confesses to the murder of Bentley too."

"You're right, Mayor," Smoke said, moving to the window and staring out of it. "What we found out about the sheriff means he's most probably a killer and is certainly a crook and a thief, but it doesn't prove he killed the doctor."

"But, Smoke!" Cal said. "We both know he's guilty as can be."

Smoke looked over his shoulder. "Knowing it and proving it are two separate things, Cal."

Then, Smoke surprised them both by grinning.

"Why have you got that shit-eating grin on your face, Smoke?" Cal asked, smiling himself because he knew that expression meant Smoke had figured out a way to get to the sheriff.

"I've got an idea," Smoke answered. He looked at Hemmings. "What was the name of that woman who helped treat Pearlie's wounds? The ex-nurse?"

"Why, uh, Hattie Monroe," Hemmings replied, blushing slightly.

Smoke smiled in return. "And you two are, uh, close friends, I take it?"

The mayor's blush deepened. "Yes, you could say that. Why?"

"Do you trust her completely?" Smoke asked.

The mayor shrugged. "I guess so. As far as I know, Hattie is an honorable woman in spite of her profession, but you still haven't answered my question. Why?"

"I told you," Smoke said. "I have an idea. . . ."

Jeb Hardy and Kid Akins were riding into town, doubled up on Hardy's mount since Akins's horse had broken his leg in the fall and had been put down.

"Hey, Jeb," Akins said, "isn't that Buck's horse over at the café there?"

"Yeah," Hardy said. "You feel up to eating something this afternoon?"

"I guess so, but I was kind'a hoping for something a little stronger to drink than coffee. I need something to ease this pain in my arm, and just about every other bone I got feels like it's been stomped on by a mule."

"We'll get to that," Hardy said, thinking to himself what a crybaby Akins was. "Let's see what Buck has to say first and then we'll head on over to the saloon."

They dismounted and went into the café, Akins still cradling his broken left arm and its splints with his right hand.

Buck raised his eyebrows when he saw them, and then he scooted over to make room for them in the booth where he and Hog Hogarth were sitting.

As soon as they'd ordered some coffee and food from the waitress, Tolliver leaned over and whispered harshly, "What the hell happened? I didn't see any commotion when I rode into town like somebody'd been killed. Did you get the old lady?"

Hardy shrugged. "I think so. We put about a hundred rounds into that rail car, and I think I heard her scream just before she dropped outta sight."

"What happened to you?" Hog asked, looking at Akins and grinning. None of the group particularly liked the brash young man, and Hog especially had no love for the boy since Akins was always riding him about his weight and sloppiness.

"Some asshole in the train started shooting back at us, an' he got lucky and plugged my hoss."

Hog nodded. "And so then you fell off and broke your little arm?" he asked, sarcasm dripping from his voice.

Akins's eyes narrowed. "Yeah, but it's not my gun hand, so don't go getting any ideas, fat man."

Hog gave a short laugh. "I don't care if'n your gun hand is good or not, little man. If'n I wanted to take you I'd take you, guns, fists, knives, or teeth," he growled.

"Shut the fuck up!" Tolliver snapped in a low, hard voice. "I'm trying to get some work done here and you two keep acting like little kids fighting all the time."

They all shut up while the waitress brought their coffee and food. Once she'd left the table, Tolliver leaned back and smiled at Hardy. "So, you think you got it done, huh?"

Hardy nodded around a mouthful of bacon and eggs. "I said I think so, Buck. Won't know for sure till we go on into town and listen to what everyone is saying. Hell, train ought'a have been here by now."

Tolliver craned his neck around to look out of the window. "I don't see no crowds around my office, nor anyone gathered in the street. Maybe the train just kept on going and didn't stop to let anybody off since they'd been attacked."

Hardy nodded down at Tolliver's empty plate. "I see you done finished your meal. Why don't you head on over to the mayor's office and see what he's heard? We'll wait here for you."

"The hell we will," Akins said, shoveling food into his mouth one-handed, his injured left arm propped up on the table. "Soon as I finish this here grub, I'm headin' for the saloon to get me some whiskey to kill the pain."

"Crybaby," Hog muttered.

Tolliver gave him a flat look and held up his hand before Akins could respond to the gibe. "All right, all right. I'll mosey on over to Hemmings's office and I'll meet you men at the saloon in half an hour."

He stood up and stared down at Hardy and Akins. "And for you two's sake, I'd better find out that train pulled into the station with at least one dead body on it."

32

Mayor Sam Hemmings was sitting in his office going over some paperwork when the door opened after a short knock. Sheriff Buck Tolliver walked in and took his hat off before sitting down, a sign that usually meant he intended to stay and chew the fat for a while.

"Howdy, Mayor," he said.

"Hello, Buck," Hemmings replied, feeling the sweat begin to gather under his armpits. Even though they'd been casual friends for a long time, Tolliver was a dangerous man when crossed, and Hemmings was about to cross him in the worst way, thanks to Jensen. Being a natural-born politician helped Hemmings keep the fact that he was lying through his teeth hidden from Tolliver.

"Haven't seen you around for a couple of days," Hemmings said, trying to keep his tone light as if he had nothing important on his mind.

Tolliver nodded and yawned, as if bored. He too was trying to keep the fact that he was lying hidden. "Yeah, well, I had to do my weekly ride around to the mining camps in the county and make sure they weren't having any problems with poachers or claim-jumpers."

I'll bet, Hemmings thought, but didn't say. "Well, you sure missed some excitement here while you were gone."

"Oh?" Tolliver asked, trying to sound mildly interested,

but Hemmings could tell it was the real reason he came by the office.

"A couple of desperadoes shot up the afternoon train from Pueblo yesterday," Hemmings said. "Probably just a couple of drunken cowboys 'cause they didn't try to rob it or anything, just shot the hell outta one of the cars as it was slowed down coming up that big hill just outside of town."

Tolliver attempted to sound casual, but his eyes gave his excitement away. "Is that so? Anybody hurt?"

"Yes, matter of fact. Miss Rule, you remember, Dr. Bentley's aunt, was shot up."

"Oh, I'm awful sorry to hear that," Tolliver said, leaning back in his chair and pulling a cigar out of his vest pocket. As he struck a match on his pants leg and held the flame under the tip, he glanced up through the smoke at Hemmings and asked, "They gonna have a funeral for her here or in Pueblo?"

Hemmings smiled. The son of a bitch is taking the bait, he thought. Now to pull him in. "Well, now, that's the good news," he said. "She wasn't killed, just wounded. That friend of Pearlie's, Cal Woods, happened to be on the train, and he took the bullet outta her and she looks like she's gonna be all right."

Tolliver gave a tiny gasp, choked on cigar smoke, and coughed for a minute like he was trying to heave up a lung. When he could breathe again, he asked, "She able to tell you anything about the night the doc got killed?"

Hemmings put a disappointed look on his face. "No, not yet. Unfortunately, she's still unconscious from loss of blood and hasn't been able to tell me anything as of yet. But we expect her to wake up anytime now and as soon as she does, I'm going to go over there and see what she has to say."

"Where . . . where are you keeping her?" Tolliver asked, trying to sound disinterested. "I might ought'a go on over there an' see if I can get a statement from her."

"She's over at the doc's house in that little room where he kept his sick patients when they had to stay overnight.

I've got Hattie Monroe staying with her, but she says we ought not bother her for a few more days till she gets her strength back. Hattie said she'll let me know as soon as she wakes up and is ready to talk."

Tolliver raised his eyebrows. "Hattie the only one staying there?"

Hemmings tried to look shocked. "Well, after all, Buck, Miss Rule is a proper lady. We can't hardly have any townsmen staying in the same house with her while she's unconscious. It just wouldn't be right."

"Of course, you're right. I wasn't thinking," Tolliver said, a speculative glint in his eye. "Besides, the only man who'd have any reason to not want her to tell about that night is already in jail waitin' to be hung."

"That's right," Hemmings agreed. "I suspect that when Miss Rule wakes up, she's gonna tell us that Pearlie killed the doc and that'll be the end of it."

"I'm sure you're right, Mayor," Tolliver said, getting to his feet and stubbing his cigar out in the ashtray on Hemmings's desk. "Well, I'd better be on my way. The good citizens of Payday don't pay me to sit around jawing all day."

"See you later, Buck," Hemmings said, lowering his head as if he were getting back to his paperwork.

After Tolliver left, Hemmings went to his window and took a handkerchief out of his pocket. He stuck his hand out of his window and waved the cloth a couple of times as if he were dusting it off, and then he went back to sit at his desk and worry about how things were going to play out.

This was a very dangerous game he and Jensen were playing, and he hoped that the right people got caught in the trap, and not the ones setting the trap.

Tolliver could hardly keep from running as he made his way straight toward the saloon down the street from the mayor's office.

He burst through the batwings and looked frantically

around for his friends. Sure enough, Hog and Jeb and Kid were sitting at a corner table across the room. As he made his way toward them, Tolliver noticed that the whiskey bottle in the center of the table was already half empty. Damn, he thought, they sure as hell weren't wasting any time getting plowed.

Hardy glanced up and saw Tolliver making his way through the crowded room, and shook his head when he saw the expression on Tolliver's face. "Uh-oh, boys," Hardy said, pouring himself another drink from the whiskey bottle in preparation for what he knew was going to be a hell of an afternoon. "Looks like we got storm clouds ahead." And he winked and inclined his head toward Tolliver.

"He looks mad enough to piss nails," Kid said, wincing as his movement caused a stab of pain in his injured arm that ran all the way past his shoulder and straight into his head.

Tolliver took a seat and without speaking, grabbed the whiskey bottle and a spare glass and filled it to the brim. He set the bottle down, upended the glass, and drained half of it in one long, convulsive gulp.

"Uh, bad news, I take it?" Hardy said, though his face showed little concern.

Tolliver turned red, bloodshot eyes on him and growled, "Damn straight there's bad news. It seems you and the Kid here didn't do too good a job yesterday."

He looked over at Kid and sneered, "In fact, about the only thing you got killed was the Kid's horse."

Hardy frowned. "Hey, Buck, I saw the lady go down with my own eyes. I know she was hit."

"Yeah, she went down but not out, you fool," Tolliver spit back at him. "You only managed to wound her, and that damn kid with Jensen was on the train, and he fixed her up good enough that the mayor says she'll be good as new in a few days and talking her fool head off."

"Did she tell him what she saw the night you . . . uh . . . the doc was killed?" Hog asked. He was on his third glass of whiskey and his words were slightly slurred because his lips were numb and weren't working right.

"Not yet, thank God," Tolliver said, finishing off his glass and pouring himself another one. "But according to Hemmings, it won't be too long 'fore she's able to send us all to the gallows."

"Hold on there, Buck," Hardy said, his voice low and hard. "None of us had anything to do with the doc's killing. That was yours and Blackie's mess, so don't be talking no gallows talk to me."

Tolliver gave a short laugh and took a deep swig of his whiskey. "I done told you once, Hardy, it don't make no never mind about who did the doc. If it looks like I'm gonna swing from the end of a rope, I can guarantee you I won't be dancing alone."

Hardy's hand dropped to the butt of his pistol. "It's beginning to look like the simplest thing for us to do is to plant you forked-end-up, Buck. That'd solve all of our problems."

Tolliver sneered. "Yeah, but my lawyer in Pueblo has all the information he needs to make sure every last one of you sons of bitches will be convicted of dozens of murders, Jeb, so you'd better get shut of that idea right now."

"Hey, fellas," Kid said, laying his good hand on Buck's forearm. "Let's not fight among ourselves. Remember, we all got a good thing going here. There's no need to let a little old lady fuck it up for us."

Hog nodded. "For once, the Kid's right, men." He up-ended his glass for another drink before he realized it was already empty.

Tolliver looked around the table. "All right then. Here's what we have to do. The mayor has the old lady being kept in the doc's house. She's being watched over by Hattie Monroe, and there's no other guards."

Hardy grinned evilly. "Then there should be no problem sneaking in there tonight and putting a lead pill in both their heads."

"Hold on, Jeb," Tolliver said, sipping his drink now instead of gulping it. "It would raise a lot of questions if they're killed like that. People might start to wonder who has something to hide."

Hog sighed heavily. "Well, then, Buck. Just what do you want us to do? Take her out to the cabin and hold her until she dies of old age?" he asked, giggling a little at his lame joke.

Tolliver laughed, more from nervousness than from amusement. "No. I just need someone to slip into the house without being seen, cut their throats, and then set the house on fire."

"But people will still know they been killed," Hog argued. "Won't they?"

Tolliver shook his head. "No, they won't, Hog. The fire will destroy the bodies so no one will know their throats were cut. Everyone knows Hattie smokes like a chimney. They'll just assume she fell asleep and set the place on fire." He looked around the table. "Matter of fact, it might be a good idea to take an empty bottle of whiskey and lay it next to her body like she'd been drinking all night and passed out while smoking a cigarette."

"Who do you want to do the job?" Kid asked.

"Not you, Kid," Tolliver said, looking down at his broken wrist. He glanced across the table at Hog. "I think Hog's the best one here with a blade, so he should do it."

"Yeah," Kid said sarcastically, "and even he ought to be able to kill a couple of women and start a fire without messing it up too bad." He paused. "Unless he's too drunk to walk by then."

Hog's eyes flashed. "I ain't drunk, Kid, but I tell you what I *am* gonna do, an' that's start a fire under your ass when I get done with them two ladies."

The men were all so intent on their discussion, they didn't see Smoke Jensen and Joshua Banks standing on the second-floor landing watching them cold-bloodedly plan the murder of two women.

Smoke had thought it might be best to have an impartial witness to the sheriff's meeting with his henchmen just in case it came down to his word against the sheriff's, and

Banks, the lawyer who'd acted as judge during Pearlie's trial, was the logical choice.

Banks looked at Smoke as the sheriff and his men got up and left the saloon. "I see your point, Jensen," Banks said. "Now that Mayor Hemmings has given the sheriff and only the sheriff the information about Miss Rule, and if subsequent to this meeting one or more of those men try to do her harm, we'll have an excellent prima facie case for conspiracy to commit murder against the sheriff."

Smoke grinned. "I take it all that highfalutin lawyer talk means we'll have him dead to rights."

Banks grinned. "Deader than a hog on a spit!"

33

Scudding clouds raced across the night sky and blotted out the moon, making the main street of Payday as dark as the inside of a black cat at midnight.

A heavyset, rotund figure moved from the alleyway just south of the late Dr. Bentley's house, and moved slowly along the boardwalk with his back pressed up against the buildings.

From the second floor of the hotel across the street, Mayor Sam Hemmings and Joshua Banks had to cover their mouths to keep from laughing at the sight of the fat man tiptoeing down the boardwalk, looking back over his shoulder every few feet or so.

"Jesus," Banks said under his breath, even though they were over a hundred yards away and couldn't possibly be overheard. "He might as well wear a sign painted on his back saying I'm up to no good—arrest me."

Hemmings returned Banks's chuckle. "Well, Joshua, if crooks were smart, the law'd never catch them and then they wouldn't need high-priced flatheads like you to defend them."

"Yeah, lucky me that most of them are as dumb as dirt." He sighed. "That's one of the reasons I thought I'd give up the law and try my hand at mining." He grinned and his teeth showed in the semidarkness. "You don't get near as dirty that way."

Hemmings cocked an eyebrow at Banks. "How are you doin' with that, Joshua? Making enough money to stay 're-tired' from the law?"

"Sure," Banks replied, smiling sardonically. "If I only eat once a week, and if I don't mind sidling up to a mule instead of a lady on the rare occasion I'm not too tired to think of female companionship."

Hemmings laughed, and then he quickly covered his mouth and looked out the window to make sure Hog hadn't heard them. When he saw the fat man was still making his way down the boardwalk, he turned and asked Banks, "So, I take it you'll be adding Esquire after your name again in the not-too-distant future?"

Banks nodded. "Yeah, but not until after these assholes are hanged." He glanced at Hemmings and said earnestly, "I wouldn't want to be in practice and find myself being asked to defend one of the bastards."

Down on the street below, Hog Hogarth felt as if his heart was going to hammer itself right out of his chest. It wasn't that he was afraid of breaking the law; he'd been doing that ever since he was tall enough to slip into shop windows in town and steal what wasn't tied down. And it wasn't the thought of killing one, or even, two women— dead was dead, he figured, and it didn't matter a hill of beans whether you were a man or a woman; you hated being killed as much as anyone. No, he thought. It was the fact that he was supposed to slip up on them and do Hattie quick before she had time to raise an alarm, and then he was supposed to kill the Rule woman, who was lying unconscious, according to Buck Tolliver.

Hog just didn't take with slitting the throat of someone who wasn't awake to possibly have a chance to fight back. As big as he was, Hog had never been a bully. He'd never had to be, and all the time he was growing up, his daddy had preached to him that he should never hit anyone smaller than him. This posed somewhat of a dilemma for

Hog, as just about everybody in town when he was growing up was smaller than him.

He'd solved his problem by never fighting anyone his
size or smaller with two hands—he'd just licked them all
one-handed and been done with it.

Now, however, he was being asked to kill not only a
woman, but a woman who was asleep at the time. This was
sticking in Hog's craw, and he didn't know how he was
going to deal with it, and wouldn't know until the very
moment the knife was in his hand and he was standing
over the lady.

When he was halfway across the last street between him
and the doctor's house, the moon came out from behind
the clouds and exposed Hog in full moonlight standing
almost on the doctor's porch.

"Damn!" Hog exclaimed, and then he clamped a hand
over his own mouth and ran up onto the doctor's porch.
Stupid shit, he told himself. Now just grit your teeth, Hog
old man, and get the job done so you can go back to the
saloon and pick up the money Tolliver promised you.

Hog reached out and tried the doorknob. It was locked.
That was no problem for him. He stuck the empty whiskey
bottle he was carrying under his arm, pulled out a thin-
bladed stiletto, and inserted the point between the door
and the jamb. He gently probed until he felt the tip of the
knife up against the bolt. He pressed the point into the
metal of the dead bolt and twisted. The bolt screeched
once, and then it moved back into the door, leaving the
door unlocked.

Careful not to make any more noise, Hog folded the
stiletto blade back into its handle and stuck the knife in
his pocket. He withdrew a large-bladed bowie-type knife
from a scabbard on his belt, enjoying its heavier weight
and more substantial feel than the stiletto. Stilettos were
all right to gut-punch someone with, but to do a good job
on the throat with all its tendons and blood vessels and
muscles, a man needed a real knife like the bowie. One
whose blade wouldn't snap like a dry twig and whose
point wouldn't get stuck in a bone or something.

Holding the knife in one hand, Hog reached down, slipped his boots off, and left them on the porch. He would be as quiet as a mouse pissing on cotton, he thought as he tiptoed into the darkness of the parlor.

He stood there for a moment in the dark, letting his eyes adjust to the gloomy atmosphere. Off to his right he could see light coming from under the door of the doctor's clinic room. That must be where they are, he thought, holding the knife out in front of him as he shuffled his feet along the floor so as not to make any boards creak as he moved toward the light.

As he eased the door to the clinic room open, he vowed to try to wake Miss Rule up before he cut her throat. He'd look into her eyes and give her a chance to try to fight him off. It wouldn't do her any good, but it might salve his conscience a little bit anyway.

He peered around the edge of the door and saw a woman sitting in a rocker with her back to the door, her long, blond hair hanging down her back. She had her hands in front of her, and it looked like she was knitting to pass the time.

On the bed in front of her, turned so her back was to the room, was the sleeping form of a white-haired lady. The covers were pulled up to her ears so he couldn't see her face, but how many grannies could there be lying in the doctor's old house, he thought, suppressing the urge to giggle at the thought.

Slowly, he crept toward the woman in the rocking chair, and as he neared her he reached out with his left hand to grab her hair and jerk her head back, exposing her neck to his bowie knife.

He was close enough now. He reached out and grabbed the hair and yanked it toward him.

He fell back and stumbled and almost went down on one knee when the hair came off in his hand. He almost screamed at the eerie feeling it gave him to yank a woman's hair plumb outta her head, but then he glanced at the rocking chair and saw Smoke Jensen turn around and grin at him. The mountain man was wearing a shawl over his buckskins and had a Colt .45 in his hand, and the hole in the end of the barrel that was pointed at Hog's head looked big enough to fall into.

The woman on the bed stirred, and Hog saw the young man who was riding with Jensen take his white wig off and sit up in the bed, yawning. "Good thing it didn't take him much longer to get here," Cal said to Smoke. "I was about to fall asleep right there in the bed."

Smoke waved the barrel of the Colt around in a little circle. "You want to drop that bowie knife, Hog? Or do you want me to shoot it out of your hand?"

Hog hesitated, trying to figure his chances of throwing the knife before Jensen could get a round off.

"Course," Smoke added, grinning, "it's kind'a dark in here and I might miss the knife and blow a couple of your fingers off instead, and they'll be calling you Lefty in the state prison for the next twenty years if you manage not to get hanged."

Hog blinked, hardly able to follow the humor in Smoke's comment, but he did hear "blow your fingers off," and that convinced him to drop the knife and raise his hands in the air.

"What do you mean hanged?" he asked, trying to force a shaky grin onto his lips. "I saw the light in the window and I knew the doc was dead and I thought I'd make sure nobody was trying to rob his place."

Smoke threw back his head and laughed. "That's a good one, Hog," he said, nodding appreciatively. "Did you think that up all by yourself?"

"Whatta you mean?" Hog asked, wondering who else was there to tell him what to say.

"Well, I thought since we have witnesses to you and Sheriff Buck Tolliver and your other friend cooking up this little assassination attempt, they might've helped you with that little story about you just being a civic-minded citizen worrying about a dead man's property."

Hog was dumb enough that he didn't realize Smoke was joking with him. He gave a lopsided grin and shook his head. "No, Jensen. For your information I thought that up all by myself. Didn't nobody help me at all."

He was so stupid he actually smiled while Smoke and Cal laughed at him. He was still smiling when Mayor Hemmings and the lawyer Joshua Banks walked into the room.

"I heard that, Smoke," Banks said, "and if I have to I'll so testify in court that Mr. Hogarth freely admitted he was lying about just checking out the place."

Hog's grin faded and he hung his head, shaking it slowly. He was thinking his daddy had been right all along—he was as dumb as a stump.

"All right, so what do we do now?" Hemmings asked, looking from Banks to Smoke.

"Well, we got one of the rats in our trap," Smoke said. "Now it's time to see if we can't entice the rest of them to join him."

Smoke put his pistol in his holster and bent over to pick up the knife Hog had dropped on the floor. As he lowered his head, he heard Hog give an inarticulate grunt. Knowing what was coming, Smoke hunched his shoulders and ducked his head just as a ham-sized fist slammed into the side of his head and he found himself wrapped inside Hog's meaty arms in a bear hug's death grip.

Smoke's vision blurred and his head swam as he heard Cal give a shout and saw out of the corner of his eye Cal's pistol being aimed at the back of Hog's head.

"No!" Smoke shouted through laboring lungs, and shook his head, causing stars to glisten and swim across his vision. "I'll handle this," he finished with a croak.

Hog grunted again and squeezed with all his might, trying to take his frustration at being not only caught in the act but also tricked into confessing out on Smoke. Smoke turned his head to the side where he could look into Hog's bloodshot gaze. He grinned at the fat man, whose face was turning red with his exertion as he tried to squeeze the life out of Smoke.

Smoke took a deep breath, flexed his own considerable muscles, and slowly moved his arms out away from his body, breaking Hog's grip and causing the big man to stumble backward a step or two.

Hog's eyes opened wide in amazement; he'd never had anyone be able to break his bear-hug grip like that, and the mountain man hadn't even seemed to have to strain to do it.

Smoke felt the lump that was already forming on the side of his head, and grinned good-naturedly at Hog. "That was a pretty good shot, Hog. You want to dance some more while I'm ready for you, or are you just good at surprising a man who's not looking?"

Hog swallowed audibly. Truth be told, he'd just as soon not test the big man any further, remembering how it'd turned out the last time they fought, but he was no coward. "Sure, I'll go a couple of turns around the dance floor with you, Jensen, but you won't like the ending."

Smoke held out his hands and wriggled his fingers at Hog in a gesture saying, "Come on and show me what you've got."

Hog made another mistake to add to the several he'd already committed that day. He ducked his head and charged Smoke, his arms out-flung, hoping to catch the mountain man unawares.

Smoke simply stepped one step to the side and popped Hog in the left ear with a wicked right jab as the big man stumbled by.

Hog yelped and grabbed his ear, whirling around just in time to catch a left hook Smoke threw from his heels on the point of his chin.

Hog's eyes crossed, he moaned, and then he went down like he'd been hit in the head with an ax handle.

"Jumping Jesus," Banks exclaimed, shaking his head. "I don't think I've ever seen anyone hit so hard in my entire life." He looked at Smoke. "You lifted his feet plumb up off the ground when you connected with his chin."

Smoke shook his hand and grimaced. "I usually take the time to put on padded gloves before hitting someone like that. It's tough on the knuckles otherwise."

"Damn, I hope you didn't kill him," Hemmings said,

stooping to put his hand in front of Hog's mouth to see if he was still breathing.

"Oh, he'll live, but he's gonna have a helluva headache when he wakes up," Smoke said, kneading his bruised knuckles with his other hand.

"How are we going to get his carcass to the jail?" Banks asked, shaking his head. "He looks like he weighs three hundred pounds."

"Who said we're taking him to the jail?" Smoke asked, grinning. "I don't think there's any need to let the sheriff know that we have Mr. Hogarth in custody. It'll be more fun to see what he does when Hog doesn't return to the saloon to tell him his mission was accomplished."

"Yeah," Cal said, nodding and smiling. "Let the dirty bastards wonder what happened when he doesn't show up."

Smoke smiled slyly. "It might just be that they'll come looking for their lost friend."

"Which will seal their fate for once and for all," Joshua Banks said, rubbing his hands together and grinning from ear to ear.

"Let's roll Hog's fat butt under that empty bed over there," Smoke said, "and then you can get back into this one, Cal."

Soon the mayor and Banks were out of sight behind an armoire against a far wall, and both Smoke and Cal were back in their assigned places. The lantern was turned down low so shadows covered Smoke and Cal's faces and the trap was once again set.

34

Sheriff Buck Tolliver looked at the big Regulator clock on the wall of his office for at least the hundredth time since they'd sent Hog off to kill the Rule woman and Hattie Monroe.

It'd been an hour and a half since Hog had snuck out the back door of the jail and disappeared into the night to do his dirty work.

"I'm telling you, Buck, something's gone wrong," Kid Akins said, nervously fiddling with the sticks still strapped to his left wrist as a brace. "Even as slow as that fat ass Hog is, he's had plenty of time to get into the doc's office and kill two ladies."

Hardy's eyes followed Tolliver's to the clock on the wall. "I'm afraid he's right, Buck," Hardy said reluctantly.

"But," Tolliver said, still clinging to some hope that things might turn out for the best, "there's been no alarm raised. No one's called for the sheriff and there's been no shots fired, so maybe he just got lost or passed out drunk or something."

Hardy snorted through his nose. "Well, as dumb as Hog is, I guess anything's possible, but one thing we do know for sure is there ain't no fire at the doc's house," he said, getting up and peering out the window toward the house in question.

"Do you think he could've killed them and forgotten to

light a fire?" Akins asked hopefully. "Maybe that's it. Maybe he just forgot, or the fire went out or something, and he's over at the saloon getting piss-drunk while we sit here worrying our fool heads off."

Tolliver turned angry eyes on Akins. "If he is, then he's a dead man 'cause I'm gonna kill him with my bare hands," he said harshly.

Hardy continued to look up and down the street. "Like you said, Buck, the good news is there hasn't been any alarm raised. If Hog had fucked up and gotten caught, then I'd expect the street to be full of men hell-bent on finding out what was going on, but it's quiet as a church on Monday out there."

"I'll tell you what, men, you two go on over to the saloon and see if Hog is there," Tolliver said. "If he is, keep him there and make sure he don't get so drunk he shoots his mouth off."

"What are you gonna be doing?" Hardy asked, his voice suspicious.

Tolliver got to his feet and hitched up his belt and holster. "Like you always said, Jeb, I started this mess, so I guess it's up to me to finish it. If Hog didn't kill the women, then I'm going to. I'll start the fire and then hightail it to the saloon. By the time someone reports it, you two can say I was there with you all the time."

"Sounds good to me," Kid said, his mouth already watering at the thought of more whiskey to ease his aching hand and arm.

Hardy stared at Tolliver for a moment. "All right, Buck, but if you ain't at the saloon in half an hour, I'm going to get on my horse and ride like hell to Pueblo, and hope I can get my money out of the bank before the marshals come looking for me."

"What? You think this is all some kind of trap, set to catch us and make us admit what we did?" Tolliver asked, his voice incredulous.

Hardy shrugged. "I don't know what it is, Buck, but something ain't right. I can smell it."

Tolliver laughed. "Hell, Jeb, Jensen ain't that smart. He's a washed-up old gunslick, that's all."

"You can laugh at me when you show up at the saloon and the fire's eating that building down, Buck. Until then, I'm keeping my options open."

Fifteen minutes later, Tolliver was easing into the back door of the doc's house, his gun in one hand and a skinning knife in the other.

He could see the light from a lantern turned low under the door to the patient's room, so he made his way quietly through the darkness, his eyes looking back and forth for movement in case this was a trap.

When he got to the door, he used his knife hand to ease it open a couple of inches, and peeked through the slit. Sure enough, he thought, there was Hattie with her hair hanging down and her head slumped to the side in a rocking chair in front of the bed where she'd fallen asleep.

Janet Rule's gray hair was sticking out from under the covers on the bed in front of Hattie. This was perfect, Tolliver thought. He didn't know where Hog was or why he hadn't done the job, but he was damn sure going to do it himself and right now.

He holstered his pistol and held the knife out in front of him as he moved across the room. His heart almost stopped when Hattie stirred and turned around in her chair.

Suddenly he was staring into the pale eyes of Smoke Jensen and the dark hole of Jensen's .45 Peacemaker.

"Good evening, Sheriff," Jensen said, and his friend Cal sat up in bed and grinned at him from under a gray wig. "Howdy, Buck," Cal said gaily, taking the wig off and dropping it on the bed.

Tolliver's mouth hung open as Mayor Sam Hemmings and Joshua Banks stepped out into the light from behind an armoire against the far wall.

Hemmings just shook his head sadly. "Why, Buck, why did you do all this?"

Tolliver grinned and dropped the knife. He was kind'a glad it was over. The strain of living a double life was gone, and it was like a weight had been lifted from his shoulders.

"Why, Mayor; you ask me why?" He moved to the side and took a seat on the edge of a bed there. "Robbing the miners was for the money, of course." He grinned. "You can't get rich off a hundred dollars a month, Mayor." And then he sobered and looked over at Jensen, his eyes filling with hate.

"The doc was just in the wrong place at the wrong time, like I told him before I shot him." He sighed and hung his head. "I hated that, 'cause I really liked him. But Blackie fucked up. He was supposed to kill Jensen's friend, and then when Jensen came back to town I was gonna kill *him*."

"Why, Tolliver?" Smoke asked, lowering the barrel of his pistol but not putting it away. "What did I ever do to you to make you want to hurt me?"

"You remember a man named Jack Tolliver?" he asked.

Smoke thought for a moment, and then he shook his head. "No, I don't."

"You and your Preacher friend shot him down in cold blood twenty years ago, him and four of his friends. It was right after you'd had a fight in a bar. They came out shooting and you and your friend killed every one of them."

Smoke's eyes lit up with memory. He stared at Tolliver. "You were the kid who shot me—the one with the peppermint stick in his mouth."

Tolliver sneered. "Yeah. Jack was my big brother and I watched you shoot him down like a dog in the street."

Smoke shook his head. "He didn't give me any choice, Tolliver. You had to know that."

Tolliver's eyes brimmed with tears. "It didn't matter then and it doesn't matter now. You took him from me and I wanted you to pay for that with your life."

Before Smoke could answer, Hog rose up from behind the bed, the stiletto from his pocket in his hand. He grabbed Hemmings from behind and stuck the knife against his neck.

Smoke raised his pistol, but didn't fire for fear of hitting the mayor in the low light of the room.

"Quick, Buck," Hog said, blood smearing his lip, "let's hightail it outta here."

As quick as a flash Buck was up and off the bed and running out of the room, with Hog stumbling along behind him dragging the mayor with him.

When he got to the doctor's back door, Hog shoved the mayor inside and slammed the door. Then he turned and ran as fast as he could after Tolliver toward the saloon down the street.

By the time Smoke and Cal and Banks picked the mayor up and got out the door, they could just see Hog and Tolliver entering the saloon.

As they ran toward it, men and women began streaming out of the batwings, screaming and hollering as shots were fired over their heads to make them scatter.

Smoke slowed to a walk, and calmly opened the loading gate on his pistol's cylinder and began to check his loads. "Looks like they're going to hole up in the saloon and wait for us to come in after them," he said.

Banks and Hemmings stopped cold in their tracks. "Hell with that," Banks said. "I'm a lawyer, not a lawman. I'm not going in there and getting myself shot."

Smoke glanced at Hemmings, who held up his hands. "I'm not a gunman, Smoke. I don't even carry a pistol."

Smoke smiled. He was used to this. He'd been here before, many times. "I'll tell you what, Mayor. You go let my friend Pearlie out of jail, give him his gun, and we'll clean up your town for you."

As he finished talking, the lights in the saloon went out, leaving the place as dark as a tomb.

"All right, Smoke. I'll do it right away."

"You might want to send him out with an express gun and some shells too, Mayor," Cal added without looking up as he too checked his pistols.

"Getting to be quite the expert at storming buildings, huh?" Smoke said to Cal with a laugh.

"It's the company I keep, I guess," Cal replied, grinning back. "I was taught by an expert."

Half an hour later, Pearlie and Cal and Smoke stood outside the saloon and discussed their options. "We could just burn the place down," Pearlie said, squinting his eyes to try and see better in the dark of the night.

Smoke shook his head. "I never held much with burning men alive," he said. "It shows no respect for your opponent."

"You think Tolliver deserves our respect after all he did?" Cal asked.

Smoke nodded. "I remember a boy of no more than ten or twelve, so small it took both his hands to ear back the hammer on a Colt. He stood there in that street with his brother and all of his brother's friends dead all around him and he tried to shoot me down while still sucking on a peppermint stick."

Smoke looked at Cal and Pearlie. "His brother had just been killed and he was man enough even at that age to try and do something about it, so, yes, he does deserve our respect. If not for the man he came to be, then for the boy he once was."

Pearlie nodded. "So, how do you want to handle it?" he asked.

"Let's give him another chance to be that brave little boy," Smoke said.

He walked up the street until he was standing in front of the saloon, well within pistol range if they tried to shoot from inside.

Hair standing up on the back of his neck, Cal joined him, as did Pearlie.

"Tolliver. Buck Tolliver!" Smoke yelled.

"Yeah, what do you want, Jensen?" came a voice from out of the darkness.

"None of you can get away, Tolliver. You got two

choices. You can stay in that saloon until the marshals get here and root you out to die at the end of a rope, or you can come out here and face me and my friends in the street."

He looked around and saw several horses tied to rails nearby. "There are horses tied up out here," Smoke yelled again. "If you get by us, there's no one else to stop you from getting on those broncs and heading into the mountains. Who knows? You might even get away clean."

After several minutes went by with no reply, Smoke called again, "It's your choice, Tolliver. Stay and die for certain, or come out here and take a chance on living. Either way, a bullet is better than a long fall on a short rope."

Seconds later, four men walked out of the saloon side by side. Three of the men had pistols on their belts, and the fourth was carrying a short-barreled express gun cradled in his arms.

"Jensen," Tolliver yelled, "this is for my brother, Jack."

Smoke nodded and all of the men went for their guns.

Jeb Hardy's eyes opened wide in surprise as he saw all three of the men in front of him draw and fire while his gun was barely out of its holster. He'd known it was going to be close between Jensen and him, but he had no idea Jensen's friends would also be faster on the draw than he was.

The first slug took him square in the chest and made him pull his trigger while his gun was still pointing down. He glanced down in amazement as his own bullet plowed into his right foot, taking three toes clean off. He grinned through the pain in his chest until a second bullet took the top of his head off and put his lights out for good.

Kid Akins never even cleared leather before two slugs knocked him backward to land spread-eagled on his back staring up at the stars in the night sky. "I'll be damned," he muttered through the blood bubbling from his mouth, "my arm don't hurt no more." Those were his last words, and the stars were the last thing he saw before he was sucked into an intense light from the sky.

Hog Hogarth got off both barrels of his express gun, firing from the hip without aiming before he was hit, and hit hard. One bullet punched a hole in his belly button, doubling him over so that the second slug went into the top of his head, exploding it into a fine red mist as he toppled over into the darkness at his feet.

Tolliver surprised even himself by drawing and getting off one quick shot at Jensen before Jensen's slugs took him in the chest and belly, spinning him around to fall face-first in the dirt in front of the saloon.

Moments later, he felt himself being turned over, and he looked up into the face of Smoke Jensen. He looked down and saw a red stain on Jensen's shoulder, and he grinned. "Got you in the wing again, huh?" he asked.

Smoke smiled down at him. "Yeah, and as I recall, it's the same arm, Buck."

"I got no right to ask, Jensen, but I need a favor."

"Yeah?"

"Take the money I got in the banks in Pueblo and have my body sent to Homestead, Colorado. There's a little cemetery there with all of my family in it. Plant me there, Jensen, next to my brother, will you?"

Smoke nodded. "I promise, Buck."

"So long, mountain man," Tolliver gasped, blood oozing from between his lips. "I gave it a good try, but came up short . . . ." And then he died.

Smoke stood up and turned, his heart aching when he saw Cal slip to his knees, the front of his shirt covered with blood.

He ran back and knelt next to Cal along with Pearlie.

"Damn," Cal said, grimacing in pain. "I'm so tired of getting shot all the time."

Smoke quickly ripped Cal's shirt open and saw four holes in Cal's chest and stomach oozing blood. Just under the skin, less than half an inch deep, he could see the outline of buckshot from the express gun Hog had fired.

Smoke took a quick breath, relieved to know Cal's wounds weren't life-threatening.

Pearlie just shook his head. "I told you, Smoke, the

boy's a lead magnet. It happens every time we get in a gunfight. The bullets just automatically head for ol' Cal."

Cal looked up and saw the blood on Smoke's shoulder, and he grinned weakly. "I'll take yours out if you'll take mine out."

Smoke nodded and laughed. "Since I heard you've been getting plenty of practice lately, it's a deal!"

THE LAST GUNFIGHTER SERIES BY
WILLIAM W. JOHNSTONE